SHEILA'S TRIFECTA

Also by Dorothy Van Soest

Nonfiction

Social Work Practice For Social Justice:
Cultural Competence in Action

Diversity Education For Social Justice: Mastering Teaching Skills

The Global Crisis Of Violence:
Common Problems, Universal Causes, Shared Solutions

Challenges Of Violence Worldwide: An Educational Resource

Challenges Of Violence Worldwide: Curriculum Module

Incorporating Peace And Social Justice Into The Social Work Curriculum

Sheila's Trifecta

A Novel

Dorothy Van Soest

iUniverse, Inc.
New York Lincoln Shanghai

Sheila's Trifecta

iUniverse books may be ordered through booksellers or by contacting:

iUniverse
2021 Pine Lake Road, Suite 100
Lincoln, NE 68512
www.iuniverse.com
1-800-Authors (1-800-288-4677)

ISBN-13: 978-0-595-41501-4 (pbk)
ISBN-13: 978-0-595-85850-7 (ebk)
ISBN-10: 0-595-41501-6 (pbk)
ISBN-10: 0-595-85850-3 (ebk)

Printed in the United States of America

The author is grateful for permission to include the poem from *Journey of Souls: Case Studies of Life Between Lives* by Michael Newton, Ph.D. Copyright 1994.
Fifth Revised Edition. Copyright 1996.
Llewellyn Worldwide, Ltd. 2143 Wooddale Drive, Woodbury, MN 55125-2989.
All rights reserved, used by permission of the publisher.

Cover Illustration: PELE Left panel of triptych by Cheryl A. Richey Copyright 2001

To all who have helped me grow—

both friend and foe alike.

...everything in this life has purpose.
There are no mistakes,
no coincidences,
all events are blessings
given to us to learn from.

—Elisabeth Kubler-Ross

Acknowledgments

A number of people have contributed to the creation of *Sheila's Trifecta*. First and foremost, I thank Hal Zina Bennett for his consistent encouragement as my writing teacher, mentor, chief critic and editor, advisor, and friend. I am real clear that this book would never have come to fruition without his wisdom.

Thank you to my writing partner, Margie Sherman, who read every word of every draft and provided suggestions and support as well as editing every step of the way.

For the support, inspiration, affirmation, and suggestions provided from beginning to end, I thank all the members of the Inner Ocean writing group: Jilly Bean, Leslie Goldberg, Karen Harris, Julie Isaac, Thelma Kidd, Beverly Kimmons, Kathi McKnight, Melanie Miller, Margie Sherman, Diane Tegtmeier and Lindsay Whiting.

Thank you to artist Cheryl Richey for graciously contributing one of her incredible paintings for the cover illustration.

A special thanks to my family and friends, who not only endured my unrelenting enthusiasm—some might say obsession—about writing in a new way, but actively encouraged me through listening imbued with love.

I'm especially grateful for the support I got at home. Thank you to my partner, Susan Seney, for her wise support and amazing patience when I was writing and to our dog, Trouble, who made me take time to walk every day.

Introduction

After publishing several academic books and more professional journal articles than I care to count, I never dreamed that I would write a book of fiction, much less one as unusual—some might say as weird—as this one. During my thirty plus years in academia, I became adept at restraining my own voice and denying my passion in the service of scholarly objectivity and neutrality.

So how did I come to write this unusual novel that tells three women's poignant and inspiring—and sometimes heartrending—stories?

It started a couple of years ago when I was re-examining my goals, as many of us do during life transitions. The idea suddenly came to me out of the blue to write a novel. I had no idea at first what kind of novel it would be, just that I had a desire to write fiction. A little voice inside prodded, pushing me by repeating three little words of instruction over and over: *write a novel, write a novel, write a novel.*

I became more and more intrigued with the idea and soon the creative part of me—the part that I suspect was behind the conspiracy from the beginning—joined the chorus with a new tune that rang in my ears: *write a novel about the meaning of life.* This was quickly followed by a second verse: *write a novel about women and shame.* Then one day when I was on vacation and walking my dog through the woods, a character named Sheila revealed herself along with the first sentence of the book—long ago discarded, I must admit, though Sheila survived as the novel's protagonist and heroine.

When I met Hal Zina Bennett and signed up, along with eleven other women, for his year-long program of writing for personal and spiritual growth, everything fell into place. As one of the characters in my book comments at one point, it was as if it were predestined. Thus began a year of adventure as ideas flowed and my newfound voice grew louder. Two other characters joined Sheila and the three took on nicknames—Spring, Sky, and Gritty—as they started to tell me their stories. It wasn't long before I found a joy in writing that I had never known before.

Setting the book in an afterlife place provided a way to review life from a standpoint outside current day-to-day experience. When Spring, Sky and Gritty tell their stories, reflecting on the lives they have just left, they show clearly what the impact of their inner world is on the outer world and how, when they undergo personal growth, their external reality also changes. As they conduct their life reviews within the context of mutual support, they come to appreciate the transformations they went through—how they grew and developed personally, how they learned how to operate in the world, how they found their way to their true selves.

Though the women's stories are fictional, their lessons are mine. It wasn't long before I realized that writing this novel was helping me reach a much deeper appreciation of my own life, what I have contributed and what I have learned on my own journey. By the time I finished writing this book, I knew I had created a reflective novel that spoke to the process of personal growth and that I wanted to share this whole process with others.

I am convinced that anyone interested in personal and spiritual growth, social injustice, women's issues, ethics and leadership, recovery from alcoholism, the discovery of one's sexuality, and the challenges of choosing a spiritual path, will find this book a good read.

My book, it turns out, is a self-help novel. I believe most of us—and particularly those of us who are women—tend to be overly modest about our accomplishments just as we often find it difficult to admit to and face our own fear, guilt, and shame. I also believe we all have stories to tell, stories that can lead to deeper insights. What I discovered is that the process of creating fictional characters as a way to reflect on one's own issues can lead to a deeper appreciation of one's own contributions as well as making peace with one's own human imperfections and struggles. Just as writing this book helped me, I believe such a writing process might help others appreciate their own lives. I believe this is true regardless of age. It can serve the older or middle aged person who wants to step back and review his or her own life, as well as the young person who is becoming more mindful of the personal growth process.

So, now that my book is in print, I see it as much more than the work of fiction I originally envisioned; it is an unusual combination of reflective novel and self-help book. I hope it will be useful to readers, whether personally, professionally or both. In order to maximize its usefulness I have included a guide at the end that suggests ways the book might be used by individuals interested in their own change process, therapists and counselors, support groups, personal growth groups, students in the classroom, individuals in recovery as well as recovery groups and substance abuse counselors, women's groups, spirituality groups, reading groups.

I am excited about the idea that my book might facilitate your personal growth in some way, provide further insights about how people grow and develop, confirm what you already know—or just be a damn good read!

Dorothy Van Soest
September 2006

PART I

▼

TRANSITION

You would know the hidden realm
where all souls dwell.
The journey's way lies
through death's misty fell.
Within this timeless passage
a guiding light does dance,
Lost from conscious memory,
but visible in trance.

Michael Newton
Journey of Souls

Sheila's longing had no name and defied explanation. An ache spread across the left side of her chest and radiated up to her throat and down to her stomach, filling her with a mysterious void. Do all human beings experience moments of loneliness when they wish for something they don't understand, she wondered? Or was she uniquely destined to search for some ever-elusive meaning in this world of pain and injustice?

Blissful ignorance of her own projections was always an attractive option during these moments. To focus outward, pointing the finger of blame and shame at others, served a completely understandable need and useful purpose. It kept her from feeling that deep emptiness, those hurts that longed for healing and understanding, that space that could not be filled by any human touch, only by the spirit in another place.

They say we are all born alone no matter how many people celebrate our coming and no matter how bright the lights and sweet the sounds of welcome. On a visceral level Sheila knew on the day of her birth that she was entering a dark, lonely place. Living on Earth would be difficult in spite of all the well-intentioned people who would try to make it not so. Even as she took her first breath she knew, without words or conscious awareness, that she did not want to be here.

The sharp pain Sheila now felt in her chest lasted for only a few minutes before the force of a transparent white light ejected it from her body, shooting it out through the top of her head. Miraculously, the terrible ache that had squeezed the breath from her was gone. Not only that, her back no longer hurt and her neck—so long a nuisance with its arthritis and bone spurs—moved freely without discomfort. Experimenting, she turned her head and her neck spun around as smoothly as a spinning top propelled by a string. She must be dreaming.

She felt lightheaded, then realized that she was floating. A puddle of fluid light carried her into a mysteriously familiar and irresistible peacefulness. There she drifted restfully like the times she floated on a raft in calm lake water absorbing the soft gentle rays of the warm sun and forgetting about time. Captivated by overpowering feelings of freedom and joy, she closed her eyes.

When she opened them a scene below mesmerized her. At first she thought she was watching a movie but as she gazed uncomprehendingly at the unfolding events, her confusion slowly turned into amazement.

"Oh my God!" she exclaimed, "That looks like me down there but I am up here! How can that be?"

She drifted downward for a better view, surprised at how clearly she could see the scene in spite of seeming to be far away. She saw that it *was* her and she was surrounded by people who seemed to think something was terribly wrong.

Then a nurse pulled a sheet over her body and a doctor, speaking with a resigned voice to no one in particular, muttered, "We did everything we could. Fortunately, the massive nature of her heart attack meant she went quickly and experienced little pain."

Sheila was incredulous. She couldn't be dead. She had never felt more alive. Besides, she felt like she was still in physical form somehow. How could that be?

Just then a gentle yet powerful force began to pull her away, drawing her toward a dark tunnel. She willingly allowed herself to be guided through its entrance, feeling as excited as a child who waits for Santa Claus in anticipation of long-desired gifts. Though a bit disoriented by the suddenness of events, she was not afraid of the surrounding darkness. Descending further into the tunnel's blackness she saw a tiny circle of light in the distance. Without effort she drifted slowly toward it until the black turned to gray and then expanded into a bright circle of light.

Emerging from the tunnel, Sheila floated among layers of light that shifted back and forth in harmony. They seemed woven together symmetrically with variations of thickness and color ranging from white to yellow to shades of blue to a touch of purple in the distance. Soft echoes of music tinkling like wind chimes vibrated with her movements.

Sheila blinked, alternating between belief and disbelief as she took in the sights, sounds, and smells. She had fleeting memories of being connected to this place. Her physical body was dead yet there seemed to be physical remnants in this magical, non-physical place. She began to remember entities she knew here. They were not human yet were related to human somehow. And the colors she saw had special significance though she couldn't recall what. It was all quite perplexing.

Then as she slowly absorbed the love and compassion surrounding her, she suddenly remembered.

"I am home again!" she whispered ecstatically.

Feeling intense joy upon returning to this place after her latest Earth death, memories began to flood through her—glimpses of places and entities that were somehow precious to her, familiar feelings of safety and belonging.

Though she couldn't remember the name of this place, she knew it was special and with a sense of gratitude deeper than any ocean, she drifted along, basking in the preciousness of the moment. Then one particular light in the distance caught her attention. It was moving quickly toward her.

"Oh my God, it's my mother!" she cried out, frantically waving, "I'm over here, Mother! Over here!"

When her mother reached her, they enveloped each other in light as if wrapped in a blanket of love.

With tenderness Sheila exclaimed, "Oh, Mother, I have missed you so much!"

They laughed as they looked at each other. Sheila remembered her mother's tiny frail body and jokingly said, "You certainly haven't gained any weight here, have you?"

Smiling, her mother reached out for her. She knew that, given the unexpected nature of her latest death, Sheila might be a bit apprehensive at first about being here so she had come in physical form to comfort her. As they blissfully floated through unlimited space, they reminisced about their life on Earth as mother and daughter. There was no need for guilt or apology. They rested in the knowledge that they had fulfilled their purpose together and their love had endured.

As her mother led her further into the light, Sheila saw rays of friendly light blue energy far in the distance, beckoning to her. Knowing she had been with them before and now longing to see them again, she headed in their direction. Then she noticed that her mother was going the other way.

"Where are you going?" Sheila asked, momentarily panicked.

"I stay in a different place than you do," her mother gently responded, "It was my job to be the first to meet you and bring you here. Now that I know you are okay, it is time for me to leave."

With resignation Sheila moved away from her mother and was directed by an unseen force toward a big open area that hovered between her and the spiritual entities with whom she wished to be reunited. Soon she was in the middle of enormous numbers of multi-colored lights of energy that were being transported in a coordinated way to a central receiving area. Hovering over the open area she listened to the sounds of excitement and marveled at the countless bright stars of varying luminescence going in all directions. It reminded her of a busy airport terminal on Earth with large numbers of travelers heading for flights that would take them to many different destinations.

Suddenly, as she was projected out toward her final destination, she found herself in a small quiet tributary away from the happy hubbub of the terminal. She glimpsed the twinkling of two light blue stars in the distance and excitedly moved in their direction.

"There you are! I have been looking for you!" she exclaimed as she approached them, suddenly remembering that she knew the one whose blue color was a bit lighter in hue as Gritty and the other as Sky.

They pulled Sheila into a circle of loving embrace; forming a swirling pattern of light and color as they sang and danced in unison and surrounded her with chants of "Welcome home, Spring! We have been waiting for you!"

Sheila, the last to arrive, smiled when she heard her name, remembering that here she was called Spring.

*   *   *   *

They entered a valley that was as familiar and beautiful to them as they were to each other. Lush foliage from countless robust grasses, bushes and trees surrounded them with dazzling shades of green. A profusion of flowers in radiant hues of red, yellow, orange, pink and purple painted dots on the green background and released delightful aromas of rose, jasmine, and lavender. A leisurely moving stream filled with scores of sacred multi-varied fish reflected the billowy white clouds floating like cotton candy in the light blue sky. In its delight the sun playfully cast Fourth of July sparklers over its rippling waters. In the soft grass next to the stream, an opulent homecoming feast was spread on a red and white-checkered cloth.

They sat in a circle eating their favorite delicacies, a tightly knit group of spiritual beings intimately united for eternity through shared human experiences. Their animated chatter was interrupted only by occasional hugs of unconditional love and the air overflowed with acceptance as they joked and teased each other, happy to be reunited in this place once again.

"Welcome back to Sweet Home, Chicago!" Sky and Gritty laughed as they toasted Spring.

Spring giggled. There really wasn't a formal name for this place but in a previous time and space, she had jokingly called it that. Always the one to want to name things she had insisted that they call it something. At one point she called it Home Sweet Home and later they had settled on a kind of compromise to humor her and called it Spirit Home. Spring smiled when she remembered how adamant she had been about naming it then and how the name didn't matter to her at all now. She was content simply to know she was home again.

There had always been three of them. Spring, Sky, and Gritty were the nicknames they had given each other many lifetimes ago to celebrate their individual personalities.

Sheila was known for her incredible passion, courage and resilience. The others named her Spring for the way her energy moved up and down and because she always bounced back from adversity in her Earth lives to spring forward in huge growth spurts. In her eagerness to accelerate her learning she spent as much time as she could in the field, even missing their reunion a couple of times.

Sky, an innocently pure spirit who was always reliable and caring, got her name from the way she floated her energy in open spaces and loved the clear blue sky. Since she had been the first to return from Earth this time, she felt rejuvenated and a bit more feisty than usual.

She looked at Sheila and teased, "Gee, Spring, I was worried that you weren't going to make it this time. I bet you finally came home because you couldn't resist finding out what happened to me, right?"

Sheila hugged her with deep affection and admitted, "I do indeed want to hear what kind of trouble you got yourself into this time, Sky. I wouldn't miss your story for the world!"

Meanwhile, true to her nickname, Gritty moved in her usual steady and diligent way, always ready to jump into the fray and take a risk. She was known for getting into situations that were over her head and the others enjoyed her determination, sometimes fondly labeling it as stubbornness.

Now Spring and Sky reached out to bring Gritty into the circle. Like a carefully balanced mobile their varied personalities danced rhythmically to the harmony of their individual vibrations.

*   *   *   *

Suddenly a graceful figure appeared. She was enclosed in a dark blue hooded robe that revealed only two intensely discerning eyes now twinkling with pleasure. Spring, Sky and Gritty knew immediately that it was Suma for she always materialized in human form at first. As she gradually softened and melted into a puddle of deep blue energy, they soared euphorically toward her embrace.

Suma was their spirit guide. She had been assigned to them when their souls were first created and they felt accountable to her as well as to each other. Spring noted that Suma's energy was a darker shade of blue—almost purple—than it was last time, a sign that her wisdom had deepened. She probably spent very little time on Earth now.

A highly skilled teacher, Suma wanted only what was best for them. She alternated between being gentle and nurturing and being firm and demanding, depending on which approach was best suited for their learning. She conscientiously allowed them to learn from their mistakes, but she still hurt for them when they had to endure pain in order to fulfill their purpose and always shared their anguish as well as their joy. Now that they were more mature, she took a less active role in their learning process than before, joining them as needed to make a point or provide support.

Suma's appearance signaled that it was time to go to the Place of Learning. In their eagerness to get to work, Sky and Gritty quickly moved away from the valley. Seeing that Spring was lagging behind, they enfolded her within their energies and carried her.

Their study was a quiet secluded room in the library, a place filled with physical images in spite of the fact that in this place physical forms were little more than a fantasy. It was an odd, sometimes confusing situation, where their own physical forms and their Earth-based senses were sheer illusion and where spiritual existence, without physical form, seemed concrete and real. Meanwhile, real or not, the present illusions were useful to them since their Earthly realities would be the focus of their attention as they reviewed the last lives they had lived on Earth.

The library itself was a massive marble structure with ceilings that hovered high above their collective energy. Stained glass windows and intricate chandeliers contributed to its cathedral-like appearance and represented the sacredness that occurred within its walls. They entered their private room through an alcove to the left of the library's main reading room. Three large life books were already at their places at the familiar table. Each one was several inches thick, although Spring's was noticeably thicker than the others because she had stayed on Earth the longest so her book contained more stories.

The storybooks were filled with live multidimensional action pictures that moved and shifted with reflected light. Inside, time was condensed and each page contained images large enough to transport them into the scenes, back to the physical, back to their Earth forms.

While they really had no form that you could see in this place, Spring, Sky and Gritty knew from past experiences that for a period of time they used physical references and, in fact, still experienced their physical sensations. They could never quite give up the memory of clapping their hands in excited applause or laughing, loving the sounds of their voices, or even the heart sensations of embracing each other. So they had agreed that while they were learning, they would use the same old language that applied in physical form, as unnecessary as it actually was. Each of them could remember the bodies they'd lived in for their short journey to Earth and, in spite of Suma's mild disapproval of their refusal to follow all the conventions of this place, they enjoyed floating back and forth between physical and non-physical descriptions.

Prepared now to study, they went to their places at the table and sat down. In this room there was a marked absence of the suspicion and competitiveness that was so characteristic of learning environments on Earth. Here the attitude was one of complete openness and acceptance. The universal bond between them made them all the same.

Suma rested at the head of the table, ready to provide a brief orientation. She solemnly reminded them, "You decided to live separate lives yet work on common issues in the field this time, choosing to live during the second half of the twentieth century because of its penchant for raised consciousness. I know you well enough to know that you will take full advantage of the learning opportunities that time period on Earth offered."

With a mischievous smile, Suma then added, "I will have some surprises for you this time. Without your knowledge I asked some souls from other spirit groups to help. So be prepared for a twist in some events. They may take you aback at first but I trust that you will welcome the revelations as gifts of love."

Suma grinned. She seemed to be enjoying their startled looks.

"Remember," she concluded, "it isn't the decisions you made or the experiences you had on Earth that are important, but what you do with them. Once you are healed and returned to wholeness, each of you will meet with your Council of Elders and then I will guide you to the Place of Life Selection to plan your next lives. But not to worry about that yet! There is plenty of time, all that you want in fact. I must now go to the other groups to which I have been assigned. I will pop in at times to help and you can call on me at any time. Godspeed, my dears!"

As the three of them waved goodbye to Suma, a mysterious mantle of intrigue fell over them, filling them with even greater anticipation.

Sheila, who was now feeling more comfortable thinking of herself as Spring, didn't like the idea of Suma making decisions about their lives without their knowledge. She had always trusted Suma, just as the others did, and wondered why she suddenly felt apprehensive.

PART II

▼

THE SCRIPT

"Things that don't matter at all to one person can hurt another so deeply it seems as bad as dying.

Banana Yoshimoto
Hardboiled and Hard Luck

Spring, Sky and Gritty always experienced both anticipation and a touch of dread about their studies at first, but this time fascination about the unknown absorbed their attention. It also enhanced their readiness to learn and they eagerly huddled together at the library table, the mystery of surprise hovering in the middle.

Spring's excitement was muted, though, and she wondered why she was so tired. She was glad when Sky said she wanted to go first, claiming it as her right since she had been the first to come home this time.

Sky enthusiastically opened her storybook to the beginning as Spring and Gritty positioned themselves on each side of her in order see without straining or stretching their energies. An Earth scene on the page came alive, no longer just a scrapbook picture but a reality that was happening as if for the first time. Sky felt an almost irresistible urge to disconnect from her feelings as images of darkness descended.

A big freestanding mahogany closet dominated one corner of a dimly lit room, a bedroom, in a very old house. Inside were Grandma's clothes and her two pairs of shoes, one for dress and one for every day. Two small girls were also in there, huddled together in the dark where they couldn't see anything—only feel the terror. The smell of Grandma mingled with the smell of wood and filled the little girls' nostrils with the promise of protection as they imagined the look of familiar patterns and touched the softness of the clothes they hung onto. Sky tried to breathe through the folds of the fabrics, pressed into the back corner of the suffocating small black space. Her body was curled into itself, making it even smaller than it already was, making her invisible against the pounding that echoed in her tiny ears, threatening to break through the door's barrier, threatening to find her and break her.

As she watched the scene, everything in Sky's consciousness came alive, filling the space she now shared with Spring and Gritty in the library. Then more scenes from her childhood filled the space, flashing by in rapid succession—over and over, the little girls huddled together in Grandma's freestanding closet, or under her bed with its loose springs catching in their hair. Sometimes they lay on top of Grandma's lumpy bed, under the thick quilt that meant safety and warmth in the quiet times, hoping its bulkiness would make them invisible in the times of the pounding, banging, yelling.

The scenes faded and Sky stepped back from the primitive feelings she had been experiencing. As new feelings and new images broke in, she looked to Spring and Gritty for support. They moved closer to her.

"Sometimes," Sky said, "my mom told us stories about how my sister and I would hide whenever Grandpa came home drunk after one of his frequent binges. Grandpa pounded loudly and ferociously on the door, demanding to be let in. The whole building shook and the neighbors yelled for him to shut up. They gathered in the hall at the ready to help if needed or maybe just out of curiosity. Mom told me how terrified I always was but since I was not yet two years old I had no words for the horror and, years later, no conscious memory of those times.

"I never saw Grandpa's face but whenever I heard him pounding I imagined a huge green monster with mean eyes all over his body and sharp scales that could slice you up in a second. Even as an adult I unconsciously carried Grandpa in my body whenever I heard a loud knock on a door."

With a turn of the page the Earth scene shifted and Sky's face revealed amazement as if remembering something that had been long buried within her.

She was three years old, sitting on top of the counter in a dark, musty bar, wishing she were outside playing in the sunshine. Putrid old men drinking foul smelling liquor surrounded her, their faces filled with rotten teeth and smiles that looked more like leering than smiling. They poked at each other and talked about how cute Sky was sitting there so primly with her white blond curls and big blue eyes. Her mom smiled at them. Then Sky put her head down, only her gravely serious eyes looking up at the men, and asked in a chastising little voice, "what are *you* looking at?" They all laughed hysterically.

Sky stepped back and looked carefully at the image of the little girl, spontaneously exclaiming, "I *was* cute, wasn't I? Look at that precious little round face! I was confused by the men's laughter but I think I was a little proud too. We were in the bar looking for Grandpa. Mom went looking for him every payday, hoping to find him before he spent all of his money on booze. She brought me along sometimes. I always wondered what Grandpa looked like so I would recognize him if I saw him in a bar or on the street or in the alley. He died in the jailhouse when I was still young and there were never any pictures of him. I still don't know what he looked like."

Sky flipped the page and the scene changed again. Her face softened as Earth images emerged and they all relaxed into the new warmth, basking in the glow in which they were newly immersed.

An older woman sat in a worn chair in a tiny living room. Her round belly moved up and down when she laughed, accenting her short, heavy body. She had a round rosy face and a sweet smile that lit up the room and seemed to say I love you without her having to say it out loud. Her hair was very long and thin and, while she usually wrapped it in a bun at the back of her neck, it fell loose now as the little girl behind her brushed it. Sky was enthralled with the look and feel of the smooth, silky streaks of blond, brown, and gray in her fingers.

The scene shifted slightly and they saw the old woman walking down the street. A dog was close by her side, a unique-looking mongrel with long black hair and very short legs that made him look like an overgrown longhaired dachshund.

"Grandma was always with her dog," Sky chuckled as she looked up from her storybook, "They made quite a pair with their short legs and round bellies! Grandma found Blackie near death in an abandoned house where he had been trapped for several days without food or water. He always looked up at her with his big brown eyes brimming with gratitude, love, and loyalty. I felt the same way about Grandma but I never told her. Whenever I looked at my mom and myself, I would see her round face in ours and feel the sweetness of her smile."

Sky turned the page and they watched as a series of scenes emerged, one right after the other: Grandma's cozy three-room apartment with hand crocheted doilies on every surface—framed pictures of very old people who looked like they lived long ago in another country—a potbellied stove in the middle of the living room—a treadle sewing machine in the bedroom covered with bobbins, thread, and colorful pieces of material—a large kitchen with a wood burning stove for cooking—a bathroom out in the hallway that was shared with the other tenants—Sky covered in black dust, playing in the coal bin behind the building, making dancing dolls with the pink wild flowers in the alley, watching Grandma work in the kitchen pantry.

Sky lingered over the image of her grandma's pantry. She breathed in its aromas and sighed, "I loved the smell of the spices and coffee in that pantry. Bowls of some kind of Finnish yogurt that Grandma called viili were always curing on the counter. I thought it was sour tasting but Dad poured maple syrup on top and ate it like it was ice cream. Jars of blueberry sauce and jam were stacked on the top shelf. Grandma spent hours picking those berries in the woods, always getting them before the bears did. Tasting that sweet blueberry sauce on warm pancakes was like savoring a slice of heaven! Cracked and mismatched plates, cups and saucers, and a variety of glasses filled the bottom shelf. I loved Grandma's dishes, just as I loved her. I never thought about how they represented poverty and a hard life.

"Grandma cleaned house and ironed clothes for a rich lady for a couple dollars a week and scraps of material. From the lady's leftover bits and pieces, she made a multicolored quilt and clothes for us. She even made a winter coat for Mom. When it was naptime I loved lying on Grandma's bed under the quilt. I felt cozy and secure there, except of course when I was hiding from Grandpa.

"Nobody ever talked about Grandpa. Years later, Mom told me how he would come home drunk with soiled pants and beat Grandma. Then she would heat water on the stove and clean him up. I imagined Grandpa standing pathetically on the cold linoleum floor in the kitchen being cleaned like a baby getting his diapers changed. How degrading it must have been for Grandma to wipe away the feces of the man who abandoned and abused her!"

Sky turned the page in her storybook and shuddered involuntarily as a new scene emerged. Spring and Gritty absorbed some of the fear emanating from her as they looked at the images on the page, unconsciously bracing themselves as feelings of tenderness for Sky surfaced from the pool of their hearts.

Tall white columns held up the roof of a small porch, making the little bungalow look much larger than it was. Inside the house, Sky was in her crib in the small front bedroom, crying. With a voice filled with anger her mom was telling her to stop. Frightened by the scowl on her face and her harsh tone, Sky cried harder. Her mom walked over to the door and sternly said, "You can just stay in your crib until you stop crying," but Sky couldn't stop. Her mom turned off the light and left the room, slamming the door behind her. Sky was alone in the stillness, abandoned. She kept crying for a long time. She wanted Mom to come back and hold her but there was no response. She cried louder. She screamed. No response.

It was getting dark outside. Blackness crept across the room like a tunnel with no light at the end and no escape. Sky stood, shaking the sides of her crib as violently as her tiny hands and arms could, putting the full strength of her determined and frightened body into it, trying to get out. Still no response. She threw herself onto the mattress, thrashing her small body back and forth like a sack of potatoes, shrieking and wailing her fear.

Then suddenly she became very still and listened. The house was eerily silent and she was afraid Mom had left. She cried louder, sheer terror now consuming her until finally, exhausted and spent, she lay her limp little body down on the mattress and whimpered. Involuntary sobs racked her body. Still no one came and there was no sound in the house. Sky felt totally alone in the world, abandoned for eternity. Everyone had left. They were gone for good and had left her behind forever. She would never see Mom again. Alone in the surrounding darkness and stillness, she fell asleep.

As the scene faded from view, Sky cried softly, re-experiencing the fear and terror of abandonment like it was happening all over again, looking to Spring and Gritty for comfort.

"The next morning," she said, "I heard Mom and our next door neighbor outside my bedroom door. They were laughing about the tantrum I had the night before. I thought my life had ended and they thought it was funny! I was hurt, confused and ashamed and, strangely, also a little proud. Even now as I remember that night, though, my stomach still feels like it is being scraped raw, its red blood turned black in the complete darkness of paralyzing fear."

That reminded Sky of another story, so she continued.

"I got stung by a swarm of bees on Grandma's front porch when I was about five years old. After that I was terrified of insects of all kinds. The sight of any bug or small animal sent me into hysterics, running away screaming and flapping my arms as if gigantic monsters were after me. Everyone would laugh and ridicule me. It became a family joke."

Flipping the pages of her storybook, Sky found the Earth experience she was looking for. Spring and Gritty looked at the emerging scene tenuously, surprised at their own uncertainty and fear. They unconsciously moved closer to Sky.

Two little girls were nestled in their bed under warm woolen blankets, safe and protected from the winter chill. They were almost asleep when their dad suddenly stormed into the room. Between his thumb and forefinger he held a mousetrap, from which a little mouse dangled helplessly by its tail. Laughing sadistically, he suspended the writhing mouse over the bed. Sky screamed in terror. She begged him to please take it away as she pulled the covers over her. Dad laughed cruelly, swinging the pathetic mouse back and forth. Then with an exaggerated flourish, he threw the mouse onto the bed and it landed on Sky's head. He left the room doubled over with laughter.

Sky was in a panic, shrieking and burrowing her head so deep under the covers that she could barely breathe. Through her muffled screams she heard Mom's voice scolding Dad, telling him to stop terrorizing his daughters. Sheepishly, he came back into the room and picked up the mouse. With a penetrating glare at

Sky who was still sniffling under the blankets, he disdainfully muttered, "don't be such a ridiculous scaredy-pants!" He left the room shaking his head in disgust.

Feeling the fear and humiliation all over again, Sky looked up from the Earth scene and said, "It took me a very long time to stop shaking and fall asleep after that. I felt very small and stupid. I wondered why I couldn't be brave like my sister. She never uttered a sound."

Sky then turned the page of her storybook to one more scene. As it unfolded, sadness flowed through her. Spring and Gritty felt it too. They all tried to distance themselves from what they were about to see but somehow knew they would not be successful.

A young girl stood at a busy corner waiting until it was safe to cross the street. Her dog, Tiny, was by her side waiting for instructions. Sky carefully looked both ways for traffic and then yelled, "let's go, Tiny!" as she started to make a run for it. Tiny took off and made it safely to the other side.

Suddenly Sky saw a car barreling toward her at high speed. Afraid that she couldn't outrun it, she turned back. She frantically screamed at Tiny to stay where he was but the poor obedient dog heard only his name and headed back toward her. As he ran into the street the speeding car hit him—hard. He flew several feet through the air before landing with a heavy thud on the pavement. The car screeched, swerved to avoid the small bleeding dog lying in the street, and left. Sky ran over to Tiny and fell to her knees. She held his bloody head in her arms just as he took his last breath, his big brown eyes looking up at her in confusion and pain.

Sky looked up from the scene, shuddering with sobs as she tried unsuccessfully to detach from the fresh, sharp pain. She felt Tiny's soft fur, wet with blood, on her arms…as if it were happening now.

"I walked home," she sighed, "carrying Tiny's limp body. I was inconsolable. I felt guilty all my life for calling Tiny's name that day and for not putting him on a leash. Even now I can see his confused eyes looking up at me as if to say 'why did you call me?'

"Eventually we got another dog. I loved Rocky but my parents said we couldn't keep him. I never understood the reason. They told me a nice family had agreed to adopt him. One day when I returned from running an errand for Grandma, Rocky was gone. I either didn't know or had forgotten that his new owners were coming to get him that morning. I howled in grief. I wailed. I threw myself on the floor and sobbed uncontrollably until my stomach burned. It was impossible to comfort me, although I'm not sure anyone tried. I remembered what happened to the precious little kittens that I had watched being born and lovingly played with for hours in the backyard. One day Dad put them into a pillowcase, took them in the car, and threw them in a lake somewhere. I wondered if Rocky was really adopted since I didn't see his new owners with my own eyes."

Sky closed her storybook slowly and waited for a reaction from the others to her childhood stories. Spring and Gritty, still tasting the bitter anguish of a little girl whose Dad had murdered the kittens she so dearly loved, entered their own private spaces of reflection.

Spring felt bad for the cute little girl with the big blue eyes and blond curls, so innocent—just like Sky really was. She knew everyone faces some trauma on Earth but it was heartbreaking to watch Sky's terror, even if she had experienced it willingly.

Meanwhile Gritty, who was both eager to learn from the stories and protect the little girl for whom she was feeling considerable sympathy, tentatively asked Sky if maybe there hadn't been too much trauma.

"Well, since one of the things that I wanted to learn was to overcome fear," Sky responded thoughtfully, "I guess I had to have enough experiences to produce fear so I would have something to overcome."

Without much forethought, Spring passionately jumped in, "But you didn't make those choices as a young child! Like you didn't choose to have an alcoholic grandpa and a sadistic father—Oh, sorry, I guess maybe you *did* make those decisions, didn't you? But it's not like you remembered them after undergoing birth amnesia. Oh, never mind! The important question is: what did you learn from your childhood traumas?"

Sky was quick to respond, guided by her raw feelings, "When I watched those scenes, my gut reeled as if I were reliving the traumas again in a primitive pre-verbal way. I get it that we know what fear feels like on its deepest level when we experience it in early childhood. I see how early traumatic experiences can unconsciously shape a person's life—though I don't fully understand how it all played out in mine yet."

In her usual diligent way, Gritty considered the choices Sky had made as a child. When she was left alone in her crib, she seemed angry as well as frightened. Her screams were like a protest against the unfairness of being punished for being scared and needy, of being *abandoned,* for God's sake! Maybe that's why she felt proud when she overheard her mom and a neighbor the next morning. When Sky chastised the smelly old men in the bar for looking at her, wasn't she telling them to fuck off? Isn't that why she felt proud when they laughed? Wasn't she expressing her anger at her parents about not making sure she had a chance to say goodbye to her dog Rocky when she howled and threw herself on the floor?

With such thoughts swirling around in her, Gritty blurted out, "You go, girl! Shit, you were something else even when you were very young. I think your screaming and yelling was a protest against unfairness—and that's a protest of the most divine sort!"

"You're absolutely right," Sky quickly responded. "it wasn't fair, none of it was. But, then, what does fairness mean anyway? It sure wasn't fair that Grandma was such a good person and had to be stuck with my drunken grandpa either!"

"Well, maybe, in the end," interjected Spring, "what you experienced as a child helped you to recognize unfairness and feel the hurt of it and maybe, just maybe, that was enough."

Just then, Suma appeared and said, "Not so fast, ladies! I have a question before you move on. If you had not been exposed to these traumas in your childhood, Sky, what would you now lack in understanding?"

Sky thought about how the impact of trauma helped her be conscious of where she was, to be tuned into her own feelings. But it didn't stop there.

"I became very sensitive to other people's feelings," she responded, "and I doubt I would have developed that ability without experiencing trauma as a child."

Satisfied with her insight, Sky waved goodbye with a smile as Suma's energy moved off into the distance.

Spring's frustration with Suma bordered on irritation and she didn't like or understand what she was feeling. Instead of appreciating Suma's ability to always aim her questions at the heart of things, she chafed at it. She hoped that she wasn't implying now that the traumatic experiences that poor Sky had endured had been a gift; she simply couldn't accept that.

Sky and Gritty sensed Spring's agitation. They glanced knowingly at each other, silently agreeing that it would be best not to comment.

*   *   *   *

Spring's energy was spent, her confusion growing. She didn't know what was wrong with her, only that something was different this time. Maybe she just needed more time to recover after living such a long life on Earth. She was relieved when Gritty announced that she wanted to tell her childhood stories next.

With a touch of apprehension, Gritty pulled her storybook toward her as Spring and Sky turned their energies in her direction.

"When I was growing up," she began, "our house was on a busy street with a bus stop on the corner, in a neighborhood that was like a stew consisting only of white potatoes. I lived in the midst of an extended family of Scandinavian relatives, neighbors, church people, and assorted merchants like the pharmacist and the clerk at the five and dime store down the street. My grandparents, six uncles and aunts and fifteen cousins lived within a few miles of our house, some within walking distance."

Gritty opened her storybook and turned to a page that transported them into the first Earth scene she had selected. Spring and Sky looked on curiously as the image of a big square building emerged, not knowing what to expect. When Gritty shrugged as if to say, "Just wait," they relaxed into it.

The Christian Elementary School was in a large foreboding building with its name boldly plastered over the main entrance. Lunchtime was over and afternoon classes were about to begin. The bell had rung and the children were already inside, the gravel playground silent and empty. A block away, a little girl and her brother were running as fast as they could, crying and gasping for breath, stumbling in their panic. They were late. It wasn't their fault—their mother didn't have lunch ready when they got home.

But they were terrified. They knew what was coming. The principal kept a big paddle in his office and beat children with it when they were tardy. Mr. Post was a tall man, stiff as a statue with little glasses on the tip of his nose that emphasized the sternness of his face. All the children were afraid of him. Some had seen the paddle. Everyone knew its story.

"It's not our fault," Gritty gasped to her younger brother between breaths, "he *has* to understand that."

Suddenly her little brother stopped, frozen with terror. He knew they would not be spared Mr. Post's wrath no matter what Gritty said. He abruptly turned to face home. Gritty begged him to keep running, told him everything would be okay even though she wasn't convinced of it herself. Unable to face Mr. Post, the little boy slowly began to walk toward home, his head drooping in defeat.

Gritty turned and bravely resumed running, the sound of her little brother's pathetic sobs becoming more distant in her ears. When she reached the school and saw the abandoned playground, she stopped and took a deep breath. This was it. She courageously walked into her second grade classroom, shaking and out of breath, bracing for the moment she would be sent to the principal's office. She could almost feel the paddle on her bottom already. She wondered if the part about Mr. Post pulling up little girls' skirts was true.

Everyone was busy working on an assignment as she quietly sat down at her desk and made herself invisible. She took out her notebook, glancing furtively at her teacher as she opened it and pretended to work. To her amazement, no one seemed to notice her tardiness.

Responding to the perplexed looks from Spring and Sky as they glanced up from the scene, Gritty explained, "The point is that I was convinced that I would get a beating that day and when I didn't I began to doubt whether Mr. Post had a paddle in his office at all and to wonder if any of the stories about him were true."

Gritty somehow knew the story about Mr. Post was significant. She knew that experiences like that raised questions for her about who she could trust, what she could believe, who was telling the truth, and if there was more than one truth.

She shook her head and looked at Spring and Sky with a shrug. She was sure things would become clear. Then she turned the page and the scene shifted from The Christian School to a small house just a block away.

The house belonged to Gritty's grandparents. Inside, in the living room, an old woman sat in a wheelchair surrounded by overstuffed furniture. The room was overheated to warm her brittle bones and it was always immaculate to suit her fancy. In constant pain from debilitating arthritis, Grandmother's frail eighty-pound body was perched like a mean little bird on the seat. Her cruel harsh voice unceasingly croaked commands at Grandfather who went about the house doing all the cooking, cleaning, and laundry without complaint. He quietly took the blame for everything that was wrong, which was just about everything if you were to believe Grandmother.

Gritty stayed a safe distance from her, never daring to touch her, imagining her hands as cold, bony, and disagreeable—just like Grandmother herself.

Gritty and her brother sat at the kitchen table eating lunch. Grandfather always made pigs in the blanket for them, knowing they were Gritty's favorite. She put her fork into the warm pastry, retrieved the little sausage from the middle, and tasted its spiciness next to the sweetness of the maple syrup he kindly poured on top. She felt sorry for Grandfather.

"Grandfather never raised his voice," Gritty said with a shake of her head. "Years later, I heard that he had abandoned a wife and children in the old country and married Grandmother without getting divorced first. One of my cousins told me his first wife was Grandmother's sister but I never knew whether to believe that or not. She also said that Grandfather never accepted a deacon position in church because he didn't feel worthy. Of course, people didn't know any of his history so they saw it as the righteous decision of a humble, religious man who worked modestly for God with no thought for his own glory. I wondered if it was his shame that silenced him in the face of Grandmother's verbal abuse.

"I was always curious about things like that. I was very careful not to let anyone know it, though. It wasn't safe to ask questions. But I was an incurably inquisitive child."

With that statement, Gritty flipped the pages in her storybook until she settled on the scene of a big white church with stained glass windows casting colorful reflections over the sanctuary. Spring and Sky tightened up, thinking that there was sure a lot about religion in Gritty's childhood and it elicited some of their own Earth memories. They looked at her questioningly and once again Gritty just shrugged and said, "you'll see."

Gritty was a little girl, leaning against the wall, invisible to adults in her silence. Light through one of the stained glass windows illuminated her pink face as she took in everything around her. Her father and uncles were taking different roles in the service—reading from their well-worn Bibles, handing out bulletins as people entered the sanctuary, ushering people to their pews, leading the congregation in singing, even preparing to preach the sermon. They were the pillars of the church. Later she sat with her parents and brother and listened carefully to the lessons that were taught each Sunday from the pulpit. Over and over again she heard that drinking, smoking, card playing, dancing, and adultery were forbidden sins. It must be true.

Another turn of the page and the scene changed to the living room in her house. It was Friday night and Gritty sat on the floor hiding behind a big stuffed chair, close to her bedroom door for a speedy retreat if necessary. She secretly watched Daddy and his brothers. They sat around card tables late into the night, playing cards and drinking beer from special glasses, unaware that little Gritty was taking in the scene. Grandfather wasn't there; Grandmother usually didn't allow him to go places without her.

"I tried," Gritty interjected, "to make sense of what I saw. They were sinning but their laughter and bantering seemed like a good thing, a sign of brotherly solidarity. I didn't understand why they smoked the foul smelling cigars, though. It was disgusting the way the tips would get slimy and squishy in their mouths. I stared with fascination at the crisp, clear sparkling beer topped off with an ample band of soft white foam in the beautifully tall and sleek glasses. Their voices got louder and their laughter more boisterous as the night wore on and as I stared at the foam caressing their upper lips I noticed who filled his glass most often. I liked Uncle Dennis best. He smoked a lot of cigarettes, drank the most beer and almost never went to church. He was kind to me but there was more to it than that. I recognized something in him, something familiar that I did not yet understand.

"Mostly I watched Daddy. He was a comedian who would go to any lengths to get a laugh. He would fall off his chair and catch his glass of beer just in time so it wouldn't spill onto the carpet. Everyone gasped, worried that he might have had a heart attack or stroke. When they realized it was just another joke they all laughed hysterically. I watched, not knowing exactly what I was learning."

Then Gritty turned to a new scene in her storybook and immediately felt the confusion that was so familiar to her as a child, only now it was clouded with sadness and a touch of anger. Spring and Sky moved closer to reassure her as they watched the images emerge.

It was the first day of April, a beautiful spring afternoon. Gritty and her brother were outside playing. They were very excited. They had thought of the best April Fools joke ever to play on Mother. Gritty was sure she would think it was very funny. She might even think they were just as clever as Daddy. Her brother hid around the side of the house as Gritty went up on the porch and rang the doorbell. When Mother came to the door Gritty screamed, "Come quick! Tom was hit by a car!"

Mother was horrified. She screamed in panic. Pleased as punch that she had been so convincing, Gritty puffed up her chest with pride. On cue Tom jumped up onto the porch and together they laughingly shouted, "April fools! April fools!" Jumping up and down with glee, they slapped their hands together, congratulating themselves for pulling the joke off so perfectly.

All of a sudden and out of the blue, Mother grabbed Gritty by the collar, pulling her into the house with such force and strength it sucked the breath right out of her. She was crying and screaming over and over at the top of her lungs, "Don't you *ever* do that again! What were you *thinking*?!"

Gritty was shocked. She had never seen Mother that upset. She didn't understand how or why things had gone so wrong. When Daddy did things like this everyone thought it was hilarious.

"So there I was," Gritty said to Spring and Sky, her voice filled with angry laughter as she looked up from the scene, "banished to my room for the rest of the day without dinner. Mother said I was supposed to sit there and think about what we did. All I could figure out is that I didn't do the joke right or that Mother was in a bad mood or that only Daddy got to be the funny one in our family.

"No one spoke about the incident again and I was afraid to ask Mother about it. I thought I should know what happened and was embarrassed about not being able to figure it out. All I knew was that bad things seemed to happen when I played the same kind of joke that got Daddy a laugh. Fear told me to be cautious, hold myself back, just watch in silence."

Gritty then turned to another page in her storybook and was flooded with mixed feelings—love, pity, mischievousness, awe—as several new Earth images emerged.

Gritty's mother scrubbed clothes in an old wringer washtub on the back porch of their small house, then hung them on the long clothesline in the back yard. Standing on her feet for hours she ironed the now dry clothes before cooking dinner. She was a hard worker who never complained.

The scene shifted back to the yard. Little Gritty was playing beside Mother who was taking clothes off the line. Mother was angry and came toward her with a stick. That meant she had been bad and was about to get spanked but Gritty didn't know what she had done. She dodged the stick aimed at the front of her legs and ducked the next swing as well, laughing and daring Mother to catch her.

Taking the bait, Mother gripped the stick in her hand so tightly that blue veins popped out on top. As she was being chased around the perimeter of the clothesline Gritty laughed and teased and joked as if it were a game. Furious, Mother finally gave up and with exasperation in her voice, threatened, "Just wait until your father gets home!"

Gritty laughed harder, figuring Mother would forget, especially if Daddy got home late from work like he usually did.

Interrupting their viewing of the scene, Gritty told Sky and Spring, "I was never afraid of Mother. I teased her when she was mad at me, just like Daddy did whenever she was mad at him. Mother was sweet, kind, long suffering, and vulnerable. I felt sorry for her. When I was ten years old, she had a hernia operation and I was sure it was because she strained herself chasing me around the clothesline that day. That surgery was the first of many that plagued her the rest of her life. I knew it was my fault that she was so sick and frail."

Gritty then turned the page of her storybook and showed them a picture of her father before continuing.

"Daddy was another matter. He would stand with his hands in his pockets, his greasy black hair combed straight back, a silly grin on his face. To me, he was larger than life. Not just to me, either. Mother would look at him adoringly like she worshipped him or something. He was a highly respected leader in the church but he was more than that to Mother. Daddy was her star, her king, her boss, her savior. Once, in school, I drew a picture of our family. Daddy was more than twice as big as Mother with gigantic hands and my brother was almost the same size as Mother. I was a dot in the corner of the page, a little eye looking down on them.

"Daddy was always the center of attention. He insisted on it. Other people saw him as a devoted family man, a strong provider who dedicated his life to the Lord and his church. They didn't see the man who would impulsively jump up in an unexpected explosion of rage and hit my brother. With the palm of his hand Daddy would hit the back of Tom's neck first. Then he would flick his wrist and hit the back of Tom's head so hard it jerked forward and flopped down onto his chest. Mother always screamed 'don't hit them on the head! Hit them on the butt!' Just as fast as it started, it would suddenly be over. Mother would then mutter that he needed to be careful not to hurt us and Daddy would look contrite. I'm sure he must have hit me like that. It's funny I don't remember.

"Daddy owned a hardware store and was kind of a handyman who knew a little about everything, having learned the trade from Grandfather. His store was in a poor neighborhood where people didn't look like us. Daddy worked eighteen hours a day, six days a week and his store was stocked with everything imaginable, all crammed into a very small space."

Gritty turned to a new page in her storybook, wanting to show them another mystery that she had tried to unravel as a child.

It was the middle of the night and the house was dark and quiet, except for Daddy's rhythmic snoring. Through her sleepy fog, Gritty heard the phone ring. Their voices were muffled and the words inaudible through the thickness of wall but Mother and Daddy sounded distressed. Doors opened and closed and a car started. Then Gritty fell back to sleep.

The next morning Daddy and Mother were gone. Gritty's favorite aunt was in the kitchen fixing breakfast.

"There was a fire in your father's store during the night," she explained to sleepy-eyed Gritty, "but I'm sure that your folks will be home soon."

Gritty watched silently as Mother and Daddy came into the house a few hours later looking haggard and tired. Daddy's store was gone, completely destroyed by a fire of mysterious origins.

Gritty thought Daddy would be more upset than he seemed. She wondered if maybe he was just exhausted. After that, he stayed home for a while and eventually opened a new hardware store in another town. Gritty never doubted that he would.

"So, now you can see," she said as she closed her storybook, "that my childhood was characterized more by confusion than by fear like Sky's was."

Gritty thought about how good it had been to tell her stories. When she considered what she learned during her childhood, it was as clear as a bell: it was safer to observe than to act and spontaneity was dangerous.

Sky felt bad for Gritty. She had tried so hard to figure out what was right and what was wrong. Just when she thought she had it figured out—like the April Fools' joke—she got slammed. Not only was she confused; she got punished for it.

Spring thought about all the mixed messages that Gritty had tried to sort out. There was the surface appearance of things that everyone seemed to believe was real: a school principal who beat children, a righteous grandfather, her father's great sense of humor, uncles who were devoted church men, forbidden sins. Beneath the surface, other things happened: the principal didn't have a paddle, her grandfather was a bigamist, her father's laughs were at other people's expense, her uncles and father drank to excess, smoked and played cards. No wonder Gritty was confused as a child.

For some inexplicable reason, Spring then hoped that Suma wouldn't appear. In an attempt to keep her at bay, she speculated about the question Suma might ask if she were here and then asked it herself, "So, Gritty, if you had not been exposed to these inconsistencies in your childhood, what would you now lack in understanding?"

Gritty paused, stumped by the question.

Suddenly Suma appeared in a burst of deep blue, alighting gently on the table like a butterfly. "Maybe it would help," she suggested to Gritty, "if you reflected a bit more about how your confusion affected you."

With typical determination, Gritty conscientiously explored the answer to Suma's question. She dug into her unconscious, shoveling through the confusion and under the conflicting messages. She dug deeper until she hit a big boulder at the bottom. She immediately knew that it was guilt—guilt about not being able to figure things out fast enough to stay out of trouble, to protect herself and others. When she took action and it was wrong, she got hurt; when she watched and did nothing, she got hurt...or someone else got hurt. She remembered feeling guilty when she couldn't figure out how to help Grandfather, to make Grandmother stop screaming at him. She had carried the heavy rock of guilt around and felt its familiar immobilizing weight on her back until finally it had become who she was.

Sky jumped in then as if reading Gritty's mind and empathically declared, "There was no way you could have been expected to sort out what was real and what wasn't, you know. You were too young. You sure were a trouper at trying to figure it out, though."

"Not only that," Spring jumped in angrily, with an intensity that surprised everyone, "your parents set you up! Why the hell was it funny when your father played jokes that scared people and hurtful when you did it? How come no one explained anything to you? I bet they didn't want to expose things for what they really were. It really wasn't fair, you know!"

Spring's seething energy boiled and bubbled, moving in all directions at once. What was she so angry about? She hovered over the others, thinking about how Suma had appeared right after her own question to Gritty had fallen flat. That made her fume even more.

Sky and Gritty exchanged worried glances but they relaxed when they saw that Suma was still there and didn't seem to be at all bothered. With the gentleness of acceptance, she responded to Spring's outburst.

"You're right," Suma said, "it was unfair in one sense. In their narcissistic way, children often feel responsible for things for which they can't possibly be responsible. In their role as teachers, parents need to help them disentangle themselves from that unfair burden. It's understandable for you to wish that Gritty's parents had been more adequate."

Then she added, "In order to gain perspective, though, it might be useful to consider how they were helpful to Gritty."

Gritty laughed. One of the issues that she wanted to confront this time was guilt and her parents had provided all the opportunities she needed. Through her confusion, she had begun to recognize that things were not always as they seem, a valuable initial lesson in honesty and dishonesty. She suspected it was a lesson that would come back to haunt her. Then she considered what Spring had said about unfairness. She would have to think more about that.

"Isn't it ironic," she said to Spring, "just as I was thinking about how I learned that spontaneity was dangerous, in you jumped with your intense feelings about fairness! Your spontaneity sure gave me more to think about."

Spring's anger subsided somewhat. They had learned a lot from Gritty's stories but once again it had been due to Suma's wisdom. Troubled by the resentment she felt toward her, she tried in vain to understand its source and the reason for its intensity. Even though her feeling toward Suma seemed old and familiar she couldn't put her finger on what it was about. As she moved to the center and picked up her storybook, she hoped her uneasiness and tiredness wouldn't interfere with her ability to focus on her own childhood.

As she looked at Sky and Gritty to signal that she was ready to tell her stories, she was relieved to see that Suma was gone.

*   *   *   *

With discomfort still lurking within her, Spring recovered enough to hug Sky and Gritty and laugh at herself.

"My passion," she said, "always seems to make it impossible for me to keep my stuff out of your stuff. It's a good thing it's my turn now."

Sky and Gritty laughed as Spring opened her storybook. Their relieved smiles evaporated quickly, though, as a scene emerged from the page and they were immediately brought into an Earth space, one that was hot and stifling and transparently serious. New feelings swept over them, feelings from which they would not be able to escape.

Four little children ranging in age from two to six were crowded in the back seat of a car among suitcases and boxes, scrunched together like sardines in the tight space. Sweat dripped from their arms and legs as they leaned against each other in the heat. Everyone was unhappy. Their father had driven for a long stretch without stopping. He was tired. He hadn't gotten any relief since their mother wouldn't drive, didn't have a license even if she wanted to.

The family was on its annual vacation, a trip for which Mother carefully planned and prepared for weeks in advance. Even though the children always anticipated it with great excitement, they were now cranky. The reality of four kids stuck together in a car traveling across miles and miles of dusty, flat and boring farmland was too much for them.

Spring, who was almost five years old, was tired of playing the little games that Mother enticed them with to make the time go faster and keep them from bickering.

"Mother, Ron is sitting in my space! Make him move! He's touching me!" Spring screamed from the backseat.

"Am not!" Ron screamed back, "She's lying!"

Spring was bored and wanted to know how much longer the drive was going to be. It seemed never ending and she wanted to know why they hadn't made much progress. When would they ever get there? She saw a sign along the road that said U.S. Highway 10. Maybe the sign held the answer.

"Are we *still* in the United States?" she asked in a curious and impatient little voice.

Mother and Father laughed and exchanged looks of pleasure.

"Well, when will we be leaving the country *anyway*?" Spring asked more insistently.

Mother and Father laughed harder. Spring's older sister laughed along with them. They all laughed for a very long time.

Spring crossed her arms in front of her chest and said nothing. She didn't laugh, didn't even smile. She just watched the farmland go by and hit her younger brother whenever he touched her. She heard their laughter long after it stopped and didn't ask any more questions.

Looking up from her storybook at Sky and Gritty, Spring stepped back from the scene in the car. It had touched a deep place of shame, so new to her as a child and so piercing in its familiarity now.

"My parents," she interjected, "never suspected how I experienced their laughter that day. I thought they were making fun of me and I felt stupid. I wondered what they knew that I didn't know—and why I didn't know it. I went into a place of shame where questions are never asked and began pretending that I understood things when I didn't."

Spring then pointed back at the car scene in her storybook and they continued to watch.

The car finally slowed to a stop and Father parked. The sun was beginning to set and the bright orange neon vacancy light in the little motel window in front of them flashed its welcome. Father said it was the best price they would find. The day had been long and boring but now everyone started to perk up.

This was Spring's favorite part of the trip. They always stayed in one room and it was crowded but she loved the white towels and little soaps and miniature bottles of shampoo and curling up in her little nest on the floor next to her parents' bed.

Everyone scrambled out of the car and stretched their legs. They pulled the suitcases out of the trunk and lugged them inside. Then they went out to eat. They never went out to dinner unless they were on vacation. After the boring breakfast and lunch that Mother pulled from the cardboard box and cooler in the backseat, eating in a restaurant was a double treat.

They all crowded into a booth in the diner next to the motel. It was long and narrow like a railroad car with handmade signs on the walls claiming that their homemade food tasted just like your grandma's. The brightly lit diner was busy, buzzing with friendly chatter as the waitress scurried from booth to booth taking and delivering orders and making small talk.

Spring eagerly reached across the table for a piece of warm, fragrant homemade bread in the basket the waitress had left along with their drinks. It smelled just like Mother's, fresh from the oven. Suddenly her hand accidentally bumped the full glass of milk in front of her and it tipped. A look of horror filled her eyes as she watched the milk flow in slow motion across the table down onto the linoleum floor, crossing the toe of her shoe before spreading outward across the diner.

Mother and Father yelled, taking turns shouting invectives at her one after another:

"How could you possibly be so stupid and clumsy?"

"Now look what you've done again!"

"Can't you even behave when we're out in public?"

"What is the matter with you?"

"Can't you do anything right?"

Mother frantically wiped up the spilled milk and with it the shame she felt at having such a stupid daughter. Some people looked at Spring with pity, others with scorn. She hung her head and looked down, frozen in place, fearful of further wrath if she tried to move or make any attempt to help. Her eyes stung and she felt like crying but she didn't. She didn't say anything, just held her hands in her lap and looked at them. She didn't speak for the rest of the meal but no one seemed to notice. The homemade bread that smelled so delicious and heavenly before now tasted like cardboard in her mouth.

Spring closed her storybook and looked away with tears in her eyes. She thought more about spilling her milk in the diner. Her three-year-old brother Ron just sat there smiling the whole time, looking angelic and innocent. It was important to tell Sky and Gritty about him.

"When I was two years old," she said, "Mother was pregnant with her third child. My parents prayed that they would finally get the boy they had wished for twice before. Just before Mother went to the hospital, I had a nightmare about a baby boy who grew into monstrous proportions and devoured me. Of course I secretly wished for a sister. When Mother brought my new baby brother home, sure enough he was the center of attention. Everything he did was a miracle and a joy, even when his little thing shot pee right into my face while Mother was changing his diapers. I figured this was just a sign of how it was going to be.

"A neighbor came to visit and put her arm around my shoulders and said 'It must be so exciting and wonderful for you to *finally* have a brother!' As if I had been waiting for one! I angrily pulled away and shouted, 'I hate him! I never wanted a brother at all. I wanted a sister!' The neighbor looked nonplussed and said nothing more.

"She didn't know what I knew: that my brother was the 'chosen one' and I was 'the disappointment.' On the day I was born Father came to the hospital with a football; he was sure his second born child would have to be a boy after what I always assumed was his first paternal disappointment—my sister. I was his second.

"I knew that I was somehow wrong and it was my brother's fault. I would make him pay. In my own way, I suppose that I did. When I wasn't ignoring Ron, I was fighting with him. Mostly we fought. I still feel sorry and guilty about some of the things I did to him—even though he usually asked for it."

Spring reopened her storybook and skipped several pages until she reached the last story that she wanted to tell about her childhood. She introduced the scene by talking about how musical her mother was, how beautifully she played the violin, piano and organ. When Spring asked for violin lessons her mother had readily agreed.

As images began to emerge from the page an ominous cloud descended over them. Sky and Gritty moved closer to Spring, huddling together to brace against the approaching storm, unsure what Earthly form or intensity it would take but knowing it would be significant.

Seven-year-old Spring and her mother climbed up several steep steps to a simple dark green house highlighted by white trim and window boxes filled with colorful pink and red impatiens. They walked hand in hand past the profusion of fragrant flowers and bushes crowding the narrow cobblestone walk. As Mother knocked on the front door, Spring tightly clutched her precious little black case. A kindly looking older woman invited them in and they entered the cozy living room where Spring would learn to play the violin.

The room was crammed with furniture. Stacks of sheet music and music books lay in disarray on the floor, a coffee table, and every other available surface. A big soft brown couch dominated the room, smelling and looking old and worn but deliciously comfortable. African violets in beautiful hues of purple were on the windowsill, providing background for a baby grand piano in the bright, cheerful room.

Spring beamed with excitement as she took out her shiny treasure. The teacher was kind and patient. During her first lesson, Spring learned about the strings and how to tune them, to hold the violin properly, to play a few basic songs. Her assignment was to practice "Twinkle, Twinkle Little Star" before her next lesson. She was so proud!

The scene then shifted to the following day. It was Sunday. Spring's family walked to church together, everyone dressed in their best clothes and looking sparkling clean from their weekly Saturday night baths.

The church was just down the block from their house. It had traditional stained glass windows and enough wooden pews to hold a congregation of several hundred. There were classrooms in a wing adjacent to the sanctuary and a big, open meeting hall in the basement.

Father, who was very active in the church, walked over to talk to the minister in the vestibule as soon as they arrived. Mother was the organist so she went to the front of the sanctuary to get ready to play the opening hymn.

Spring headed toward her second grade Sunday School class. The teacher stood by the door greeting the children as they arrived. Spring excitedly told her about her new violin.

"Why, that is wonderful news!" the teacher said encouragingly, "Maybe you could play for us sometime at the Sunday evening children's hour!"

Spring was delighted and told her that she would play that very night.

The scene shifted and it was Sunday evening. Filled with pride and eager to perform at the children's hour, Spring walked briskly toward the church. She sat in the front row of the basement meeting room, setting her violin case carefully on the floor beside her. Soon the room was filled with reverberating sounds of jostling and chattering first through sixth grade children. Spring sat quietly and looked straight ahead with nervous anticipation.

Finally a heavy-set woman went to the front of the room and called for quiet. Everyone complied. They liked the round and jolly children's director and sang boisterously as she led them in song. She told a story about a little child who was lost and then found by his father and how everyone was happy in the end. The children listened with interest until she read Bible verses that told a similar story about a lost sheep but in words they didn't understand.

Then it was time for Spring's performance. The children's director introduced her warmly, telling everyone how proud she was of her for learning to play such a difficult instrument.

Spring proudly walked to the front of the cavernous room. Everyone was very quiet as they watched her open the black case. She looked admiringly at her shiny new violin. How she loved the look and feel of its polished brown wood! She took it out of its case, stood up and looked out at all the little upturned faces watching her. Suddenly her violin felt very heavy and she lifted it up in slow motion.

Then she froze. She tried to put the violin under her chin but couldn't remember the proper way to hold it. She tried to put her fingers on the strings but they wouldn't move; she didn't know which strings or fingers to use. She stood in front of the room motionless, barely breathing.

An eternity passed. Children fidgeted in their seats, then someone giggled. Soon the twittering turned to laughter echoing off the walls of the big open room.

In a fog, Spring hung her head and put her violin back in its case. The room went silent as she walked slowly back to her seat in the front row and sat down. The children's director looked at her sympathetically and said something soothing about looking forward to hearing her play some other time.

The only thing Spring heard was the laughter.

Closing her storybook with a slam, Spring startled Sky and Gritty as she abruptly pulled them from the scene, hoping for a reprieve from her pain back in the spiritual space of the library.

"Then it happened again," she said emphatically. "I went into my deep pit of shame. By then it was very familiar to me. I heard nothing else the rest of the evening as I sat stiffly in the little metal folding chair like a humiliated statue until children's hour ended. Then I walked drearily down the street to my house. I went straight to bed. I told no one what happened…and no one asked.

"My view of the world and my place in it was quite simple by then. Having to practice or learn something meant I was stupid, deficient. Knowing this influenced everything.

"But another side of me also emerged—a stubbornness that kept me going to violin lessons. I did learn to play and in high school was promoted to first chair in the orchestra. I was certain it was either because the teacher liked me or felt sorry for me. There could be no other explanation for I allowed nothing to disturb my belief in my defectiveness. After I graduated, I never picked up the violin again."

Spring bowed her head for a few minutes, immersed in deep reflection. One of her goals had been to overcome shame. Now she saw how the foundation for that work had been laid in her childhood. She wrote her shame-based script at a very young age and it convinced her that she was not good enough, smart enough, talented enough. At the core of it, she was unacceptable as a human being. The proof was all around her: she didn't know what others knew and couldn't do things without practice. The birth of her brother confirmed her unacceptability for he was clearly acceptable in every way—even when he peed in her face. Now if *she* had done that you can bet there would have been a very different reaction. Of course, there was no way she could have done it without the right physical equipment…just more proof of her inadequacy.

Sky was incredulous. Spring's mother and father had failed to explain even the most basic things to her—what highway signs mean, that accidents happen in life, that everything requires learning and practice. As a little child Spring had to figure everything out herself. The best she could do was to conclude that something was wrong with her. That made Sky angry.

Gritty thought about how *none* of their parents had explained things to them. Nor had they been sensitive to how children think and feel. Had they all purposely chosen ineffectual parents? Even though they were provided with what they needed to accomplish their goals—to overcome fear, guilt and shame—did it have to entail not getting what they needed to grow as healthy, happy children?

Then Gritty thought about her own guilt about not being able to act appropriately and how different that was from Spring's shame about herself as a person. The antidote to guilt was learning to act with discernment, to change behavior; but what could you do if you were unacceptable no matter what you did? She couldn't think of an antidote for shame.

Suma had not appeared to join in the discussion. Spring felt both relieved and hurt about that. Figuring she would just have to ask the question herself, she interrupted the silence and asked, "So, what did I learn from my childhood experiences?"

Gritty, still unable to find an antidote for shame, was anxious about whether Spring would be able to find a way out of the dark cavern into which she had been plunged. Her shame seemed so deep and entrenched at such an early age. She had never worried about Spring before, but this seemed different. She wanted to help, to somehow find a solution.

"Not so fast!" she cried, "I hear your shame loud and clear, but there were other ways in which you were affected by your experiences. Your violin story revealed tenacity as well as shame. You didn't quit taking lessons. You kept going and even excelled."

Spring was quiet for a few minutes. Once again Gritty had diligently pushed her to dig deeper.

"Ahhhh, yes," she finally responded, "I was so convinced of my unacceptability that I had to make sure that no one else found out about it. So, my solution was to study and practice very hard—but keep it a secret. I pretended to just know things without having to learn them, to automatically have skills without having to practice them. This was all unconscious, of course, which only increased its power."

"That proves," insisted Gritty, "that you were a *survivor*! You didn't succumb to your shame. Something wouldn't let you be a victim. Something made you determined to overcome—kept you going to those violin lessons."

"But my goal," Spring argued, "was only to avoid exposure and public humiliation. Accomplishing things was my way to cover up the secret of my unacceptability. When I did achieve something—like being moved up to first chair in the orchestra—*I* still knew I was deficient and therefore undeserving."

Gritty sat quietly, disappointed that her attempts to help Spring feel better had failed.

"There's something else," Sky suddenly interjected, "that we haven't talked about: your *anger*. It was most obvious when your brother was born but when you became silent in the car and the restaurant, there it was and…"

"Indeed!"

Spring surprised Sky with her spontaneous interruption but her insights were coming with the intensity of a multitude of flashing light bulbs, so blindingly illuminating that she felt she couldn't communicate fast enough. She was coming into a new, deeper understanding—and had more questions.

"Yes, I *was* angry!" she said. "You know what I think it was? Even as a child, I recognized unfairness and it pissed me off!"

That was all Spring could say about it right now. She knew she had never been able to tolerate life's unfairness. Once, as an adult, she told her therapist about something that she thought was unfair and her therapist asked, "So you think things *should* be fair?" That response confused her and she still wondered what her therapist meant.

Yes, she thought that life should be fair and she was angry at the unfair things that happened to all of them as children—like Gritty getting punished for her April Fools joke with no explanation—like Sky's parents not letting her say good-bye to her dog Rocky—like her own parents laughing at her and criticizing her.

Then she wondered what they were supposed to learn from their collective experiences: that life was unfair and they should just accept it? To recognize unfairness so they could do something about it? To know how painful it was so they would be sensitive to others?

Spring wished for Suma's wisdom now. She wondered why she hadn't appeared after her stories like she had for both Sky and Gritty. She considered calling for her, knowing that she would always help if asked, but something kept her from doing so and she hid her thoughts from the others.

Sky and Gritty were absorbed in their own reflections and collective insights. They didn't notice Spring's restless and increasingly disturbed energy, oblivious to the dangers that loomed like threatening storm clouds in the distance.

PART III

▼

STEALTH IDENTITIES

"The self can be imprisoned and caged,
but as long as the person is breathing…
some part of [her] song will be sung."

Clark E. Moustakas
Loneliness and Love

Trying to shake off her uneasiness, Spring moved her energy in rapid spurts back and forth, up and down. Yet the feelings lingered unpleasantly, refusing to dissipate. Attributing her negative feelings to Suma was not an option here in this spiritual place, yet it seemed that projection was the only way out of her confusion. Earth's irritating finger of blame pinched her like tight-fitting jeans and she wished to be free of its frustratingly elusive hold on her. She began to think of herself again as Sheila, an entity that seemed both unrelated to Spring and at one with her at the same time.

Her only option was to proceed in spite of her unsettledness, calling upon the wisdom of her eternities to lead the way. She hoped her trust would hold.

"Spring! Where did you go? Your energy just went swoosh and for a time we couldn't find you!"

It was Sky, calling through the haze of her thoughts. Spring found her way back to the library and saw her and Gritty focusing on her inquisitively, concern coloring their energies.

"I'm sorry," she apologized, "I needed some time alone. I'm ready to get back to work now if you are."

Assuming that Spring might still be thinking about her childhood, Sky and Gritty suggested that she go first this time.

"Oh no," she adamantly replied. She definitely was not ready to be the focus of study and hoped that, by concentrating on Sky and Gritty's stories, she would gain perspective or at least forget about her discomfort for a while.

"I think it would be good," she suggested, "to start with you again, Sky, like we did before."

That suited Sky just fine and she eagerly opened her storybook. Suddenly new and hard to understand feelings seized all three of them. Terror gripped like a vise as a church steeple rose ominously upward from the page. They involuntarily cringed and clung to each other.

Hundreds of people poured into a large church, filling every pew, spilling over into the glassed-in section intended for mothers with crying babies, additional folding chairs set up in the back. The sanctuary was remarkably plain, its dark wooden pews, walls and ceilings devoid of color. The whiteness of a huge movie screen pulled down from the ceiling behind the altar provided an almost shocking contrast to its gloominess.

Sky sat in the front row of the balcony with several other thirteen-year-olds from her church youth group. They fidgeted and giggled as they looked down at the drab people in the dimly lit sanctuary, eagerly waiting for the movie to start. Even though Pastor said it was highly acclaimed around the world, they would have been excited to see a movie of any kind.

Pastor preached that movies were sinful and whenever she wanted to go to one, Sky's mom always asked the same question, "What if Jesus returned to take us up to heaven and you were at the movies?" Now Sky tried to figure out why it was okay to show movies in church, guessing that they must be exempt somehow. Maybe it was because if Jesus came back he would know to look for the saved in a church rather than at a movie theater.

Suddenly the lights were extinguished and a hush fell over the crowd.

Scenes from the movie then emerged in rapid succession: Fires burning, bombs dropping over cities, explosions everywhere—people running in all directions—women, children, old people on crutches and with canes stumbling through streets that crumbled under them—sirens blaring, voices shouting instructions on bullhorns—chaos everywhere—people being blown up and consumed by red hot flames—piercing shrieks of terror and horrible sounds of pain and dying.

Sky sat in a pool of frozen fear, gripping the railing of the balcony as she watched the movie, wondering if it was about the evil of the godless Communists or if it was about World War III.

She saw people frantically running to escape the flames that chased them with terrifying speed, nipping at their ankles, turning their feet into charcoal. She heard the sizzling sounds of burning flesh, deafening explosions, and roaring fires and saw that there was no escape. A desperate man lay on the ground amid the chaos, only a few seconds of life left in him. He had lived a reprehensible life of boundless sin filled with sex, adultery, gambling, stealing, drinking, lying, cheating. Now he prayed, a look of terror in his eyes, and pleaded to Jesus for forgiveness with his last breath. Hearing the sincerity in his voice, Jesus forgave him.

Others were not as lucky. Before they had a chance to be saved their bodies exploded in a burst of heat and fire, incinerated within seconds.

When the movie took a joyful turn Sky realized that it was about the end of the world. The righteous were on their knees thanking Jesus for coming back, praising him, singing with joy and happiness as they were lifted up into the heavens. The man who had been saved at the last minute floated in the clouds above the misery, relief and gratitude on his face. Below him, the condemned screamed in pain as they were thrust into the eternal flames of hell.

Immobilized, Sky sat perfectly still, hands folded in her lap, not a muscle moving. A familiar terror grabbed the pit of her stomach, throwing her back into Grandma's dark closet with the screaming, pounding, threatening.

Then the lights in the church came up and the movie credits faded. A minister stood behind the altar with his arms outstretched.

"Just in time!" he shouted. "He was saved from the flames of hell *just in time.* What about you, my brothers and sisters? Will you wait until the last minute to confess your sins or will you tell Jesus that you are ready *now*?"

Organ music played softly in the background and soon a woman's clear strong voice rang through the sanctuary.

"Just as I am, without one plea, but that Thy blood was shed for me...."

Scores of people stood and began making their way toward the center aisle. They were crying, sobbing, holding hands.

"...and that Thou bidd'st me come to Thee..."

They shook in terror and shame, afraid that Jesus might come back before they reached the altar, that they wouldn't be as lucky as the man in the movie.

"O Lamb of God, I come...I...come."

Desperate people crowded into the aisles. Many had made the walk to salvation before; now fear compelled them to walk it again. They tripped over each other, hands folded in supplication, arms raised to the heavens as they prayed, begged and pleaded for forgiveness. They fell to their knees at the altar where volunteers lay hands on their bowed heads. Together they wailed in a writhing mound, heaving with sin and humiliation.

People around Sky were getting up and leaving the balcony, sobbing as they made their way down the stairs.

Sky's eyes were dry, her body stiff as a statue.

"Will you risk hell," the minister screamed, "or will you tell Jesus that you want to be saved now? To those of you still sitting, I ask, what if Jesus returned tonight while you were sleeping? Would you be ready?"

Sky was now nearly alone in the balcony. She sat glued to the seat. The man in the movie got to live an entire lifetime just the way he wanted and he still went to heaven. All it took was a one-minute confession. She just might hedge her bets like he did.

"Come *now*," the minister urged, "before it's too late!"

She still didn't move, didn't even wiggle. Pastor always said that if you turned it all over to Jesus he would make everything all right. Just like that! Maybe she *should* go forward. Then, when she died, she would go to heaven no matter how much she sinned because she would have been saved.

Still, she didn't get up. How embarrassing to confess your sins in front of everybody! She wouldn't make a spectacle of herself like the others. Her jaw stubbornly protruded in refusal. Then she felt guilty.

She wondered if the devil was in her.

With a sigh Sky closed her storybook, returning to the spirituality of the library, smiling when she saw how relieved Spring and Gritty were to see the church scene disappear.

"Not long after that," she told them, "Pastor asked me if I was saved. I mumbled that I didn't know. The next day while we were washing dishes, Mom said that Pastor had told her what I said. She asked if it was true. I was in a quandary. If I told her the truth, everyone in the damn church would be praying for me and would be on my back until I finally caved in and got on my knees in front of everyone in the universe and confessed my sins. There was no way I would do that! So I lied and said that I was saved but didn't want to talk to Pastor about it because I didn't like him. Mom sighed with relief. She didn't want to talk about it anymore than I did."

Sky remembered how hard she had tried to be a good girl, a desire that was strongly reinforced by her church. Their religion was simple, concrete, black and white. You were saved or doomed, good or evil; what you did was right or wrong—there was nothing in between. The notion of becoming saved was particularly confusing. Since she was already a good girl, why did Pastor call her a sinner in need of salvation? Would something magical happen if she was saved so she wouldn't have to think about what it meant to be good anymore? It seemed to her that conversion was a way to squirm out of things, to take the easy way out somehow. She never dared ask questions that might illuminate things for her, though. That would reveal her doubts and doubting was a sin.

Spring was fascinated by Sky's story and the memories it triggered. She had to go to church, too, but it had no significance for her. It was just another way to conceal her unacceptability; that was why she was president of the youth group, sang in the choir, and taught the little ones in Sunday school. Being good was the same as being successful and being successful was a way to avoid humiliation. Being good for Sky had been different; it was a way for her to feel safe.

Then a long forgotten memory struck Spring with a newness that caused her to impulsively shift the focus from Sky to herself. She opened her own storybook, turning the page with such decisiveness that her intensity penetrated Sky and Gritty, causing them to urge her to tell her story right away. As the scene began to unfold from the page, they found themselves in crisis, filled with Earthly uncertainty and pain.

Spring was fourteen years old. She and her twelve-year-old brother were home alone. He was a brat and they fought all the time. Spring tried to do her homework in spite of Ron's antics. He jumped around like a wild monkey—teasing, taunting, and whining for no particular reason. Increasingly distressed, she screamed at him to knock it off. He echoed what she said. She told him to shut up. He said shut up back at her. Exasperated, she threw her books on the floor. He laughed gleefully at his victory.

Suddenly, Spring flew into an uncontrollable rage. Before he had time to even think about defending himself, she grabbed Ron's hand and pulled it to her mouth. Her fury screamed, "take that, oh special one," as she sank her teeth into the soft webbing between his thumb and forefinger, biting down so hard she felt her upper and lower teeth meet inside his flesh. When she released his hand, blood gushed from the holes made by her sharp teeth and sprayed onto the kitchen floor, slowly spreading its sticky red tentacles across the linoleum.

Spring jumped back in horror at what she had done. Mortified, she looked at the red stains on the floor and then at the stricken face of her brother. She grabbed a towel and wiped the blood from his hand, ordering him to hold it there while she got some bandages. Stunned, he obeyed. Neither of them spoke as she covered the perfect teeth marks in his flesh with ointment and a bandage and he went to bed.

Shame crept across Spring's face and moved down to her gut. It finally settled heavily at the very center of her being and told her she didn't deserve to live.

She fell to her knees on the kitchen floor, clutching her chest with her left hand and opening the door to the oven with her right. Wracked with shame and remorse, she sobbed uncontrollably as her shaky hand reached for the knob to turn on the gas.

Her head fell to her chest as she knelt there. Then both hands abruptly fell to her sides. Without consciousness, she folded them together in prayer. Brought down by her shame, she sobbingly confessed her sin and promised she would never do such a horrible thing again. Then she asked Jesus to forgive all of her sins, to save her from her whole sinful self.

A rush of relief followed, quickly replaced by embarrassment. She looked around in fear that someone, worst of all her brother, might have seen her. She turned off the gas, got up off her knees at once and, acting as if nothing had happened, went back to her homework. It was over.

Spring closed her storybook and the scene evaporated. She was amazed how well she had kept her confession a secret. Not only did she never tell a soul, she had tucked it away so deeply in her own memory bank that it was inaccessible even to her until Sky's story jolted it loose. Her violent behavior that day only confirmed what she already knew. She never believed that Jesus saved her that day. She knew He found her unworthy.

Sky thought about their two salvation stories. It was ironic that Spring, who didn't take church seriously at all, ended up on her knees while she, the one who always tried to be good, refused to get down on hers.

The idea of good and bad dominated Gritty's thoughts. She chuckled. It appeared that she was the only one who tried to be bad. She saw their combined feelings and solutions as a three legged stool: Sky was good as a way to cope with her fear, Spring was successful to cope with her shame, and she was bad to cope with her guilt. Fear, shame, guilt—good, successful, bad—three legs, same stool.

Gritty decided this would be a good time to tell her own church stories. Spring and Sky nodded in agreement.

"When I was a child," she began, "church was a cozy seamless extension of family. After Daddy's hardware store burned, though, he opened a new one in a small town far away and we moved. My parents and a small but determined band of others founded a church there.

"From then on I hated church. It was a place of strangers, totally separate from the rest of my life. Most people in town were Catholic and not Scandanavian like us. Suddenly I was different and I didn't like it one bit. It meant being judged as inferior based on myth and speculation. Just as the country kids were thought to live mysterious and primitive lives without running water or indoor bathrooms, our church was thought of as a fundamentalist cult.

"Daddy was its most prominent leader—founding president, head of the Sunday school, and even preacher of sermons on occasion. When he wasn't working in his store, he was busy being religious. In both places he was the center of attention, as usual, and always joking.

"Our preacher was Reverend Anders, a short ugly man with a smirky smile and black-framed glasses. I detested him. I disliked his three little boys, too. They had the same smirky smiles and thick glasses and thought they ran the church just because their father was the minister.

"Daddy and Reverend Anders were pretty tight. When he dropped by our house unannounced—one of his many annoying habits—Daddy ran to the bathroom to flush his cigar down the toilet. Unbelievably, Reverend Anders never mentioned the sour cigar smell lingering in the air. It was disgusting how he colluded with Daddy's duplicity especially since he always preached that lying was a sin.

"When Reverend Anders said that Catholics would go to hell unless they became saved and stopped worshipping Mary, I was worried. Two of my new best friends, Kristen and Cathy, were Catholics. Reverend Anders also said the Jews killed Christ so they would for sure burn in hell, but I didn't know anyone who was Jewish or what that meant. He gave us pamphlets with instructions about *bearing witness* to the nonbeliever—which included anyone who didn't have the same religious beliefs as ours.

"So here's my salvation story. I didn't want my friends to burn in hell. I decided to save Cathy first. I gave her the pamphlet and told her that she needed to be saved and stop praying to Mary. When she got all huffy I was afraid she wouldn't want to be my friend anymore so after that I decided not to risk trying to save Kristen. A short story, I know, but one with a lot of significance."

Gritty stopped talking and remembered how guilty she felt about not trying to save her friend Kristen, how Cathy's reaction confirmed her belief that things went awry whenever she did act. There it was again: the "guilt about not taking action" mantra and the belief that she was damned if she didn't and damned if she did.

"My rebelliousness increased as Daddy's religiosity intensified," Gritty then continued. "I hated church and found excuses to get out of going. Whatever I was told not to do I did—and then lied about it. Dancing was forbidden so I secretly went to school dances by sneaking out of the house or staying at a friend's house overnight. I went to beer parties. I wore makeup. When I was specifically ordered to stay away from a group of older boys from a neighboring town, I drooled over them with a fervor that almost equaled my thirteen-year-old desire for Elvis Presley. Those boys were everything my parents feared: they had a car, drank beer, wore black leather jackets and engineer boots, combed their greasy hair into ducktails with little curls drooping over their foreheads, and they were Italian and probably Catholic. Of course, I fell madly in love with a couple of them and rode around in their cars at every opportunity.

"My parents despaired, prayed over me, worried that I was a bad seed. Over and over they grounded me and took away my privileges. Nothing worked. When they threatened to send me to a Christian boarding school hundreds of miles away, vividly describing it as a rigorous military academy, I dared them to do it, acted like I didn't care. It was a good thing they didn't follow through. Years later, when I met some girls in college who had gone there, I discovered it was actually a private school for rich kids and those girls were the wildest little gang of rebels the campus had ever seen.

"My parents and Reverend Anders always insisted that dancing was a sin because it led to sex, drinking, and all kinds of perversions. Yet, when I was a senior in high school, my parents let me go to the prom. By then, I was so familiar with inconsistencies between what was said and what was done I didn't think much about it.

"The truth was, I had become one big inconsistency myself. I played the bad girl but I really was a good girl. You could tell I was good by what I did *not* do. I was probably the only girl in my graduating class who didn't have sex before marriage. The biggest hoot was that I didn't drink until after high school even though there were six bars in town and it was both the norm and a source of pride to start drinking at a young age—a boy who got drunk thirteen weekends in a row was our ninth grade hero. I went to beer parties where we stood around huge bonfires in the country, in the middle of nowhere, and while everyone else was drunk on their ass I held the same plastic glass of beer all night without even tasting it.

"You could also tell I was a good girl by how hard I worked to keep Mother well. I worried whenever she had surgery and did things I thought would ensure her survival. I cleaned out the linen closet, transforming it from its usual state of chaos into something worthy of a before and after feature in *Better Homes and Gardens* magazine. I cleaned the house, cooked, did the laundry. Keeping Mother happy was my way of keeping her alive. Later, when she became addicted to pain pills, I tried to keep them away from her."

Gritty then closed her storybook. In her usual determined way, she searched for the insights tucked away in her Earth memories. She had learned to be duplicitous just like her father by acting bad when she was really good. How ironic that she adopted such negative surface appearances that belied who she really was! Then she thought about how she felt guilty when she didn't take action and how she believed that she got in trouble when she did act. Maybe she really wasn't a good girl after all; maybe she just tried to avoid negative consequences. Maybe she was afraid—like Sky.

Sky thought about how all their stories exposed the powerful role religion played in both creating and reinforcing their life scripts. She was awed by how creative and adaptable each of them had been, how they had fiercely protected their individuality in the face of tremendous pressures to conform.

Spring was surprised at how engaged she had become in the stories. She mused about the way their individual personalities were slowly revealing themselves, even though who they really were was still a mystery to them at that time in their Earth lives. Probing and pushing through the mist, their stealth identities waited for the air to clear so they could emerge from the darkness of ambiguity and incongruity and enter the light of wholeness. It would be a long time coming.

Just then Suma appeared and, without any preliminaries, started talking, "As children you saw the world as being all about you and that was absolutely essential for the development of your ego so you could break away in adolescence. Your stories show how organized religion threatened to bind you to your childhood scripts and subvert your life purpose. Yet you found ways to disentangle yourselves. As you did little seeds of insight began to sprout, their tender roots reaching for the light, leading you to who you were meant to be."

"As teenagers," she continued after giving them a few minutes to absorb her words, "you were given hints mostly about who you weren't: Sky's refusal to be saved whispered the truth that she may not be her fear—Gritty's rebelliousness whispered that maybe she wasn't her guilt—Spring's determination to avert humiliation intimated that she might not be her shame. Of course, you didn't know any of that for a long time. What you did know intimately was your woundedness."

Then Suma drifted away in a cloud of blue that seemed even darker than before. They watched her disappear and thought about how, once again, her insights were right on the mark. After a few minutes of relaxation, Spring and Gritty invited Sky to continue, acknowledging that they had interrupted her turn with their own religion stories.

$$*   *   *   *$$

Without a moment's hesitation, Sky re-opened her storybook. As new images emerged, the three of them were drawn into the Earthly scene with a combination of exhilaration, excitement, and confusion.

An attractive young woman walked up the winding stairs of a grand old stone building with massive columns on each side of its entrance. Sky was a seventeen-year-old wide-eyed freshman on her way to class. This was her first semester at the religious college affiliated with her parents' church. To her right a white cupola on top of the main administration building marked the center of the small, well kept campus. Couples embraced in the midst of a profusion of mature trees that were a sign of the school's long institutional history.

Sky went into a classroom and sat down. It was a required religion class. The professor was a tall slim man of middle age wearing a tweed jacket with patches on the elbows and sophisticated wire rim glasses. He lectured about the Bible and metaphor, challenging the students to consider the story of Jonah and the whale as a myth used to teach moral truths. Sky was fascinated by the idea that the Bible might not be a literal reporting of facts. That was what she had always been taught. This new information was explosive…and exciting.

A quick shift in scene and Sky was in her dorm. A small group of freshmen girls sat on the cold black and white marble floor of the large bathroom late into the night. As they talked about the professor's lecture about the Jonah story, several of them cried. With a wringing of hands in anguish and confusion they faced their first crisis of faith. One girl rocked back and forth against the hard tile wall.

"If Jonah wasn't really swallowed by a whale," she complained, "then what can we believe? My entire faith is being challenged and shattered! This is *not* what I expected from this college!"

Some of the girls were emotionally and psychologically exhausted from crying but Sky felt strangely exhilarated. She sat quietly to the side keeping her thoughts to herself, her arms wrapped around her bent knees. Maybe she wasn't bad or crazy or stupid or a sinner because she had doubts and because she hadn't been saved. If this very smart theology professor could ask questions, then maybe she could too.

Another scene change and it was Thanksgiving vacation. Sky was home for the holiday weekend. It was Sunday and she was in the adult Bible study class taught by Pastor.

She raised her hand and asked, "What do you think about the idea of the Bible as metaphor?" and then shared her professor's ideas about the story of Jonah and the whale.

Pastor's face turned red. A small gasp moved up his throat and escaped through his mouth, his head positioned condescendingly as he squinted at Sky.

"The Bible," he argued righteously, "can only be understood literally. It is God's word revealed to man!"

Sky looked amused, a glimmer in her eye as Pastor launched into a tirade.

"You young people," he concluded, "come back from college thinking you are smarter than the rest of us. Well, let me tell you, too much education can be a bad thing!"

Sky looked up from the scene of the pastor's face turning redder and with a bright smile said to Spring and Gritty, "That is the precise moment when a miracle happened. I didn't go into my old familiar fear. Instead, I laughed. I knew—in the deepest part of my soul—that Pastor was wrong."

Sky remembered how worried her parents had been when she started questioning the tenets of their faith. Their concern was alleviated, though, when she started dating Don. He belonged to the same church, planned to become a pastor, and they were old friends of his parents. They secretly hoped their daughter would become a minister's wife.

"I met Don," Sky then continued, "during my freshman year. He was smart in a quiet, thoughtful way and planned to go into the seminary. His mother suffered from mental illness when he was a child and did bizarre things like paint all the doorknobs in the house green. Later she was hospitalized and had electroshock treatments. When I met her, she seemed like a dutiful and sweet, though somewhat dull and muted, wife and mother. The part of her brain that gave her thought and passion had been fried along with the part that created strange voices that she no longer heard.

"I saw Don as a little neglected and confused boy and my heart went out to him. Whenever he stuck out his lower lip in a pout I felt a fierce maternal protectiveness and would spontaneously hug him. Those were the only times I felt any affection for him, though."

Sky thought about her complicated feelings toward Don. She didn't really like him though she thought she might love him—or maybe she just loved the little boy she imagined he had been. Something mysteriously familiar drew her to him.

"Everyone," she told Spring and Gritty, "thought Don and I were perfect for each other. I didn't want to be a preacher's wife, but it would make my parents happy and it would certainly validate my good girl status. When he proposed, I was unable to say no. That seemed to please everyone. The night we were engaged, the girls in the dorm gathered around, screaming ecstatically, gushing over the tiny diamond ring on my outstretched left hand. It was every girl's key to heaven, a promise of the MRS degree they had all come to college for. I acted happy."

Sky remembered how, when she was a junior, she fantasized about getting a master's degree in sociology and attempted to break off the engagement. Don was devastated, said he was going to quit school and join the army, and when he begged her to reconsider, she relented and stopped thinking about graduate school. The good girl won. Sky shook her head at the insanity of agreeing to marry someone she didn't even like.

By then Spring and Gritty were shaking their heads, too, as they watched a series of new scenes emerge in rapid succession: Sky, hair in rollers and wearing a tee shirt and shorts, alone in the church basement decorating for her wedding reception, arranging the tables with white tablecloths and vases of pink roses—Sky driving to the beauty shop to pick up her mother and sister from their hair appointments—at home, Sky fixing her own hair in its usual style, refusing anything special for her wedding—a photographer taking pictures of the beautiful young bride, looking perfect except for the slight hint of a cold sore on her upper lip that always appeared when she was anxious or unhappy—the mothers of the bride and groom standing next to each other, smiling bravely in their pink floral chiffon dresses, identical except that one was a size five and the other a size twenty-two—a beautiful wedding cake made by a woman in the church according to Sky's instructions, with real pink roses on the top, no bride and groom—the attractive couple by the cake, his hand over hers, ready to cut the first piece—Don, looking happy and contented—Sky looking condemned.

As she watched the succession of scenes, Sky remembered how numbly she had gone through her wedding without feeling, how unaware she was that her marriage was a sacrifice to her fear, how she held her denial close, how she watched everyone else being happy.

After the reception, she and Don were suddenly alone. They went to a hotel in a neighboring town, stopping for hamburgers and malts at an all night diner on the way. Don wanted a beer but the bars were closed.

"So there I was, married," Sky said, looking sadly at Spring and Gritty. "I was nervous on my wedding night. Our hotel room was drab and sparse and imagining the illicit activities that had gone on within its walls made me nauseous. Fortunately, the sex was over quickly—after all, Don had waited for four years. It wasn't so bad—the pain and blood were minimal—but I hoped we wouldn't have sex too often."

Again Sky went into her private reflections. It seemed that Don wanted to have sex a lot and she became a master orgasm-faker. One night during their first year of marriage when she discovered a Playboy magazine on their bed, she ran out of the apartment, filled with despair and rage, leaving the door wide open, the magazine thrown on the floor for effect. Don, in a panic, found her a few hours later walking the city streets. At first she refused to get in the car, relenting only after she thought he had suffered enough even though she suspected that her frigidity was the problem. When they got home, Don made love as a way to apologize and she forgave him by faking an orgasm.

"That about says it all for our sex life," Sky said knowingly to Spring and Gritty.

Sky continued to review her life as a minister's wife-in-training and assessed that she hadn't done too badly. After she graduated from college she got a job as a social worker and was the breadwinner while Don was in the seminary; that meant she had some friends and colleagues of her own. She set limits with Don: when he said he wanted to be a missionary in Africa she told him there was no way she could live with all those bugs, terrified as she was of the tiniest spider; when it was time for Don to do an internship, she said there was no way she would live in a small town. He relented both times. She found perverse pleasure in little things: how the sidewalk across the street from seminary housing looked like a perfectly shaped penis and scrotum when viewed from their second floor apartment; playing cards with another seminary couple on Friday nights; rebellious conversations and raucous laughter with some of the wives.

She stayed away from the couples with children, having decided that she would not contribute to an already overpopulated world. She secretly knew the real reason was that she didn't want to have children with Don. She conscientiously took her birth control pills and later Don had a vasectomy; not until many years later did he confess that he always wanted children.

Sky remembered how quiet the apartment was when she and Don were alone. He was the strong silent type. They pretty much lived in separate worlds so didn't have much to say to each other anyway.

Flooded with new memories filled with passion, righteousness, and rightness, Sky eagerly began to tell Spring and Gritty other stories.

"I wasn't a traditional seminary wife or a good minister's wife. The part of me that refused altar calls grew larger, its force overwhelming common sense or any thought of propriety. I read *The Feminine Mystique* and encouraged other seminary wives to read it; a group of us stridently rejected the traditional roles expected of us, specifically refusing to raise money for highly polished silver tea sets or even to serve tea at all. Instead, we organized fundraisers to end hunger, disdained the church's racism, became involved in equal housing actions when Dr. Martin Luther King Jr. came to the city to organize. One weekend, when our husbands were living on skid row for a few days with only a dollar in their pockets as part of a class immersion project, we went downtown to a bar and got drunk."

"All right!" Gritty interjected excitedly, "I knew even when you were a mere child that you were something else! What else did your deliciously rebellious self do to give you the message that you were not your fear?"

Sky responded with pride, "There was a socially active church next door to the agency where I worked. It was in a deteriorated concrete building with a community center attached. Don and I went—at my urging, of course—and eventually joined. The minister sat at a card table in front of the altar on Sunday mornings and talked about current events, urging us to feed the hungry, house the homeless, clothe the poor, stop the war, and eliminate discrimination. Once he held up a shredded Bible as he preached, its few remaining tattered pieces fluttering between a worn black leather cover. He had cut out everything related to social justice. When I saw that there was almost nothing left, I realized that my church had left out the heart and soul of the Bible.

"Sometimes my passion was aroused so powerfully it took my breath away. I took a class about the Vietnam War, joined anti-war protests, became active in the civil rights movement, and started a tutoring program at the church community center. Don and I engaged in lively conversations with the minister about radical ideas, which I embraced with the zeal of a convert. I could relate to a religion that championed the abolition of slavery, the cause of women's suffrage, human rights, labor's right to organize, eradication of child labor, and the end of war.

"I also asked some of the seminary theologians questions I never dared ask before. During the 1967 War in the Middle East, I asked whether it was a sign of Armageddon, whether it would bring about the end of the world in a fury of fire and brimstone—like the movie I saw as a teenager. I breathed a sigh of relief at their rational responses, so different from Pastor's fear mongering."

Sky closed her book. What happened to her during those years had been nothing short of amazing. Pastor's worse predictions had come true; she never should have questioned whether or not a whale had actually swallowed Jonah. Just see where doubt had led, she thought with a triumphant smile.

With a flourish of dark blue energy Suma then made her entrance, enveloping Sky in a warm embrace as she spoke.

"In your childhood, so many attempts were made to obliterate the passionately curious, bright and oh so precious part of you. Your attempts during adolescence and young adulthood to rebirth that part were nothing short of heroic, Sky. You refused to be annihilated by the fear that rose from the head of your childhood trauma like lava from the head of a volcanic mountain. Unconsciously, you were coming to understand the brutality with which innocence is often treated and…"

"…and I chafed at the unfairness of it," Sky chimed in with fresh revelation, "that's why I resonated to the suffering of others who were innocent victims of poverty, war, discrimination. That's why the social justice message of the Bible caught my heart and passion so immediately and completely."

"More will be revealed," Suma said with a smile and then she was gone.

Sky thought about what Suma said about her fear. She knew she had succumbed to it by marrying a man she didn't love but, on the other hand, had subdued it by the way she managed her life as a seminary wife. It seemed that, without her knowing it, her passion for justice and her fear had been engaged in battle. It was something to think about.

$$\ast \qquad \ast \qquad \ast \qquad \ast$$

Spring marveled at how Sky had jumped into situations wholeheartedly, maneuvered the labyrinth of others' approval and expectations, welcomed discovery and a path to herself. She wished that she had been as bold in her youth.

Suddenly she felt envious of Sky, of Suma's wisdom, of their warm embrace. In an attempt to fight against making comparisons, she circled the cavernous library several times, preparing to talk about her own very different path. She tried to shake off the disappointment she felt in herself for choosing to live without passion or excitement.

Finally she settled into her place at the table as Sky and Gritty watched her open her storybook to a new page. She pointed sadly to a picture of herself on Earth—a studious, frightened teenager.

"By the time I reached my awkward, pre-teen years," she began, "I was already adept at playing the role of natural born star, trying to fool others into thinking I never had to work for anything. In the sixth grade, when I won first prize in narrative reading at the regional debate contest, I didn't tell anyone about the hundreds of hours I practiced. I just modestly hung my head as if to say, 'I really don't deserve this award because I did so little to win it.' How effortlessly I played the lead role in the school opera, won the spelling bee contest, edited the school newspaper, made the cheerleading squad. No one saw how hard I worked behind the scenes. I didn't want people to know how hard I had to work. I made it look easy.

"With each success, I became increasingly self-critical and felt more and more unworthy. After all, I had to work hard for each accomplishment and still nothing was ever good enough. Any failure—big or small, real or perceived—was a catastrophe in my mind. Successes that fell a little short of what was possible—like getting a grade of A- rather than an A or A+—confirmed my inadequacy."

Spring remembered how shame had dictated everything in her life, even her choice of boyfriends in high school. Consumed by sadness and grief, she turned back to Sky and Gritty and found comfort in their eagerness to hear more.

"My boyfriend in high school," she said, "was Donny, an all around popular and nice guy who was captain of the football team. All the girls considered it a coup to land him. I felt lucky and proud. To me it was another success. Maybe being Donny's girlfriend would finally make me acceptable. Of course it didn't and there was even public proof of it when Donny was elected homecoming king just as everyone expected and I wasn't even elected to the homecoming court, much less as queen."

At that moment, Spring felt her shame as deeply as she had then. She remembered watching the homecoming king and queen and their court procession down the football field, golden scepters held proudly, jeweled crowns resting tentatively on their heads, velvet capes flowing behind in a swirl of royal red. She stood in her cheerleader uniform on the sidelines and clapped as they passed, a fake smile pasted on her face. During that night of public humiliation, she knew her unacceptability had been exposed for all to see. Even as an adult, when she recognized the folly of such juvenile displays, it still hurt in a hidden place that no one could touch.

"It was amazing to me," she continued, "that Donny still seemed to like me after that. I loved him for it. One night we were at his house alone, lying side by side on the couch quietly talking, nodding off to sleep now and then. I lay in his strong muscular arms, overwhelmed with gratitude and love, willing to do anything he wanted. I cautiously whispered 'I love you' in his ear. When he didn't respond I was relieved that maybe he hadn't heard me. Then he sat up, clearly uncomfortable, and said he didn't want to hurt me.

"His comment surprised and confused me. I had been so sure he wanted to have sex. Just the night before when he kissed me I felt something hard against my leg. That was the first time I realized what a hard-on was.

"A week later my girlfriend saw Donny hugging and kissing another girl. He never even broke up with me, just let my girlfriend do the dirty work. I cried so hard during Chemistry class that the poor teacher felt compelled to take me out to the hall and ask if I was all right."

Spring knew she had been more than heartbroken—she was ashamed, sure that she had screwed up by telling Donny she loved him, that he didn't bother to break up with her because she simply wasn't worth the effort. This latest public humiliation convinced her that the secret of her unacceptability had been confirmed once and for all.

"I felt like my life was over," she told Sky and Gritty. "I went into the kitchen and found a long sharp knife in a drawer, taking it to the bathroom, where I looked in the mirror at my tear-stained face, brought the knife up to my neck, pressed the blade against my skin. Just one quick deep cut across my throat and I would bleed to death before anyone discovered me. I looked in the mirror and positioned the edge of the blade at my jugular vein, mustering my courage. Then I thought about how my death would affect Mother, how embarrassed she would be to have a daughter who killed herself. I slowly brought my arm down to my side and my shame shifted from being dumped by my boyfriend to lacking the courage to commit suicide. I hid the knife under my blouse and went out to the kitchen to return it to its place in the drawer. I never told a soul what happened. My parents didn't even know Donny and I broke up."

Spring thought about the elaborate web of shame that she had conscientiously spun until it became so deeply woven into her psyche that no evidence to the contrary could penetrate its tangle. With each achievement as well as each perceived failure, the web tightened as her fear of being found out, of others discovering that she was a fraud, motivated her to work even harder at being perfect.

Others saw her as a quiet unassuming leader, her nonchalant stance convincing them that she was unusually brilliant and talented. No one was surprised when she decided to go to a big university after high school. It was expected.

She, on the other hand, was terrified that she was not smart enough to make it in college. The first book she read as a freshman confirmed her worse fears. She didn't understand a word of it; it was as if it were written in a foreign language. Her solution was the same as always: to study harder than ever. When she got good grades she explained them to herself as mysterious undeserved gifts. Learning was never her primary focus; it was always about protecting her secret.

Feeling weighed down by the bleakness of her youth, Spring's throat clenched in terror at the possibility that she had failed in her life's purpose. She kept her fears to herself, the old familiar shame raging inside her, even in this spiritual place. She figured that if she had been successful Suma would have appeared by now with her usual encouragement. Her absence was proof of the veracity of her bleak prediction.

Then her earthly pride lifted its ugly head, reminding her that misery loves company. Trying to recover by shifting attention onto someone else, she said, "let's hear one more time from you, Gritty. It seems to me that you were pretty miserable in your youth too."

Just at that moment, Suma materialized. Spring's heart leapt in joyful anticipation. Now her unhappiness would be explained and made meaningful.

"You have all the obstacles you need to reach your goals," Suma said in a matter of fact voice, then vanished as quickly as she had appeared.

Spring belligerently wondered what the hell that meant and how it was supposed to help. When she looked to Sky and Gritty for support, she realized she had been the only one to see Suma.

*   *   *   *

Gritty, oblivious to Suma's brief appearance, felt sad that Spring had considered suicide twice as a teenager. It confirmed her earlier thoughts about how much deeper and more pervasive shame was than guilt! Knowing that Spring needed a reprieve, Gritty responded to her prompt to tell more of her own story.

"I was pretty miserable all right," she said. "On the outside, I looked like a normal boy-crazy teenager. Inside, guilt swirled through me like a harsh wind, sometimes as brutal as a raging hurricane. It harangued me about being bad, not doing stuff I should do, screwing things up, losing no matter what I did."

Gritty opened her storybook to a new page and the three of them watched as a series of scenes shifted quickly from one to the next: Gritty, slim with long blonde hair, walking up and down Main Street with her girlfriends, looking for boys—Gritty wearing tight black and white leopard-patterned pants, their bold design disguising her skinny ninety pound Twiggy body—drinking her daily weight-gain malt concoction of five scoops of ice cream with thick chocolate syrup—walking hand in hand with a cute boy with dark greasy hair, Gritty wearing her boyfriend's black leather jacket—smiling painfully as the same boy hissed into the phone, "you're not the only pebble on the beach"—hugging a different boy who looked amazingly similar to the previous one—Gritty's parents wringing their hands in distress over their out of control daughter—Gritty reading stories in a dirty magazine she'd found tucked under the porch steps, suppressing the sick feeling in the pit of her stomach that told her they had been hidden there by Daddy.

"Oh, I was so bad!" Gritty said as she watched the scenes of her teenage years on Earth go by, "To my parents' dismay I married Mike, who was Italian and Catholic, right after graduating from high school. We rented a small house in town and he worked in his mom's bar. I went to junior college twenty miles away and worked in Daddy's hardware store on weekends. Life was pretty boring. There wasn't much to do but study, work and go drinking at one of the town's six bars on weekends.

"I chafed under the constraints of small town pettiness. Main Street was the center of everything where people greeted each other, shared the latest gossip, knew everybody else's business—or thought they did. Mike was a true native, being in the fifth generation to claim the town as its own. His large family was in-your-face boisterous, quite a contrast to my lack of spontaneity. They thought I was shy. After a while, most of them stopped trying to talk to me.

"After I finished two years of junior college, Mike and I got divorced. I wasn't unhappy about it at all and he seemed relieved. Our marriage had been little more than another hasty action that had gone awry, that was all. I left for the anonymity of the big city to attend a four-year college, planning to finish my degree so I could teach. I hoped to never look back."

Then Gritty turned to another page in her storybook and a new scene appeared. Immediately sensing new feelings and awareness Spring and Sky moved in for a closer look.

It was a hot summer day. A thin pale man lay on a couch with his compromised, frail body covered by thick wool blankets even though the room was oppressively warm and stuffy, his head propped up on a soft mound of white fluffy pillows. Gritty sat in an adjacent chair. She had just finished her junior year in college and was unhappily at home for the summer, helping out in the hardware store while Daddy recovered from a heart attack.

They watched the live television broadcast of Dr. Martin Luther King Jr. leading a massive civil rights march on Washington. Throngs of people with hopeful eyes—their numbers stretching far beyond the reflection pool—listened to Dr. King's historic "I have a dream" speech. He spoke about being at the mountaintop, about little black and white boys and girls holding hands.

Tears flowed unbidden from Gritty's eyes as she heard the cries for justice. Turning her head away, she furtively wiped away the tears on the sleeve of her white cotton blouse, hoping Daddy wouldn't notice.

Just then he looked at her with surprise as he spotted her tears. In a sympathetic tone of voice that she had never heard from him before, he said, "Come over here, Honey."

Now Gritty was surprised. She didn't think Daddy understood the significance of what they were witnessing.

She walked over to the couch and sat on the floor next to him. He put his arm around her shoulder and said, "Everything is going to be all right, Honey; I am going to get well and be my old self in no time. There is no need for you to worry or feel sad."

Gritty looked at Daddy through her tears and nodded. She didn't tell him that she hadn't even been thinking about him or his health.

"Something happened to me," she interjected, looking up from the scene, "when I went away to college in Chicago. That summer I came home with new ideas that hurled my outsider status into an even deeper place than it was before. My ex-husband Mike came into Daddy's store to get something. He seemed cautiously happy to see me and greeted me with a hug. Then, making conversation, he asked with a lopsided grin, 'So…how do you like living in the big city with all those jungle bunnies?'

"I looked at his sinister and provocative grin and responded defensively, 'I really love it. All the people there are wonderful! Your ignorance is showing big time, Mike! Have you ever been to the city, *any* city? Where do you get your information anyway?'

"He grinned, then sneered, 'Yeah, right' and walked out of the store without buying anything."

Gritty remembered how surprised she had been by her audacity and spontaneity. It was so unlike her.

The truth was that almost everyone at her college and in the neighborhood around the campus was white and her new and limited experiences with black people had been uncomfortable. The first time she went downtown she missed her stop and was frightened to find herself alone at night in a black neighborhood waiting for a return bus. When she worked the night shift in a nursing home, all of the other staff members were black; they pointed and laughed at her thin lips and straight blond hair while she looked at the floor and smiled awkwardly in response. When she worked in a candy factory, she made only a few feeble and unsuccessful attempts to make conversation with other women on the assembly line.

Nonetheless, there she was implying to Mike that his ignorant self had just insulted her and all of her black friends. With a combination of youth, self-righteousness, and passion she held fiercely to new unformed ideas that were tiny buds a long way from flowering into full bloom. A similar thing had happened in high school. In a social studies class when she was the only student to answer an exam question related to racism correctly, she unabashedly defended it in the face of her classmates' unanimous skepticism and derision.

Gritty looked at Spring and Sky and, shaking her head, said, "I wonder where my passion came from."

Then she turned the page of her storybook and feelings of despondency suddenly descended as a new Earth scene unfolded. Spring and Sky experienced the feelings as somehow familiar, as if they too had been there.

It was a brisk November day. After enduring a dreadfully boring and alienating summer at home, Gritty was glad to be back at school. She headed for the dorm where she was the senior resident counselor, anticipating a nice afternoon nap.

As she walked into the building, she heard cries coming from the lounge where several girls huddled in a circle, holding each other, weeping and keening in unison.

Between sobs, a voice filled with despair and disbelief responded to Gritty's unspoken question, "President Kennedy was shot and they don't know if he is dead or alive. They are pretty sure he is dead."

Gritty usually enjoyed the way the girls played jokes on her but this one crossed the line. She was pissed.

"That is *not* funny!" she exclaimed irritably.

The girls sobbed louder. Wailing pierced the air as Gritty stood immobilized, at first refusing to let the news penetrate. In the midst of the confusion, the dorm housemother came in to announce that a prayer vigil had been called.

It was eerily quiet except for the rustling of leaves under hundreds of feet as students and faculty headed toward the campus chapel. They streamed into the sanctuary where they sat in dazed incomprehension, the silence interrupted only by an occasional muffled cough, a nose being blown, a sob escaping a throat.

Gritty numbly watched as the college chaplain prayed at the podium, hearing the sound of his voice but not his words. She remembered how Daddy wouldn't vote for Kennedy because he was a Catholic and wondered how he felt now. She had always liked President Kennedy.

She would be forever grateful to him for saving the world from a nuclear holocaust. For three long days during the Cuban missile crisis, she had been terrified, vigilantly watching the sky for bombs, fearing the end of the world, standing on a precipice waiting to fall. She couldn't believe that now he was dead. Who would do such a thing?

Gritty turned away from the scene and looked sadly at Spring and Sky before speaking.

"I kept a candle burning in my dorm room for a long time after President Kennedy's assassination," she told them, "Next to it, I put a rose in a wine bottle and replaced it every Friday in his honor. I framed a newspaper cartoon and placed it on the other side of the candle. It was a picture of the memorial statue of

President Lincoln, his body bent over, head in his hands—but the head was clearly that of President Kennedy. He was crying."

Spring and Sky quietly remembered where they were when President Kennedy was shot and killed in Dallas that November day. Tears filled their eyes as they felt the shock and pain once again and thought about how things were never the same on Earth after that.

Spring thought about the Cuban Missile Crisis and imagined what it must have been like for Gritty as she waited for the bombs to fall. New memories then flooded her with such force that she spontaneously opened her own storybook. She looked at Gritty, apologizing for the interruption.

"No problem," Gritty responded with a shrug. She liked the way their stories intersected.

With the new scene unfolding from Spring's page came familiar feelings of fear, anxiety, and confusion. The three of them huddled together as they watched.

Spring was in school, her sixth grade class disrupted by the sound of a loud siren in the hallway.

"Walk in an orderly single file," her teacher commanded urgently, "and line up against the wall in the hall!"

With the ringing alarm vibrating in their ears, the children silently followed orders. They stood wide-eyed in the hall, some holding their ears to block out the terrible sound.

"Sit down!" the teacher shouted. They quickly sat.

"Now tuck your heads between your knees and place your hands on the backs of your necks. Do not move until I tell you to."

With their little backs against the wall they followed her instructions to the sound of the insistently shrill alarm. Spring sat perfectly still, her head covered protectively as she looked at the floor. She was confused and scared, not knowing what was going on but sure that whatever it was must be terrible. Was this practice or was something bad really happening? She didn't remember the teacher telling them they would be having a drill.

After several minutes the siren stopped as suddenly as it had started.

"Please rise," the teacher instructed, "and walk back into the classroom in a single file."

They silently obeyed and sat at their desks, waiting for an explanation.

"Now you are to go home immediately," the teacher said very seriously, "and do not dawdle along the way!"

Spring thought she heard the teacher say something about getting home as quickly as possible, that if this were the real thing that is what they would have to do.

Though warned to leave in an orderly way, the children ran out the door and dispersed from the school in many directions, scattering like ants when something upsets their hill.

Spring made her way quickly down the street, headed toward home. She was half running, half walking, her fear-filled eyes focused on the sky. She wondered why the teacher would send them out in the open where a nuclear bomb could drop right on their heads. All around her girls and boys silently walked or ran toward their homes. There was no laughing or playing, no calling out to each other.

When she finally made it home she ran into her bedroom and shut the door. It took a long time to stop shaking.

"That night," Spring interjected, "I dreamed that soldiers in red uniforms were pounding on the door, demanding my father. They took him away into the night and we never saw him again. I woke up screaming but no one seemed to hear."

She then looked up from her storybook, surprised at the terror she felt in her gut at that moment. Even as a child she knew that no one could survive a nuclear attack. She thought about the impact those drills had on her, how they led her years later to make decisions that would have a profound effect on her life.

Sky and Gritty just nodded, remembering the terror of those times.

$$* \qquad * \qquad * \qquad *$$

With their storybooks closed on their adolescence and young adulthood, the three of them pulled back from the table, eagerly anticipating Suma's appearance. They didn't have to wait long.

With a nod and a smile, Suma arrived and gathered Spring, Sky, and Gritty into a circle like a mother holding her children to her breast, providing the comfort and wisdom they had so longed for on Earth.

"You have chosen your stories well," Suma said as she released them, "and you already understand much. In a most intimate and painful way you know how cruelly innocent children are too often treated. You did your best to cope with the resulting residue of deep feelings that penetrated the core of your identity and out of your woundedness found ways to survive through pleasing, rebelling, and succeeding.

"As children you were full of what you were meant to be. And in spite of attempts—albeit unintentional—to extinguish your humanity, you refused to let the most precious parts of yourselves be annihilated."

Suma's words sank into the heart of each of them, touching them with gentleness and love that filled a void they weren't even aware existed.

Sky thought about how she had been filled with fear from the traumas she experienced as a child, how being good had helped to assuage it.

Gritty remembered being confused by the hypocrisy around her; she had withheld her natural spontaneity out of guilt over screwing things up whenever she didn't understand what lurked beneath surface appearances, and eventually she played the role of bad girl as a defense.

Spring knew her deep shame grew out of the criticism that was heaped on her as a child and she had tried with all her might to be successful in order not to feel it.

"Your true self then began to sneak in during adolescence," Suma continued. "The strength of your character was revealed in your determination not to stay on the limited path of your parents and their church, a path that actually prevented you from seeing the light. As you paid attention to the contradictions before you and followed the questions that led toward a new path, you were beginning to rebirth those parts of you that had been thoughtlessly slaughtered."

Sky's mind was swimming with thoughts about all the ways that she had opened herself to new ideas as a seminary wife, how she began to recapture the determination that had always been within her.

Gritty thought about how, by moving away from home and small town thinking, she had found the freedom to be curious again.

Spring struggled to find examples from her life that would give truth to Suma's words. She thought about how the brutal criticism she experienced as a child left her with a distorted sense of who she was, how in her youth she seemed to have limited coping mechanisms with which to defend herself.

With a seriousness that immediately caught their attention, Suma interrupted their reflections.

"Too many children," she said, "never make it to what they were meant to be. There is another lesson in that for you. When you were very young, you chafed at the brutal treatment heaped upon you in your defenselessness. In your youth you transferred your childhood experiences to a concern for others who suffered unjustly, especially when it was based on something over which they had no control—such as the color of their skin or the country in which they were born or a war in which they were innocent victims.

"Sky and Gritty's stories as young adults reveal a developing commitment to social justice. When you instinctively recognized unfairness, you hated it and couldn't accept it…and that is what helped you begin to recapture your own humanity."

They sat in silence, contemplating the significance of Suma's words.

Sky understood her automatic reaction against injustice in a new way. She remembered the passion with which she worked to end housing discrimination. She and a white man masquerading as her husband would be shown apartments right after the black couple that preceded them by minutes were told by the same landlords that there was nothing available for rent and turned away. She now saw that her intense anger about that and other injustices circled back to the unfairness of having to hide from Grandpa, being abandoned by Mom, being subjected to Dad's sadistic exploitation of her fears. No wonder she decided to become a social worker, she thought. Then the phrase *physician, heal thyself* crept into her mind, increasing her curiosity about what she was yet to learn.

Gritty basked in the light of new insights. She remembered how convinced she had been of the truth about racism in high school, how she had implied that she had black friends when she didn't, how moved she was by the 1963 March on Washington for civil rights. She too completed the circle back to the unfairness she felt in childhood about being lied to, about surface appearances disguised as truth. For a brief moment she caught a glimpse of future experiences with injustice that would affect her greatly. She involuntarily shuddered, feeling a bit of dread mixed with an eagerness to get on with more stories.

Spring's reflections were very different from those of Sky and Gritty. Plunged into despair, she was unable to complete the circle from her own childhood pain to a concern for others. Suma's insights about injustice came from the stories of Sky and Gritty only, for Spring had no such stories to tell. With her shame blocking any curiosity that might lead the way, she could muster no compassion for others or for herself. She couldn't even feel any passion about the unfairness of her childhood. She could only relate to Suma's words about coping. She had survived the excruciatingly painful years of adolescence in spite of two suicide attempts. At least that was something.

Caught in the intricate cloak of shame and striving that she herself had so carefully woven, Spring felt that in this spiritual place, just as on Earth, she was simply not enough to achieve her purpose, not smart enough to learn what she was supposed to learn. She envied Sky and Gritty who seemed to be moving along with great courage and ability. She was sure that Suma favored them. She saw herself as a desperate creature who had gone broke on her perfectionism and all or nothing thinking, having nothing left to reach understanding, much less compassion, and certainly not acceptance. She didn't think she could put up with herself any longer. Her only option was to give up, admit her failure, and leave. She began to plan her exit strategy.

PART IV

▼

COURAGE TO FEEL

Pain softens us to one another.
It fosters empathy.
It helps us to reach out
and realize our need for one another.

—*Each Day a New Beginning*
Hazelden Meditations

Spring moved her light blue energy restlessly through infinite space. Millions of stars of many sizes and colors soared around her. While they headed purposely to their places of study or perhaps to the Place of Life Selection to plan their next lives, Spring darted aimlessly. Her energy waned. She was agitated about her many Earth lives and their repetitive theme of regeneration and transformation, the many times she had crashed and burned only to spring back like Phoenix rising from the ashes. Each time she reentered the planet of pain and suffering she wanted it to be different...but it never was. Now she was tired—too tired to do it again. She wanted out.

Just then a flash of light appeared before her. Like skywriting in fluffy white clouds, messages came into view then gradually faded into nothingness: I have enough—I do enough—I am enough—Curiosity—Compassion—Humor—When I grow old I shall wear purple—Look to the ancients for the wisdom you seek—Be honest—Don't use your word against yourself—Your best is good enough—Fear makes you stupid—Hope makes you strong—Curiosity leads to solution—Compassion creates loving communities—Humor keeps you sane—How important is it, really?—Acceptance is the answer—The stories you tell yourself determine your life.

Strung together in quick succession, the messages formed a collage that contained all that Spring needed. Yet, like a drowning person desperately reaching for a lifeline, she could only grab onto the last message.

She thought about how the stories she told herself had determined her life as Sheila on Earth. She had despaired about how more and more fundamentalists screamed and pulled people back to the primitive, how their fear spread across the Earth like a plague, leaving cruelty and devastation in its wake. She told herself the right wing was winning, that it was strong, powerful, and omnipotent. Even those who professed to doing good were too often driven by primal instincts, heaping destruction on the planet in the name of justice. In her hopelessness she wanted to crawl into her own little corner and hide.

She also saw the numbers of seekers increase and sensed that something new was in the air. In the midst of the ongoing culture wars, she told herself a tidal wave of change was in the wind. When she sniffed the air for hope and inhaled the delicious aroma of kindness and love, she felt optimistic and joined with others to create change.

Hope and despair, two sides of the same coin, different stories leading to different outcomes.

With those thoughts, Spring realized that she was at a crossroads.

Moving her energy resolutely, she headed toward the terminal through which she had come, to the central receiving area filled with the anticipation of innumerable multicolored energies being dispersed to their final destinations. She smiled as she remembered her own excitement when she was transported back to Sky and Gritty. Then she thought of Suma's dark blue—almost purple—wisdom and her light blue energy faded. Familiar *less than* feelings captured her, telling her she was not as wise, as evolved, as good.

Suddenly, Spring's own light was extinguished and she unexpectedly found herself sitting in a coffee shop in an airport on Earth, once again Sheila in human form. The luminescent energies had been replaced with physical forms that revealed the diversity of humanity. People passed by with their lattes, chais, and decaf coffees. Walking with determination, they pulled their carry-on suitcases on wheels. Small children clutched their little pink and blue backpacks as they clung to adults. Stewardesses, pilots and other airport personnel rushed to their assigned duties.

Sheila watched a young Indian woman in her twenties as she pushed a cart loaded with luggage toward an international check-in counter. Tight blue jeans hugged her slim hips and her long black hair flowed gracefully down her back, brushing her diminutive waist. Each of her two gigantic suitcases was easily larger than her. She leaned over, took a deep breath, then grunted and heaved her body as she lifted each one onto the scale, anxiously watching to see if she met the weight limits. Suddenly realizing there was no identification on her baggage she quickly grabbed a handful of paper ID tags from the counter, hurriedly wrote on them, and attached one to each suitcase just before they were put on the conveyor belt and taken away.

How could anyone wait until the last minute to fill out identification tags, Sheila wondered uncomprehendingly. She had two plastic tags on each of her suitcases at home, which she always re-checked before leaving for the airport.

There seemed to be two basic types of people in the world: on-timers who were usually early and last minute folks who were usually late. Each was frantic in her own way, the only difference being the point in time in which their franticness kicked in. The on-timers were much better organized, though. She gave them the edge on that.

Just then Sheila panicked. She had forgotten that she needed Euros. As she rushed to the money exchange booth she started to laugh. She had been an on-timer all her life and here she was getting Euros at the airport at the last minute, something she had never done before. Even on-timers run into last minute times, she thought.

With that, she realized she had found an answer.

The physical form of Sheila dissolved and Spring's glowing light blue energy was back. With determination, she moved it up and away like a flash of lightning and headed back toward the central receiving area.

She thought about how her stories about fundamentalism on Earth were a projection of her own black or white—all or nothing—thinking, of her fervent belief in her unacceptability. Her personal extremism had taken the form of perfectionism and success at all costs. The stories she told herself had ruled her life: being on time for everything had been a way to ensure that things would not get out of hand. She realized now that her fear had made her stupid, that her faith in her shame-based identity was as stubbornly fanatic and absolutist as any of the right wing religions she had so vociferously decried.

Yet she had more than one story. There was also a story about responsibility and action but because her contributions hadn't been perfect, she had discounted their significance. This was something she needed to think about.

As Spring's curiosity returned, with it came a surge of happiness. She wanted to learn more. She had only to choose where to do the work.

She lingered at the crossroads between two possibilities. She could return to the Earth school where there was plenty of passion and bravery to be called upon. Yet learning was much more insecure and difficult there. She knew first-hand how that learning environment was filled with resentment, fear, antagonism, conflict, quarreling and cruelty.

It was so different in the library with her beloved Sky and Gritty. There was constant questioning about each other's motivations but there was never judgment or condemnation. In that spiritual place with no name, there was always forgiveness.

It didn't take Spring long to decide which direction to take. Her self-imposed exile had provided time to think, to reflect, to wrestle fear back into its cage.

Though she still dreaded the difficult work ahead and chafed at her unresolved feelings about Suma, she was ready to go back.

She floated purposely toward the library.

*   *   *   *

Sky and Gritty waited anxiously for Spring. It wasn't like their sister to leave without telling them where she was going and how long she would be gone. They had consulted with Suma about their concerns and knew what to do. *If* she returned, that is.

Just then Spring's light blue energy landed at her place in the library and they heaved huge sighs of relief, smiling at her even more radiantly than when they were first reunited.

Yet they didn't stretch their energies to embrace her, knowing it was important to give her space, to let her be the first to talk. When she was ready she would tell them where she had been, what she had done, why she had returned.

Spring immediately reassured Sky and Gritty that she was all right. She told them about her journey, what she had learned, how she had contained her fear— at least for now. She left out the part about her discomfort with Suma. Then she indicated she was ready to get back to work. She looked at Sky, assuming that she would go first as usual.

Sky and Gritty sat on each side of Spring, wedging her between them in a protective embrace. They glanced at each other with an unspoken question about which one of them should speak. Gritty, always a risk-taker, wound her energy around Spring like a reassuring arm.

"We want *you* to go first this time," she said.

"If you don't mind," Spring responded, curbing her impatience, "I'm not quite ready. I would be okay with going second but not first."

"It's best that you go first now," Sky said gently.

Spring's resistance increased. She wondered how they could determine what was best for her. Their behavior was baffling at best and irritating at worst. She wondered what they had talked about in her absence, suspecting a plot. This was not the way we operate here, she thought.

"Suma insists," Gritty said in a slow firm voice that signaled finality as she pulled Spring closer to her.

Spring said nothing as she wrestled with the myriad thoughts and feelings tumbling over each other. She was pleased to have Suma's attention. Maybe she hadn't been abandoned by her after all. Irritation followed close behind relief, though, bringing out the rebellious teenager in her that wanted to argue.

Yet Suma always knew what was best. Spring had never defied her before and she would not do so now. With reluctant acquiescence she reached across the table for her storybook—but it wasn't there.

"*This* is the page you are to start with," Sky said, pointing to Spring's story-book that lay open on the table directly in front of her.

Offended, Spring started to object. Then she thought about why she made the decision to return, how she had subdued her fear and opened herself to faith and curiosity.

With a deep sigh of acceptance, she nodded that she was ready.

$$*\qquad*\qquad*\qquad*$$

As Gritty called her attention to images on the selected page, Spring gasped with profound sadness, sinking into Earth memories lost long ago, things she wished to keep buried. She really didn't want to see them now. Sky and Gritty sighed and braced themselves for Spring's reactions, wanting to protect her as a scene unfolded.

Spring was two years old and cute as a button, sitting in a high chair in the kitchen, a little bowl of food on her tray. She laughed as she smeared the gooey mixture on her face, hands, arms, in her hair. Squealing with sheer pleasure, she felt the warm mush between her fingers, delighted in each spray of food that hit her face when she slapped her little hands together, enchanted with the bright orange color of carrots.

Without warning, a shadow fell over her. Suddenly Mother's huge imposing face was inches from hers. It was a scary face, dark and foreboding, its big red mouth spewing harsh cruel sounds. Then the face receded as big hands grabbed the bowl away and slapped Spring's tiny hands.

Her delight changed instantly to horror and dismay. Spring cowered, hurt and afraid. She screamed and cried wetness onto her cheeks. There it mixed with food as Mother slapped her tears.

The scene on the page then shifted. Spring swallowed hard and pinched her eyes to hold back tears. As different images emerged so did new memories and a fresh painful sadness. She held tightly onto Sky and Gritty, forcing herself to watch.

Spring was four years old. She looked perfect in a beautiful white dress with ruffles around the sleeves, bodice, and skirt. She stood primly by the sandbox where children were intently building a castle from mud created by the morning rain. Fascinated and bursting with desire to be part of this amazing project, Spring fell to her knees and joined in the fun. With each new creation came laughing bursts of satisfaction. Alive with creativity, she bloomed like a bright daisy lifting its face to the sun as she added turrets to the castle, made statues for the courtyard, dug around for sticks to build a bridge over the river that flowed around the expansive playground they were creating for the little prince and princess who would live there.

Suddenly, an all too familiar shadow materialized. Darkness fell over the children and their beautiful creation, extinguishing their delight. Spring felt the hand before she saw it, grabbing her arm and jerking her to her feet. It slapped her face, her behind, her legs. A fierce brutal voice screamed about how bad she was for getting dirty, for spoiling the beautiful dress her mother made. How could she be so evil...so evil...so evil! Then two hands dragged her across the playground and away from her dazed playmates.

Sky and Gritty moved closer to Spring, turning the page in her storybook once again. As a new scene appeared Spring's sobs became moans. Feelings of defeat enveloped her being, new memories, old pain, so much pain.

Spring was now six years old. Dressed in a perfectly starched light pink dress with white ruffles, she looked adorable. Everyone said she was so cute, a perfect child. They told her mother how lucky she was to have such a beautiful and well-behaved little girl. Spring stood stiffly, watching the other children from a distance as they played on the swings and the teeter-totter in the park. She moved to a bench, out of sight of the others but still with a view. She wiped the leaves and any possible dirt from the seat and, being very careful not to wrinkle or soil her dress in any way, she demurely sat down.

There she waited with hands folded primly on her lap. If she was very careful, the shadow would not come, the brutal voice would not shriek and she would not be bad, she would not be evil. She would be the perfect little girl that made Mother proud. Everything would be okay as long as she didn't get dirty.

Spring looked up from the scene pleadingly, almost unable to bear any more. Sky and Gritty held her close as they turned the page and a new scene emerged. Spring knew that she was about to be confronted by more memories that she wished to shove back into the deep recesses of her mind where she had banished them long ago.

An attractive young woman sat at a table in the school library. Spring was a bit on the thin side but pretty and neatly groomed, every hair in place in her beehive hairstyle. Deeply engrossed in the book before her, she didn't look up at all. Anxiety seeped from every pore. Her fingers were in her mouth, her nails bitten down to bleeding cuticles. She appeared to be studying but no learning could get past her fear. She barely contained her terror long enough to memorize, to hold onto tidbits of information long enough for the test, for the A. She *must* get an A. If she didn't, her secret would be exposed and she would die.

"One more scene," Sky reassured Spring as she turned to another page and new images appeared. Even Sky and Gritty cringed at the dreadful sight that emerged and they clung to Spring tightly, as much for their own comfort as for hers.

A multitude of dark hairy creatures encircled the young woman. They had sharp uneven teeth, bulging eyes, big ears, and claws with long sharp nails for hands. They completely surrounded Spring, shrieking and waving their arms and legs. With high-pitched mocking sounds they penetrated her skin, burrowed their way into her abdomen, and nested in her solar plexus, making it their home.

The inside of Spring's stomach was a black cavern where the ugly gargoyles flew around, sneering and taunting whenever she studied, made a presentation in class, got a test back with an A on it, was successful. Whenever she tried something new and potentially risky, their shrieks became deafening: "Who do you think you are? Who do you think you are? Who do you think you are?"

As the scene faded from view, Spring collapsed.

Sky and Gritty moved away, giving her space and time to recover. They were proud of her for having the courage to feel—in the depths of her being—the pain and unfairness that she had kept at bay for so long.

The breakthrough sapped Spring's energy but even though she was exhausted, she knew that what she had experienced was good. She had recovered her passion. No longer stuck in her defenses, she was less afraid of the other stories yet to emerge. And it didn't even matter to her whether Suma appeared or not—at least for now.

Just then, a mass of dark blue energy circled her like the string of a yo-yo winding around and around, tighter and tighter, until it merged with Spring's light blue energy in a long warm embrace, then spun her off on her own once again.

Spring received Suma's unspoken encouragement with gratitude, basking in the glow of her caring. Rejuvenated and with her feelings now accessible, she felt a new empathy for herself. With renewed strength she was ready to move on.

*   *   *   *

Spring's mind wandered back to her college days. She remembered how surprised she was to graduate with honors, how in spite of her fear she applied to a graduate program in nonprofit management and was accepted. She decided she would pick up her story there.

Sky and Gritty returned to their places on each side of her as she opened her storybook to a new page. The scene of an urban university emerged and with it came new memories, some confusion, a lot of sadness.

It was the first day of fall semester. Spring rode her three-speed bike to the large Chicago campus from the nearby boarding house where she rented a room. Surrounded by the promise and energy of youthful protest, she fit right in with her faded jeans and an overly large pea green army surplus shirt without a bra, her face untouched by makeup, and her long blond hair falling naturally down her back. She stopped now and then to sign a petition, listen to an impassioned speech against war and racism, and accept a flyer announcing an upcoming event.

When she reached the building that housed the College of Business Administration, Spring locked her bike up next to hundreds of others. She took the elevator to the ninth floor and entered the room where her first class in graduate school was about to start.

The professor was a short and stocky middle-aged woman with mousy brown hair and wire-rimmed glasses. After introducing herself she handed out an exam saying she wanted to assess their pre-existing knowledge of the subject. The room was quiet except for the sound of pencils filling blue books as everyone tried to answer the four essay questions on the test.

After writing copiously on the first three questions, Spring tapped her pencil on the desk. She was bored. Since the professor said the exam wouldn't be graded she stopped writing and handed in her blue books.

She left the building thinking that the first day of class hadn't been too bad and headed toward the university bookstore to buy her books.

Then it was the next morning and Spring was back in the business administration building where she found a note in her mailbox in the student lounge. The professor wanted to see her in her office that afternoon.

All day she worried. Maybe her responses were so inadequate that the professor doubted her ability to successfully complete the program. Maybe the professor wanted to know why she didn't finish the exam. She kicked herself for not answering the fourth question.

As the day went on, the shrieking of the ugly little gargoyles became insufferable. Over and over they twittered gleefully, "See, we knew you'd screw up! Who do you think you are? Who do you think you are?"

Spring wondered how she ever could have thought that she could make it in graduate school.

Finally it was afternoon and time for her appointment with the professor. Two other students were already there when she arrived. Upon entering the office she was immediately distracted by a mass of clutter that assaulted her senses—papers seemingly thrown in every direction and uneven stacks of books and papers blanketing every inch of surface. Finding the last available place to sit down, Spring wondered how anyone could keep track of anything in such a mess.

"The three of you," the professor began, "clearly do not belong in my course."

Spring froze. Sure that her worse fear had come to pass, she braced herself for the inevitable. Through her terror fog, she heard the professor continue.

"Your responses to the essay questions were very sophisticated and I think you would be terribly bored. So, I took the liberty of removing you from my class roster and registering you for the advanced course."

Spring mumbled a word of thanks and left the office. She was in shock. Surely a mistake had been made.

The other two students suggested the three of them go for coffee. Marnie and Janice didn't seem at all surprised at having tested out of the course and she didn't tell them how she felt.

"Marnie and Janice were very bright," she interjected, looking up from the scene, "and they assumed that I was, too. That was the basis of the friendship we forged that day."

Spring remembered her time in graduate school as mysterious. When the three of them took an advanced statistics course, she got an A while Marnie and Janice got Bs. She couldn't figure out how that happened when they seemed to understand statistics so well and she was clueless. All the professors gave her A's and treated her as if she were one of their best students, yet she still felt stupid. She told herself that the graduate program was outrageously easy and undemanding, that she fooled the professors by never speaking in class. She held onto her belief in her inadequacy like a religion and when she slept with her internship supervisor out of fear about her grade, her shame flourished.

All she did was study and her efforts paid off. She graduated early with a master's degree. There was a downside, of course. She had no other life but school. It seemed the only other thing she did during that time was watch the Nixon impeachment hearings on television.

Spring looked up from her reverie and saw Sky and Gritty waiting patiently for her to continue.

"I graduated with straight A's," she said, "and was immediately hired to do supervision and management training for nonprofit organizations around the region. My workshops were successful so my secret seemed safe for a while but sometimes the shrieking of the gargoyles got out of control. Then I increased my efforts and worked even harder. I didn't know what else to do.

"My neediness and insecurity left me desperate for affirmation so when one of the managers noticed my work, naturally I was thrilled. He was a debonair older man with a graying beard and a slightly bent slender frame who was known as a scholar in his field. One day he invited me to his office.

"In a soft, intelligent voice that was melodic and reassuring, he said, 'I have heard so many wonderful things about your workshops. How did you become so wise at such a young age?'"

Spring remembered how the positive regard of this wise elder promised to fill a hunger in her that ached to be satisfied. She was fascinated by his philosophy of helping and social change and even timidly shared some of her own ideas.

"I pointed out to him," she said to Sky and Gritty, "that I wasn't that young, thus implying that I really wasn't as wise as he thought I was. When he invited me to dinner, I eagerly accepted. Like a hungry puppy feasting on attention, I reveled in the stimulating and informative dinner conversation and admiringly listened to him talk about being a strong family man, having a good relationship with his wife, worrying about his grown children.

"He walked me to the door at the end of the evening like a true gentleman and hugged me goodnight. Only he held me too tightly. I gently pushed him away but he persisted, releasing his hold only when I insisted more firmly. Then he said he would like to have sex with me. I said I was flattered but declined and went into my house.

"With my back against the closed door, I slid down onto the floor with my face in my hands…and cried."

Spring stopped talking, feeling anew the keen disappointment and stinging disillusionment. She had regarded him as a noble mentor. She had even begun to consider the possibility that maybe she was smart, that she had some good ideas. How could it be that the accolades she so eagerly consumed were merely part of a seductive dance to get her into bed? The shrieking gargoyles in her gut danced with delight.

Spring then turned to another page in her storybook. As she watched new images appear, she saw something else she didn't want to remember and braced herself, hoping for the courage not to cringe or look away. With concern, Sky and Gritty moved closer and watched the scene unfold.

Spring was a trim and attractive young woman in her twenties. She was in a hotel suite with a group of officials from non-governmental organizations who were drinking, flirting, gossiping, laughing, and generally carrying on at the end of a day of conferencing. Sophisticated in an understated navy blue business suit, Spring held a glass of wine as she quietly engaged in individual conversations, periodically deflecting sexual moves with a cool professional demeanor.

A tall, imposing man with wavy gray hair looked over at her. Though Spring had never met him, she knew he was an important person in upper administration. He weaved his way toward her through the crowded room—so drunk he could hardly walk—and almost fell on top of her before thrusting his face within inches of hers.

In a hoarse slurred voice that reverberated through the room he exclaimed, "Who do you think you are anyway, doing management training? What experience do you have that makes you think you're qualified?"

All conversation stopped as curious eyes turned toward his loud abusive voice. A matronly woman quickly appeared, wagging her finger, scolding, as she pulled him away.

Spring turned and fled, hiding her face as it flooded with horror and humiliation. She ran to her room, shaking so hard she could barely manage to unlock the door, and threw herself on the bed. She had been found out. Even someone who was drunk knew the truth—that she was a fraud.

Spring looked up from the scene in her storybook and breathed deeply. Her monsters had found expression in the man's voice, apparently now able to appear directly and at will through others. The public humiliation that night stung at the core of her. Her worst fear had come true. She had been found out and was found wanting.

The next day, the man's administrative assistant apologized for him. She said he had been very drunk and felt bad about his behavior but he never apologized himself. It didn't matter. The damage had been done.

Most people would have quit at that point, but Spring continued to work hard in the organization for two more years. When she was asked to direct a national training project, she jumped at the opportunity, once again working very hard and achieving notable success. When she thought about how she persevered in spite of the shrieking gargoyles who had taken up permanent residence inside her, she found a new appreciation for her tremendous grit and determination.

That reminded her that there was another story besides her shame narrative. She had also been a seeker who longed to comprehend the meaning of life, to know her soul, to understand her despair and loneliness. Her quest for spiritual answers twisted and turned, sometimes leading to interesting places on Earth: transcendental meditation, short-lived experiments with organized religion, Yoga meditation, transactional analysis, Gestalt therapy—to name a few.

Spring smiled when she remembered how her most intense interest had been reincarnation. She read voraciously about past lives and the spirit world between lives, wanting desperately to believe such a place existed. She asked questions like: What if I chose my own parents? How do my former lives influence me now? Why did I come back this time? She wondered if the habit she had of pulling on her ear lobe came from living in the sixteenth century and having part of her ear cut off under the English Poor Laws as punishment for begging. Might her decision to help others be traced back to that time and place?

She turned to a new page in her storybook, eager now to immerse herself in Earth experiences that held the promise of understanding and healing. Sky and Gritty sensed her positive energy and enthusiastically watched as a new scene emerged in her storybook.

Spring made her way up the back stairs and into a small room above a metaphysical bookstore. A man sat cross-legged on a chair, an expression of great serenity on his face. He stood to greet her, warmly shaking her hand, inviting her to sit in the comfortable chair opposite him. As they sat facing each other, their knees almost touching, he carefully explained the process of recalling past lives. While she was under hypnosis, he would ask questions and instruct her to raise her right index finger when her answer was yes and her left index finger when her answer was no. He then began the hypnosis session. After a while, Spring felt flushed. Her cheeks burned.

"What are you remembering right now?" the man asked.

"Oh my God!" she responded, "We're going so fast! I don't know if I can hang on!"

Spring felt the wind blowing on her face, a terror clutching her chest as she clung to the outside of a carriage. Her desperate grip tightened with each bump in the uneven path.

"Are you running away from something or are you running to something?" the man then asked.

No response.

"Raise your right finger if you are running away and your left finger if you are running to something," he instructed.

Spring's right index finger went up involuntarily.

"Who are you? Where are you?" came the next query.

"I am a Roman soldier. I am wearing a breastplate that is very heavy and leather sandals with straps up to my knees holding leg guards trimmed with studs. Several of us are hanging on to the chariot. It is moving so fast but I don't know where we are or what we are running away from. Something terrible has happened. Oh my God! Now I remember!"

Spring sobbed, unable to continue.

"Did someone die?" the man asked softly.

Spring's right index finger went up automatically.

"I was there. I helped them crucify him."

Her uncontrollable sobbing increased and the man quietly suggested that she leave that life. After a short period of silence, he moved her into another time where she recalled being a powerful speaker and advocate for women's rights. Later she wondered if that previous life explained her natural proclivities at public speaking and conducting workshops.

As the session came to a close, the man gently guided Spring through a visual meditation, saying it would help her understand what she had learned.

She walked through an enchanting valley, filled with the incredible beauty and wonder of nature, the sounds of singing birds filling the air with exquisite music.

A fish called to her from a bubbling creek. She knew his name was Nathan.

"When you are swimming against the current and you get tired, just get on my back. I will carry you," Nathan said.

She got on his strong wide back and was carried smoothly through the water until they reached the foot of a hill where she disembarked.

She walked up toward a sacred place at the top of the hill. A figure robed in rich dark blue from head to toe stood waiting, facing away from her. As Spring approached, the figure slowly turned, looked at her with the most extraordinarily compassionate smile and stretched out her arms to embrace her.

Spring looked up from the scene in the storybook, delighted at her discovery.

"It was Suma!" she exclaimed to Sky and Gritty, her energy jumping up and down with excitement.

"Suma came to me at that moment! She showed herself to me on Earth. She was reminding me of the connections between my purpose in this life and other previous lives. She was telling me that she was with me, that I was not alone!"

Spring remembered how the ninety-minute past life regression session had seemed like it was only ten minutes long. When it was over she still didn't know whether she believed in reincarnation or not but she had gained some insights.

She shook her head in wonder. Even though her memories of this spiritual place in the library with Sky and Gritty had been erased on Earth, she had sure worked very hard trying to recover them.

Then she realized that Suma, in the guided meditation, had been telling her that there was a reason for everything—even when she couldn't understand it.

Like her seemingly irrational behavior at two anti-nuclear weapons protests. Each year a small group of peace activists gathered on Good Friday at a nuclear weapons production site. Led by a man carrying a large wooden crucifix on which rested a nuclear missile, they silently walked toward the entrance in single file while singing the Easter hymn "Were You There When They Crucified my Lord?" Upon reaching the gate, they formed a circle and prayerfully got down on their knees where they waited for the police to arrest them for trespassing.

The first year, Spring planned to leave when the police gave their warning: "You are on private property. If you do not leave immediately, you will be arrested."

Instead of leaving, she fell to her knees, sobbing uncontrollably, unable to move. Without intending to, she was arrested, her limp body carried to the squad car that would transport her to jail.

The next year Spring went to the Easter protest again, determined that this time she definitely would not get arrested. But the same thing happened and she spent the day in jail.

Now she understood. She *had* been there as a Roman soldier when Jesus was crucified. That experience and the unrelenting shame that stalked her in her latest life had been connected: no matter how hard she worked, no matter how hard she tried, nothing could make up for what she had done.

Then she realized that her shame reflected a deep passion, ancient in its origins, powerful in its manifestations. Birthed in both her parents' criticism and her life as a Roman soldier, she had focused that passion on a push to excel—but that was only her initial focus. Her passion had led her to other places as well. For the first time, Spring considered the idea that there might have been positive aspects to her shame.

As Sky reflected on Spring's stories she admired her more than ever. In spite of her all-consuming demons, she didn't lose sight of life's unfairness to others. She had, after all, chosen a career dedicated to helping people through nonprofit organizations and she had searched courageously for larger truths. Somehow Sky knew there were convergences between her and Spring's lives, even though fear had been her own motivation while shame had been Spring's. Further insights were beyond her comprehension at this point but she was glad her curiosity was alive to receive them when they came.

Gritty was awed by what Spring uncovered during her experimentation with hypnosis, how she had made incredible connections to previous lives. She marveled at Spring's courage and resilience, how time and time again she seemed defeated but would then spring back, never quitting like most people do.

Suma did not appear with words of wisdom or more hugs. But it didn't matter. Spring got comfort from knowing Suma had appeared to her on Earth and from remembering Suma's warm embrace after she allowed herself to feel the pain of her childhood. Right now Spring was saturated with new awareness and insights. She needed a break from both the bleakness and complications of her life. Though she still had a negative premonition about what was to come, she was glad that her discomfort about Suma seemed to have abated. She looked hopefully at Gritty, who indicated by opening her storybook that she wanted to go next.

PART V

▼

HUMAN
CONTRADICTIONS

My soul has taken me to task
and taught me…
to treat as a friend the one whom they insult.

Kahlil Gibran

Gritty had so many Earth stories to tell she had to think carefully about her selections. As she turned the pages of her storybook and saw a picture of her daddy, she decided to start with him.

"My daddy," she began, "recovered from his first heart attack but a second one laid him low a few years later. I was teaching by then but took time off to go home. When I got there Daddy was still in the hospital and the doctor asked to meet with my brother and me. Dr. Foster had performed several surgeries on Mother—he removed a tumor, her gall bladder, a large portion of her stomach (bleeding ulcer), and all her female organs (hysterectomy). Her adoration and trust in her doctor was so obvious that sometimes I wondered if she was secretly in love with him. I suspected that she asked him to meet with us.

"Dr. Foster was a kind, patient man whose desk and bookshelves in his comfortable office were filled with pictures of his wife, children and grandchildren. In a voice that sounded like it was coming from somewhere far away he tenderly said, 'Your father will not leave the hospital this time. I am very sorry.' He was right. Daddy died that night.

"I drove everyone home from the hospital. Mother said nothing during the hour-long drive from the city to our small town. Mother sat next to me in the front seat, staring out the window, tightly clutching Daddy's few belongings in a brown paper bag as if she were holding part of him. My brother sat in the backseat next to Uncle Ben who had arrived by plane just in time to say goodbye to Daddy. The car was silent except for Mother's muted weeping.

"I have only snapshot memories of the next week: our house filling with church people, casseroles covering the dining room table—a neighbor calling from her backyard to ask how Daddy was, then running into her house in tears when I said he had died—Mother behind the closed bedroom door for hours with her best friend—my uncles and grandfather arriving for the funeral—Reverend Anders telling me that I should be happy that Daddy was in heaven and me barking back at him, 'What the hell do you know?!' I wrote hundreds of thank you notes for Mother, taking care of everything until I fell exhausted into bed."

Gritty turned the page and a new scene began to unfold. Sky and Spring wondered about the half smile on her face that masked a tear sneaking into the corner of her eye.

The austere sanctuary of a small church was filled to overflowing with hundreds of people. Latecomers stood outside craning their necks to see, straining their ears to hear. Holding tear stained handkerchiefs in clenched fists, they talked in hushed sad tones about what a shame it was, what a good man he was, how he was too young to die, how hard he worked, how wonderful he was to have founded this church.

Gritty sat in the last pew with her mother, brother, grandfather, and six uncles. The family hoped to have privacy by breaking with tradition and sitting behind everyone rather than in the front row. This caused Gritty to wonder if crying was supposed to be bad or embarrassing. She saw people looking at her and knew that, to small town eyes, she looked like a city-savvy professional woman in her trim black suit with the skirt landing just above her knees.

Gritty's private reverie was interrupted by Reverend Anders' words. In a cheerful voice he proclaimed that Daddy was in heaven; this was a celebration, they should all be happy. He read verses from the Bible to support his contentions and talked on and on.

Soon Uncle Albert fell asleep, his chin resting on his ample chest. When he began to snore, the other uncles snickered. Then Uncle Dan's nose honked like a goose as he tried to contain his laughter. The pew wobbled from the shaking of Uncle Ben's round stomach as the contagion spread down the row, threatening to burst into a riot of laughter. Gritty covered her mouth to hold back her own giggles. The pew began to rock, snorting sounds intensified the hysteria, white handkerchiefs over mouths contained the sound of air bursting from nostrils, tears flowed down cheeks.

Reverend Anders droned on, oblivious to the drama in the back of the church. Gritty hoped people would think they were all crying. She thought about how Daddy the jokester would have loved this scene. He would be laughing right along with them. She even wondered if he had provoked it all in the first place.

Then she looked at Mother, the only one crying. The million broken pieces of her heart lay in her lap, her grief so profound that Gritty could almost taste it. She hoped Mother was so inured to inappropriate humor that she wouldn't feel bad about the laughter. Maybe she didn't even notice.

"For the record," Gritty interjected as she looked up from the scene, "I never cried for Daddy."

She thought about that. Tears would have been appropriate; laughter was not. Once again, she wondered what was going on, but she didn't want to dwell on her daddy's death any longer. There would be time to make sense of it later.

Turning to a new page in her storybook, Gritty's confusion took another form. She knew the emerging scene was laden with significance related to her life purpose though she didn't yet fully comprehend its meaning.

"With a bachelor's degree in English literature and a teaching certificate in hand," she explained, introducing the upcoming scene, "I began teaching at an inner city middle school in Chicago. There were three thousand students in grades eight and nine, more than twice the number of people in my hometown and more than ten times the number of students in my high school."

Spring and Sky watched with curiosity as images of the school then emerged from the page.

Gritty wore three inch spiked heels and a stylishly trim bright red suit on the first day of school, hoping this uniform would lend a look of authority to her usual skinny, teenage blond appearance. Dutifully she went into the school auditorium at 7:30 a.m. for teachers' welcome and orientation, as instructed in the principal's letter she received the week before.

Making her way down the poorly lit aisle in the massive dark room and sitting in a seat at the end of an empty row in the back, she saw that hundreds of teachers were already there. From the high-pitched buzz of animated conversation it seemed that everyone knew each other. As she sat silent and alone in the dark, Gritty felt anxious and when the principal asked all new teachers to convene in his conference room right after the meeting, her nervousness increased.

After the orientation, she and about twenty other new teachers gathered around the table in the principal's conference room where they were asked to complete some paperwork. The principal then instructed five of them to stay. Gritty was one of them.

After the others left, the principal stood, his large pot-bellied frame and red face looming over the remaining handful of teachers as he bellowed, "Your personnel records will indicate that you defied my authority on your very first day by not attending the orientation session as instructed!! From now on, you will follow the rules or you will be fired!"

Stunned, Gritty sat frozen in disbelief, her gut recoiling from such an unexpected and unwarranted blow. She stayed behind as the other four teachers sullenly marched out of the room.

In a small, timid voice carefully modulated to disguise her growing anger, Gritty looked at the principal and said, "Excuse me, sir, but I *was* at the orientation."

Disdain flitted across his eyes, then settled around his mocking lips.

"Well, you may *say* that you were there," he sneered, "but your name is not on the sign-in roster."

"What sign-in roster?"

Gritty was incredulous. She wondered how she could have missed it. Old familiar guilt stirred, telling her that once again she'd done something wrong, that she hadn't been able to figure things out fast enough.

"There was a clip board with an attendance roster on a chair at the back of the auditorium. You are to sign your name whenever there is a required meeting," the principal huffed.

Gritty saw that he looked disgusted, as if she were the biggest dummy in the world for not knowing the procedure. She wondered why no one had told her. The auditorium was so poorly lit that surely no one could have seen the roster unless they already knew exactly where it was.

"I'm very sorry, sir, I didn't know anything about signing in, but I *was* there," she said meekly.

The principal didn't respond. Gritty picked up her papers and as she left the room with her head bowed, she bravely held back the tears constricting her throat and begging to be released and tried to purge her guilt.

"So that was how my first day of teaching began," Gritty said, looking up from the dismal scene.

"Shit!" Spring shouted, "how did that dumb-ass principal think you all knew to meet in the conference room anyway if you hadn't been at the orientation session to hear his instructions?"

Gritty shook her head. Such logic hadn't even crossed her mind. Turning the page of her storybook, she shrugged and whispered, "It gets worse."

Powerful memories poured over Gritty like a raging river as a new scene revealed more of the huge worn-out school building, with its scuffed and chipped marble staircases and institutional gray walls. Spring and Sky marveled at how small and innocent Gritty looked in contrast to the high ceilings and wide halls.

Then Gritty was in one of the drab classrooms, walking around its perimeter, searching the tables that lined the walls, looking for the books for her students. But her search proved futile. Seeing the distress on her face, a stern-looking secretary told her that there were no books for her classes. No explanation. Just no books. Gritty left the room feeling confused, wondering what to do.

Then she thought of a possible solution and with determination headed down the hall to find the classroom where she was assigned to teach five ninth grade English classes each day. Maybe the textbooks were already there. When she arrived at the room that matched the number on her schedule, though, she discovered it was the school cafeteria.

Assuming there must be a mistake, Gritty walked back to the principal's office. Another secretary, more kindly disposed than the previous one, seemed eager to help.

"I'm sorry," she said sympathetically, "our school is terribly overcrowded so all of your classes will have to meet in the cafeteria. To the left of the door you will find a blackboard in front of tables and chairs that have been set up for your students. I'm afraid that's the best we can do."

Gritty went back to the cafeteria, wondering how she was going to teach without textbooks or a classroom.

She arrived just in time to see twenty expectant black faces looking up at her. Hoping they wouldn't notice the nervousness and stress in her voice, she said good morning and introduced herself. She went to the blackboard to write her name on it but there was no chalk, only an eraser. She kept her composure as she slowly spelled her name for the students so they could write it in their notebooks, then asked them to identify themselves.

The students yelled to be heard above the din of clanging dishes, shouting workers, intermittent peals of laughter, and sporadic crashing sounds that echoed off the cafeteria walls. Gritty asked them to write short essays about themselves, promising to read them that night as a way to begin to get to know them. She was amazed to see that as the students dutifully wrote, they seemed oblivious of the noise.

Throughout the day, Gritty continued to smile warmly, greeting one class of students after another, fighting exhaustion and a creeping demoralization. By three o'clock her voice was so hoarse it was barely audible, yet there was still a discernible resolve in her step when she left the building carrying the student papers in her arms, heading for home.

The scene then shifted and Gritty was in her apartment, reading the essays, dismay clouding her face and a puddle of anxiety pooling in her gut at what she faced. None of the students could write at anywhere near grade level. To make things worse, there were no textbooks and their classroom was a jumble of cafeteria clatter and chaos.

She did the only thing she could think of. She went out and bought a box of chalk, then clipped articles from newspapers and magazines late into the night.

These would have to serve as substitutes for textbooks for a while. She hoped it wouldn't be for long.

"I went back to teach the next day," Gritty told Spring and Sky with a tone of sadness as she looked up from the Earth scene, "and the day after that and the day after that. I fought for textbooks and a quiet space for my classes to meet but never got a response. Not even an excuse. Finally, one morning, I just laid in bed, unable to get up. I never went back."

Gritty never forgot the faces of those ninth grade students or their desire to learn, which was so strong that they kept coming to school day after day in spite of incredible obstacles and inhuman conditions. When she read Jonathan Kozol's book *Death At An Early Age* about the intolerable learning environments of inner city schools her guilt intensified for having left them behind. With a force that increased with each familiar story in the book, her anger churned, forming a cyclone in the pit of her stomach. When friends who taught in resource-rich environments talked about what bright achievers and eager learners their students were, Gritty's anger turned to rage. Her ninth grade students hadn't been any less eager or bright.

It was then that the truth of life's unfairness was irrefutably etched into her brain. It was a truth she would never accept.

Gritty then turned the page of her storybook and with the new images came deep feelings, long forgotten but readily resurrected—a combination of love, sadness and guilt. Spring and Sky, who had been gripped by outrage about the educational injustices they had just witnessed, looked at Gritty with concern as they watched the new scene unfold.

It was summertime in the South Bronx and Gritty held the hand of a tiny black girl who was chattering away as the two of them walked purposely down the street. Sylvia was four years old, precocious and adorable, bright red ribbons in her neatly braided hair. Every morning they walked the same route to the dilapidated building wallpapered with graffiti where Head Start classes were held.

As soon as they walked into their classroom, Sylvia ran over to the toy box to find her favorite doll while Gritty prepared for another day of teaching. She placed juice and crackers on the tables so they would be ready when the students first arrived. It was the only breakfast some of them would have. Then she retrieved the art supplies from the cabinet and organized the books and toys.

Gritty looked over at Sylvia, happily playing in the corner. What a joy she was, such a bright child, so sensible at such a young age, so in need of attention and love. Her mother, who was in jail, had asked Gritty to care for Sylvia until she was released in a few months. Sylvia had been a gift, filling Gritty's apartment and life in a new way. She would miss her terribly at the end of the summer.

Soon the other students arrived. The scenes shifted from one to another, revealing a series of typical Head Start days: twenty four-year-olds mesmerized as Gritty read a story; walking single file on a field trip to the country, learning where eggs and milk come from; learning to write their names and add numbers; squealing with delight as they ran through the hose in the playground to ward off the sizzling heat of summer in the city; finger painting, their hands and arms covered with bright vibrant colors; Gritty visiting their homes at the end of the day whenever they didn't come to school.

Then a new image emerged. A little boy named Jasper came into full view, his bloated stomach and hollow brown eyes revealing endemic malnutrition. Gritty always gave him extra food, which he secretly hid in his pockets, stowing it away for his dinner. She suspected abuse as well as neglect and planned to make a home visit but one day Jasper didn't come to school. There had been a fire in his apartment building the night before. He didn't get out. Gritty sobbed, crying over and over, "it's not fair, it's not fair!"

"I was assaulted each day," Gritty interjected as she looked up from the sad scene, "by the injustices of life on Earth."

She thought about the summers she taught Head Start in New York, realizing it had been her way to compensate for quitting on the ninth grade students in Chicago. She loved the little children with their bright curious eyes, their quick minds not yet defeated by the cruelty of life that threatened to pull them down at every turn.

During the school year, she taught third grade in a Chicago suburb, telling herself she was doing what she could…but it wasn't enough. After three years she took the New York City teacher's exam and moved to the South Bronx permanently. She would teach middle school there.

Another turn of the page in her storybook and Gritty smiled, remembering a time when she got in over her head, how she hadn't known what she was getting into. Sensing an unfolding Earth drama, Spring and Sky drew closer for a good view.

It was the first day of school at P.S. 457 in the South Bronx. Gritty was up early, eager and ready to start teaching eighth grade. She nervously sipped her morning coffee and opened the newspaper. The front-page headline was bold: the teachers had declared a strike. There would be no school that day.

Three weeks passed and finally the teachers' union successfully negotiated a salary increase. School now officially began.

Gritty arrived at P.S. 457 at six-thirty in the morning to meet her first hour class of thirty-five students in the gymnasium and escort them to their classroom. A seasoned teacher, trim and debonair with salt and pepper hair and a handlebar moustache, warmly welcomed her and introduced himself as head of the school's chapter of the union. He looked out at the sea of excited brown faces and then at Gritty, his hand gesturing toward them dismissively.

"Let me give you a tip," he said in confidence, "These kids are nothing but animals. All you have to do is train them to behave and you will be fine. Just don't expect them to learn."

Gritty angrily looked up from the scene in her storybook, the man's lethal advice still ringing in her ears. Over twenty-four hundred students were enrolled in P.S. 457 but its broken down building was barely adequate for one thousand. Mobile classrooms occupied every available space on the playground but the students still had to attend school in shifts. Half of them came for the morning shift from seven to noon; the other half had school from noon to five in the afternoon. One-third of her eighth grade students didn't speak English and most of the others, with one or two notable exceptions, read at about the third grade level.

The contrast from her previous suburban school could not be more blatant. Yet this time—unlike her brief stint at the Chicago middle school—Gritty was aware of the starkly substandard conditions and more than willing to tackle the challenges. Her creativity flourished in spite of insufficient resources. She embraced the students with protective mother fierceness, patiently nurturing their potential, and they eagerly responded to her high expectations. After school she visited their parents or caretakers in the projects and crowded tenements surrounding the school. When the head of the union—the man with the first day tip for her—slammed one of her students against the wall, Gritty helped his parents file a grievance that resulted in a formal reprimand on his record. At the end of the school year, she tearfully said goodbye to her students and looked forward to coming back in the fall.

Gritty then turned to a new page in her storybook and, with a knowing glance at Spring and Sky, declared, "wait 'til you see this!"

It was the next fall, the first day of school, and Gritty was excited to begin her second year of teaching at P.S. 457. But once again the morning news announced a teachers' strike. This time the issue was union opposition to an initiative that would give more control of the schools to the community.

Gritty listened to the radio, thinking about the issues. She supported community control of schools but she also supported unions. Mostly, though, her heart was with the students. Already so far behind in their learning, they couldn't afford to miss any time from school. When it was predicted that the strike would last a long time she became more concerned. Feeling she had to do something, she arranged for her classes to meet in the basement of a church for the duration of the strike. One other teacher joined her.

A week passed. Gritty was in her apartment, preparing for the next day of classes at the church, when the phone rang. It was the district superintendent.

"I understand," Superintendent Alexander said, "that you are teaching your classes in a church, is that right?"

"Yes?"

Gritty wondered if she was in trouble. Why was this important person calling? Had she miscalculated again and taken an inappropriate action?

"Please forgive me," Superintendent Alexander quickly said, picking up on the uncertainty in Gritty's voice, "I should explain why I asked and why I'm calling. The principals have joined the teachers in a sympathy strike. All schools in the city are effectively shut down. I'm terribly worried about the kids in our district. They desperately need to be in school."

Gritty agreed but still wondered what the superintendent wanted from her. It quickly became apparent.

"I think you can help," Superintendent Alexander went on, "I want you to keep P.S. 457 open for the duration of the strike. I am prepared to appoint you as Acting Principal."

Gritty was dumbfounded.

"I need a few days to think about this," she mumbled and hung up.

She fell onto the couch, holding herself tightly, attempting to subdue the fluttering of her heart and the butterflies in her stomach.

Two days passed. It was the weekend. Gritty was deep in thought, feeling the pressure of the looming decision when the ringing phone startled her. It was the man who was the head of the teachers' union at her school.

"How are you?" he asked pleasantly.

"Fine," she answered curtly. Given their short but unpleasant history, Gritty was understandably suspicious of his friendly tone. She wondered why he was calling. Surely there was no way he could know about the Superintendent's request, she thought.

"I understand," he went on, "that the district superintendent asked you to keep the school open. What have you decided to do?"

He didn't reveal his source of information and Gritty didn't ask. When she simply said she hadn't decided yet, he gently urged her not to do it. She listened carefully and found a few, though not all, of his arguments convincing. Then he ended the conversation with a final assertion:

"You know, the district superintendent is just another black person who has it in for white teachers. You need to seriously think about that."

That settled it. Gritty's decision was made. As soon as she hung up the phone, she slowly but determinedly dialed the home phone number that Superintendent Alexander had given her.

"Hello," she answered pleasantly. "I'm hoping that you're calling with a positive decision."

"Yes," Gritty quickly responded, "I will do it."

With surprised gratitude in her voice, the Superintendent said a messenger would deliver a letter of appointment the following day, designating Gritty as acting principal effective immediately.

Gritty hung up the phone and sat on the couch in a daze, wondering what she had done and what would happen next.

With a mischievous smile, Gritty looked up from her storybook at the delighted faces of Spring and Sky.

"You did it again, didn't you?" Spring shouted. "Jumped right into the fray! How old were you, anyway, about twenty-five? How did it go?"

"I was twenty-six years old," Gritty smiled. "I'll show you how it went."

She turned the page and Spring and Sky excitedly watched as one scene after another rapidly emerged: with a small cadre of regular teachers, many substitute teachers, and committed parents as teachers' aides Gritty kept the school open for two and a half months—most of the teachers and parents going into the school each morning were black, all of the teachers on the picket line were white—Gritty got death threats on a regular basis, mostly by phone, but never took them seriously—when the maintenance staff changed the locks on the doors before walking out in a sympathy strike, Gritty met a locksmith at the school at four o'clock the next morning to restore access before classes started.

Then a new, longer scene unfolded.

It was a Sunday afternoon, early in the strike. Teachers and parents gathered in Gritty's living room for an organizing meeting. Some drank coffee as they talked strategy while others made posters containing positive messages aimed at establishing dialogue with the picketing teachers. Hearing a knock and thinking it was a latecomer, Gritty answered the door.

Three very tall men with dark brown skin and berets on their heads smiled down at her.

"Is this where there is a meeting about keeping the school open?" one of the men asked in a friendly tone.

"Yes, it is," Gritty answered.

"We're members of the Black Panther Party," the man then said with a big smile, "and we're here to help."

She invited them in.

Looking up from the scene, Gritty smiled as she remembered how the men ensured the safety and protection of P.S. 457 over the next two months. With their German shepherd guard dog, they arrived at the end of each school day and spent the night in the principal's office—Gritty's office during the strike. Each morning when the teachers and parents returned, the men welcomed them with the aroma of coffee and sweet smelling donuts before going home to sleep.

Grinning, Gritty turned the page in her storybook. Spring and Sky shook their heads in disbelief wondering what possibly could happen next as a new scene unfolded.

Two months had passed. The teachers' strike was finally over and P.S. 457 was alive with the hustle and bustle of happily returning teachers and students. Gritty was in her classroom when she got a message that the principal wanted to see her. She walked down the old winding stairs and the long wide hall to the office that had temporarily been hers, bracing herself for the unpleasant encounter she expected. She figured she would probably be fired or maybe transferred to another school for what she had done.

Nervously, she knocked on the principal's office door and was invited in.

Miss Traskett, who had been head of the school for thirty-five years, looked like a lumpy mass of clay slouched in the high backed leather chair behind her big mahogany desk. With a gesture of her short flaccid arm, she indicated that Gritty should sit down. Then she smiled at her for what seemed like a very long time.

Gritty squirmed, wondering if this was some kind of sadistic game.

"I just want to thank you," Miss Traskett finally said in a gruff, raspy smoker's voice, "Ours was the only school in the city that was not vandalized or broken into during the strike. I know that you were responsible for that."

Gritty sat quietly for a few minutes. Surprised and pleased, she smiled back at Miss Traskett.

"You can thank the Black Panthers for protecting the school," she said. "They stayed in your office every night to make sure nothing happened."

Silence. Miss Traskett stared at her with a wide-eyed look that was worth a thousand words, yet defied description. Fully pleased with herself, Gritty smiled back for a very long time.

"Excuse me," she said finally, then left the office and went back to doing what she loved—teaching.

"It's funny," Gritty said to Spring and Sky as she returned to the library from the Earth scene, "that I didn't mind when none of the teachers spoke to me for the rest of that year. It was kind of amusing how they went out of their way to avoid me—they moved away in the teacher's lounge if I happened to sit next them; they pretended not to see me in the halls by looking down at the floor. They even crossed the street so they wouldn't have to say hello. Trying to understand my motivation, they made up bizarre stories about why I agreed to be acting principal. Hell, I didn't even understand why I did it myself!"

Gritty closed her storybook and the scene in Miss Traskett's office disappeared. She was smiling and so were Sky and Spring.

"That was really exciting!" Sky said giddily.

"Your unrelenting passion," Spring added, "and commitment to your students were impressively intense."

Gritty thought about how that intensity had threatened to drain her soul. Though her work was fulfilling, there was plenty of heartbreak. She knew it was time to talk about the other very different life she led.

"That wasn't the whole story, though," she responded sadly. "There was another side to my life and, believe me, it wasn't pretty."

*   *   *   *

With a sigh, Gritty re-opened her storybook. The emerging scene quickly wiped away the smiles of Spring and Sky, replaced now with new feelings of loneliness and powerlessness.

They saw a group of young professionals in a dark, upscale bar laughing and carrying on, having a good time, letting go of the work week. Gritty sat in the middle, expounding on the meaning of life. She was known for her sardonic wit and the passion with which she proffered solutions to the world's problems when she was drinking. The others laughed, extolling her dazzling insights about politics, philosophy, and religion, encouraging her and egging her on. At closing time, she was the last to leave.

The scene shifted and it was late the next morning. The ringing phone woke Gritty. It was a friend, who went on and on about how insightful she thought Gritty had been the night before, how her ideas were gloomily pessimistic and at the same time brilliantly inspired.

Gritty sat in the middle of a pounding headache and listened. She recalled none of what she had said that so thoroughly impressed her friend. The only thing she remembered about the night before was the world spinning out of control as soon as her head hit the pillow. She didn't even know how she got home.

Looking up from the scene briefly with a melancholy nod to Spring and Sky, Gritty turned the page of her storybook. A new series of scenes appeared, taking a different and ever more gloomy turn: Gritty alone in her apartment grading papers, a bottle of wine and filled glass at the ready—later half-sitting, half-lying on the couch with her head drooping, the wine bottle almost empty—going out the door and walking down the street, headed for a liquor store—back in the apartment, passed out on the couch, nothing but snow on the television screen—staggering to her bedroom, collapsing on the bed fully clothed—the next morning, holding her head, pulling herself together with a cup of strong coffee—throwing the empty wine bottles in the trash on her way to school—stopping at a different liquor store on her way home at the end of the day.

Gritty looked up from the scenes. This sad and lonely side of her latest Earth life had been her carefully guarded secret. No one knew she did things she didn't want to do or that she was unable to stop. A Bible verse, one of the many she had memorized in church as a child, suddenly came to her: "I do not understand my own actions. For I do not do what I want, but I do the very thing I hate"— Romans 7:15. That was how she felt.

"During the day," she candidly told Spring and Sky, "I often helped students who showed signs of having alcohol or drug problems. I even talked with some of their parents about their own drinking, encouraging treatment, and on rare occasions when a parent agreed to seek help, I worked with the school social worker to make the arrangements. Sometimes when I saw a parent heading for a neighborhood bar, I would go in and talk to them in my eagerness to help them find a way out of their addiction.

"Then, at night, I would turn around and go to a trendy bar in a neighborhood across a busy street that marked the territory of the *haves* from the *have-nots*. There the beer was more expensive and we thought we were sophisticated, yet our slurred speech and unsteady gait revealed the truth: the outcome for people who stayed until closing time was the same in both bars.

"Wearing bellbottom jeans that hugged my hips, a tight tank top without a bra, and my hair in two long blond braids gracing my shoulders, I danced my heart out in the bar on weekends...even though I still felt a little guilty about dancing. I slept around a lot, always bringing the man of the moment to my own turf, pushing him out the door the next morning, wondering how the hell he got there and wanting him to be gone. I had blackouts regularly although I didn't know what they were and thought everyone had similar memory lapses.

"I had a wild affair with a student intern at my school. Our time together was filled with alcohol, drugs, and fast riding down the highway on the back of his motorcycle, my long blond hair flowing out from under a bright red helmet. When Dick went to Boston to finish his graduate degree, I visited him there over Christmas vacation. Before he left for work each day, he drew a line on the vodka bottle he kept on his kitchen table so he could see how much was gone when he returned. Insulted, I carefully rationed my consumption. We spent Christmas Eve alone in a dark, desolate and god-forsaken bar where we got drunk and had little to say to each other. Desperately lonely and with shame so deep it threatened to obliterate my soul, I boarded the plane for my trip back to New York and wondered how I had sunk so low."

Gritty remembered her behavior during that time with disgust—brazen promiscuity, vomiting and urinating in public, blatant dishonesty. While keenly aware of the problems of some of her students and their parents she was clueless about her own. It was funny how, even though she felt guilty and ashamed, she assumed that others still perceived her as a good person, a sober, competent and dedicated teacher. She was genuinely shocked by evidence to the contrary, like when an older teacher called her a slut and a man in the bar assumed she wanted to sleep with him even though she wasn't the least bit interested. It was ironic how she desperately wanted a good girl image as an adult in spite of her negative behavior. When she was younger, it had been just the opposite. She wanted a bad girl image then even though she really was a good girl. She thought about how things were never as they seemed, how her insides didn't match her outsides, how she lived a double life just as Daddy and her uncles had.

Shaking her head, Gritty cleared her thoughts and continued telling her story to Spring and Sky.

"Then I met someone at a teachers' workshop and woke up the next morning in his hotel room. Chuck was a well-loved and highly esteemed member of his community, a strong family man with a wife and three children. I was drawn to his respectability and the seriousness with which he seemed to listen to me. I desperately yearned to be cared for and in exchange I happily provided him with the sex that he loved and craved.

"I had pursued Chuck relentlessly until he succumbed, eventually leaving his wife and moving in with me. As soon as his divorce was final we married and bought an attractive four-bedroom home in the suburbs with a large swimming pool on several acres of prime land. Chuck's children lived with us three days a week and I tried my best to be a good stepmother."

Gritty closed her storybook with an air of finality, remembering how she had hoped that marrying Chuck would make her respectable, that it would solve her problems. She didn't know her troubles had just begun.

Sky reflected on Gritty's stories—how committed she was to her students, the risk she took when she became acting principal of the school, her certainty about the rightness of that act. But had her inability to accept the injustices heaped upon her students almost destroyed her? Was Gritty's drinking a way to numb the pain so she could continue jumping through hurdles each day in her quest to make things better?

Spring was absorbed in her own private reflections as well. She thought about how complicated life was on Earth, so filled with contradictions and unfairness. As young adults she and Gritty had been similar in many ways: their passion, commitment, persistence, risk-taking, and desire to do well. Gritty's flaws were bold and raw yet, in spite of her barefaced imperfections, she was an outstanding teacher, cared for little Sylvia as if she were her own child, tried to make up for her first failed teaching experience. Spring had many questions: Did Gritty's strengths outweigh her flaws? Might one noble act outweigh many imperfections? Did it really matter?

Then Spring wondered why Suma hadn't appeared. While trying not to engage in conjecture or make assumptions, she was secretly comforted that she wasn't the only one who told her stories and then heard nothing from Suma when she was finished.

✳   ✳   ✳   ✳

When they realized that Suma was not coming, Spring and Gritty looked at Sky expectantly, a signal that it was her turn again. Sky continued her story where she had left it—as a seminary wife with a questioning mind.

"When it was time for Don to do his internship," she began, "I was determined not to go to any podunk town where I would have to serve tea to the church ladies. We were lucky to be assigned to a church in the South Bronx. Our card-playing friends were not as fortunate. They tried to make the best of being assigned to a small depressed town in Indiana, despondently joking that if God ever gave the United States an enema, surely He would insert the tube there. Happily, we moved to New York with plans to return to the seminary for Don's final year while our poor friends went to the pits.

"Reverend Nelson, Don's internship supervisor, was kicked out of a rich suburban church in Connecticut, a real feather in his cap as far as I was concerned. He reminded me of the minister in our socially active church. The small South Bronx congregation of one hundred people was evenly divided by diversity. One-third were loyal old-timers, Swedish people who remained active in the church even after moving to the suburbs when the neighborhood changed, one-third were Puerto Rican people who lived on the same block as the church, and, one-third were black people who lived just a block away.

"Attached to the old worn church was the parsonage where Reverend Nelson, his wife Rebecca, and their three teenage daughters lived. They were the only white people in the neighborhood until we moved across the street. Their home was a beautiful oasis in the bowels of the inner city with Victorian furniture, a grand piano, even a little concrete patio in the back surrounded by carefully tended bright flowers and lush greenery in clay pots. Every Sunday Don and I joined the Nelson's after church for a delicious meal of pot roast, potatoes, and carrots that Rebecca put in the oven before the service. During warm weather we ate out on the patio."

Sky then opened her storybook and pointed to a new Earth scene. With it came a sudden wave of nostalgia, fond memories of city sights, sounds, and smells.

The image of a neglected apartment building emerged. Its former grandeur whispered in wide marble stairs now chipped and stained, faded ornate tinwork on high ceilings, and walls that produced daily portions of peeling paint. The entry reeked of urine, which combined with the pungent smell of Mister Clean on Tuesdays when the janitor cleaned.

Sky and Don's apartment was on the second floor, its door weighed down by four locks, a chain, and a bar. Two tall living room windows, covered with heavy metal security bars, opened to a fire escape with a clothesline that was operated by a pulley system stretching across to the next building. Filled with used furniture and brick and board bookcases, the three-room apartment was cozy and eclectically comfortable.

"An elderly Jewish woman lived there for fifty years," Sky interrupted, "and because of city rent control laws we paid very little for that apartment."

The scene in the storybook then shifted slightly. It was Saturday and Sky was cleaning the apartment, marveling at how much black soot could accumulate on the windowsills in just a week and how the stubborn mushroom in the shower's moldy grout had re-sprouted once again. After cleaning the apartment, she removed everything from the kitchen cupboards and sprayed them for roaches.

Sky looked up from the Earth scene, remembering how hard she tried to keep their apartment roach-free. It was no wonder her efforts had been futile. Once a month her fastidious neighbor moved her furniture into the hall and sprayed her whole apartment, causing her roaches to escape the encroaching fumes by marching like a little army across the hall to Sky and Don's apartment. When a building across the street was demolished as part of urban renewal, legions of roaches crossed the street to seek a new home in their building.

"At least they didn't bite," Sky said, smiling at Spring and Gritty, "and the bugs would have been much worse in Africa where Don had wanted to go as a missionary."

"I read about how resilient roaches were," Spring said, unable to resist commenting. "They could survive anything and it was said they would flourish after a nuclear holocaust."

Sky nodded in agreement as she turned the page in her storybook and a new scene came into view.

Stepping gingerly over the dog poop and garbage that littered the sidewalks, Sky walked toward the grocery store in her South Bronx neighborhood. The garbage workers had been on strike for several weeks and she held her breath from the worst of the stench. It had been a mistake to wear sandals even though it was unbearably hot. With a friendly smile she greeted people sitting on their stoops. Some nodded and half-smiled while others looked puzzled like she was a creature from another planet dropped into their territory by mistake.

Once she was in the grocery store, Sky realized she had made another mistake. It was Mother's Day, the first of the month, when families received their welfare checks by mail. On that day prices for the over-ripe fruits and moldy vegetables at the small neighborhood store always mysteriously increased. She bought only a few necessities and headed for home.

As Sky looked at the scene she remembered the remarkable statistics. Over ninety percent of the two thousand people living on her block were on welfare. With rent due to absentee landlords and inflated grocery prices, they often found themselves out of money within days of getting their checks. The rest of the month they lived on powdered eggs and peanut butter provided by the government in gallon cans. Sometimes a neighbor gave Sky her extras.

"Our block was a microcosm of urban poverty," Sky explained, "and soon I was busy working as a social worker in the neighborhood elementary school and helping to organize projects in the community. My role as a minister's wife was limited to joining the women's group in the church."

Sky then remembered when she and six others from that women's group went to a retreat together. A wonderfully diverse group of Latina, black, and white women, they piled into a van and several hours later arrived at a camp in New Hampshire, providing the only color among two hundred very white Swedish women. Over the weekend each church group made a presentation to the others with most of them singing a hymn or reading scripture. The South Bronx women dramatized the story of Harriet Tubman helping slaves escape to freedom in the north and the church's role in the abolitionist movement. Sky remembered how their presentation was greeted with uncomfortably polite applause; how later, at the social hour, the white women fell all over themselves to be friendly to the black women in her group.

With a smile, she filled Spring and Gritty in.

"Several women in the church created a historical production about slavery and took it to suburban churches. After each performance we dialogued about the need for churches to promote social justice and excoriated the white parishioners for their racism."

Sky shook her head, shuddering with memories of those turbulent times—how she despaired as she watched the riots at the Chicago Democratic National Convention on television, angrily protested the Vietnam War by demonstrating in New York and Washington, D.C. with thousands of strangers, and mourned the assassination of Dr. Martin Luther King Jr., commemorating his message of nonviolence by joining a memorial march through Central Park. The world would never be the same again and neither would she.

"We ended up staying in the South Bronx," she then told Spring and Gritty, "Don went to a liberal seminary in New York to finish his theological studies and continued working as assistant pastor of the church. I didn't realize that he was changing. It was so slow and imperceptible at first. When he went to a weekend retreat at the new seminary, the group leader suggested something about his personality that was baffling at the time. Later it would slowly threaten to devour us, as sinister in its guile as it was cunning in its invisibility.

"I don't remember exactly how I ended up being a housemother for seven emotionally disturbed adolescent girls. It started when Don decided he no longer wanted to be a minister. Relieved that my days as a poor excuse for a minister's wife were over, I hoped he would find a job in the city but things didn't work out that way. When a childcare organization offered him a houseparent job in a new group home, I guess I was just part of the deal."

Sky remembered intuitively knowing it was a mistake but reluctantly agreeing to the houseparent idea anyway and they moved from the South Bronx to an integrated middle class Long Island neighborhood. In stark contrast to their tiny roach-infested apartment, their new home had five bedrooms and three bathrooms with a wrap-around front porch looking out on a street lined with mature elm and maple trees.

"Our first assignment," she continued, "was to set up the house. We bought sturdy furniture built to withstand adolescent abuse, appliances, linens, dishes, pots and pans—the works. Creating a warm family atmosphere was like playing house...until Patti, Wanda, Sylvia, Carmen, Yolanda, Vera, and Susie arrived, clutching little suitcases in which they had carefully packed all their belongings. A trembling sense of dread lurked in the pit of my stomach. Suddenly there I was, someone who had never wanted children, in the role of pseudo-mom with an instant family of seven girls, all of whom were at an age when many parents want to give their children away."

Sky thought about the hard lives the girls had led. Some of them had languished in an institutional treatment program for years, abused and abandoned by their parents. Their stay in the group home marked the first step of their transition back to the community. Some of the girls would move on to live independently, others would live with relatives.

Sky opened to a new page in her storybook, eager to introduce the girls to Spring and Gritty. As she watched their images emerge, her heart filled with caring and regret.

Carmen, the oldest, was eager to prove she was capable of living on her own. She was a strikingly beautiful seventeen-year-old Latina, a mother hen to her two little sisters who she planned to care for once she reached eighteen. Yolanda, wide-eyed and innocent at age twelve, and Vera, slim and sensible at thirteen, adored Carmen. The three of them were inseparable.

Susie was the only white girl and at age fourteen clearly the most disturbed of the seven. With sad eyes crossing involuntarily and mousy blond hair falling haphazardly on her shoulders, she was a lost soul with no known parents or relatives.

Patti and Wanda, multiracial thirteen-year-old twins, carried deep and unhealed scars from years of horrendous abuse. Still, they fantasized about living with their drug-addicted mother once they left the group home.

Sylvia was the only black girl and the youngest of the seven. Her wisdom and maturity belied her mere eleven years and revealed a brutal life that had robbed her of innocence at an early age.

Suddenly Gritty jumped, interrupting the Earth scene with a flurry of questions: "Where did Sylvia come from? Where did she live before? Who was she? Please tell me about her!"

Not grasping the urgency behind the questions, Sky responded factually.

"Her mother was in and out of jail for years and Sylvia was passed from relative to relative—an uncle who sexually abused her, a grandmother who cared but was too old and tired to provide what she needed, an aunt who was drunk most of the time. She lived many places—Manhattan, Brooklyn, South Bronx, even down South, maybe in Mississippi. When her mother was found dead in an abandoned building with a needle in her arm, Sylvia was placed in the treatment center and shortly thereafter our group home.

"Her strengths were phenomenal. Even though she was so young and just a little bit of a thing, she was the most sensible of the girls. She mediated conflicts, found solutions to problems, talked like a little parent. Once when there was a food fight in the school cafeteria Sylvia jumped up on a table, whistled for attention, and stopped the melee. I was so proud of her!"

Gritty interrupted again, her energy jumping up and down with excitement, darting in every direction.

"The Sylvia you describe," she shouted in spurts, "*had* to be my Sylvia—little Sylvia who lived with me for three months—when she was four years old—when I taught Head Start during the summer—before I moved to the South Bronx to teach middle school!"

Sky suddenly realized the truth of what Gritty said.

"So that was *you*!" she exclaimed breathlessly, "Sylvia's case record indicated that when she was about four years old she lived temporarily with her Head Start teacher. Of course that was you! The timing is right. It all makes sense!"

Overwhelmed by the unexpected convergence, Sky and Gritty each went into her own mental space, trying to absorb its meaning, realizing this was one of Suma's surprises.

Gritty remembered how bright and curious Sylvia was, how eager and quick to learn, how she chattered all the time, how tightly she hugged her when saying good night as if she were afraid that Gritty would leave before morning. Filled with remorse, she grieved that Sylvia had suffered sexual abuse, neglect, and trauma at the hands of several caretakers and ended up in a group home at a young age. Then guilt hit her: if only she hadn't left the city at the end of that summer, if only she had been successful in her attempts to find her after that, if only she had kept Sylvia with her, if only she could have rescued her, protected her—if only, if only, if only.

Sky's thoughts were very different. When she was the group home mother, she was impressed by Sylvia's resilience and knew that she was going to be okay. Sky was certain that Gritty had played an important part in her development at a critical age, that the care and protection she provided that summer might have made all the difference in the world.

Both Sky and Gritty wondered what Sylvia's life had been like. Seeking assurance, they spontaneously called out for Suma.

With an impressive flourish and the sound of laughter, Suma's dark energy immediately appeared. Impatient for answers, Sky and Gritty accosted her, their energies fluttering nervously around hers.

"I have been waiting for this moment," Suma said with a mischievous smile, "and to satisfy your curiosity, I will first show you what happened to Sylvia."

All of a sudden, snapshots of her life appeared before them: Sylvia holding Gritty's hand, skipping happily by her side—the two of them hugging and crying as they said goodbye at the end of the summer—between dirty sheets in a dingy little room, Sylvia cowering in terror, praying the old man wouldn't come to her in the night—Sylvia hugging her grandmother tightly, helping her walk, hoping she would live—stealing money from her drunken aunt's purse to buy food— Sylvia as star of her third grade class in reading—as top of her class in middle school—as a leader in the group home—living with caring foster parents, doing well in school—as a tough, smart and determined teenager—giving an inspiring graduation speech as valedictorian of her high school class—graduating from college and going on to graduate school with a full scholarship, earning a doctoral degree—teaching at a large prestigious research university, moving up the ranks to full professor in record time—serving as dean of a college of education—marrying a kind professor—loving her two happy sons.

"Enough!" Sky and Gritty laughingly shouted as they celebrated Sylvia's triumph in the face of staggering injustice.

Gritty then got it that she *might* have played a small but important role after all. Maybe both she and Sky had helped Sylvia along her life's path, had made a difference somehow.

"Exactly!" Suma said, reading Gritty's mind, "and Sylvia's lesson is for all of you. It is about accepting what you can do even when it isn't everything you wish you could do. Gritty and Sky couldn't protect Sylvia from trauma and brutality, but they could help her at critical moments in her life.

"You see, when most people see what they can't do they cut and run. You saw that you couldn't eliminate all injustice, but you didn't cut and run. Even when you began to realize your powerlessness you stubbornly persisted, making what was yet to come possible."

As they contemplated Suma's words their collective questions and wonderings swirled around the library and bounced off the walls. Had they learned that life was unfair only to suffer from their own inability to change it? If there was only so much one person could do, then how much was enough? Had they tried to do too much and how much was too much? If it was good that they didn't cut and run, was it enough to just persist?

Suma quietly allowed them to wander in the darkness of their uncertainty for a while.

"I know," she then said after a few minutes, "that this is a lot to take in. Even though your passions are glowing with desire to understand, it is impossible to absorb everything at once. We'll take it one step at a time."

And with that, she was gone.

Spring had been quiet for a long time. Now she wondered how many more surprises Suma had in store for them. She had a premonition that not all of them would be as positive as Sylvia's story and shuddered in anticipation of what the next one might bring. Troubling fear still nibbled at the corners of her mind and, even though she didn't want to, she resented Suma's surprises.

Keeping her doubts to herself as usual, Spring looked at the others with a weak smile, acknowledging with a nod that Sky had re-opened her storybook and was ready to continue.

*   *   *   *

Without missing a beat, Sky picked up the strands of the story she had been telling about life in the group home before it was interrupted by Suma's surprise.

"Don worked part time as a security guard to bring in a little extra income and I stayed at home full time, playing house and mom. We all had assigned roles. A chart on the refrigerator told each girl what her weekly tasks were—setting the table, doing the dishes, sweeping the floor, dusting the furniture, vacuuming, cleaning the bathrooms. Each girl did her own laundry. Don and I did the grocery shopping, filling two carts to overflowing each week. I did all the cooking for the nine of us and Don mowed the lawn.

"I hated all of it, especially being a pseudo mom. I didn't know what that meant and neither did the girls. I hated cooking. I hated it when I was home alone and I hated it when the girls were there. The house felt like a prison either way. I hated trying to manage the inevitable conflicts, worrying and feeling responsible for everything, feeling inadequate, being on call twenty-four hours a day. I hated that the girls had such hard lives and, even more, I hated that I couldn't make up for that.

"I felt overwhelmed and alone especially when there was a crisis—like the school calling because of someone's behavior and Susie having another emotional breakdown. One night Patti crawled out her bedroom window, jumped to the ground from the porch roof and ran away. The next morning I found the purse she had dropped and searched it, hoping to find a clue about where she had gone. A double-edged razor blade Patti had tucked away for protection sliced my finger so badly it took nine stitches to sew it back together. I called our supervisor from the hospital emergency room and he said not to worry. He sounded stoned.

"Don wasn't much help either. He was often at work when there was a crisis and when he was home, I tried to protect the girls from his sternness and emotional detachment. Something was wrong with him. He had always been the strong silent type but now he seemed even more distant and preoccupied.

"One day Susie drew a picture of Don and me for her therapist. His large looming frame filled the page. I was a very small shadowy figure standing beside him, my tiny hand swallowed by his huge one. It was a frighteningly accurate portrayal of how I felt—like a very small, inconsequential, and incompetent person.

"Sensing my growing anxiety, our supervisor suggested tranquilizers. As the days went by, I took more and more of them, retreating to our bedroom at every opportunity until one day I didn't come out at all."

Sky remembered how Don had agreed to quit the job even though it seemed to suit his purposes just fine. When they told their supervisor there were problems in her family and they needed to move back home, he exchanged a conspiratorial look with Don as if to say they always knew Sky wouldn't be able to cut it. A new housemother was hired and the girls liked her a lot. At least that was a relief.

With sadness, Sky remembered the morning they left before dawn. The night before she and Don said goodbye to the girls before they went to bed; when they woke up, they would be gone. She felt guilty about leaving them behind but her own survival was at stake. As they passed New York in their rented truck early that morning she wistfully longed for her previous life in the city, having no desire to go back home to her family. But it was too late. Plans had been made. With a sigh she threw the tranquilizers out the window and tried to be optimistic.

"It was January," she told Spring and Gritty, "when we left the group home and moved to the town where Grandma lived. When we arrived, pure white drifts of snow several feet high greeted us and twenty below zero winds slapped our faces and burned our hands as we unloaded the truck. The small two-bedroom house we had arranged to rent wasn't much but it was warm. The next week Don found a temporary job and left for work every morning at six. I stayed in bed, sometimes for the whole day."

Sky remembered how depressed she had been during that time. She created a studio in the spare bedroom where she painted gloomy pictures that gave expression to her pain about the state of the world—the Vietnam War, racism, injustice, you name it. One picture portrayed a small Vietnamese boy carrying his dog in his arms, clutching a small bag of meager belongings as he ran from his village, a look of sheer terror on his face; his thatch-roofed house burned in the background and bombs fell from the sky. Another was a large abstract painting that oozed anger and rage in bold swirls of red and orange juxtaposed with gloomy lines of brown, black and dark blue that exuded sadness and despair. It wasn't until years later that Sky understood the underlying reason for her depression.

"My family was happy to have me home," she said sadly to Spring and Gritty, "but I seldom saw them and chafed under the weight of their expectations. They wanted me to be happily married, spend time with them, go to church. Most of all they wanted me to love them but my heart was cold. Sometimes I invited them over for dinner for which they gratefully praised me but when they left I heaved a sigh of relief, glad I wouldn't have to do it again for a while.

"Grandma, whose love and protection I had always cherished, had become a burden to me. When I took her to the store I was impatient with her for moving so slowly and embarrassed when she paid for her groceries with food stamps. Then she was diagnosed with late-stage cancer and I was with her when she greeted her mother on the other side just before taking her final breath. Bereft and ashamed of how I had treated her since my return, I left the hospital with sadness so deep it numbed my entire being. It was a long time before I could look at pictures of Grandma with the same deep affection I felt as a child.

"A year later, Don and I bought a small cabin on three acres of land by a lake wrapped in a blanket of white birch and tall regal pine trees. With the help of friends, we insulated the large one room cabin, papering its walls with beige burlap, carpeting its floor in orange and brown shag, and covering its windows with homemade macramé curtains. The kitchen area at the far end of the room proudly sported an old round oak table with claw feet that we found at a garage sale. The living room was in the middle, marked by a black leather couch and chair and a high-backed ornately carved wooden bench from the church in the South Bronx. Our bedroom at the lake end of the room consisted of a mattress on the floor and two antique dressers, my favorite one having belonged to Grandma. A tiny bathroom off the bedroom was wallpapered with huge bright pink and lime green flowers. In the fall we stacked hay bales around the cabin to keep the pipes from freezing and a slow-burning woodstove kept us toasty warm during the cold harsh winters.

"We reveled in living a simple life. Don chopped wood, gardened, and spent many hours fishing, the electric motor on his canoe silently zigzagging him across the placid lake water. I fried the perch and northern pike he caught, canned the vegetables he grew, and spent hours in the root cellar below the cabin painting pictures and making a variety of candles. For bathing we heated the little sauna at the edge of the lake and threw water on the steaming rocks until we couldn't breathe and our skin burned. Then we jumped into the cold lake. In the winter, we rolled in the snow."

Sky remembered the parties they had during the summers and how their simple lakeside home became known as the place to be on weekends. Drinking, pot smoking, and folk singing around a campfire followed nude saunas on Saturday nights. She and Don fancied themselves as hippies, refusing to pay phone taxes to protest the Vietnam War and feeling proud when the federal government garnisheed their paychecks.

"Don and I worked as social workers," she continued, "for the county. Our office was a mammoth open room in the basement of the courthouse with rows of desks occupied by thirty social workers. Cigarette smoke wafted through the room, its stench filling the air along with the constant buzz of ringing phones and muted voices. In the winter, the fat tape-wrapped pipes on the ceiling pounded erratically as steam surged through them on its way to heat the old courthouse. At one end of the cavernous room was a row of cubicles, each equipped with a small microphone for dictating client information that would later be transcribed into case files. At the opposite end were four enclosed cubicles for the supervisors.

"My supervisor was Mary Ann. She was impressively competent and caring and played a significant role in my professional development. Don was assigned to an older woman who was an active alcoholic, a fact that was ignored since she was close to retirement and was a drinking buddy of the agency director.

"My caseload covered one hundred miles of farmland, woods, and logging camps and included a Native American Reservation of several hundred people. I drove the forty-mile round trip to the reservation in a county car three times a week.

"It was spring and thick mud from the melting snow formed deep ruts in the reservation road. Soon it became impassable. Reservation leaders told me that the same thing happened every year and no matter how much they complained nothing was ever done. At their request, I wrote a letter to the Bureau of Indian Affairs emphasizing how dangerous it was for elderly people to be cut off from essential medical care because of the blocked road. I copied the letter to my supervisor and the agency director."

Sky then turned to another page in her storybook to show Spring and Gritty what happened. As she saw the new Earth images emerge, she felt her anger anew and instinctively tightened herself to hold it in, even though that was unnecessary in this non-physical place.

The three of them watched as Sky was summoned to the director's office the day after she sent the letter to the BIA. As she knocked on his door, she drew herself up proudly, expecting to be commended for her advocacy effort.

"Come in and close the door," came a voice from within.

The director was a short heavy man with graying hair. His rumpled suit fell loosely on his torso suggesting recent weight loss. Looking unhappy and waving her letter in the air, he signaled to Sky to sit down.

"I am troubled by this letter," he said sternly. "It should not go to the BIA. The county maintains the reservation road. Didn't you think to ask who was responsible instead of making assumptions? You are not to go around me like this again. It is not your job to talk with anyone about roads in the first place. It is your job to work with your clients. I will talk with the county about the road myself."

Sky was devastated. She knew she should just apologize and leave.

Instead, she said, "I was told by knowledgeable people that the county always insists that the BIA is responsible. Neither agency ever does anything about the road and this happens every spring."

She could see that it was a mistake to argue with the director but she couldn't seem to stop.

"I'm sorry," she said though her apology was insincere, "the important thing is to get the road taken care of somehow. I hope you are able to get some results."

She stood and walked to the door, then turned toward the director and hesitantly added, "My clients asked for my help. I guess I saw advocacy as part of my job."

With that she left his office, knowing he had no intention of doing anything about the road.

"Years later," Sky interjected, looking up from the scene, "that director told me I was the best damned social worker who had ever worked for him. He was drunk at the time but I laid into him anyway, reminding him of his reprimand of me when I was new to the agency. I told him that I had done more research and found that the BIA was indeed responsible for the road. I added that it still wasn't fixed. He responded with a dismissive wave of his hand.

"Don's first visit to the director's office was far different than mine. After being with the county for only six months, he was commended for his work and offered a promotion. Don's strong silent demeanor was often interpreted as super intelligence—and don't get me wrong, I always acknowledged his intellect—but I knew he was lazy. He would leave work early and take long lunch breaks—sometimes even stopping at a lake to do a little fishing—and I suspected he might be drinking on the job. Knowing he didn't deserve the promotion, I was hurt and angry but kept my silence, focusing instead on the challenges of my own job."

The horrendous conditions on the reservation were still vivid for Sky. Most families lived in one or two-room wooden houses with no plumbing, inadequate or no insulation, and dangerous wood stoves that didn't begin to provide the necessary warmth during the long hard winters when harsh strong winds blew across the fields and whistled through the cracks in the walls. Medical care was an hour's drive away at a clinic known for its poor and disrespectful treatment of Native people, not a single child from the reservation had ever graduated from high school, and the unemployment rate was over seventy percent.

"Under the War on Poverty," Sky told them, "people were hired by the Office of Economic Opportunity to make improvements on the reservation. They gathered in the community center for coffee and lunch breaks and to get their job assignments each morning. That's where I hung out a lot, engaging in conversations about individual and community problems, getting information, strategizing with community leaders about ways to make things better.

"One cold winter day as I drove toward the center, I saw an elderly woman—she was at least ninety years old—laying in the snow. On her stomach, pulling her body along the frozen ground with her arms, she was headed toward an outhouse fifty feet away. I stopped to offer help but she didn't speak English so I knocked on the door of the house where she lived. Her two sons, bachelors in their sixties who lived with her in the tiny one-room cabin, told me their mother had been unable to walk for weeks but refused to go to the medical clinic. With their agreement, I asked my own doctor to make a free home visit, which he did, and together they found a solution.

"As a result of that experience, I worked with community leaders to launch one of our most successful projects—setting up a medical clinic on the reservation. My doctor and his wife, a pediatrician, held a free clinic once a week on their day off. At first it was operated in the community center kitchen where medicines were stored in the padlocked refrigerator and exams conducted on the large table. For the first time people got preventative health care. They came in droves to see about sore throats and coughs, cuts and bruises, prenatal care. An elderly man who had his hearing restored after the doctor convinced him to have ear surgery worked with others who had also been helped by the doctors to raise money for a small building to house the clinic. Then we arranged for two people to get paramedical training so clinic services could be expanded to three days a week and emergencies.

"There were several successes, though none as impressive as the clinic, during my years as a social worker for the county—but many more failures. There is one I still grieve."

Sky then turned the page of her storybook and with the new scene came poignant sadness, a profound sense of failure, thoughts about forgiveness.

Parking in front of a small house on the reservation, Sky reached for her notebook on the seat before getting out of the county car. Josie and John Buckley lived in the decrepit two-room house with their six children who ranged in age from eight to seventeen.

Sky remembered her first encounter with the family at the community center when Josie came to her to ask for help. Their refrigerator was broken and they didn't have any money to buy another one with their meager monthly public assistance check. Sky immediately obtained county authorization for a new refrigerator and after that stopped by their house weekly to help in whatever ways she could. She and Josie's relationship had slowly developed over several months of visits.

Sky now waved hello to Josie who smiled and waved back. As usual, she was standing in the doorway waiting and the coffee was on. This day she seemed to have something particular on her mind.

"I was wondering," she began nervously, "if you could find out how my son is doing."

"Your son?" Sky asked.

Confused by the question, Sky wondered if one of Josie's sons had run away or had gone to live with relatives in the city. People often moved back and forth between reservation and urban life, finding work where they could.

"My son Jamie," Josie responded.

"Jamie?"

"He's in a foster home."

Josie went on to explain that she had another son, a seventh child. Several years before, during a particularly difficult juncture in their lives when she and John were drinking heavily, all of their children were placed in foster care. Jamie was born during that time. Josie held him in her arms only briefly before he too was taken from her. As she and John slowly pulled their lives together their other six children were returned one by one.

Sky thought about how the family was barely able to hold life together from day to day. What a huge task it must have been for them to quit drinking on their own and get their children back with so many strikes against them. She made a note to get more information from the previous social worker and wondered why there were no foster care records regarding Jamie in the family's file. She leaned forward and listened attentively, worried about what was to come.

Josie continued to tell Sky about Jamie. For some reason he was not returned to them with the other children. At first they visited him regularly but Josie was uncomfortable in the foster home with its potted plants, manicured lawn, and affluent atmosphere. It was painful when her own son saw her as a stranger, when he clung to his foster mother as protection from her. She and John visited less often, then only occasionally. Finally they stopped seeing him altogether.

"I just want to know how Jamie is," Josie said, "that's why I'm telling you about him. I think he is better off living with his foster parents. If he is doing okay, I wonder if they will adopt him. He doesn't even know us."

Sky agreed to see what she could find out, shuddering in anticipation of the difficulties that inevitably lay ahead.

Back in her office, Sky researched the situation, voluminous pages of archived case files spread across her desk. Just as she suspected, Jamie had become lost in the system. She rubbed her eyes, tired from the strain of reading the moldy pages of reports written years ago. Shivering from the chill of an ominous gut feeling, she picked up the phone to call Mary and Jack Williams, Jamie's foster parents.

The scene from her storybook then shifted and Sky shook her head, bracing herself to relive the story, her heart breaking all over again. Feeling a wave of sadness mushroom through the library, Spring and Gritty moved closer and watched as new images emerged.

Sky sat in the Williams' living room. Jamie, an energetic and bright six-year-old Native American child, played happily with his toys, wrapped in the cocoon of his comfortable middle class family. The home was filled with tenderness and the smell of freshly baked bread and he was surrounded by loving, caring parents and grandparents who adored him and met his every need.

"We love Jamie as our own," Mary Williams told Sky, "If only we could adopt him! His parents stopped visiting at least four years ago. He never asks about them. They were strangers to him when they did visit. He was too young to understand."

Sky sighed as she got in the car and drove back to her office. Jamie had been placed in the white foster home when he was only two days old and as far as he was concerned, Mary and Jack were his parents. She had seen how exuberantly happy and precocious he was. He was obviously thriving. Then she thought of Josie and her grueling day-to-day struggles. She would visit her tomorrow.

Then it was the next day. Sky sat on a tree stump in front of Josie's house. The wind blew across the barren field, swirling dust at their feet and specks of dirt into their eyes as the two of them talked.

"I saw Jamie yesterday," Sky told Josie, "and he is doing very well. He looks healthy and happy. His foster parents are taking excellent care of him."

Josie nodded but didn't say anything. Sky wondered what she was thinking.

Taking a deep breath she then added, "Mary and Jack Williams would like to adopt him."

Josie nodded. They sat in silence until Sky suggested that they talk more the next week. Josie agreed and they said goodbye.

Then it was a week later and Sky sat in one of the Buckley's two rooms with Josie, sipping coffee from a cracked mug and waiting.

"John and I talked it over," Josie finally said after a period of silence, "and we made a decision. We want to give up our rights as Jamie's parents. We think it would be best for him if he was adopted."

Sky felt Josie's intense sadness and even deeper love. This was the ultimate sacrifice she could make for her son. There was no greater love than allowing him to live permanently with the only parents he had ever known.

She told Josie that she would file the legal papers and explain every part of the process to her and John thoroughly as they went along, that they would have plenty of time to change their minds. Josie nodded.

Several weeks passed and finally it was time for the Buckley's to appear in court to terminate their parental rights. Sky drove to the reservation early in the morning to pick them up and found them waiting for her outside their door. Josie wore her only dress, worn and faded but freshly ironed, and John looked ill at ease in a suit that was far too big for him. During the long drive to the courthouse Sky explained the legal proceedings again, making sure they understood what was about to happen, giving them another opportunity to change their minds.

They sat together at a table in the front of the courtroom. Awkward and uncomfortable in the formal setting, Josie and John sat quietly with their hands folded on the table. Mary and Jack Williams sat unobtrusively in the back of the room, containing their excitement about adopting Jamie out of respect for his parents. The juvenile court judge, a kind and thoughtful man with whom Sky had worked many times, was devoted to finding solutions that were in the best interests of the child. He questioned Josie and John about their understanding of the court action, explaining in detail what it meant.

"Do you understand" the judge then asked, "what terminating your rights as parents would mean for you in relation to Jamie?"

Josie and John hesitated, looked at each other before nodding in response. As he gently probed for more information, concern slowly crept across the judge's face.

"I am appointing a lawyer for you," he finally said, "and setting a new date for your hearing so you have time to meet with him."

After announcing a three-week delay, the judge left the courtroom.

As she drove them back to the reservation, Sky explained that the judge wanted to be sure they understood what termination of parental rights meant. She encouraged them to tell their lawyer the truth about how they felt about their decision, assuring them that it was his job to be their advocate.

Three weeks passed and it was time for the new court hearing. Josie and John arrived with their lawyer. From her conversations with Josie, Sky knew things had changed. Mary and Jack Williams sat in the back of the room looking anxious.

"Your honor," the court appointed attorney began, "I have talked extensively with Mr. and Mrs. Buckley and I find them to be ambivalent about their decision to terminate their rights as Jamie's parents."

Josie and John sat stoically at the table. Mary Williams gasped and Jack put his arm around her shoulder, pulling her close to muffle the sound of her weeping.

This case was an excruciatingly difficult one for everyone, Sky thought angrily. It could have been prevented if the system hadn't failed. If Josie and John were able to adequately care for their other six children there was no legal justification for keeping Jamie in foster care. On the other hand, returning him to the Buckley's now when he had spent his entire life of six years with the Williams' could cause him irreparable damage.

The pounding of the judge's gavel startled Sky from her thoughts.

"I am ordering," he said, "the immediate return of Jamie to his birth parents."

The judge went on to cite both legal and human rationale for his decision. Jamie had a right to live with his birth parents and his siblings and he had a right to his culture. His parents had a right to their child and their community had a right to raise its children in their indigenous ways. He chastised the county for being remiss when it returned the other children to the Buckley's and left Jamie to languish in the foster care system.

"I am further ordering," he concluded, "that Mr. and Mrs. Buckley's social worker transport Jamie to their home within three days. I hope the two families will work together to help Jamie make the transition and that Mr. and Mrs. Williams will be able to visit him…although I want to make it very clear that that decision belongs to his legal parents, Mr. and Mrs. Buckley, alone."

Spring and Gritty sighed as they looked up from the courtroom scene. As new images began to emerge from her storybook, Sky was not sure that she could bear to watch. Words could not adequately describe the overwhelming pain that cut through her, threatening to shut her down completely. Yet she persevered, watching as the new scene unfolded.

Three days had passed since the judge's order. Mature trees formed an umbrella of shade and lush flowers brightened green lawns as Sky drove the county car down the paved street toward the Williams' home. Her gut churned as she pulled into their driveway. She was about to take Jamie from the parents he loved and the only home he knew and bring him to a place filled with strangers who, to his uncomprehending mind, were his parents and siblings in name only.

Mary and Jack greeted Sky at the door, their eyes red and puffy, shoulders drooped in defeat. Softly and lovingly they soothed Jamie, told him they would visit soon, and coaxed him into the car. His little body was rigid as a stone as he allowed himself to be hugged and kissed and he sat in shock as his carefully packed suitcases were placed in the trunk. As Sky slowly backed the car out of the driveway, Mary and Jack stood arm in arm, bravely waving kisses to Jamie before turning to pick up the broken pieces of their hearts.

When Sky pulled the car onto the highway and it picked up speed, Jamie's shock broke. Suddenly he seemed to realize the horrible fate that had befallen him and began to cry. Soon his soft weeping gave way to choking, heartrending sobs. Tears flowed from his swollen red eyes like a broken damn, a river flooding down his little brown cheeks, threatening to drown him. Finally he laid exhausted on the car seat, hiccupping in his stupor, a sob rising sporadically from his throat. Then he fell asleep.

With tears in her eyes Sky drove, listening to the sound a heart makes when it is breaking.

When they reached the reservation Jamie woke up to a new and very different world—one of dirt roads, barren land, rusted car parts scattered in front yards with no grass or trees or flowers. A group of strangers—supposedly his parents and six brothers and sisters—stood by the road waiting for him.

With a discomfort so palpable it hung in the air like a shroud, Josie moved awkwardly toward Jamie, softly encouraging him to get out of the car. She hugged the stiff wooden statue that was her son, the child she had failed so miserably, and wondered how she could ever be enough for him.

Through their tears, Sky and Josie looked at each other, forever bonded by the knowledge that they could never make up for the injustice done to this precious little soul.

As she closed her storybook, Sky wept inconsolably. Spring and Gritty enfolded her, feeling her grief as if it were their own. Jamie's face loomed, filling all space in their minds, rendering them speechless, unable to think. They sat in silence, then went off in separate directions to recoup, recover, and reflect.

Sorrow burrowed into the depths of Sky's soul where Jamie's cries became those of the little girl that had been her, abandoned and alone in her crib. How could she have traumatized an innocent child when she had been traumatized herself? She wondered what other options she might have had, then thought about the things she did. She had encouraged bonding between Jamie and his parents as well as continuation of the bond between Jamie and his foster parents and Josie and John were generous in allowing them frequent visits. Yet Sky knew that nothing could erase the trauma. When she wondered how things turned out for Jamie her energy cowered in fear. It was quite possible that he had never recovered. She thought about how terribly brutal and complicated life on Earth was.

Gritty tried to contain her sorrow by stepping into the familiar. There she immediately recognized Sky's double bind situation and the impossibility of a win-win outcome. There were so many conflicting rights—those of Jamie, his parents who birthed him, his tribe's culture and spiritual traditions, and the foster parents who raised him. She thought about how life's complications had become increasingly apparent to both her and Sky. When she agreed to be acting principal during the New York teachers' strike, conflicting rights had been at the core of that situation as well—the rights of children sorely in need of an education, the rights of teachers to strike, the rights of the community to control its own schools. Both situations had been impossibly complex and both Sky and Gritty had done what they could do.

Spring was off to the other side of the library room immersed in her reflections. She thought about how Sky had balanced her good girl proclivities with the strength of her convictions. The result was often a boldness of spirit and positive changes for people—like the medical clinic on the reservation. Driven by her passion, Sky—like Gritty—sometimes innocently jumped into situations and got in over her head when her only desire was to do a good job. Sometimes that hurt her.

The three of them rested in their contemplations, storybooks closed as they waited. They felt spent after hearing so many stories, seeing so many scenes of themselves as young adults, gaining glimpses of understanding. They relied on Suma's wisdom to pull together their collection of individual insights, to weave the common strands of their separate Earth lives into one purpose in this spiritual place. They waited patiently, each of them holding different puzzle pieces, trying to figure out how and where they fit together.

∗   ∗   ∗   ∗

So deep were their reflections that they didn't notice Suma. She had been sitting there all along. Out of respect for their reveries, she didn't speak, knowing each of them held the key to her own understanding. Suma was always careful not to give them what they already had by moving too fast.

One by one, they discovered Suma's presence. Only when all three of them were looking at her with readiness did she speak.

"You have learned much," she said, "about the brutality of life and the extraordinary and surprisingly unexpected heroics that come from just trying to do a good job, to be an advocate for the human heart. You jumped in where angels fear to tread but often didn't know it and even when you did know it, you didn't know how to stop caring long enough not to go there. Unrelenting passion and the innocence of youth blinded you to potential dangers.

"You suffered greatly when you realized you couldn't change humanity. Because you were unable to accept the powerlessness, you always felt that what you did was never enough.

"So it is important to recognize and honor what you were able to contribute— Spring's achievements were extraordinary, especially in the face of persistent shame that threatened her very soul. Gritty helped many children by teaching, keeping the school open, caring for Sylvia; Sky facilitated many changes on the reservation and even in the church.

"Life's complications also manifest themselves in your human contradictions—Sky was a good girl and minister's wife but also a religious skeptic and rabble rouser. Gritty was a great teacher but she was also a lonely and increasingly desperate woman. Spring was a notably successful achiever but also a nail-biting shame-filled woman. You often despaired about your shadow sides but even though your childhood scripts still survived you were beginning to understand that you were not your fear, guilt or shame—that you were much, much more.

"It is enough," Suma said, taking a deep breath, "Later you will see how your despair, though understandable, held the key to understanding for you. Now you must rest and prepare yourselves for you will need all your strength to face what is yet to come. Remember that you can call on me when you tire—and you will surely tire at times."

Suma then slowly floated away while Sky, Gritty, and Spring watched in silence until her energy was no longer visible. Then they rested.

At least Sky and Gritty rested. Spring was agitated. Suma's words of wisdom unsettled her somehow. What was she trying to tell them about the human condition? What did she mean by despair being the key to their understanding? Even though she grappled intently for clarity it remained stubbornly elusive and she was left with only her old unsettling premonition.

PART VI

▼

HOPE AND REDEMPTION

Hope begins in the dark,
the stubborn hope that if you just show up
and try to do the right thing,
the dawn will come.

—*Anne Lamott*

Spring was already in the library when the other two returned. Sky and Gritty felt renewed and were surprised to note that Spring's energy was weaker than it should have been after a period of rejuvenation. They exchanged concerned glances. Something was still amiss with Spring though they didn't understand the nature or extent of her distress.

Thinking it best not to comment, Sky opened her storybook and readied herself to continue with her turn. Spring and Gritty signaled their agreement.

"After what happened with Jamie," she began, "I worked hard to be on top of everything, desperate to make sure no other child would be traumatized under my watch. My supervisor talked about boundaries, warned me to stay in my own lane, said that controlling was the antithesis of helping. I tried to take her advice by listening less to my own heart and limiting those times I went the extra mile to help others who were in great need. Yet I still couldn't stop worrying and soon was in serious danger of burning out.

"Then there was my relationship with Don. Instead of my usual indifference, I felt totally responsible for everything he did. After a liquor store called to say he owed them a thousand dollars, I paid attention to how often he came home late with slurred speech, passed out on the couch, missed work, drove when drunk. Of course I told him everything I noticed and soon, like a fly caught in a spider web, I was trapped in a vicious cycle. The more I tried to control Don the more we argued—the more we fought the more he stayed away from home—the more helpless and angry I felt, the more I tried to control him."

Sky paused to reflect on how much she had changed in relation to Don. In the beginning she was passive and subservient like her mom but later, as his drinking progressed, she became dominant and overbearing like her dad. She was ferociously unrelenting in her watchfulness and criticism and the more she nagged the further Don retreated into his bottle. With increased regularity tensions magnified, angers flared, tears flowed, and sadness loomed.

"I became a shrew," Sky decried sadly, "shrieking against the despair that hovered just below the surface of my aggression. One night when Don came home drunk, the ugliness reached its lowest point. I nagged him like I always did but instead of his usual silence, he yelled at me to shut up. I kept shrieking, unable to stop. Then he hit me, slapped me right in the face. Instinctively my hands flew up in self-protection, my cheek throbbing from the blow, turning red and swelling. Time stopped. Like a photograph capturing the incident in all of its hideousness, we stood frozen in stunned horror and dismay, tears in our eyes as we wondered how it had come to this."

Sky knew at that moment that if she didn't do something both of them would be destroyed. She left the house and went to see a friend and for the first time confided in someone, telling her about everything, even a disastrous affair she had with a co-worker. She remembered how surprised her friend was to discover such incredible pain and disorder hidden under Sky's carefully maintained image of perfection.

"My friend," Sky told Spring and Gritty, "then made a suggestion. She knew other women like me who somehow found a way to live with alcoholism by going to Al-Anon meetings. She didn't know how the program worked but suggested that I find out and in my desperation I was willing to try anything."

Sky then settled on a page in her storybook. Sensing a move in her energy away from despair, Spring and Gritty grew hopeful as they watched new images from Earth emerge.

Twenty people—mostly women, only a couple of men—sat on metal folding chairs in a circle in a church basement, laughing and drinking coffee as they waited for the Al-Anon meeting to begin. Sky tentatively entered the room and, noticing all the seats were taken, stood uncertainly by the door. A woman quickly walked toward her. She was in her sixties with a gray ponytail, dressed comfortably in a t-shirt and blue jeans.

Sky thought the woman looked like a hippie who grew old but never grew up. She was relieved to be rescued by her warm smile.

The woman stretched out her hand, said her name was Donna, and enthusiastically welcomed her into the circle. A middle-aged man immediately jumped up and unfolded another chair while everyone shifted to make space for her. Just as she sat down another woman handed her a cup of coffee.

Sky accepted it with a nervous smile, feeling a bit overwhelmed by all the friendliness. She didn't recall ever feeling as welcomed anywhere else.

Soon the meeting began. The woman leading the meeting was named Edna. She recited a preamble that explained that Al-Anon was a fellowship of men and women who were living with or affected by alcoholism. Then Donna—the woman who had been the first to greet Sky—told her story about finding Al-Anon when her alcoholic son landed in jail.

Sky wondered how Donna could speak so openly, why she didn't seem depressed, why she focused on herself rather than her son's troubles. Feeling skeptical and hopeless, she wondered why she had come. Part of her wanted to run from the room but desperation glued her to the chair. Besides, what options did she have?

People listened to Donna with smiles of warmth and friendliness, accepting whatever she said without criticism or judgment.

"Thanks to Al-Anon," Donna concluded, "I learned how to take care of myself and my life is good today, even though my son still struggles. I know who I am now and I like me."

As she listened Sky realized she had no idea who she was anymore, if she ever did. She had focused on other people for so long, trying to make their lives orderly, safe, secure, comfortable. She had scurried around trying to meet everybody else's needs and expectations—like becoming a group home parent when she knew it was the wrong thing for her to do, marrying Don when she didn't love him, having sex when she didn't want to, and on and on.

When Donna finished telling her story others took turns talking. When someone mentioned God, Sky cringed. A young woman sitting across from her, who later identified herself as Cindy, looked agitated, anxious to speak.

"All this God talk," Cindy blurted out, "confuses me. Well, my God is my cat and that's the best I can do."

Everybody just smiled and nodded. Someone else talked about coming to believe in God as she *understood* God and said something about that being what the program was about.

Sky didn't know what that meant. It was baffling that no one in the group told others who or what to believe about God. After all, her parents taught her that there was only one way to believe. Their God came in a very small box. They used religion to keep her in line. Fear was the weapon of choice—burning in hell the ultimate punishment for not believing the *right way*. Sky had always been afraid of God even when she rejected him, even when she dared to not get saved. Well, she didn't want that punishing, scary God!

She wanted a God who loved her, cared for her, accepted her for who she was, wanted the best for everyone. She wanted what the people in the circle seemed to have: a God to treasure, not to fear.

Just then Edna asked Sky if she wished to share.

"I just want," Sky began with considerable discomfort, not knowing what to say, "my husband to stop drinking and my clients—especially the children—to be safe. I've been considering getting a divorce. I just don't know what to do but I know I have to do something!"

When Sky finished talking, she looked up at the smiling, nodding, sympathetic faces around her. Several people gently said, "Keep coming back, we're glad you're here."

A woman named Linda then spoke. About the same age as Sky, she looked youthfully attractive in a three-piece pinstriped pantsuit with a white silk blouse. It looked like she had come to the meeting directly from work.

"When I first came into Al-Anon," Linda said, "I thought divorce was the magic pill to happiness but my sponsor advised me not to make any major changes for six months. She said her thinking always became distorted when she tried to force solutions. So I took her advice. Even though my husband and I did eventually split up, I'm glad I waited for my head to clear before doing anything."

So many thoughts swirled around in Sky's mind that she felt dizzy from the spinning. Maybe she should just come to more meetings before deciding what to do about Don—or anything else.

Sky looked up from the scene of her first Al-Anon meeting on Earth and glanced at Spring and Gritty as she brought her focus back to the library.

"That night," she informed them, "I decided to wait six months before making any decisions. It was quite a struggle. I prayed to my new loving God for guidance and made a list of reasons to leave and to stay. Often I thought the pain would kill me and I wanted to sidestep it and head directly for divorce. The longer I waited, though, the clearer it became that it was not so much the pain I wanted to avoid—it was me. I didn't want to look at who I'd become."

Suddenly the image of her old college theology professor popped into view, his forehead tattooed with the words *stories as parables*. Sky thought about how Jonah was swallowed by a whale during a storm, how he finally stopped struggling and prayed as he descended into the depths of darkness. There he waited for three days and three nights before emerging as a new person. Like Jonah, she descended into her own darkness during those six months of waiting and she prayed like she had never prayed before. It was the start of her re-birth.

"I learned a lot during those six months," she told Spring and Gritty, "and my mantra soon became the three C's of Al-Anon: *I didn't cause it, I can't control it, I can't cure it.* The message 'I didn't cause it' allowed me to let go of my guilt. I always told myself that Don wouldn't be an alcoholic if only I had loved him, if only I hadn't married him, if only I had been a better wife, if only I had been willing to have children. I believed that Jamie and other children wouldn't have been hurt by life if only I had been a better social worker. Now I knew that in reality Don's suffering from alcoholism—and my clients' suffering from their life situations—would have occurred even if I didn't exist. I didn't cause it! What a relief!

"The message 'I can't control it' released me from focusing on others and gave me permission to take care of myself, to live my life. Finally I could stop trying to manipulate Don into drinking less. There was nothing I could say or do—or *not* say or do—that would have any effect on his choice to drink. That choice was completely in his hands, not mine.

"In meetings I heard a new definition of insanity—that it *was doing the same thing over and over and expecting different results.* The message 'I can't cure it' freed me from the insanity of trying just one more time to stop Don's drinking, hoping that this time it would work. I learned that the sanest thing to do was to focus on my own recovery.

"I read the Al-Anon literature and meditation books and copied messages on little pieces of paper that I carried in my purse to remind me that alcoholics don't drink because of you or me. They drink because they are alcoholics. Don had a disease. He had had it for a long time; even the retreat facilitator in New York had identified the problem many years before. I started to feel compassion for Don and at the same time began to discover my own needs. Finally I understood that focusing on myself might actually give other people the opportunity to solve their own problems.

"A calmness came over me each morning as I sat with my cup of coffee and my meditation book, regardless of what Don had done the night before. I learned about acceptance, that it started with accepting myself and then accepting everything else as being exactly the way it was supposed to be. How different it was to look at something that was wrong and not immediately jump in to fix it. I learned to sit still, feel my fear and passion, accept it, and then take action or not, depending on what seemed to be required. Sometimes the best thing to do was nothing or, as my sponsor would say, 'Don't just do something, sit there.'"

Worried that she was beginning to sound like an advertisement for Al-Anon, Sky stopped talking. It's just that she was so grateful for what she learned in that program—that she was powerless over Don's drinking and didn't have to carry the burdens of others. She became gentler with herself, sometimes even accepting herself as a human being.

Her journey of faith and healing had been a slow painful one. She meditated and prayed to a God that didn't have a church or even a name, placed her problems and worries as well as her joys and gratitude in the hands of her new loving God, and finally climbed into those hands herself. Sky smiled as she realized that somewhere along the way she had finally been converted. It didn't happen in a moment of magical thinking when God erased all her fear, doubt, and pain. Instead, it was a surprisingly long, slow re-birthing journey that brought her to the self she was meant to be.

"I stayed with Don," Sky then said, "not out of guilt or pity but because I felt serene and happy in spite of his inability to face his demons. I learned more productive ways to cope with his alcoholism, ways that no longer resulted in a loss of myself. I found a way to live without regrets and stopped reproaching myself for not seeing the messy tracks that alcoholism had left all over my life for so long. Denying the problem had been my way to survive the constant crises, embarrassments, broken promises. Starting with my grandpa and ending with my husband, it had been my way to cope with alcoholism's unpleasant and sometimes terrifying reality.

"I learned to detach with compassion from my clients' problems and stopped worrying about them as well. There were things I could do to help but their decisions and their journeys were theirs, not mine."

With a deep sigh of gratitude, Sky stopped to reflect. Her new identity still included caring about others but now she defined her humanity by the degree to which she was able to know other people's pain and joy—without needing to remove their pain. Taking care of her own fear and pain led her to where she needed to go in this life; the same could happen for others if she didn't rob them of the opportunity to find their own way.

She had become more effective as a social worker. Instead of taking her clients' problems on as her own, she looked for ways to eliminate institutional barriers that blocked their progress—like working for legislation to prevent children from getting lost in the child welfare system, protecting clients' rights through mandatory legal representation, and developing a foster care network on the reservation so children could remain in their community when they had to be separated temporarily from their parents.

*   *   *   *

With an air of finality and resignation, Sky looked solemnly at Spring and Gritty as she turned to the last page of her storybook. With new emerging Earth images came tense anticipation. The three of them sat perfectly still, intuitively aware of the enormity of what they were about to experience.

An attractive, youthful-looking woman in her mid-forties, Sky greeted people as they came into the meeting room in the church basement, her face aglow with serenity, a peacefulness wrapping itself around her sweat suit clad body like a halo.

It had been many years since her first Al-Anon meeting, but Sky had never forgotten the friendly welcome she received. Now she was always the first to greet newcomers with a warm handshake and a cup of coffee. It was a way of giving back.

The Al-Anon meeting then began. Sky's eyes welled with tears of gratitude when she talked about her recovery.

When the meeting ended, she lingered over coffee with one of the young women she sponsored. Randi, a computer programmer with a high-paying position, looked fit and trim like the savvy professional she was. But her life with two little children and an alcoholic husband—even though he was in recovery—was a mess. She was distraught that life had not improved in the few months she had been coming to Al-Anon and questioned whether investing in the program was worth it. Sky quietly soothed her, telling her not to quit before the miracle happened. Soon Randi relaxed and smiled, saying she now knew she could make it another day. They hugged and said good night.

Sky breathed a prayer of thanks as she turned out the lights, locked the church door and walked out into the night. She unlocked her car and got in, making sure to fasten her seatbelt before putting the key into the ignition and starting the engine. She waved to a couple of people talking in the parking lot and then slowly drove down the streets of the quiet town, headed toward the highway and home.

As they watched Sky's car picking up speed on the highway, an ominous feeling consumed Spring and Gritty. For a moment, they distanced themselves from the Earth scene to replenish their energy, then moved closer together for mutual support.

They watched as the car slowed for one of many curves on the highway. Sky turned on the radio and sang along to one of her favorite folk tunes, the big smile on her face reflecting the joy in her heart. She rounded the last curve before the turn leading to her house, looking forward to getting home and going to bed.

Two headlights glared into her eyes from the other side of the road. The flash of light temporarily blinded her but her mind was clear as she instinctively swerved to the right.

In the next moment the night filled with deafening sounds—metal twisting, glass breaking, tires screeching, screaming. The two cars crashed head-on. Suddenly there was only silence, an eery stillness disturbed only by the sharp hiss of a punctured radiator releasing its fluids all over the pavement.

A man staggered out of the wreckage of his car. He was in a daze, his hand holding the back of his head, blood oozing through his fingers. He slowly made his way to the other car. The window on the driver's side was crushed. He couldn't see anything inside. Painstakingly he wrapped his bent frame around the front of the car and little by little pulled himself to the passenger's side. With blurred and uncomprehending eyes, he looked through the opening that was once a window. He recoiled as he saw the lifeless body, bloody, mangled and oddly twisted beyond recognition. He backed away, his hand over his opened mouth, his mind filled only with confusion.

In that instant, Don recognized the mass of smoking wreckage. It was Sky's car. He collapsed onto the highway, limp as a rag doll, a sob spewing from his mouth along with vomit as his face hit the pavement.

Shaken by what they had just witnessed, Spring and Gritty were speechless but Sky remained calm as she closed her storybook for the last time.

"My purpose on Earth had been accomplished and it was time," she declared with a smile.

"Congratulations, Sky," said Suma, her dark blue energy descending from above without warning and landing in their midst. "You achieved your purpose—you overcame fear and found the courage to accept and love yourself.

"There is much more that you accomplished as well: you became your own person and after that you made your sacrifices willingly and without any loss of self. Your spiritual journey led you to an unshakable faith. You were even able to learn from your family's fear-based religion that spirituality is a deeply serious business. You learned compassion in its truest sense. You learned about powerlessness and were thus able to accept your limitations as a human being. You learned that a little forgiveness is necessary everyday and, in the end, that sometimes a whole lot of forgiveness is required all at once."

"Yes," said Sky with contentment, noticing that her light blue energy seemed to be darkening just a little.

"Wait just a minute!" interjected Spring with a passion that startled everyone, "Don had every opportunity to do something about his drinking and he didn't do anything and in the end he killed you. He murdered you, Sky! And you talk about forgiveness? How could you forgive him? I'm really sorry but I am having a little bit of trouble with all this."

"Don didn't kill me, Spring," Sky responded with a calmness that was impressive even to Suma, "His disease killed me—though of course he was ultimately responsible for his choices. What I feel is compassion and sorrow for him. As for me, my Earth death was timely for I had reached my goals. I was done."

"Well, you were certainly a better person than I," Spring retorted, once again comparing herself to another and coming up short, "I would sure feel better knowing that Don paid somehow for what he did!"

Suma smiled sorrowfully and told them what happened to Don after Sky's death. There was an investigation of the accident and he was charged with manslaughter, but somehow he made it through the ordeal without going to jail. His drinking worsened, eventually he married someone who was not in Al-Anon, He lost his job and eventually died of alcoholism.

Enclosed in the lingering sadness Sky, Gritty and Spring thought about how there had been no redemption for Don. Finally Sky broke the silence with words of faith that confirmed a lesson she had learned well, "Everything happened just as it was supposed to. Don was on his own journey just as I was on mine."

Then they noticed that Suma was gone.

Though Spring knew it was time to move on, she held back. She felt uneasy and wondered if sometimes people forgave too soon. Unexpectedly, like a bolt of lightening, an image of little Jamie appeared before her briefly. He was sobbing as Sky took him to his birth parents. He was wearing a white t-shirt with one word on the front in bold red letters: *forgiveness.*

*   *   *   *

One by one, when they were ready, Spring and Sky moved back to the library table. Gritty had already opened her storybook and was ready for her turn when she noticed Spring's still perplexed energy. She looked at her inquisitively, wondering whether to continue or wait. In response, Spring shook herself briskly as if waking from a dream and indicated with a weak smile and nod of encouragement that she was ready to listen.

Gritty continued her story where she had left off—with her marriage to Chuck. She glanced knowingly at Sky with a look of expectation, thinking she would understand better than anyone what life had been like for her.

"No matter how disgusted I was with my drinking I was unable to quit," she began, "I thought that marrying Chuck, moving into a nice house in the suburbs, and becoming a step mom to his young children would help. I tried in every way to be respectable like him. I kept the house immaculate, cooked everyone's favorite meals even after long days of teaching and commuting, drove the children to their activities, supported Chuck in his work. For the first time in my life, I tried to be good. It didn't help."

Gritty remembered how she went underground with her drinking. She only drank wine and disguised it in a large coffee mug diluted with ice, went to different liquor stores for her supply, carefully hid the empty bottles in the garbage to avoid detection, and didn't touch the full bottle of wine in the refrigerator while secretly drinking instead from the stash she kept carefully hidden in laundry baskets, garbage cans, and closets. On rare occasions when she and Chuck went out socially, she would sneak a couple of drinks before going and then have just one drink at the event. Before, during and after dinner each night she drank wine from her big coffee mug, passing out on the couch after the children went to bed and Chuck watched sports on television downstairs. No one suspected.

"I was completely faithful to Chuck," she continued, "laughing about my former sexual escapades as vestiges of a foolish youth long gone. Because Chuck loved having sex I told myself that our marriage was happy but I always worried that he would have an affair. I knew that karmic payback time would eventually come and sure enough, he slept with another woman in our bed. My respectable world crashed down around me, exposed as the empty charade it had always been. Too slowly and too late, I discovered that Chuck loved sex so much that he would have it with anyone at anytime and anywhere."

Gritty remembered how she screamed hysterically, throwing her heavy drinking mug at Chuck, barely missing his head, nicking the edge of the coffee table instead. Her tears flowed like a relentless waterfall, quickly becoming a raging hurricane. Utterly devastated and convinced her life was over, she charged furiously through the house, family pictures crashing on the floor in her wake as Chuck looked on helplessly.

"I left my comfortable home in the suburbs," she went on, "and rented a small furnished apartment in my old neighborhood in the South Bronx—right next to my favorite liquor store. My heart burned from the fresh wound that oozed pain from the latest blow, while all the blows that had come before centered their scars and still open sores on the new wound, compounding my agony. My eyes, red and puffy from the salty tears that flowed with only intermittent breaks, were impervious to the cold wet teabags I used each morning to reduce their swelling."

Gritty sighed as she remembered how tired she was, more tired than she had ever been. Tired of drinking. Tired of feeling lonely. Tired of giving men a piece of her self-esteem and watching them leave with it. Tired of feeling guilty. Tired of feeling like a pile of shit. Just tired, tired, tired.

She went about her teaching duties as if she were comatose, unsuccessful in her attempts to disguise the pain that permeated her being. At the end of each day she was relieved to go home where, after a stop at the liquor store, she quietly drank and grieved until she passed out. She was oddly happy to be in a strange and lonely apartment with furnishings that were not hers. It was a place where she could drink with abandon.

"On the advice of a friend," Gritty went on, "I made an appointment to see a therapist. Like a worm crawling along the baseboards and then curling up in a self-protective ball I walked into her office with my head down and sat stiffly on the couch hugging myself."

Gritty remembered how uncomfortable and fidgety she was when the therapist silently waited for her to begin. She then turned to a new page in her story-book. As Sky and Spring watched the scene unfold in the therapist's office they felt themselves absorbing Gritty's tension and anxiety as if they were on Earth with her.

The office was decorated in warm soothing colors and comfortable stuffed furniture. The therapist, a middle-aged woman with expressively liquid brown eyes that smiled from behind large rimmed glasses, exuded warmth that filled the room. Gritty sat on the couch, her back straight, body rigid as a board. After several awkward minutes she finally blurted out her story.

The therapist listened deeply as Gritty berated herself for always doing the wrong thing and despaired over her failure as a wife and stepmother. Then, looking at her gently and directly, she asked, "So where is the addiction?"

Gritty looked down at her hands—so carefully placed in her lap—and thought about Chuck's obsession with sex.

"I...I...don't know," she mumbled.

"The reason I am asking," the therapist continued, "is that I have a very strong feeling that addiction is involved in your situation. I don't know where the feeling is coming from but I trust it. I am going to refer you to a substance abuse counselor and I want you to see her before our next session. I also have a weekly therapy group and there will be room for a new member in about a month. I want you to consider joining the group in conjunction with individual sessions with me."

Totally defeated yet intuitively trusting the therapist, Gritty agreed to everything she suggested.

Another scene unfolded as Gritty turned to a new page in her storybook. Sky and Spring looked on with hopeful expectation.

Gritty sat in a waiting room, its walls covered with information about alcohol and drug addiction. With a wax-like affect like a plastic Barbie doll, she was dressed perfectly in a stylish royal blue suit trimmed in black, her hair freshly shampooed and blown dry, her makeup expertly applied.

As she walked into the office of the substance abuse counselor Gritty glanced at the posters on the walls, smugly confident that she would pass the alcoholism test. At that moment she was certain that she didn't have a problem. Maybe the counselor would suggest that she not drink for a year to see how it went. She could handle that.

"What do you remember about your first drink?" the counselor asked.

"It was just a little sip from a glass of gin and tonic when I was twelve years old. I was at a wedding reception and someone asked if I wanted to taste her drink. It was clear and sparkling in a little plastic glass with ice shimmering in it and a beautiful green slice of lime floating on top. I liked the taste but only had a little sip. That was it, no more than a sip!"

"Tell me what you remember about your second drink," the counselor continued, the hint of a smile forming in the corners of her mouth.

"I was twenty years old and a group of friends and I ordered a bottle of wine with dinner. It was a rich, heavy burgundy. I can still see the bottle sitting in the middle of the table with its beautiful deep red color and the fancy wine glasses at our places. But it tasted horrible! I don't think I even drank half of my glass and have never had any red burgundy wine since."

Smiling and feeling proud, Gritty relaxed in her chair, uncrossed her legs. Certain she had impressed the counselor with her ability to resist drinking on those two occasions, she was more convinced than ever that she wasn't an alcoholic. After all, if she were, those first two drinks would have been very different.

The interview continued and Gritty minimized the amount of alcohol she currently consumed, saying nothing about her daily stops at the liquor store or her ritual of passing out each night.

Finally the counselor looked at her candidly and asked, "Would you feel better if I told you that I am not going to put you into treatment?"

Gritty was shocked. She had no answer, just stared numbly at the counselor.

"It's not the amount you consume," the counselor went on to explain, "but your relationship with alcohol that I'm looking for…and it is clear that you have a very strong relationship…the reason I am not going to put you into treatment is because I know you wouldn't go."

You've got that right, thought Gritty sarcastically.

"Instead," the counselor continued, "I want you to go to a Monday night women's meeting of Alcoholics Anonymous on Center Avenue Northwest. You will be very surprised at who you see there. I also want you to read all the literature about alcoholism that you can. Here is a reading list. If these things don't work, we will then look at treatment. Do you have any questions?"

Gritty had no questions. She agreed to give the Monday night meetings a try. Then she mumbled her thanks and walked out of the office gripping the AA schedule and reading list tightly in her fist.

She had not acknowledged that she had a problem but inside she knew she did. A part of her had known it for a long time. That is why she had secretly prayed on several occasions—to a God in whom she didn't believe—that she would not turn out to be an alcoholic.

She went back to her apartment, opened the refrigerator, and lifted an almost full bottle of White Zinfandel wine from the shelf. Slowly she poured its contents down the drain in the sink while crying and whispering lovingly, "goodbye, my dear, best friend."

Gritty closed her storybook and retreated into her memories. Sky and Spring smiled at her, breathing a sigh of relief as the Earth scene disappeared.

Gritty remembered how the next day she went to look for the books on the list the counselor had given her. The first one she found was *The Booze Battle*. It was a little paperback that seemed safe enough since the book cover said it gave practical advice about how to deal with the alcoholic. Gritty was comforted by the detachment it seemed to promise.

She started reading about how in people's minds alcoholism is a moral issue instead of a disease. The alcoholic's embarrassing, disgusting and even shameful behavior helps the whole process of stigmatizing and moralizing along since she often does the very things that society deems most improper when under the influence of alcohol, thus seeming to ask for its value judgments.

Gritty found the information interesting, keeping her distance from it. But when she read a chapter about how the alcoholic views the world, she suddenly felt like she was being torn apart, exposed, her life slowly and painfully unraveling on the pages. She read how the alcoholic's drinking and behavior were frequently different from the way she meant them to be and thought about how she usually drank more than she planned to and behaved in ways she didn't intend. Just as the book said, her thinking had become totally distorted; she either accepted as real that which was unreal or rejected as unreal that which was real.

Painful memories continued to flood through her until Gritty looked up and saw that Sky and Spring were anxiously waiting to hear more about what happened.

"Sorry about the lapse," she said, "I was just remembering the first book I read about alcoholism. I wondered how the author could know me so well. It seemed that she knew that I made rules about drinking that I would always break like *never before noon, never alone in a bar,* and *never drive when drunk.* She knew how devious and cunning I was in order to be sure that alcohol would always be there, how I would sneak drinks, gulp them down quickly, hide the amount of my consumption. She even knew that because of all of my rationalizations about drinking I had buried my feelings to the point that I was entirely alienated from them.

"By the time I read about how the alcoholic's feelings of inadequacy soon became a chronic self-loathing, I was sobbing uncontrollably, holding the book close to my heart, drenching its pages with my tears. Never before had someone told my story so vividly."

Then Gritty remembered how nervous she was about going to the AA meeting so during the weekend she drove to the building where it was held, just to be sure she knew where it was. When she got to the address she had been given, she was amazed to see a liquor store there. She wondered if it was some kind of cruel joke. It turned out that the AA meeting was downstairs in the same building. The door was in the back. How clever, she thought, to have meetings where there was a constant reminder of why you were there!

Gritty then turned to another page in her storybook and the three of them watched as new images emerged.

It was Monday and Gritty was headed for her first AA meeting. She passed people going into bars, laughing as they made their way to happy hour at the end of the workday. Suddenly grief flooded through her, threatening to drown her good intentions.

"I don't want to go to any fucking AA meeting!" she mumbled to herself, "I want to go to happy hour!"

As she imagined ordering two-for-one drinks her anger turned into a full-blown tantrum. She railed against a God she didn't believe in, screaming at the top of her lungs.

"Why me? Why do I have to be an alcoholic? Why did you do this to me?"

Then she burst into tears.

"After I blew my nose and wiped my eyes," Gritty interjected, looking up from the storybook scene, "I discovered that I was lost. Since I was now going to be late for the meeting I considered turning back and going to a bar for happy hour. For some reason I stopped and asked for directions instead. I soon found the liquor store just a block away and drove around to the parking lot in the back."

Gritty again turned the page of her storybook and as they watched the emerging image they saw a little sign on a door that said *Women's AA Meeting, Mondays, 5:30 p.m.*

Gritty opened the door and walked down a dangerously steep flight of stairs. Dozens of well-groomed professional-looking women were gathered in the large open room at the bottom; several other women drank coffee and smoked cigarettes in a smaller room off to the side. The walls of both rooms were covered with lists of the twelve steps and twelve traditions of Alcoholics Anonymous and with slogans like—*live and let live, one day at a time, how important is it anyway.*

An elderly woman with a welcoming smile walked gingerly toward Gritty, her outstretched hands offering a cup of coffee. With the steaming cup in her hand, Gritty sat on one of the cold wobbly metal chairs that were arranged in a circle in the middle of the room.

She thought irritably about what a poor substitute the bitter coffee was for her favorite glass of wine, yet she knew she was exhausted and totally defeated. There was not an ounce of fight left in her.

Soon the meeting started, with each woman introducing herself by her first name. When it was Gritty's turn, she quietly surrendered and said she was an alcoholic.

She had just taken the first step.

Gritty looked up from her storybook and retreated into her private thoughts. Her obsession with alcohol had been lifted at that moment, never to return. She knew she didn't deserve to have her compulsion to drink removed when so many other people had to struggle with theirs. It was an act of Grace for which she would always be grateful.

"I remember those Monday night meetings fondly," Gritty then said to Sky and Spring, "how comfortable I was with the women there, most of them professionals like me with stories like mine. I became a regular and looked forward to arriving early to join the women in the smaller room before the meeting. The raw honesty of their laughter and tears helped me to not feel so alone.

"The first year I cried at every meeting. Held captive by years of drinking, my tears had filled a reservoir to overflowing. Little by little, week-by-week I released the tears I withheld at Daddy's death. The tears I stoically withheld whenever I felt hurt, rejected, pained, scared, disappointed. The tears I turned into anger over the injustices I witnessed as a teacher.

"When I stopped philosophizing and started crying, the tears cleansed me. My heart softened. I began to understand who I was.

"But I was a bit worried about the God part of AA. Step Three of the program said that as alcoholics 'we made a decision to turn our will and our lives over to the care of God, *as we understood Him*'—but I didn't believe in God. I certainly didn't understand God to be a male. My therapist suggested that I share my concerns with a minister that she recommended. So I did.

"A kindly man who had been in recovery for twenty years, the minister listened intently as I talked about my spiritual quest—how I had rejected Christianity, attended Quaker meetings for a while, tried transcendental meditation, and finally decided I was an agnostic. After probing some more in order to understand my worldview, the minister assured me that my spirituality was as valid as any, that it wasn't counterfeit just because it wasn't one of the five traditions. He said I would have no trouble with God in AA. After that conversation I knew my Higher Power would do, even though I didn't know what it was. In my wildest imagination, I never would have predicted that I would find my spirituality through my alcoholism but that's what happened."

"Nor," Sky interrupted with a chuckle, "would I have ever predicted that I would find my spirituality through someone *else's* alcoholism...especially ironic since the active alcoholic in my life was a preacher."

Sky and Gritty smiled at each other with the kind of deep understanding that comes from shared experience.

All beliefs or lack of belief were welcomed in AA and Gritty felt surprisingly tolerant of others. She was even amused when she attended a meeting in the deep South where they recited the third step as "made a decision to turn our will and our lives over to the care of God, whom we choose to call *Jeeesssuuuuss!*"

"Did you ever hear anyone say that religion was for people who were afraid of going to hell and that spirituality was for those who had been there?" Sky asked with a grin.

Gritty nodded knowingly not only because she had heard that said many times, but mostly because she knew what it had been like to live in hell.

Turning to another page in her storybook and a new Earth scene, Gritty was eager to show Spring and Sky some of what she had experienced early in recovery.

Gritty had just arrived in Las Vegas to attend a teachers' conference. There she was, walking through a noisy, neon-lit casino, her senses assaulted by smells of stale alcohol and tobacco and sounds of raucous laughter as she made her way to the hotel lobby.

By the time she reached her room she was in a panic. To be surrounded by the glamour of cheap alcohol and enticing gambling for several days was a slippery slope for someone in recovery only a short time. Knowing she had to find a meeting, she reached for the phone book and called the Alcoholics Anonymous Intergroup number, then grabbed her coat and ran down to the lobby and out the door to hail a taxi.

The AA meeting was in a desolate and deserted part of town, in a run down house with rickety wooden steps leading up to a ripped screen door hanging loosely from its hinges. Inside, a couple dozen people gathered in a room lit by a single bulb hanging from the middle of the ceiling. Large spots of multicolored paint were exposed on the walls where several layers of ancient wallpaper had peeled away. The color of the worn carpet was indistinguishable except for the brown of large coffee stains.

Smartly dressed in a trim bright yellow business suit with a short skirt, Gritty sat primly on the tattered and stained cushion of a chair and looked around the drab room. A white woman with no teeth joked with a black man whose arm was in a cast. An elderly brown-faced man in a dirty threadbare trench coat moved slowly to his seat with the help of a walker. A heavyset white woman in a housedress resembling a nightgown looked dazed as she sat staring into space. A black businessman in a smart gray suit, starched white collar and red tie looked over at her with a broad friendly smile. A man of indistinct ethnic heritage with a bloody bandage around his head, looking and smelling like he lived under a bridge, walked around the room cheerfully providing coffee with cream and sugar from a tray carefully balanced in his shaking hands. Gritty graciously accepted the offered cup with its chipped rim and missing handle.

For the first time in her life she felt like she belonged. She wondered how that could be. After all, she couldn't be more different from most of the people in the room. Yet, even though she couldn't understand it, she knew she was home.

When the meeting ended, the woman with no teeth offered Gritty a ride. She gratefully accepted. As the woman drove she told an incredibly heroic story of her recovery from heroin addiction. When they arrived at the hotel, the two of them hugged as they said good night.

Gritty waved as the woman drove away, then smiled at the bewildered look on the doorman's face. How conspicuously opulent the hotel looked compared with the old beat up and rusted out car that had just deposited her at its door.

"Alcohol and drug addiction," she interjected, looking up from the scene, "were the great equalizers. They didn't discriminate based on race or social status or any other status. I came to understand that, in the rooms of AA, we were all the same—a bunch of drunks and addicts who needed each other to stay clean and sober.

"My life slowly got better. I was promoted to department chair, so often traveled to teachers' conferences and meetings around the country. When my colleagues gathered in the hotel bar at the end of the day I went to AA meetings. I met business and professional people, politicians, movie stars and musicians, tattooed men and women, people who haltingly told their stories in broken English, writers who eloquently shared theirs with dramatic humor, illiterate people who could neither read nor write, rich people and poor people, people who were Native American, African-American, Asian American, Latino, White, gay, lesbian, transgender. I went to meetings in sterile or moldy church basements of all denominations, pleasantly decorated recovery centers, shabby rooms above and below bars, and even meetings *in* bars."

With deep affection, Gritty remembered some of the people she met. There was the black man in his sixties who had been illiterate all his life. When he quit drinking he took reading lessons and one night volunteered to read from the AA big book during a meeting. She would never forget the proud look on his face. His victory brought tears to her eyes even now.

"My honeymoon with the program ended, though, after six months. Even though it had been helpful, I was tired of going to meetings. When I told my therapist, she acted fast."

Gritty then pointed to a new page in her storybook and immediately they saw that she was back in the substance abuse counselor's office.

"So, why don't you want to be an alcoholic?" the counselor asked Gritty.

Stumped and feeling in a double bind, Gritty thought for a long time before answering.

"Alcoholics don't care about anyone but themselves and that is not me. If anything I care about other people too much. I was always told that alcoholics were skid row drunks, immoral sinners with no self-control. I definitely don't want to be like that."

The counselor looked at Gritty, the familiar little smile beginning to form in the corners of her mouth, and nodded.

"What else?"

"Well," Gritty continued, squirming in her chair, "I don't believe in the God that my family believes in. They think I'm going to hell. In the eyes of them and their church, I'm a bad person. I know I've done some bad things but I still think I'm basically good. If being an alcoholic means I'm bad, I guess that's why I don't want to be one."

Until that moment, Gritty had been unaware of harboring such thoughts.

Then the counselor proposed that she participate in the family program at a treatment center in upstate New York. Gritty wondered why she didn't suggest the treatment program for alcoholics instead. Wouldn't that be more appropriate? Though she was confused by the suggestion she was even more surprised and bewildered by her readiness to follow it.

As she pointed to a new scene in her storybook, Sky and Spring's curiosity peaked.

A car slowly entered the gate to a treatment center. The expansive grounds were beautifully groomed with many roads leading to buildings surrounded by parks, ponds, and gardens. As she slowly drove along the winding road Gritty passed several small buildings, making a mental note to visit the bookstore and gift shop and a new meditation center during her weeklong stay. When she reached the large central administration building, she pulled into the parking lot, retrieved her suitcase from the trunk, and walked through the main entrance. A nurse in white uniform sat behind a white counter with protective glass across the front. She greeted Gritty with a friendly smile and said she would check her in.

"Do you have any medications with you?" she asked.

"No, all I have are vitamin pills."

"You will need to leave them," the nurse said pleasantly, "each morning you can come here to get your daily dose."

"I don't think so," Gritty responded, feeling insulted and degraded. "I will be participating in the *family* program. And, besides, what do you think I am going to do with vitamins—overdose or something?"

The nurse noted Gritty's attitude with a smile, calmly informing her that the treatment center was drug-free and that the policy was applied consistently—to everyone.

Gritty smarted, feeling like an inmate in a prison or mental hospital. She opened her suitcase with an exaggerated shrug and handed her vitamins to the nurse.

As they watched the scene, Sky and Spring smiled at Gritty's typical spunkiness. Eager to see how she handled any other strictures of the treatment program, they moved closer to view the next scenes unfolding on the page.

Gritty walked through the front door of the family building and into a pleasant lounge with overstuffed chairs arranged in small conversation areas. On the way to her assigned room, she walked by several people who were talking quietly or meditating. Two men played chess at a table next to a brightly burning fireplace.

Her room was sparse but comfortable. She was glad she had her own bathroom. She unpacked her suitcase and then headed for an orientation session for newcomers.

After that she met with her assigned counselor to set goals for the week. She agreed to make a searching and fearless moral inventory of herself by writing out Step Four of AA's twelve steps. At the end of the week she would admit the exact nature of her wrongs by taking Step Five with a chaplain.

Time went fast and soon Gritty joined others from the family program to walk to the main dining hall for dinner. On the way they told her that each group ate their meals together and they were not allowed to speak with anyone from other programs.

Sky and Spring smiled as they watched Gritty acquiesce to each instruction. Gritty smiled back, knowing what they were thinking. She remembered how hard it was to resist satisfying her curiosity about what movie stars or famous people might be in treatment that week.

"After dinner," she interjected, "there was a lecture in a large auditorium. Three hundred people filled the seats, sitting together as assigned by program. I looked for the alcoholics, wondering if I might be more comfortable with them than with the family group. At the end of the lecture, we went back to our building for the rest of the evening to work on our goals, make phone calls, or just sit around and talk or play board games.

"I went directly to my room the first night to work on my fourth step, effortlessly filling four pages with a list of my character defects—the bad things I had done, the resentments I held. My counselor's instructions, though, had been to write a page of positive characteristics for each page of negatives. So I started working on the positive list but immediately got writer's block. I turned out the light and tried to sleep.

"Every day the routine was the same until one night something happened that changed everything for me. A medical doctor lectured about alcoholism as a disease, showing pictures that demonstrated how alcohol affected the brain of a person with the disease differently than it affected the brain of someone without the disease. With each piece of scientific evidence offered, my excitement grew. When the lecture ended, I flew back to the family building, burst into the lounge and exclaimed, 'Did you hear the lecture tonight? Wasn't it wonderful? I am so excited! I have a disease...don't you see? I have a disease!'

"People glanced at each other with confused expressions, the kind of look that suggested maybe I wasn't quite right in the head. Finally, a woman cautiously responded as if talking to a child, 'Yes...we know. You told us you were an alcoholic when you first arrived.'

"'No, you don't understand!' I countered loudly, 'I knew I was an alcoholic. What I didn't know was that I have an inherited *disease*. My uncle had it, my mother is addicted to painkillers so she must have inherited it too, and who knows who else was secretly addicted to something—Daddy was addicted to work and who knows what else.'

"Ignoring their perplexed looks and not waiting for a response, I charged up the steps and headed toward my room laughing and singing, 'I have a disease! I have a disease!' I took out my fourth step inventory and soon filled four pages with a list of my strengths, then turned out the light and slept better than I had in a long time."

Gritty smiled, remembering the relief she felt that night when she realized that alcoholism was not a sin or a moral deficiency, that it was a disease—like diabetes. She was not a bad person after all; she was a sick person. She thought about her favorite uncle. He had the same disease. That was why she liked him so much.

The next day it was time to do her fifth step. She was excited about sharing all her strengths and weaknesses but the chaplain said he wanted to hear only the highlights. Disappointed, she read selections from her inventory, choosing the ones she thought most outrageous. He looked bored. She detected a slight rolling of his eyes. She wondered if he didn't care, if he had heard so many fourth step inventories they bored him, or if her defects were not as bad as she thought—that, maybe, in fact, they were pretty humdrum. Could it be she wasn't the worst scum of the earth after all?

She left the treatment center the next day with a huge gift—the knowledge that she had a disease for which there was no cure. Nonetheless, as long as she kept going to AA meetings she wouldn't have to pick up a drink. She could deal with that.

Gritty looked up from her reverie to see Sky and Spring patiently waiting to hear more about her story. They were eager to know whether she quit drinking for good or not.

"I kept going to meetings regularly," she told them, "and things kept getting better. Every morning I read my meditation books while drinking coffee and then jogged through the park for thirty minutes, carefully keeping an exercise record. Each night I wrote an inventory of my day based on AA's tenth step—

'continued to take personal inventory and when we were wrong promptly admitted it.' I held on to the word *when* like a precious gem. It reminded me I was not responsible for everything, that I could discern when I was wrong and when I wasn't. I began to taste freedom from the guilt I had carried all my life."

Sky smiled at Gritty with understanding.

"I know just what you mean," she interjected, "So many times I felt guilty and apologized for Don's behavior. So often I felt it was my fault when he drank. I found peace only when I accepted my powerlessness over his alcoholism and over him."

"Ah, acceptance," Gritty said with a nod, "I struggled with that a lot. When I first heard the idea that acceptance was the answer to all of life's problems, I just couldn't buy it. Was I supposed to accept the injustices of the world? Inequality? Oppression? Poverty? War? Should I just roll over and accept that life was what it was and there was nothing I could do about it? If that was what accepting life on life's terms meant, then it wasn't for me."

"Yes," said Sky with the radiance of hard-earned wisdom, "I had the same struggle. Finally I understood that acceptance meant accepting *everything*, including my anger and sadness about injustice *and* my unwillingness to accept it."

"Most importantly," Gritty interjected as she merged her energies with Sky's in the understanding that each of them had reached in her own way, "it meant accepting myself. I had to get right-sized to know that I was neither a useless piece of shit nor queen of the universe. I was just a human being who was powerless to change everything. When I could accept that, I could accept what I *could* do about injustice."

Sky nodded in agreement. She knew they could discuss the complicated concept of acceptance for a long time but it wasn't necessary. She rested in Suma's earlier insights about how each of them anguished about what they couldn't do, unable to accept things as they were. She was glad they didn't cut and run, that they did what they could, that they didn't give up even as they were learning to accept their limits.

Gritty seemed eager to continue with her recovery story so Sky and Spring turned to her and indicated they were ready to listen.

"I had a lot to learn about living without alcohol," Gritty said, "Learning how to ask for help and how to take care of myself physically were the most difficult. In my family only Mother was allowed to be sick and get medical attention. Life revolved around waiting for her next illness to strike, her next surgery, her next trip to the hospital, her next long period of recovery, her next round of pain pills. In the service of attending to Mother's body, I ignored my own."

Gritty remembered what it had been like: once when she had the flu as a child she lay in the dark of her room for three days terrified she would die, worried no one would notice, yet unable to call for help—she assumed total responsibility for Mother's health, convinced she would get well if only she were good enough so she cleaned the house, organized closets, cooked and froze meals, all so Mother wouldn't die and would come home from the hospital.

Gritty then looked at Sky and Spring, gratified by their engrossed attention, and continued, "When I first quit drinking, I had terrible headaches. My therapist asked what my doctor said about them. I told her I didn't have a doctor. She was incredulous and asked me where I went for my annual physical examination. I told her I didn't have annual examinations.

"With tears in her eyes my therapist then gently explained that normal people have a physical once a year. My homework assignment was to find a doctor and go for an examination. She told me I shouldn't go alone, that I could ask someone from our therapy group to go with me. That was the most difficult part.

"So at age forty-three I had my first physical exam—blood tests, urine and stool samples, vaginal exam, the works. When the doctor said she would call with the results in a week, an old familiar terror gripped me. It was the same fear I had whenever Mother got sick. I was sure I had a brain tumor and was going to die.

"My fear led to another excruciatingly difficult assignment from my therapist. I was to ask someone to be with me when I got the test results. I did as I was told. When the doctor reported that I was in perfect health and that my headaches were a temporary symptom of alcohol withdrawal, I was so relieved that I didn't realize what a huge step I had taken."

*   *   *   *

"Oh Gritty!" Spring blurted out, "Your story reminds me so much of something similar in my Earth life. If you don't mind my interrupting, I would really like to talk about it."

Glad to have a break, Gritty responded by nodding and closing her storybook. Spring smiled gratefully and opened hers. As a scene began to unfold from the page, Spring's heart involuntarily tightened. Sky and Gritty stiffened beside her.

It was the middle of the night and Spring was asleep, her bedroom ominously dark and quiet. Suddenly she awoke, a tight pain squeezing her chest, running across her back and shoulders and down her arm. Instinctively she hugged herself tightly as if to keep her heart from collapsing. Taking slow deep breaths, she cautiously walked to the bathroom and drank a cold glass of water. The pain subsided. She went back to bed, carefully placing a glass of water on the bed stand, making sure it was within easy reach if the pain returned.

She lay perfectly still, not daring to move, too fearful to think, not knowing what to do. She breathed deeply to ward off the ghostly terror that hovered over her as she waited for the pain to either go away or come back. An interminable two hours of watchful dread passed with the pain subsiding, then returning, lessening then increasing.

Finally Spring looked at the clock. It was five a.m. She shook her head, got out of bed, carefully put on a sweatshirt and jogging pants and went out to her car. She got in and slowly backed out of the garage.

"I prayed," Spring interjected, "that I wouldn't die on the way to the hospital. I walked through the automatic double doors of the emergency room and calmly said, 'I have pain in my chest, back, and arm and I'm afraid I might be having a heart attack.' Suddenly a wheelchair appeared out of nowhere and whisked me to a bed surrounded by a white curtain. When an oxygen tube was inserted in my nose, I immediately felt better. I thought it all must have been my imagination—until they moved me to the cardiac intensive care unit. Frightened and alone, I lay in bed listening to the rhythmic beeping of the heart monitor. I pledged to stop smoking, a habit that had grown into a full-blown three-pack a day addiction. The next morning I was released and drove myself home. The doctor's diagnosis was stress, not a heart attack. I did quit smoking, however.

"This is the most important part of my story: I didn't ask anyone for help even in the face of possible death. Can you believe it? I could think of only two solutions that night—to lie in bed and die or drive myself to the hospital. It never even occurred to me to call an ambulance or ask a friend to take me!

"Your story, Gritty, about having difficulty asking for help was *my* story as well. I never asked for help in my entire life. I always kept my thoughts and feelings to myself. I've been doing the same thing here. I haven't even been able to ask you or Suma for help in the safety of this spiritual place!"

Realizing that some of her discomfort with Suma was related to her inability to ask for help, Spring timidly called out to her.

Suma's dark blue energy appeared immediately, even before Spring finished saying her name.

"Can you help me understand why I am unable to ask for help?" Spring pleaded.

Suma responded with a smile and hug of complete acceptance.

"I think," she then said, "you are afraid that asking for help means that you are deficient or 'less than.' If asking for help is unacceptable to you, then doing so would prove that *you* are unacceptable."

Tears flowed profusely and unexpectedly, covering Spring's energy like a blanket as she wondered why she hadn't thought of that, why she wasn't as wise as Suma. She should have been able to figure it out herself. As usual she felt inferior, inadequate—yes, unacceptable.

"I'm playing out the same old script here that I played out on Earth," she sobbed.

Suma smiled and gently folded her energy around Spring in a warm embrace.

"You know so much more than you realize, Spring," she said comfortingly, "it's your fear that keeps you from knowing how much you already understand. Asking for my help now was a big step. I hope you will be able to do so again as your story progresses for more will be revealed that will further challenge your feelings toward me."

Spring smiled and relaxed. Though she didn't know what was to come and still hadn't fully incorporated this new understanding, she knew that Suma was right on target and had her best interests in mind. That made all the difference.

Gritty was happy that her story facilitated Spring's breakthrough with Suma. Sky thought it was ironic that they all had worked so hard to help others yet didn't know how to receive help themselves. They were all pleased with the way they were learning from each other.

✳   ✳   ✳   ✳

When it was time for Gritty to continue with her story, she thought more about her recovery journey. It was a time of personal and spiritual growth that turned her life upside down, especially during the first couple of years. So many things she previously believed to be true were actually not true and things she believed to not be true were actually true. Then she remembered how her view of her mother changed during that time.

"I hadn't had a drink for more than a year," she told Spring and Sky, "when I confronted my mother. It was my therapist's idea, another homework assignment. Tightly gripping my one-year AA chip in my hand for support, I sat face-to-face with Mother and told her what it was like for me growing up. How neglected I felt…How worried I was about her health and her dependence on pain medicine…How Daddy's jokes were abusive and disrespectful.

"Mother listened passively at first. Then she talked about how hard life had been for her, that she and Daddy didn't have a very good relationship, she was jealous of other women, and she didn't trust him. Though her revelations surprised me, they didn't respond to my needs. In fact, it was as if Mother really wasn't listening. She was too wrapped up in her own issues to hear about mine."

Gritty felt her frustration as if she were experiencing it all over again. She remembered how, instead of focusing on Mother's needs that day, she grasped her chip even more tightly and forged ahead, expressing her own needs as clearly as she could. When she finished, Mother's response no longer mattered. She had done what she needed to do. By giving voice to her own experience, she had affirmed herself.

"To my surprise," she continued, "Mother suddenly reached out for me. With tears in her eyes she held my hands firmly in hers and told me everything I longed to hear. She told me she loved me. She was sorry she had been unable to be the kind of mother she wanted to be and that I deserved. Even though she gave what she could, she knew it was not enough. I was a beautiful, smart, and wonderful daughter. She was proud of me for quitting drinking. She was grateful that I loved her enough to tell the truth.

"Then we hugged for a very long time, my veins and arteries rhythmically pumping relief and joy to my heart, filling it with peace. Our smiles lit up Mother's dusk-filled living room with the warmth of love and the brilliance of release. Beginning in that moment, love and gratitude replaced the guilt and resentment I had felt toward Mother for too long."

Gritty was filled with warmth when she thought about her mother. What a gift it had been to see her as she really was.

Facing the truth about Daddy had been an entirely different matter. The family myth was that he walked on water. It was an unspoken rule that he be worshipped and adored, an imperative carefully nurtured by Mother. Others admired him, too. The mayor even named him Family Man Of The Year when Gritty was a teenager. The church relied on him as their most stalwart leader and lay minister. People loved his humor, seemingly unaware that his jokes were always at the expense of others. When people didn't think Daddy was funny, he thought *that* was funny—like the time a traffic cop stopped him for speeding and warned him to drive more carefully. In response Daddy immediately put his car in gear and drove it into the ditch, then laughed when the angry cop gave him a ticket.

Gritty struggled mightily to understand her daddy. Her therapist suggested the book *People of the Lie* by M. Scott Peck. She was fascinated by what she read:

that evil was the use of power to destroy the spiritual growth of others for the purpose of one's own narcissistic needs—that evil people are dedicated to preserving their self-image and are unceasingly engaged in efforts to maintain the appearance of moral purity, their goodness in fact being only a pretense and thus a lie—that it is seldom possible to pinpoint their maliciousness because they are experts at disguise and the disguise is usually impenetrable.

"My view of Daddy changed next," Gritty then told Spring and Sky, "I read in the book my therapist recommended that evil people are likely to exert themselves more than most in a continuing effort to obtain and maintain an image of high respectability. At that moment the scales fell from my eyes and my illusions about Daddy were exposed in the blinding light of truth. The things he did at other people's expense—with no remorse or guilt—revealed a complete absence of empathy for others. He hurt people for his own narcissistic pleasure—making fun of an elderly person's feeble-mindedness, faking food poisoning in a restaurant and then laughing hysterically at the owner's terror of a lawsuit, calling attention in public to the physical characteristics about which I already felt humiliated as an awkward teenager, cruelly pinching mother's nipples while her hands were occupied so she couldn't defend herself."

Gritty thought about how Daddy laughed at people's discomfort, how he would double bind them so they couldn't respond. It was a form of psychological and emotional torture. She remembered finding a large black and white photograph of him. His dark greasy hair was combed straight back from his face, emphasizing his gleeful eyes and sinister smile.

"I brought a picture of Daddy to a therapy session," she continued, "and looked at it while telling him what I now knew about him. It was brutal. When I finished, I burned his picture, my fingers trembling as I lit the match. An indescribable emptiness descended on me as I watched the flames flare, then quickly die. The staggering shift was completed—from Daddy as a Savior to be glorified to Daddy As Evil."

Gritty then re-opened her storybook. She shivered as a scene of her in her apartment began to unfold. Spring and Sky moved closer, suddenly afraid.

Gritty had just come home from the intense therapy session and she felt numb. She blindly dropped her keys onto the kitchen counter and flung her depleted body heavily onto the couch where she sat staring into space. She heard faint whisperings that hinted at the enormity of what she had done. She smelled the burning photograph and saw the Daddy she knew disappear.

Then she felt him hovering over her shoulder. Daddy was annoyed.

Convinced that his angry, cajoling and joking spirit was in the room, Gritty spoke to him firmly.

"Go away and leave me alone! I know what I know and you are not going to change my mind!"

Restless and agitated, she walked toward the kitchen to get a soda. On the way she tripped over the telephone cord, catching herself just before falling by grabbing the edge of the dining room table.

Gritty knew it was Daddy.

"Leave me alone!" she screamed, "That is not funny! You are evil!"

Still she felt his presence. She tried to ignore him, telling herself it was her imagination. Trying to keep herself busy, she headed for the laundry room in the basement. When she returned, she realized the keys to her apartment were inside. She had never locked herself out before.

"Leave me alone!" she cried, sliding her body down onto the floor outside her apartment door. "This is not funny!"

She heard Daddy laughing.

When she went outside to find the landlord in the next building, she slipped on the wet surface of the alley and screamed at Daddy again to leave her alone.

A few days passed. Daddy's pranks persisted. So did Gritty's determined resistance.

"When I felt the calmness of surrender and acceptance," Gritty interjected as she looked up from the Earth scene, "I knew that Daddy was finally gone. He had been a sociopath, a master who had fooled everyone. I was the only one who saw him for who he really was.

"Then I began to see how similar Chuck and Daddy were. Both were highly respected in their communities. Both were workaholics. Chuck had multiple affairs and there were rumors in town about Daddy's adulterous behavior. The pornographic magazines I found under the front porch belonged to Daddy. I found Chuck's pornography stash in the bottom drawer of a dresser.

"I began to challenge my view of Chuck as an honest family man and myself as the seductress who had led him away from respectability. When I dared to open my eyes, I saw Chuck for who he was—a sociopath, philanderer, narcissist, sex addict and liar. When I derided myself as stupid for once again not being able to see below surface appearances, my therapist emphatically pointed out, 'It was *not* that you were stupid. It was that he was *that* good. He was a master who fooled everyone, not just you. But I can guarantee that from now on, when you see a sociopath, you will see what you are dealing with as clearly as you see the top of this table. Even when other people are fooled, you will not be.'"

Gritty remembered the moment she realized how good Chuck was at fooling people, just like Daddy. With eyes now open and wary, very different from her customary wide-eyed innocence, she began to learn how to protect herself. She filed for divorce without telling Chuck. When he called, angry and embarrassed at the public exposure of being served the papers at his office, she matter-of-factly told him she was simply following the advice of her attorney and offered no other explanation or apology. When he called to smoothly beg for forgiveness, she told him she didn't have time to talk and hung up.

"Wow!" exclaimed Sky. She was awed by the power of the truth and the courage it took Gritty to stand by it even in the face of the supernatural intensity of her daddy's spirit.

Captivated by Gritty's risk-taking, Spring blurted out, "That was really heavy, Gritty! You kept digging through the layers of confusion and discomfort until you came to the truth of who Chuck and your daddy really were. As if that weren't huge enough, you came face to face with the reality of human evil."

To their amazement Suma instantly appeared, stopping quickly and firmly before them, her determined seriousness rendering them speechless.

"Your personal and intimate encounter with evil," she said, looking directly at Gritty, "helped you to heal, to understand your pain. But it was a gift to be treated with care."

Suma then looked at Sky and Spring, indicating that her words were meant for them as well.

"On Earth," she continued, "the idea of evil is often misinterpreted and misunderstood. It is easy to label people as evil just because they hurt us or don't like us or don't behave the way we would like them to. It is important to note that Gritty recognized the truth about her daddy only when she had a sense of what evil was, when she understood some of its characteristics. She did not use the word lightly.

"So the first lesson is this: it is very difficult to identify and understand human evil, there is considerable ignorance about it and misuse of it, and it needs to be handled with extreme care.

"Evil people are easy to hate and that is *not* a lesson you are to learn. Notice that Gritty did not express hatred for Chuck or her daddy. Instead, once she saw the truth, she focused on protecting herself from the havoc they could play in her life. That is the second lesson.

"Because of Gritty's intense struggles with her own shadow side, with the good and bad in herself, she also knew the truth of the old adage 'There but for the grace of God go I'. And that is the third lesson."

Gritty thought about how Suma's lessons seemed to be related to those she learned in AA. She had learned that rigorous honesty was essential if she were to stay sober. That's what motivated her to seek and face the truth in the first place. Another lesson was the need for humility. That's what helped her detach from evil rather than be consumed with hatred and anger.

"Yes, another gift you were given," Suma said with a smile of acknowledgment, "was the gift of recovery."

Gritty loved it when Suma read her thoughts. She felt blessed to have inherited the disease of alcoholism for she had gained so much in recovery—spirituality, acceptance, humility, peace, joy, love, and more. The list was endless.

Suma waved farewell and slowly drifted off into space. Gritty turned to face Sky and Spring, thanking them for listening to her story of change and healing. As she closed her storybook she looked at Spring, indicating it was now her turn to take center stage.

*   *   *   *

Spring's thoughts led her to a challenging time on Earth, the time of the Reagan Administration, a time when her passion for justice and fairness found new expression. She had conducted research about poverty, taught a course at the local university about peace, co-founded a small empowerment group against nuclear proliferation, wrote a book about how ordinary citizens can be peacemakers, chaired a coalition of non-governmental organizations for human rights.

When she opened her storybook it automatically flipped to a page that brought back surprisingly poignant memories. As new Earth images began to emerge, Spring's deep emotions radiated energy over Sky and Gritty and they moved closer.

It was summer. Spring lived in a tent on hard, drought-parched ground in an open cornfield with hundreds of women. She was at a Women's Peace Camp located near an army base where it was suspected that nuclear weapons were stored. When they weren't protesting at the base the women shared daily tasks like preparing meals, building a barn, and facilitating workshops. They took turns providing security—especially at night when the field was enveloped in darkness like a shroud and army helicopters conducted voyeuristic surveillance over their camp.

"Living and working together," Spring interjected as she looked up from the scene, "was a challenge. A group of middle-aged women grumbled about how some of the younger women were topless while working on the barn roof. They thought it indecent and offensive to the Amish farmers in the adjacent field with whom they wished to have an amiable relationship. The young women protested that if men could work in the hot sun without shirts, why couldn't they? Then some heterosexual women were offended when lesbians held hands and expressed affection for each other and worried the camp would be seen as a lesbian stronghold. A community meeting was hastily called to talk about the conflicts."

Spring pointed to a scene on the next page and the three of them prepared for the meeting.

A hundred women gathered in the partially finished barn, forming an oscillating circle of diversity: faces of many colors—bodies of all shapes, sizes, ages— clothing ranging from farm wife housedresses to saris to jeans and tank tops to no clothes at all.

A middle-aged woman chaired the meeting. She stood in the center of the many-layered circle, a tall imposing presence in her floor length flowing peasant skirt topped by a simple sleeveless white blouse and long hair streaked with silver strands.

Spring sat on a bale of hay, curious and prepared to listen objectively to all sides. Several women stood to speak, tremulous voices and shaking hands illuminating their sincerity and depth of feeling.

Then an elderly woman stood, trembling as she took a deep breath and mustered the courage to speak. With painful honesty she talked about how all the men in her life had been emotionally unavailable, how she only found genuine love and affection with women. She begged for understanding of the incredible beauty of its expression.

Involuntarily Spring stood, propelled by an impulse that came from a place deep within that she did not understand. There was a lump in her throat and her voice was filled with sadness.

"To be perfectly honest, I really don't know what my sexual orientation is but the only authentic relationships I have experienced have been with women. I don't know what that means. I do know that if we are going to be able to stop the nuclear arms race, we need to do it together and in peace."

Brushing away a tear, Spring sat down.

Immediately a young woman who was openly gay and had been intimately involved in the conflict stood. She turned to look directly at Spring and said, "I appreciate your honesty. We really like you and..."

Spring heard the words *we really like you* over and over like a welcome song, a mantra of acceptance. She didn't hear anything else that was said.

When the meeting ended, the young woman approached her. She smiled brightly as she asked if Spring was planning to get arrested at the army depot the next week.

Spring's heart fluttered. The beauty of the slender young woman captivated her.

"I plan to be at the action," she responded awkwardly, "but I'm not going to engage in civil disobedience. Why?"

"I would like you to be my support person," the young woman said, "when I am arrested. I will give you my drivers' license and credit cards so you can get me out of jail if necessary."

A sudden bolt of electricity surged through Spring's body as she told the young woman she felt honored to be asked and immediately agreed to help. She didn't understand the depth or significance of her feelings at that moment. She just knew something very special had happened.

Then it was nighttime. Hundreds of women from the peace camp carried burning candles and walked in silence as they marched in single file along the side of the road. They were headed toward the army depot for a protest vigil, their numbers stretching for half a mile or more. Spring was at the front of the line.

A group of men and women from the neighboring town stood across from the army depot. Wearing baseball hats and clutching bottles of beer, they waited for the protesters to arrive as they leaned on their cars and watched, ready for their evening sport of taunting the women.

As Spring led the marching women toward the gate of the depot, the local folks started shouting.

"Go home, bitches! You're nothing but a bunch of feminists, communists, lesbians...and vegetarians!"

Spring laughed out loud. Wouldn't they be surprised to know how much she craved a hamburger and fries from the local drive-in right then? She was amazed at how lighthearted she felt. Somehow she was a different person after the community meeting though she comprehended neither the magnitude of the change in her nor the extent to which she did not understand.

"After my summer at the peace camp," Spring said, looking up from her storybook, "I was ready for more involvement. I joined a coalition of peace organizations planning a protest action at the corporate headquarters of a major nuclear weapons producer. In preparation for my arrest, I attended nonviolent civil disobedience training and joined a women's affinity group. At the crack of dawn, over a thousand people showed up for the peaceful, symbolic action at Corporate Plaza—and over two hundred of us were arrested. With our hands behind our backs and plastic bands tightened around our wrists, we were loaded onto waiting buses and taken to jail where we were fingerprinted, photographed, and booked. After spending the day in jail, we appeared before a judge who gave us a trial date before releasing us without bail."

Spring then turned to a page in her storybook that revealed an old courthouse. She sat back with Sky and Gritty as if watching a movie, choking back tears that signaled something other than sadness.

A trial was just beginning. The court clerk declared that the proceedings were matters of the State versus the eight defendants as named and delineated the charge as Trespassing. The judge acknowledged that the defendants had chosen to defend themselves, then potential jurors were questioned for two days until a panel was selected. On the third day, the jury sat on the left side of the court-room, the eight defendants at a table facing the judge, and the prosecutor at a table adjacent to them with about four feet of space in between. The judge asked Mr. Elder, the assistant district attorney, if he was ready to proceed.

Mr. Elder responded, "Yes, Your Honor. I would like to make a very brief opening statement, if I may. The State's case will show by means of four wit-nesses that on April 10, 1987, at a place known as the Corporate Plaza, the folks who are seated at this table were arrested for the crime of Trespass. Now, what led up to this was that about a thousand people approached the Plaza area, as the testimony will show. Eight hundred of these people left voluntarily after they were warned that they were trespassing. The State will show that there was intent on the part of each of these eight ladies to trespass by the fact that subsequent to a warning that was collectively made and individually made to each one, they did remain on the premises."

Pausing briefly to look at the defendants seated at the table behind him, Mr. Elder continued, "The State will further show that they did not have a claim of right under the controlling case, State v. Brogness, 523 N.W.2d 745 (1983) by the Supreme Court, which refers to a claim of right as a property right, such as that of an owner, tenant, lessee, licensee or invitee. And that, in essence, Your Honor and members of the jury, is the State's case. Thank you."

The judge then asked if any of the defendants wished to speak. Spring had been designated by the group to make an opening statement for all of them. She stood and began with a disclaimer.

"As you know, Your Honor, we are representing ourselves. Since we have not been trained in the law, we may do some things that are objectionable and we understand that you may need to point that out to us from time to time."

Spring paused, attempting to suppress her fear by referring to her notes, and then continued.

"Ladies and gentlemen of the jury, we want to talk directly to you as the conscience of the community. Each of us will be presenting testimony in turn. I will briefly summarize what that testimony will cover. First, each of us will describe what we did at Corporate Plaza on April 10th beginning at six-thirty in the morning with a prayer service at St. Mark's Church to the point when we were arrested. We will testify how a thousand people held hands and encircled corporate headquarters in an *arms against arms* legal presence. We stood in groups at each door to the building although management and other employees could enter at all entrances."

Spring felt the heavy responsibility of speaking for her co-defendants and was awed to find herself before a judge and jury in a court of law. She straightened her body, took a deep breath, and bravely continued.

"We will testify that at one entrance, ten to twenty people sat in front of the main door and were arrested. After their arrest, about ten more people sat in front of the door, each group taking turns in a symbolic action that did not keep anyone from going to work that day. We will also testify that it was a peaceful, orderly protest. Each of us will state our motivation and what we hoped to accomplish, emphasizing that we took action with no criminal intent but with a longing for peace and a plan for ending the arms race. Finally each of us will talk about what our rights were to be at corporate headquarters that day. I would like to give an overview of those rights."

Spring took a deep breath. She was about to plunge into foreign legal territory.

"First, we will claim we have rights based on the enormous significance and urgency of the statement we are making. Second, we will claim we had rights because the dangers and consequences of the nuclear arms race are imminent and not remote with the dangers growing greater with each passing day. Third, we will claim we had rights because the harm from the corporation producing nuclear bombs clearly outweighs the transgression of trespass. Fourth, we will claim we had rights because we were obeying international laws by being at corporate headquarters. Fifth, we will claim we had rights because as taxpayers our money is paying for the weapons of our own destruction and the corporation cannot claim sole right to property that is financed with our money. Sixth, we will claim we had rights because of freedom of speech and religion. And, finally, we will claim we had rights because of moral and economic imperatives."

Spring now felt more confident and slowly looked at each juror before concluding.

"We know that the prosecutor must prove us guilty beyond a reasonable doubt. We believe that after you have heard our testimony and weighed the evidence, that you, as the conscience of the community, will find us innocent of a criminal act, and on that basis will find us not guilty."

Spring returned to the table and sat down. It was only then that she started shaking.

Mr. Elder then called his first witness, a security officer who testified in detail about the human chain of a thousand people that surrounded Corporate Plaza. He told how, using a bullhorn, he read an announcement to each group sitting in front of the entrance that they were trespassing and if they did not leave immediately they would be arrested. He identified each of the defendants as refusing to leave when warned, stating that he turned each of them over to the police. Mr. Elder then called three police officers each of whom identified the defendants he had arrested that morning. Several of the defendants cross-examined the witnesses and, surprisingly, the judge often upheld their objections.

Spring felt proud to be part of such a savvy group as the defendants then testified. Their voices were filled with passion as they eloquently articulated their motivations. Spring was the last to make her statement.

"I work in a helping profession like many of the other defendants," she began, "I also teach part time at the university and many students from a course I am currently teaching about the peace movement are in court today as observers."

Spring looked at the young enthusiastic faces of her students and smiled before turning to again face the jury and continue.

"Being at Corporate Plaza on April 10th was the culmination of many actions I have taken against the production of nuclear weapons. When I asked myself 'how much more do I have to do?' I thought of people from the past whose commitment to bringing about justice and a respect for human rights in both our country and other countries never faltered. So when I went to Corporate Plaza on April 10th, those people were with me. As I waited to be arrested, I thought about how slavery was legal in our country but because people broke the law and took other actions to help slaves escape, slavery is now illegal. I thought about how it was legal to deny women the right to vote but people broke various laws to change that and because of their actions, today it is illegal to deny women the right to vote. I thought about how it was once legal to deny workers the right to organize into unions but they organized anyway…and it was bloody…and because of their actions union organizing is legal today. I thought about how it was once legal for restaurant owners to refuse to serve black people so black people sat at their lunch counters anyway and because of their actions it is now illegal to discriminate because of race. I came to Corporate Plaza because I realized that it is now legal to produce nuclear weapons and other bombs in violation of human rights and we are working to make nuclear weapons illegal."

With the full strength of her passion and commitment Spring faced the jury. Her voice was compelling as she went on.

"On April 10th, as I drove early in the morning to Corporate Plaza, all of these considerations were with me…and more. I thought about how 55 percent of my tax money was going to the military, forcing me to participate in war making. When I considered what I would do when asked to leave the premises, I thought about extraordinary people who took responsibility to change things, people like Martin Luther King, Jr., Rosa Parks, Gandhi, Jesus Christ.

"I thought of ordinary people like you and me, how we hold the key to democracy in our hands when we exercise our freedom of speech and work to change things. And I was certain to the core of me that human rights must always supersede property rights."

By now, Spring was unstoppable.

"So I was asked to leave the premises and I stayed. I was arrested. And I ended up here, appealing to you to understand that my intent was to take responsibility for saving lives, not only those lives that would be destroyed by the weapons, but the lives that are being lost today because people's basic needs are being ignored in order to use our limited resources to build weapons and promote war-making. I'm appealing to you to understand that it was not criminal intent, but a sense of responsibility, that motivated me on April 10th. I'm appealing to you to understand that my sense of legality includes a right to be on the property—the tiny little piece of land that I paid for with my income tax dollars in order to finance nuclear weapons—and I am responsible for that. I'm ashamed that I do not have the guts to stop paying those income taxes. At the same time, I realize that if I did stop paying my taxes there would be even less money for poor people and for improving the quality of life for all of us. So this is what I felt I *could* do…take a symbolic act to call attention to the situation…and I did it. I do not believe that I am on trial here today, but that corporate headquarters is on trial. Thank you."

Mr. Elder jumped to his feet and began his cross-examination of Spring.

"Is it not true that on the date in question, you were not the owner, tenant, lessee, licensee, or invitee of the Corporation in question?" he asked irritably.

"I do not believe that is true," responded Spring.

With a tone of incredulity in his voice, Mr. Elder impatiently and sarcastically asked, "*If* we were to check the property records in this building, we would find *your* name as the owner of Corporate Plaza?"

"No," responded Spring, "but if I might expand, my belief is that the little piece of land that I sat on, I owned, at least for a few minutes. Even though I do not have legal title to it, I have moral title to it because my money is going into financing that property."

"Thank you. Nothing further," Mr. Elder concluded. He threw his hands up and his head back, looking at the jury as if to imply that Spring was out of her mind.

After all testimony had been offered, it was time for closing statements. Mr. Elder went first.

Facing the jury and looking at his notes, he said, "Ladies and Gentlemen, we have heard a lot of very moving testimony here today. And I don't mind telling you it was moving to me too. But what I think doesn't matter. We've heard statements that refer to historical events, which, while appalling, are not a part of this trial. We have heard about the horrors of the Nazis and the Nuremberg trial, the holocaust. We've heard about the terrors of what has happened to civilians in Lebanon. The foreign policy of the United States with respect to furnishing or permitting the sale of weapons is not on trial here. Israel is not on trial for what it did in Lebanon, regardless of how you or I may feel about that. The tax policy of the United States is not on trial. The military policy of the United States is not on trial. The only persons who are on trial are these eight ladies on my right.

"Now, good motives do not excuse violation of the law unless there is a showing of necessity. Now, necessity requires imminent danger. No one has shown that by this act an imminent danger existed in that split second, in those minutes, in those hours and that a disaster was prevented or could have been prevented by what happened here. Now, what did happen here?"

Mr. Elder droned on about the thousand protesters and what they did, making his legal arguments and refuting each claim the defendants had made.

In closing, he said genially, "These defendants are honest people. They told you the truth. They were not the owners of that piece of land known as Corporate Plaza. They were there to make a statement. They had a simple choice to make. The issue before you is very simple, despite the complex motivations that are behind what transpired. The issue before you is whether or not the State Trespass Law was broken. I believe the State has shown, regardless of their good motives, that these eight ladies broke the law intentionally. We have shown beyond a reasonable doubt that all the defendants did, in fact, trespass on that day. Thank you very much."

The judge then asked, "Who wishes to speak for the defense?"

Marian stood. She had been a social worker for over thirty years and her confidence and caring heart were evident as she approached the jury.

"Ladies and gentlemen," she began, "we do not believe that we should be convicted of a crime for four primary reasons. First, we did not go to Corporate Plaza with criminal intent but with a sense of great urgency. We believe that we *do* face an imminent danger. The Society of Atomic scientists has an atomic clock, which they adjust every year. It is now three minutes before midnight. As one of my co-defendants said, it feels like we are in a little car and we are being pursued by a semi that's completely out of control. If we broke a speeding violation in order to get out of the way of that vehicle, we do not believe that we should be charged with a crime.

"Second, we do not think we committed a crime because we were peaceful and non-violent and did no harm to any person or property.

"Third, we should not be convicted of a crime because we have rights as citizens and taxpayers to speak out at Corporate Plaza. Because our taxes are supporting their production of nuclear weapons we believe we had a right to be there for a few minutes. In fact, we should be invited as guests to come and sit on the Plaza for a short period of time even though we might not have actually signed a lease. I also believe that we were singled out because of our convictions. You just can't tell me if we went there to say that more nuclear weapons are what the community needs and to applaud the corporation's efforts that we would have been arrested. I do believe it was a political arrest over and above the trespassing charge.

"The fourth reason we believe we should not be convicted of a crime has to do with looking at what we did in a larger context. To me, it is almost beyond belief that our country could at this moment drop nuclear weapons anywhere in the world, and it would be legal. Yet, we are here in a criminal court because we are publicly stating this is a terrible abridgment of humanity's rights. And I think that there is such a double standard here that it's hard for me to see how we can be convicted of a crime when to start a nuclear war would not be considered criminal. I also think that any time social change has come about in this country, it's been through an orderly testing of laws in our courts.

"We did go to Corporate Plaza to make these statements. And basically, what we are saying is that the arms race is wrong and we believe that what we did was right and we should not be convicted of a crime. In your role as the conscience of the community, we ask you, ladies and gentlemen of the jury, to find us not guilty."

The judge then gave instructions to the jurors, excused them, and sent them to the deliberation room. Spring and her co-defendants went to the cafeteria to wait. They felt anxious. The judge had a reputation for being punitive and if the jury found them guilty, it was likely he would send them to jail immediately. In anticipation they had brought overnight bags with them.

Spring's students gathered around a table a few feet away. Seeing that their anxiety matched her own, she joined them as they enthusiastically shared their observations, asked questions, and fervently expressed their concerns about the verdict. Two hours passed quickly. Spring had gratefully forgotten that she might be spending the night in jail.

Another hour passed before they were summoned back to the courtroom. Tension filled the room as the defendants, Mr. Elder, the jurors, and the students sat in quiet anticipation of the judge's appearance. Spring looked intently at the jurors' faces hoping for a clue about the verdict. Their impassivity revealed nothing.

When the judge arrived he asked the foreman of the jury if they had reached a verdict. The foreman was a professional-looking man with gray hair and wrinkles of kindness around his pleasant mouth.

In a neutral tone of voice, he responded, "Yes, we have, Your Honor."

Spring's heart pounded in her chest. The foreman passed a folded piece of paper to the judge. He read it without expression before returning it to the foreman.

"Please state your verdict," he then instructed.

The foreman looked first at the judge and then at the defendants. With a slight smile forming in the corner of his mouth, he announced the verdict in a bold voice:

"Your Honor, we find the defendants *Not Guilty.*"

Everyone gasped. Spring grabbed Marion's hand. The students' spontaneous cheers and applause immediately turned into mute smiles when the judge sternly warned that there be silence in the court. Satisfied and proud, the jurors smiled broadly at the defendants. They looked angelically radiant.

Though Spring was exhausted, her students' enthusiasm was irrepressible, so over pizza she held class late into the night.

As the Earth scene faded from view Spring looked up from her storybook. She thought about what a ride her first experience with civil disobedience had been. She was arrested six more times after that. Five times they were found not guilty. The one time her group was found guilty the judge sentenced them to take a *legal* action to protest the arms race; so they organized a workshop about the nuclear threat and invited the judge to make an opening statement. Spring remembered how firmly she had believed that their actions would make a difference.

Sky and Gritty were impressed by how clearly Spring articulated her case in the courtroom, what an effective change agent she had become.

Just then Suma appeared and said, "You all became powerful advocates for change. Think for a minute about how that happened."

Sky thought about her own early experiences as a social worker, how sometimes her passion ruled her head. Even though she tried to do a good job she often failed to make a difference. Sometimes it seemed she even made things worse—the painful memory of what happened to Jamie immediately tugged at her heart. Through her own pain and healing she came to know herself and her limits. Only then had she become more effective.

Gritty was having similar thoughts. She too had jumped into situations without thinking—like keeping the school open during the teachers' strike. After she hit bottom with her drinking and learned to accept herself and her limits, she was positioned to be more influential in her school.

"Exactly," Suma said, blending with their reflections, "You could not really be powerful until you were aware of who you were, until you understood what it meant to be human. When you gained a deeper understanding of your powerlessness, you became more powerful. Then you were able to see the big picture and you learned how to operate in the world."

Spring jumped in, her energy bouncing with excitement at the insights she was gaining.

"It is fascinating how we became more effective when we realized our limits. I came to understand that I was only one ordinary person among millions but, if each of us did our part, our combined actions could and indeed have changed the world. When Sky accepted her powerlessness she was able to join with others to bring about changes in the child welfare system. Once Gritty found genuine humility through recovery, she was more effective in influencing school policy."

"Yes," Suma affirmed, "Gandhi's wise exhortation to *be the change you want in the world* was certainly manifested in your lives."

*　　　*　　　*　　　*

Spring beamed like a ray of sunshine, her uncertainty and discomfort gone as she watched Suma leave the library. Eager to tell another story she collected her energy, signaled her intentions to Sky and Gritty, and began.

"Something happened when I was middle-aged that changed my life forever and overshadowed everything that came before. It started when I hired an attorney to help with a real estate matter at work. Tess was a feisty top-notch lawyer with luminescent green eyes and blond hair streaked with brown tones. Her buxom figure screamed eroticism in spite of the manly tailored suits in navy blue and black that she always wore. With dewy eyes and fluttering heart I lingered breathlessly over our conversations, finding the slightest excuse to call her just so I could hear her voice, not caring about the fee minutes that ticked away on her attorney's clock with each encounter. Like a schoolgirl with a crush I burst into song at the thought of her—'Sister, you've been on my mind, Sister, you're one of a kind, Sister, I'm keeping my eyes on you!' I had never been happier."

Spring paused to turn to a new page in her storybook. The fluttering of her heart even now surprised her as she watched the Earth scene unfold. She was taking an afternoon nap, smiling as she slept. When Sky and Gritty suddenly realized they were privy to her dream they bubbled with curiosity and excitement.

Two beautiful women lay with their naked bodies wrapped around each other, sensuality oozing from every pore, affection permeating the air with fragrant lilies. Tess moved her beautifully sensuous body over Spring like a slow moving stream, her voluptuous melon breasts brushing against the delicious apple-sized breasts beneath her. Spring joyously welcomed her, tension building with every touch. She finally exploded grandly in the most magnificent orgasm she had ever had. Just as she opened her eyes and whispered "I love you" she discovered that the face looking down at her was her own! Then she woke up.

With a wide smile, eyes as bright as the sun, and arms outstretched with joy, Sky interrupted the Earth scene with the exclamation, "Congratulations, Spring! I am so happy for you! You waited so long to love yourself!"

"That's exactly what a friend said when I told her about the dream," Spring said, "but I was baffled. Was I in love with myself or was I in love with Tess? Did my growing self-love portend authentic love with someone else? And might that someone be a woman?

"I felt nervous and excited and thought it might help to talk with my friends until I realized that my sexuality was too precious to give away. I should treasure it, nurture it, and let it be mine alone. I didn't tell anyone.

"I was learning an important lesson about honoring and protecting myself, one that proved to be enormously beneficial in an unexpected way when I was research director at the Women's International Development Institute, a non-profit organization run by the Catholic archdiocese. I had worked there for four years when my department conducted a search for an associate director. We were excited to find the ideal candidate, a perfect match for our team. I expected the administration to approve our recommendation without question."

As Spring turned to a new page in her storybook a wave of nausea crested in her churning stomach. Sky and Gritty looked on with concern as the scene appeared before them.

Six gray-haired white men, content in their privilege, sat at a massive mahogany table in an elegant Boardroom with high ceilings and impressively carved wood. An elaborate crucifix dominated one wall.

Spring entered the room, dressed impeccably in a red power suit that matched the plush red chairs around the table, her short blond/gray hair swept up like frosted feathers. The Vice President, who as chair of the meeting sat at the head of the long table, invited her to sit next to him. He was a tall, slender man who was highly respected as a thoughtful and fair administrator. He and Spring had a good relationship.

In spite of the sea of male faces gathered around her—three of them wearing priestly collars—Spring felt comfortable. With amusement she noted the contrast of her red suit from the somber black attire of the others. The meeting was called to order and after Spring presented her department's hiring proposal with articulate confidence, the Vice President thanked her and opened the meeting for questions.

A few innocuous queries followed, confirming Spring's expectation that she would have the administration's support. Then someone asked about the candidate's research on women. This was followed by a groundswell of more focused questions: What is her research methodology? Aren't qualitative methods less rigorous than quantitative research? Why did the candidate select her particular line of study?

Spring fielded each question evenly, maintaining an objective and professional manner even as she felt her heart slowly moving up to her throat.

An administrator who was particularly close to the CEO was the last to speak. He was an exceedingly ugly and gross man with a red bulbous nose that belied his evening vodka consumption. His face was pimpled and scarred, his belly fell over his belt, and his fat neck overflowed from the sides of his clerical collar like too much batter in a cake pan. Using his index finger for punctuation his voice thundered, "Well, *I* have serious reservations about this person's scholarship and integrity. Look at her resume, just look at it! Feminist! What the hell is *feminist* research methodology anyway? And look at this, throughout her resume, you see it—Lesbian! Lesbian! Lesbian! It makes you wonder, doesn't it?!"

His face was rage red as he looked knowingly at the other men as if to say "you all know exactly what I am talking about, don't you?"

The Vice President countered uncomfortably that the candidate's credentials indicated solid scholarship and asked if there were any other questions. In the silence that followed, Spring struggled to maintain her calmness, searching for a helpful or appropriate response to the tirade but finding none. She held her breath, almost gasping from the stench of the polluted, foul air that had filled the room. All she could do was nod when the Vice President politely thanked her and invited her to leave them to their deliberations.

Feigning composure, Spring walked out of the room, shut the door, and immediately collapsed against the outer wall, desperately breathing in the fresh air. She trembled as she whispered to herself, "We are in serious trouble."

The Boardroom scene disappeared and Spring continued telling her story to Sky and Gritty.

"The administration did not approve my department's hiring recommendation in spite of several strong appeals on my part. Even though I was terrified that the secret about my own sexual exploration might be exposed I had to do something. So I called a trusted friend who was influential in the community. I said I was going to tell him something that happened in my organization, that I hoped he would take appropriate action, that after I gave him the information I would never speak of it again with him or anyone else. I told him I wanted him to agree that we never had this conversation and that I would deny that we had ever talked.

"I know that what I did was honorable and right. I also knew I had to protect myself like hell from that point on…even if it meant lying. One thing I knew for sure. It was time for me to leave that organization."

Spring was flooded with memories about what happened after her phone call. All hell broke loose in the nonprofit community. It even reached national proportions with separation of church and state issues flying like boomerangs. Through it all, no one suspected the role she had played.

Gritty smiled, immediately understanding Spring's predicament. She remembered how her own perspective about right and wrong had shifted over time.

"Doing the right thing," she said thoughtfully, "is not always simple. You were so brave to expose injustice and there was nothing wrong with lying about it to protect yourself!"

Sky smiled at how far removed she was from the simple thinking of her childhood. She understood that decisions about right and wrong depended on the situation and considerations of the higher good.

"Just think," she said to Spring, "if you had not lied, *you* would have become the focus of attention rather than the organization's discrimination."

Spring thought about what Sky and Gritty said and wondered what Suma might have to add. Just then, as if on cue, Suma appeared but her response was brief.

"Well done, ladies! Now it is time to rest so you can absorb the enormity of the changes you have been through and the many things you have learned."

They gathered in a circle embrace, basking in the glow of mutual acceptance and support, feeling gratified about their hard work. Suma's dark energy radiated through them, warming them while reinforcing and strengthening their bond. One by one they drifted off to float peacefully in the broader expanse of space beyond the library.

PART VII

▼

TRANSFORMATION

*The heart that breaks open
can contain the whole universe.*

—*Joanna Macy*

Enjoying the multitudinous bright lights bobbing and weaving both near and far, Sky glided serenely through space until she felt rested and revitalized. Then she went back to the library, the first to return. Though she was finished telling her own stories more understandings awaited her from the stories of Spring and Gritty. She was glad the three of them had decided to work on common issues during their stay on Earth this last time. She was in no rush to move to the Place of Life Selection. There would be plenty of time to think about her next life after all three of them had completed their learning and healing. Smiling at the thought of Sylvia having lived with both her and Gritty at different times, Sky welcomed Suma's surprises and looked forward to more disclosures.

Spring returned to the library next. Wishing to assuage her uneasiness with Suma and her nervous premonition about what was to come, she preferred not having too much time for reflection. She was ready to work, more determined than ever to accelerate her development and thus reduce the times she would return to Earth. With great resolve she moved quickly to her place at the table. She glanced furtively at Sky, feeling envious of her calm, peaceful spirit. She wondered if Sky's energy had darkened a bit or if she was only imagining things.

During the rest period Gritty thought about another gift she had been given: serenity. When she was drinking she seemed able to tolerate considerable emotional discomfort but when she was in recovery that tolerance decreased. When something was wrong her serenity came only when she found a resolution, driving her to truth, to apology, to amends…and ultimately to faith. In her eagerness to share more of her recovery story, she moved back to the library, opened her storybook and simply began speaking. Spring and Sky exchanged glances, at first a little put out by Gritty's eagerness but then, with a shrug, they made a mutual decision to let her go unchallenged.

"I still went to my regular Monday night women's AA meeting but my spiritual home was another meeting that focused on the eleventh step, which was 'sought through prayer and meditation to improve our conscious contact with God, praying only for God's will for us and the power to carry that out.' At that meeting I talked incessantly about not understanding who or what God was, still clinging to my problems like a toddler clutches her favorite blanket, unwilling to let go. How could I turn them over to a God I didn't understand?"

Gritty then turned to a page in her storybook, smiling playfully. Sky and Spring knew that smile well. It reminded them how much they enjoyed Gritty's stubbornness and grit. That is, after all, how she got her nickname. They watched curiously as a new Earth image emerged from the page.

Gritty was in bed, alone in the darkness, listening to the persistent leak of the bathroom faucet. Drip, drip, drip—with each drip came a reproach. Why didn't she just get the damn thing fixed? She didn't know how to fix it herself and would have to call the landlord. It was simple. So why hadn't she done it? It was just like a problem at school that wouldn't go away and that she couldn't seem to fix. She looked at the clock. It was two a.m. Another sleepless night, worrying the problem to death. With each tick of the clock and drip of the faucet her distress grew, turning the room into a turbulent cauldron of powerlessness and voices she didn't want to hear but couldn't silence.

"Please, dear God," she whispered in despair, "tell me what to do. Please show me the way."

Like gentle musical chimes, a voice as clear as a bell rang in her ear:

"Get on your knees."

Silence. Gritty stubbornly stayed in bed, arguing with the voice. Images of the church of her youth tumbled into the darkness, hovering ominously over her bed, taunting her. She saw people on their knees, consumed by fear and guilt, cowering with insincerity. The memories blocked her mind, keeping her mired without hope in the muck of impotent responsibility.

"No way!" Gritty adamantly objected, "I am *not* getting on my knees.'

Minutes passed, then an hour. Gritty tossed and turned, looked at the clock. It was three-thirty a.m. At least it was the weekend so she wouldn't have to go to work in the morning, tired like she had been all week.

Exhausted and desperate, she again pleaded, "Please help me!"

"Get on your knees."

Consumed with worry yet still obstinate in her refusal, Gritty lay awake for another hour. Finally in anguish, she threw back the covers, lifted her head from the pillow, slid her body from the bed…and fell onto her knees. Holding her hands together in prayerful supplication, she meekly whispered, "Please!"

Nothing happened. There was no voice. No answer. No solution. Gritty got back into bed, pulled the covers up to her neck, and immediately fell into a deep restful sleep. When she awoke several hours later the problem was gone. In its place was peacefulness and simple awareness that she had been given the gift of Grace once again.

Gritty looked up from the scene and saw that Sky and Spring were laughing.

"When I told that story at my eleventh step meeting," she said with a chuckle, "they laughed, too, recognizing their own resistance. I had finally turned my will and my problem over to the care of some power greater than me. That night I was plunged into surrender and came out changed. Yet part of my old defiance held on and I hoped that I would never have to get on my knees again!"

Sky and Spring bounced up and down with laughter. Gritty just smiled, thinking about the number of times she had in fact gotten back on her knees after that.

"As my recovery deepened," she continued, "The promises of the AA program came true for me. I found a new peace and a new happiness. I didn't regret the past nor did I wish to close the door on it. I had no fear of financial insecurity. I was able to handle situations that had previously baffled me. I was a gentle miracle, just as you were, Sky, through your Al-Anon recovery. The greatest gift my alcoholism gave me, though, was faith."

Gritty turned to a new page in her storybook, eager to show Sky and Spring an example of her faith. As the scene unfolded they saw Gritty at her Earth home with her younger brother and his wife.

The three of them sat at the dining room table, lingering over a candlelight dinner, reminiscing about Reverend Anders and having to go to church as children, enjoying each other's adult company.

"You know," her brother acknowledged, looking at Gritty with compassion, "We pray for you all the time."

"Why?" Gritty asked, "Do you think that I'm a sinful person? Do you think I'm bad?"

"That isn't it," he replied, "We're all sinners. It's just that we know that you don't believe in God and we love you too much to let you go to hell. We pray that you will be saved."

"I *do* believe in God,' Gritty responded non-defensively, "It's just that my God doesn't look like yours. I don't believe in translating the Bible literally, either, but none of that means I don't have faith."

Gritty was surprised at how calm and centered she felt, grateful that her previous judgment and anger about her family's religion were gone.

Gritty's sister-in-law, who had been looking sincerely perplexed as she listened, then thoughtfully asked, "How can you say that you believe in God and that you have faith when you don't believe what the Bible says about God?"

"Let me ask you," Gritty responded, enjoying the conversation, "how do you know who or what God is, really? Human beings, who defined God, wrote the Bible, and human beings decide how to interpret it. It seems to me that we're playing God when we do that. How do you know the God that Reverend Anders defined so specifically and narrowly is really God and not just what you want God to be or were simply taught that He is? And, by the way, what in the world makes people think God is male?"

Gritty's brother and sister-in-law seemed stumped at first. They sat in silence for a few minutes.

"The Bible says," her brother finally answered, "that we are to have the blind faith of a child. It also refers to God as the Father. If He isn't your God, then who or what do you believe in?"

"That," Gritty said with a big smile, "is a very good question to which I have no answer. I can't begin to comprehend God. I stopped trying. Sometimes, I just think that God is something inside—a wise part of us—and that gives me something a bit more tangible to believe in. Even though I have no idea who or what God is, I have the utmost faith in a power greater than myself. My belief is unshakable. I even get down on my knees before that power. I never thought that I could believe in something about which I had no understanding but I do. I just do. It's a mystery to me. I guess the thing I could probably say I feel most sure about is that God must be Love."

Gritty's sister-in-law, who had continued looking skeptical throughout the conversation, now spoke—a bit defensively, "Well, *we* believe that God is Love, too."

"Maybe, then," Gritty smiled, "we can all agree that at the core of it, God is Love. Still, I'm not willing to believe that any human being—especially not Reverend Anders—can define God for the rest of us. What I really don't understand is why people create a punishing God who sentences them to burn in hell for eternity."

Gritty then looked up from the dinner table scene and closed her storybook. She thought about how, as she talked that night—within the context of the fundamentalist religion of her upbringing—she had realized for the first time how deep and unwavering her faith had become. She said a quiet prayer of thanks to a God she still didn't understand and had no need to understand.

Spring, inspired by Gritty's story, glowed as she thought about her own faith journey. With the help of a women's spirituality group, she had finally found a personal God that worked for her in midlife. At first her God was the hooded woman robed in rich dark blue that she met during the past life regression session. Of course she now knew that woman was Suma. Whenever she was distressed or worried, she visualized her and treasured her words: *Be gentle with yourself, Sheila. You are loved.* Eventually she didn't need a visual image or a gender in order to believe. Her faith had become unwavering. She knew she was in tune with her higher power's will at those times when life was beautifully harmonious in its symmetry—when her mind, body, gut, and behavior were all aligned.

Suma then appeared and said, "Your spiritual quests took you from repressive religious upbringings to a steadfast faith in something that bore no resemblance to tradition or institutions. Because the fear, shame and guilt of your childhood religions had such a profound affect on you, it wasn't easy to overcome their narrow ideas. Yet, as you stood face to face with false beliefs you held tightly to your core—the part of you that knew the truth and always had—until you landed in the arms of your own deep spirituality. Well done, ladies!"

They received Suma's dark blue blessing with a joyful dance of the spirit. It had indeed taken courage to plunge into doubt's turbulent waters and flounder through the chaos that threatened to drown them, but they did. And now they emerged into a faith that was real and strong and good.

*   *   *   *

After the three of them returned to their places at the table, Gritty re-opened her storybook with determination and a complicated look of acceptance, sadness and deep understanding as she began another story.

"I had been in recovery for several years when Mother became very ill, which was nothing new. She had been sick on and off all my life. Each time I feared she would die but each time she lived. This time was different. Mother hovered between life and death, briefly rallying, then plunging into a pre-comatose state only to rally again. This yo-yo pattern continued for several days and I grew impatient.

"When I talked honestly about my frustration in the safe environment of my Monday night women's meeting, my selfishness was revealed with startling clarity. I wanted the painful waiting process to end for *my* sake. When I surrendered that truth to others, I was able to accept that this was *Mother's* death and she would get to do it her own way.

"That night I called her like I did every night. In a voice barely a whisper and so halting that several seconds and even minutes passed between her weak utterances, she was trying to tell me something. Employing all my powers of concentration, I listened intently to each labored word. A yearning to understand erupted from the depths of my soul, a place so deep it was unknown to me, having never been touched before."

Gritty then pointed to a page in her storybook and they saw her in human form, talking with her mother on the phone.

Mother said, "Well…I…have…had…quite…a…time."

"What happened?" Gritty asked.

"They…took us…away."

"Who took you away, Mother?"

"I…don't…know…The doc…tors…I…thu…thu…think."

Gritty knew Mother had something staggeringly significant to tell her. She continued to probe in spite of the weakening voice on the other end of the phone.

"Where did they take you, Mother?"

"…to…a…fur…furnace…I…was…in…a…box…there…was…fire…a…big…fire."

For a moment Gritty felt frantic. She could see Mother in the middle of a fiery furnace and wondered if she was in a coffin, if the fire symbolized hell—or maybe cremation. She felt like she was being transported to another world, a place unknown yet somehow known to her. She continued to probe.

"You were in a box in a furnace? Wasn't that uncomfortable? Were you burning? Did it hurt?"

"It…felt…good…it…was…warm…and…peace…ful."

Gritty wondered briefly if Mother was hallucinating yet in her gut she knew that though she was weak her thinking was quite lucid.

"Where are you now, Mother?"

"In…the…hos…pi…tal…in…my…bed."

Her mother's voice was now almost inaudible. Gritty worried that she might die right there in the middle of their phone conversation.

"How did you get back to the hospital? How did you get out of the box, Mother?"

Her mother's adamant reply took her by surprise. With her last ounce of strength she responded—clearly and with no hesitation in her voice:

"By *refusing* to *die!*"

Suddenly Gritty knew what had happened. Mother had returned from a near death experience. She wasn't ready to go.

She then assured her mother that this was her death and she would get to do it her way, that she would know when it was the right time to go. Then she tenderly told her mother that she loved her very much and would miss her terribly. Tears ran down her cheeks, a lump in her throat blocking any more words.

In a barely perceptible whisper, Mother told Gritty that she loved her very much, too, and then said goodbye. Gritty knew it would be the last time they talked. She was sure Mother knew it too.

Gritty lingered in the scene, lovingly holding onto her mother awhile longer and then, with tears in her eyes, slowly turned toward Sky and Spring.

"I was both stunned and exhilarated," she told them, "I had accepted Mother's invitation to be with her on her death journey. The defiant acceptance I found there was staggering.

"The next day, my brother called. He said I should come home fast. Mother was delirious. I smiled, knowing she was not. I had run to her deathbed so many times in the past out of fear. Now that she was really dying I had no need to be there. I heard her when no one else could and she showed me there was nothing to fear. She died that night."

Gritty thought about how that long goodbye said so much about their relationship as mother and daughter. When she heard Mother had died all she felt was compassion, love, and complete forgiveness, total acceptance, closure. She knew who Mother was and loved her for it. She hadn't been the weak, passive, non-person Gritty had once thought she was. Mother was tough and resilient. The way she died said it all. She refused to go until she was ready.

"I inherited my addiction from Mother," Gritty then told Sky and Spring, "and was always sad that she never found her way out of her disease like I did. But when I learned to detach with love I was able to value what I learned from her. For that I have always been grateful."

Gritty's story once again touched Spring deeply. In her later years, Spring too had come to understand her own mother and in that understanding found peace. Trapped in her own shame bath, her mother had pulled Spring into the murky pool with her. There they had suffered together. Her mother wanted to be perfect just as she wanted her daughter to be perfect. Compassion filled Spring's heart when she imagined what terrible things might have happened to her mother as a vulnerable child. Sadness flooded her soul to know Mother had never found a way out.

Sky was thinking about her own mom, too. From her she had inherited the characteristics that adult children of alcoholics so often wear like a burdensome and baffling cloak. It was quite natural that Sky had gravitated to something familiar in Don even without conscious awareness of his disease. Her compassion for him—and for Mom and Grandpa—carried sadness with it for recovery had eluded them, too.

Suma had quietly appeared while they were reflecting. She now chimed in. "Only when you could accept your own humanity could you find love and compassion for your mothers."

"...and because your healing was complete," she added with an affectionate grin, "you are now free from the need to live over and over with their spirits—and they are no longer obliged to live with you!"

Like a bullet piercing her heart, Spring felt a sharp pang of loss. She remembered how her mother had been the first to meet her this time when she came home again, how grateful she had been that their love had endured. She had forgotten that the strength of that love came from their spirits having been together in different relationships over many Earth lives. Oh how she would miss her!

Suma congratulated them for learning patience and love for their mothers. "...and for others as well," she added with a fond farewell wave.

Spring immediately wondered whom Suma was referring to. She had lived over and over on Earth not only with those she loved—like her mother—but probably many times with those she hated and feared as well. She was pretty sure she hadn't learned patience and love for them, whoever they might be—she couldn't remember. Fear then gripped her, so surprising in its intensity that she tightened defensively as its power surged through her, pushing her into her seat at the library table with such force that she landed with a thud—almost as if she were still in physical form.

In unison, Sky and Gritty cried out with alarm, "Spring? Are you okay?"

Spring mumbled, "It's Suma's damn surprises. I can feel another one coming."

They looked at her questioningly, wondering if she had inside information, if she knew what was going to happen. Shaking her head, Spring assured them she had only a premonition though it was a powerful and persistent one. She insisted that they continue, saying there was nothing to do but wait, she was sure that things would be revealed in due time. She hoped that focusing on Gritty's life would calm her.

*   *   *   *

Once they settled down, Gritty searched for a page toward the back of her story-book. A new glow emanated from her light blue energy. It was a radiance that Sky and Spring intuitively understood. With sighs of resignation they moved closer, unconsciously bracing themselves as an image of Gritty in Earth form appeared before them.

She was in a doctor's office, deep in conversation with a kindly woman in a white lab coat. There was a look of acceptance on Gritty's face.

Other images then flashed by in quick succession: different hospitals, labs, medical centers—Gritty in her apartment, her bald head proudly displayed with-out cover as friends brought food, read to her, took her to the neighborhood park in a wheelchair, kept her company, loved her.

"My death," Gritty said as she looked up from the scenes, "was considerate. It took its time so I could prepare, and my ending was peaceful and happy. With close friends surrounding me with faith and love the last words I heard were *and acceptance is the answer to all my problems today.* What a wonderful thing!"

Sky and Spring floated silently around Gritty, words failing to express the depth of their joy. Suma joined them so quietly it was as if she had been there all along. She hugged Gritty, then winked at the other two.

"You were so ready to come to your Spirit home," she said. "that you never looked back. Your friends knew that you were happily gone. They partied all night, celebrating your life and how much you meant to them. Then they had a memorial service, which of course you missed as well, so…"

Suma, who had no trouble navigating backward and forward in time, circled the library before gathering the others to her and magically transporting them to P.S. 457 in the South Bronx. There they watched with eager anticipation, know-ing what they were about to see would be good.

Hundreds of people gathered in the school auditorium—students who had been in Gritty's last class, former students of all ages, teachers, administrators, parents, members of AA, friends, her brother and sister-in-law in the front row. People walked slowly in single file down the left aisle and then across the front, looking at scores of pictures of Gritty artfully arranged on the stage. There was Gritty laughing, with different classes of students, as a little girl, as a teenager, as a young bride, with friends, hiking in the mountains, cross country skiing, jogging, with little Sylvia and her Head Start students, with her parents and brother. As they reviewed Gritty's life in all its complexity, people smiled, laughed, grinned, sniffled, cried, nudged each other, shared memories. They added their own mementos to the already burgeoning collection and soon the stage was filled with symbols of the footprints Gritty had left on so many people's lives.

At the far right of the stage was a large picture of Gritty with no hair, a huge serene smile filling her face. Next to it were a framed copy of the serenity prayer, the big book of Alcoholics Anonymous opened to page 449 and her favorite excerpts about acceptance, and a pottery bowl in which twenty-eight AA chips rested, one for each year of her sobriety.

Gritty wept as she watched people go up to the podium. One after another they talked, their words like musical chimes ringing the whole truth of her life in gentle beautiful harmony: "She taught me to have faith in myself," "If it weren't for her I wouldn't be sober today," "She faced her cancer like she faced life—with passion, curiosity, anger, humor, and finally acceptance," "Ooohhh, you should have seen her when she was angry!," "I couldn't stand here and tell you honestly that I thought she was a great woman or a good woman or a bad woman or a great teacher or a decent person or anything else although she was certainly all of those things—what I can say is that she was a human being, a complex and rich human being who did her best and finally understood that her best was enough," "She was the best sponsor I ever had!" "Her faith was a mystery to me but so what? It was a mystery to her, too!"

"Enough!" cried Gritty with a full, boisterous laugh, "I get it! Honestly, I get it! Enough!"

Sky and Spring laughed with her as they floated away from the auditorium and landed back in the library.

Suma then congratulated Gritty.

"You accomplished much," she said, "You overcame guilt. You diligently dug under surface appearances and rejected the hypocrisy hidden there. You sought and embraced the truth. You took risks that caused you to stumble and fall yet picked yourself up again and again. You moved from troubling questions about good and bad to a much more profound awareness of yourself and others—to an intense spiritual consciousness that defied explanation and surpassed religion."

Gritty grinned and jokingly summed it up in the simplest of terms, "I learned how to be right-sized and faith found me!"

Yet she knew her path had not been as easy as that sounded. It had been damn hard—and slow. Life had asked much of her—nothing less than total transformation. Her faith had not come smoothly. She had resisted, defied, questioned, probed, and scorned—until finally she had no alternative left but surrender. Her spiritual journey was not a sprint; it was a long, laborious and awkward marathon—often through dry deserts, deep waters and seemingly impassable mountains. She had taken the excruciatingly painful, sometimes tortuous and seemingly endless journey in the only way she could—one step at a time, one day at a time. It had taken a lifetime for her to re-birth the self she was created to be.

*   *   *   *

Spring was now the last one standing. Since once again she stayed on Earth the longest, she had more stories to tell. She moved to her place at the library table and opened her book, primed to pick up the strands of her last story. Sky and Gritty remembered she was at a critical time in her life—the moment when she knew she had to leave her position at the Women's International Development Institute. Intensely curious about her next venture, they moved in close, like kindergarten children excitedly crowding their teacher at story time, and looked eagerly at the emerging scene.

Back in her Earth life, Spring sat on the living room floor surrounded by boxes, carefully inspecting their contents. The box labeled "Kitchen" contained everything she thought she would need—one medium sized pot, a frying pan, a large serrated knife, one small paring knife, a few essential utensils, and enough silverware and dishes for four. Other than tablecloths, placemats, blankets, pillows and two sets of sheets and towels in the box marked "Linens" the other boxes contained only clothes. When she was satisfied that she hadn't forgotten anything, she taped the boxes shut and wrote her new address boldly on the top of each with a black magic marker. The next day she would ship the boxes to Washington, D.C., where she would live for a year. She would put all her other belongings, including her car, in storage.

Spring marveled at how things had worked out. After she quit her job a plan unfolded with amazing ease—as if preordained. She would work part-time on an international human rights project on Capital Hill and do some university teaching. It would be a good break. She was still outraged about what happened at the Women's Institute. The universe had plopped an enormous lesson in her lap without warning and she needed time to take it in.

Spring looked up from the scene, remembering how she boarded NWA Flight 373 for Washington, D.C. a week later. The path before her was but a shadow, daunting in its dimness. If she had known that day all that awaited her on the East Coast, it would have been too overwhelming to contemplate and surely she would not have gone.

"I arrived at Washington National Airport," she told Sky and Gritty, "blissfully ignorant about the adventures to come. Navigating through the rush hour chaos with my knapsack and sleeping bag, I made my way to the Metro station, getting off at the Farragut North stop. I walked in the direction of the affordable efficiency apartment I found during my last business trip to the district. It was in an enormous square building that consumed an entire city block, adjacent to one of the city's circles sporting a General on horseback, someone I'd never heard of. A group of men standing in front of the building smoking cigarettes, drinking beer, and speaking a language I couldn't decipher didn't seem to notice me as I walked through the automatic double doors. I checked in at the reception desk to pick up the keys to my apartment.

"When I stepped off the elevator on the second floor my senses were assaulted by the clanging sounds of dinner being prepared behind closed doors and deliciously rich smells of Indian, Afghani, Mexican, and Salvadoran cooking. My new neighbors, I thought."

Spring remembered opening the door to her apartment and her surprise at how large the one room looked. Its walls were freshly painted in gleaming white. The polished linoleum floor glistened as the setting sun's rays streamed through a large picture window. Along one wall was a compact kitchen with a sink, stove, refrigerator, and cupboards hidden behind a folding door. One wall of the hall off to the side held the apartment's one large closet. At the end of the hall was a huge bathroom with an old claw foot tub.

"That first night," she continued, "I slept on the floor in my sleeping bag, the eerie emptiness of my new home matching my creeping loneliness. Car horns and squealing brakes formed a continuous cacophony of unpleasantness outside my window. Inside, the building was a beehive abuzz with the sounds of hundreds of people coming and going at all hours, babies crying, people yelling, Johnny Carson on television. Later I learned—with a kind of perverse pleasure—that several apartments in the building housed a robust prostitution business, accounting for some of the rowdy nocturnal activity.

"The next morning I selected some furniture at a rental store and it was delivered that afternoon. I arranged the beige hide-a-bed couch and matching chair along with a coffee table, two end tables and lamps on an attractive area rug splashed with shades of brown and gold. I placed the round dining room table with four chairs in the kitchen area and a desk and chair along the opposite wall. Instead of curtains on the window I lowered the old Venetian blinds as needed for privacy—but mostly I welcomed the light from the sun in the day and from the moon and stars at night. I decided to buy some framed posters for the walls.

"The next day UPS delivered my six boxes. It didn't take long to unpack. After carefully putting everything in its designated place I gazed admiringly at my new nest, reveling in its simplicity. During the day, the comfortably inviting living room/dining room/kitchen easily accommodated three to four guests. In the evening, the room was transformed into a large yet cozy bedroom with moonlight drifting lazily over my bed."

Spring opened her storybook to a series of new Earth scenes that revealed the rhythm of her new life that summer in Washington, D.C.: there was Spring running weekly errands, pulling a cart filled with groceries and a bouquet of flowers—stopping at her favorite coffee shop in DuPont Circle on her way home and later placing the flowers lovingly on her dining room table—jogging her regular thirty minute trek to the White House and back each morning—buying a *Washington Post* from the machine outside her apartment building—walking leisurely down Embassy Row on Massachusetts Avenue Northwest—going to a different Smithsonian Museum each week—riding the Metro just for the fun of it.

"Life was delicious," Spring broke in with a grin, "each day my senses filled with the sights, smells, and tastes of independence, freedom and possibility. At first it was a bit lonely but it wasn't long before I made friends with transients like me who planned to be in Washington for a short time. When fall came I took the bus three afternoons a week to Capital Hill to coordinate the human rights project. One night a week I taught a nonprofit management course at a nearby university. The days and weeks flew by and soon my year was up, but my spirit of adventure was not. I made plans to stay another year and settled a little deeper into my new life."

Spring then turned to a new page in her storybook. Sky and Gritty were surprised at the feelings of anxious anticipation that engulfed them. Instinctively knowing another momentous change was imminent, they gathered close and watched as a new scene sprang from the page.

Spring strolled through the DuPont Circle neighborhood with no particular destination in mind. Enjoying the briskness of fall in the city was enough. When she came to the gay and lesbian bookstore on Connecticut Avenue she looked longingly at the brightly colored rainbow flags displayed in the window. She had walked by the store many times but never dared to go in.

This time a powerful urge wrestled her fear to unconsciousness. Something beyond her control propelled her through the door. Suddenly she was inside the brightly lit bookstore filled with thousands of books, videotapes, gifts, magazines, and greeting cards—all for or about gay, lesbian, bisexual and transgender people.

Spring felt nervous. She had entered forbidden territory. What if someone she knew saw her there? Glancing furtively over her shoulder, she took cover behind a stack of books and tried to absorb the enormity of finding herself in such a startling new world.

A middle-aged woman with short grey hair smiled at her. She seemed to be flirting. Spring quickly looked down, excited and terrified at the same time. She walked away.

At the back of the store, notices were tacked up on a large community bulletin board. One of them was about a support group called "Coming into a lesbian identity." Spring secretively slipped one of the phone numbers attached to the notice into her pocket.

She nervously headed toward the exit, pretending to look at books on the way. On her way out of the store she picked up a copy of *The Washington Blade,* the gay and lesbian newspaper, tucking it discretely under her arm. She anxiously looked both ways as she stepped onto the sidewalk, moving quickly away before anyone could recognize her.

Spring hurried home, fleeing to the safety of her little apartment where she collapsed on the couch. Her nerve-wracking foray into the bookstore left her feeling vulnerable and exposed but also keyed up with excitement.

She pulled the little piece of paper out of her pocket and laid it on the table. Finally garnering the courage to call about the support group, she dialed the phone number. A friendly woman named Cindy answered. The first meeting of the group was next Sunday and six women were signed up so far. Cindy told Spring she would be most welcome and gave her detailed directions to her house.

A week passed and then it was Sunday. Apprehensive yet determined, Spring rode the Metro for forty minutes, then caught a taxicab for the final leg to Cindy's condo, discouraged by the idea of making such a long trip every week.

At Cindy's doorstep, she pulled her scarf tightly around her neck as protection from the cold biting wind, then nervously rang the doorbell. Cindy swung the door open and greeted Spring warmly, ushering her into the living room. She was the last to arrive and was met by the welcoming voices of the other women who were already gathered in a circle, drinking coffee and tea.

Spring joined the circle and Cindy opened the meeting by asking each woman to introduce herself. Maureen was the first to speak. A woman in her thirties, with strawberry red hair and a vibrant smile, her enthusiasm belied a desperate need to be liked. She had been married for fifteen years to a man with who she was still deeply in love. She was exuberant about discovering she was a lesbian and her husband was happy for her too.

Spring was impressed with how Maureen seemed to be making the transition from married woman to divorcee to lesbian with such ease. She suspected there was more to her story than Maureen was letting on.

Sandy was the next to speak. She was in her fifties and had an overall dull gray appearance, from her mousy hair to her ashen skin and drab loosely fitting clothes. She shared a very different story from Maureen's. Her husband had come out as gay, as had one of her two adult children. Soon after coming out, her husband moved in with a man he'd been having an affair with and cruelly cut off all contact with her. Sandy felt no sexual desire but was beginning to feel attracted to women and wondered if she too was gay.

Spring sensed the depth of Sandy's depression and apprehension and wondered how the group would manage the contrast between that and Maureen's over the top enthusiasm.

Other stories revealed the diverse experiences of the women in the group. A young blond woman had lost custody of her two-year-old child after she told her ex-husband that she might be a lesbian. A middle-aged woman was in a same-sex relationship for the first time. An older woman had never before told anyone that she was a lesbian.

As the stories unfolded, Spring focused on what she would feel safe revealing about herself. When it was her turn, she decided to make her introduction brief.

"Well," she began, "I always considered myself hopelessly heterosexual and just thought I was sexually frigid. Then, last year I became super attracted to my attorney, a woman. It was an incredibly powerful feeling, one that I have never had before in my life. When I realized that it was not safe for me to explore my sexuality while working at the job I had at the time—I can tell you *that* story later—I decided to take a break and come to Washington for a year where I might feel free to explore and find out what this was all about.

"Last week," she continued, "I worked up the courage to go into the gay and lesbian bookstore in DuPont circle and just about freaked. That's when I saw the notice about this group. I think it will really help to be with others who are going through similar experiences and I am glad to be here."

The women seemed more comfortable with each other after the introductions. Cindy then noted that she had heard anxiety in their stories—with the notable exception of Maureen, of course. She suggested that some of their apprehension might come from their perceptions of gay people and asked them to share what they had heard about lesbians. Cindy wrote what was said on a large piece of newsprint with a black magic marker. Soon the page was filled with images: Black leather jackets. Short, spiky hair. Dykes who look and act like men. Chains. Topless. Motorcycles. Mean-looking. Ugly. Fat. No makeup. Drive pick-up trucks. Man-haters. Ball breakers.

Spring was appalled by the preponderance of negative images that they seemed to have collectively internalized. Yet she was worried. She had seen women in the bookstore and other places that fit some of those images.

With determination in her shaking voice, Spring said, "I know these are stereotypes but I'm still worried that there might be expectations in the lesbian community about how you should act, what you should look like, what you should wear."

"Well," she then announced, "I am too old to conform to someone else's perceptions of who I should be. I simply won't do it any more. If I turn out to be a lesbian, I will be a lesbian in my own way!"

Spring saw herself as a little girl in a spotless white ruffled dress, the ultimate in femininity—pretty, demure, docile, sweet, charming. She wasn't that little girl anymore and she damn well wasn't going to be defined by anyone again. No one would be the author of her life but her! She wondered where this wonderful spunkiness came from.

Soon the meeting ended and Maureen offered Spring a ride home. She said she'd like her to see her new apartment in Crystal City on the way. Spring agreed but wondered if Maureen was interested in her and how she would respond if that were the case. She was not attracted to her at all; in fact she was a little put-off by Maureen's neediness and hyperactive non-stop talking.

Maureen's apartment was on the twenty-first floor of a tall white building. It was a small L-shaped efficiency cluttered with books, papers, and boxes. Maureen walked over to the two large picture windows and excitedly pointed out the lights of the city.

"Isn't it just amazing," she exclaimed, "what we are discovering about ourselves? Isn't it *too* wonderful that we each have our own space and the support group to help!!"

Maureen then spontaneously reached out for Spring and hugged her.

For some reason Spring's apprehension dissolved as she fell into the embrace. She hoped that she and Maureen would become friends.

Weeks went by. Every Sunday, Maureen pulled into the circular drive in front of Spring's apartment building to pick her up for the support group. Together they started going to other lesbian gatherings where they twittered and giggled about potential romance like thirteen-year-old pubescent girls.

One night they went to an event about the dynamics of lesbian dating. After a lecture, they were divided into small groups to discuss the question, "How do you know if you're on a date?" A woman named Jody facilitated Spring's group.

Fifteen years her senior, Jody was short and stocky with dyed black hair and big glasses framing her round face. She reminded Spring of her high school gym teacher, Miss Kelly, who ran class like a military training camp and entertained them by flexing her huge arm muscles.

The women in Jody's group told funny stories about how confusing lesbian dating could be. Spring was fascinated to hear about how difficult it was sometimes for a woman to know whether she was just having dinner with a friend or if she was on a date. She'd always gone out to dinner with women friends and it was never an issue before. Things were different now.

Suddenly Jody looked over at Spring as if she had just discovered her presence and said, "Well, we haven't heard from you yet. How do *you* know when you're on a date?"

"I am so new at all of this that I don't have a clue," Spring answered, "I'm just here to listen."

Jody was drawn toward Spring like a powerful magnet. With a suggestive half grin that oozed seduction she asked, "How new *are* you?"

Feeling both uncomfortable and excited Spring looked down at the floor and mumbled something about how she guessed that she was about as new as you could be.

When the discussion ended everyone dispersed to socialize over refreshments. All of a sudden, Jody was by Spring's side, full of questions and earnestly interested in everything she said.

When it was time for Spring to meet Maureen and go home, Jody quickly asked, "Would you go out to dinner with me? And just so I am clear—I *am* asking you out on a date."

Like a teenage girl who had just been asked to the prom, Spring's insides jumped up and down, screaming silently with nervous excitement. She and Jody agreed to meet at a restaurant for dinner the next week. When she told Maureen she had a date, the two of them squealed like teenagers.

The week passed and then it was time for Spring's first date with a woman. When she arrived at the restaurant, Jody was already there and had ordered dinner for both of them. She had even told the waiter she would be paying the check. It was clear that she was taking charge.

They engaged in conversation aimed at getting to know each other. Spring talked about her peace activism and the human rights project she was coordinating. Jody responded that she was retired from the Marine Corps and that Hitler would have destroyed the world if everyone had been a Pacifist. Spring talked about how much she valued her freedom and independence. Jody countered that independence was overrated and talked about her last relationship, how she took such good care of her partner, even writing term papers for her while she was in school.

Looking up from the scene, Spring readjusted to being back in the library. She saw that Sky and Gritty were trying not to laugh as they too turned away from the storybook scene in the restaurant. Spring shrugged and smiled at them. Admittedly, she had allowed herself to be taken in.

"Of course I ignored those red flags," she acknowledged, "even though they fluttered frantically in my gut and the rational voice inside me screamed in warning. My teenage sexuality completely subdued all middle-aged prudence and the strength of my physical attraction to Jody rendered me helpless to resist. Three weeks later it was over. The essence of our brief encounter was simple. Jody was a controlling woman who loved to introduce new lesbians to sex and I was desperately curious about what it was like to have sex with a woman.

"Once my curiosity was satisfied, I broke off the relationship, not realizing that Jody took hostages. Freeing myself from her clutches was not easy. I stopped answering the constantly ringing phone and the frantic knocks on my door. I ignored the short stocky figure lingering in the park across the street as Jody looked up at my apartment window, hoping for a glimpse of what she had lost. When I went on vacation for three weeks over the Christmas holidays without leaving a trace of where I had gone or for how long, she finally gave up."

Spring thought about what she had discovered about herself through her brief relationship with Jody. Though she shied away from any more sexual relationships for a while after that, she knew she had turned a corner on her journey. She set about to learn about gay culture and in the process met many interesting men and women. The richness of their talents and experiences was awesome. She discovered gay people everywhere in every imaginable role: filmmaker, civil rights lawyer, professor, congressional aide, human rights advocate, successful writer, poet, minister, lobbyist. She became lifelong friends with several of them.

"I learned so much," Spring told Sky and Gritty, "about courage, compassion, and humor from my new friends. I learned about love when I saw how it overcame major differences between David, a hospital administrator and proper New Englander, and his partner Roy, a construction worker and authentic small town Texan with a southern drawl so thick it was like hearing a foreign language. I learned the power of humor from Sandy and Rachel when Sandy, wearing a tuxedo, danced down the aisle to Pink Panther music at their wedding, followed by Rachel who walked demurely to traditional Here Comes the Bride music wearing her grandmother's wedding gown. I learned about acceptance from Dennis who always said, 'If people could do better they would.' I learned about living in the present from David, who bought himself a brand new convertible in his last days before succumbing to AIDS. I learned that opening your heart to someone is more important than protecting yourself from possible disappointment from Maggie, a therapist I dated briefly.

"And," Spring concluded with a flair, "I learned how to howl at the moon with my women's spirituality group."

"I wonder," Sky said jokingly, "how many of those people were recruited by Suma to teach you those lessons."

Spring shrugged. Somehow she hadn't thought of Suma's surprises as positive ones. Perhaps Sky was right. Maybe Suma's hands were all over her simple joys as well as her hurts and growing pains but she preferred to ignore that possibility. At the moment, other thoughts absorbed her attention.

She was thinking about how exciting it was to be immersed in the gay and lesbian community but also how troubling it was. She lived in two different and incompatible worlds—her personal life and her professional life. She didn't feel safe revealing her emerging sexual orientation at work. All she had to do was remember what happened at the Women's Institute and any ideas she might have about coming out were quickly squelched. More and more she felt like she was living a lie. She didn't want to end up like the older woman in her support group who had never told anyone she was a lesbian.

Then she remembered how help had come from an unexpected place and as she filled Sky and Gritty in about her double life she turned to a page in her storybook. Together they watched a new Earth scene unfold.

Spring and one of her colleagues were on their way to a meeting. Sarah, who was driving, had worked in the field of human rights for decades. She was an elegant brown-skinned woman with a brilliant mind and a heart of gold. Spring liked and admired Sarah and was glad to have some time to get to know her better. They talked about work and other things and then the conversation turned to their mothers.

"My mother," Sarah confided, "is getting too old to live alone. I want her to come and live with me but I am not sure she will. She doesn't approve of my lifestyle."

"What doesn't she approve of?" Spring asked innocently.

"She doesn't like the idea of my having a housemate," Sarah replied.

Spring was confused. She wondered what the problem was with having a housemate.

"Why doesn't your mother like your roommate?" she asked with curious naiveté.

With a tone of amusement revealing a slight frustration that her carefully disguised code word had not registered with Spring, Sarah looked directly at her and said, "I'm a lesbian. I want you to know because I would like us to be friends."

Spring flew back in the seat in surprise. She hadn't had a clue!

"No shit!" she blurted out, "So am I!"

Sarah was so shocked she almost drove off the road and Spring had to grab the steering wheel. First they looked at each other with amazement. Then they burst out laughing and hungrily told each other their stories—about how they knew, when they knew, who else knew, what life was like, how they felt, who accepted them and who didn't.

That night Sarah called Spring and handed the phone to her partner, Jane, who wanted to meet her and talk about what had happened in the car that day.

Jane's voice sounded excited yet a bit suspicious when she said, "It's nice to meet you. When Sarah told me what happened, I asked her if it was a sting. When she said it was for real, I couldn't believe it!"

They both laughed but it was bittersweet.

Jane's initial suspicion that Sarah might have fallen into a trap aimed at exposing her as a lesbian hit Spring hard. As she thought about how lonely life was for people who were secretly gay and lesbian, she felt the depth of her own loneliness. She was grateful to find an island of safety with Sarah. When she was with her, she felt her two separate lives move a little closer together and overlap at a precious spot.

"Sarah and I," Spring interjected as she turned the page and the Earth scene vanished, "developed a deep and lasting friendship. Through Sarah and Jane I discovered an invisible lesbian community. I knew that gay and lesbian people were everywhere and represented all segments of society, but I didn't have a clue about the vibrant secret communities they created."

Spring then took a deep breath and rested. She thought about what a journey her coming out process had been. At first she was troubled when people asked her things like if she was married or if her husband was coming to the holiday party. Years later she comfortably answered such questions by saying she was married to a woman or that her wife was coming to the party. She was even amused when people would awkwardly respond with statements like, "I'm so sorry, I didn't know!" or "Oh, well, that's okay with me." After living for many years with her own discomfort and ignorance, she figured she surely could allow other people theirs.

Just then Suma appeared in the library with a flourish, surprising Spring from her reverie.

"Your road in life was difficult," Suma said, "not only because of your shame script but also because of the sexual stigma that being gay carried in society, particularly during that period in Earth history."

"My sexual orientation," Spring explained, "was an important teacher. It immersed me in a reality that required me to confront the injustice of that time head-on."

Spring then thought about how she had found so much more than experiences of oppression and discrimination as a lesbian: she had come to know empowerment, resilience, and strength.

"Yes," Suma said, reading Spring's thoughts, "and that led to something more. Your sexual journey was a form of emancipation that helped to free you from your shame as well."

Suddenly Spring began to make new connections, to see the contradictions that had been there all along. The illusion she had carried all her life was that she was unacceptable and she had worn her mask of shame for so long that she had come to believe that was who she really was. Opening to the possibility that she was a lesbian—a *source* of shame in the eyes of her family, church, and much of society—seemed only to reinforce her unacceptability. But, in reality, facing her sexual orientation did just the opposite. Instead of dishonor and humiliation she found strength and beauty. In the process she got unstuck from her shame mask and took a giant step forward toward liberation from her dark illusions of herself.

"In midlife," Suma added, "your false self wrestled with your true self through your sexual exploration. Your true self won that round."

Spring remembered how she had worried that her sexual journey could bring her down professionally. Now she saw it had been about much more than losing a job or a career. When she pitted her star status against her true self, the ultimate risk was exposing the inner shame she had so carefully hidden under a long list of shining accomplishments. In the end she had chosen who she was over what she did.

Spring then understood that her sexual orientation had been a spiritual gift. She looked up in gratitude to thank Suma but found only a whisper of her energy remaining in the library space.

*   *   *   *

There was one more story about her sexual journey that Spring was eager to tell. Sky and Gritty were enthusiastic, anticipating another transformative experience. As a new scene emerged from the page Spring felt her heart melting with a longing so compelling that—for the first time—she wished to be back on Earth.

It was nine o'clock on a Saturday morning. Spring and Maureen walked into a city high school to attend a conference for older wiser lesbians—known as OWL. They sat in the balcony of the grungy auditorium, feeling slightly awkward and out of place as they looked down at a rainbow sea of faces with well-worn wrinkles. Hundreds of bright smiles illuminated the dark room as women embraced old friends and greeted new ones.

The opening session of the conference began with the usual uninteresting introductions and words of thanks followed by an opening speech. The speaker was a longtime gay rights activist, a diminutive elderly woman with pure white hair and a shockingly deep and strong voice that belied her frail appearance. Her brilliance and enthusiasm brought the women to their feet and soon the auditorium vibrated with the music of stomping, clapping and cheering.

Inspired, Spring looked forward to the rest of the conference as she made her way from the opening session to a workshop she had selected from the schedule. She sat down at one of the battered desks arranged in a circle in the dreary classroom and smiled at a woman sitting directly across from her. When the woman looked away, Spring wondered if she was shy.

The workshop was about Lesbians and Peace. Even though the subject deeply interested her, Spring was preoccupied with the woman across the circle. Drawn to her like a moth to a flame she looked at her long and hard, trying to understand the power that pulled at her. The woman was in her late thirties or early forties with shoulder length light brown hair and a smile that lit up the room. She was dressed modestly in a rust-colored L.L. Bean jacket and loose-fitting blue jeans.

When the woman noticed that Spring was staring at her, their eyes locked and Spring looked into the bluest eyes she had ever seen, eyes that captivated her and wouldn't let go. She tried to look away but was unable to tear herself from their powerful spell. She *had* to meet this woman.

A few minutes before the workshop ended, the woman stood up, quietly left the room and disappeared into the hall. Spring panicked, thought of running after her, decided against it, then realized it was too late. She worried she had missed her chance, that she would never see her again.

When Spring met Maureen for lunch all she could talk about was the woman with the sky blue eyes and beautiful smile. Maureen, ever the optimist, declared with utter certainty, "You will find her this afternoon and get her phone number!"

Spring wasn't so sure.

After lunch they went back to the auditorium. Spring didn't hear anything the speaker said. Completely absorbed in her assiduous search, she scoured the audience with a sense of urgency that was beyond her control. Consumed with fear that she wouldn't find the woman again, she told herself to calm down. As the speaker concluded, she finally gave up, thinking it probably was just not meant to be.

Soon several hundred women surged toward the exit, heading toward afternoon workshops. Spring walked toward the door with heavy disappointment, hardly noticing the crowd pushing against her on all sides.

Just then, as if compelled by a strange force of nature, Spring turned around and there the woman was, right behind her. Spring's face lit up as she looked directly into those gorgeous blue eyes and in a spontaneous voice that didn't sound like her own, proclaimed, "Oh! *There* you are! I have been looking for you!"

The woman nodded knowingly and in a voice as calm as the sea said, "I've been looking for you, too."

Time stopped. It seemed that they were the only two people in the room.

"At that moment," Spring interjected as she looked up from the scene, "I was certain I had known her before. We walked out of the auditorium together and introduced ourselves. Becca lived an hour and a half away in rural Virginia and was a single mom with a young daughter. She was afraid to drive in the city and had come to the conference with a friend. I silently kicked myself for leaving my car in storage. I suggested that each of us could take the train and meet somewhere for coffee. Becca seemed to think the idea was ludicrous, something that occurred to me as well—but not until much later. A wall of caution began to rise within me. There were too many obstacles to getting together and I was too old to get involved with someone with a child. We exchanged phone numbers anyway and said goodbye. Becca headed toward an afternoon workshop and I headed toward a different one in the opposite direction. I decided I wouldn't call her. It was all too complicated."

Sky and Gritty looked at her sadly. With no further explanation, Spring re-opened her storybook and directed their attention to the Earth scene that popped off the page.

Spring walked slowly down the hall, feeling let down, certain she would never see Becca again. She went to the workshop she had selected but a sign on the door said it had been cancelled. Another damn disappointment, she thought. She pulled out the schedule, found another workshop that sounded interesting, and half-heartedly headed in its direction.

When she arrived, she saw that the room was packed and the workshop had already started. Bent over and trying to be inconspicuous, Spring found her way to the only remaining seat in the back and quietly placed her coat and notebook on the floor, then unfolded her body and sat down.

There was Becca, sitting right next to her, a warm mischievous smile revealing her surprise and pleasure. Spring's heart soared. Maybe this was meant to be after all.

Just before the session ended, Becca quietly left the room and disappeared. Once again Spring's heart collapsed in disappointment.

The conference ended and Spring went home. That evening the phone rang. It was Becca, calling long distance. With a mysterious comfortableness and the familiarity of old friends they talked for two hours. Then Becca invited Spring for dinner and a movie at her house with some other women in two weeks. Spring immediately accepted and asked if she could bring a friend, hoping that Maureen would drive. Spring and Becca talked on the phone every night after that.

Two weeks passed and it was time to go to Becca's house. As Maureen drove her little white Honda along the winding country roads, Spring's already high expectations inflated with each mile until she was about ready to explode.

The winding driveway up to Becca's house, flanked by lush raspberry and blackberry bushes, opened to a rambling white house topped with skylights and solar panels. A huge garden in the back lay dormant after the long winter, bordered by a grove of apple trees just beginning to come alive with the promise of spring. Nervously knocking on the back door, Spring heard the sound of laughter inside. Becca opened the door with a radiant smile and tender hug for her, then a warm welcome for Maureen. The kitchen was bustling with women preparing food.

Spring looked around and immediately felt the warmth of the house enfold her with something familiar. The evening passed pleasantly enough, but no matter how interesting and enjoyable it was, for Spring it was merely background noise. Becca was foreground.

Spring's heightened senses magnified everything to a place of electrifying significance. When Becca asked her to carry the burning sage during a ritual to bless her garden, she took it as a sign of having a special place in her heart. When Becca commented about the full moon and suggested she go outside to see it, Spring imagined them turning toward each other for a hungry long-awaited kiss as they gazed at its beauty together. When Becca invited Spring and Maureen to spend the night to avoid driving home in the dark, she took it as an invitation to her bed. When she said her daughter was spending the weekend with her father, Spring heard it as confirmation of Becca's desire to be alone with her.

By the end of the evening Spring was practically jumping out of her skin in anticipation of her fantasies being realized. She could hardly wait for the other women to leave but it was almost midnight before they finally said good night and dispersed into the cool evening air. With a wink and a nod Maureen considerately went to bed in the guest room. Spring and Becca did the dishes together and then Becca suggested that she sleep in her daughter's bedroom so she wouldn't waken Maureen. With a broken heart, Spring said goodnight. She lay awake most of the night, wallowing in pain and disappointment until it turned to anger.

The next morning, she dragged herself out of bed. She and Maureen planned to spend the day in Alexandria before going home. She would keep her promise to go but at that moment she just wanted to curl up and escape into an invisible ball. All night she wondered how she could have been so wrong about Becca. She still didn't have an answer.

When Spring reluctantly emerged from the bedroom, Becca was sitting at the dining room table. She offered her a cup of coffee. Spring was surprised at how comfortable it felt to sit together in silence. She hoped Maureen would sleep awhile longer.

"I can't stand this any more," Gritty exclaimed, tugging at Spring and Sky so they would look away from the scene in Becca's house. "The tension between the two of you is almost unbearable. Why was she so elusive? Just tell us what happened! Please!"

Spring smiled. The tension had felt unbearable at the time to her too. She understood Gritty's desire to get it over with and know what happened.

"That morning as we talked," she responded, "Becca and I felt a deep spiritual connection and something shifted in both of us. When we hugged goodbye, there was a radiant warmth and love in our embrace that was familiar, like an old bond. I was again certain I had known Becca before. Naturally, my Earth self

soon forgot and when she invited me to a concert on Saturday I found myself
back in the human mating dance with all its tension and intrigue.

"Becca and I went to the concert the next week. Suede was the first lesbian
singer I had ever heard. Every rich tone and suggestive word that flowed from her
sensuous lips breathed the fire of my own budding sexuality. Its flames exploded
through my body and headed straight for my heart whenever Becca's arm or hand
lightly brushed mine either by accident or design. We found excuses to whisper
in each other's ears. I ached to reach out for her hand but was immobilized by
fear of possible rejection."

Spring remembered how that evening was like a roller coaster ride—excitement and exhilaration one minute followed by slow uphill anticipation of a steep
fall the next. One minute she was desperately attracted to Becca and convinced
the feeling was mutual; the next minute she didn't know if they were on a date or
if they were just new friends going to a concert together. One minute she felt
Becca's desire, the next minute she sensed her ambivalence.

"The concert ended," she continued, "and when we said goodnight Becca
pulled me into the warmest longest embrace I have ever experienced. It was then
that I knew I was home. Like an angel floating on air, I drove back to Washington in the little car I had rented, the hour and a half drive seeming like only five
minutes. When I opened my apartment door the phone was ringing. I picked up
the receiver and said, "Hi Becca," before hearing her voice, so certain I was that it
was she.

"In spite of her insistence that she would never drive in the city, Becca came to
visit the next weekend. With a big smile and outstretched arms she arrived with
the announcement that she was in love with me. We kissed for the first time—a
long, passionate kiss.

"But my humanness quickly took over. Confounded by what I had perceived
as Becca's mixed messages of *come here* and *go away*, I felt cautious and self-protective. So I replied that I liked her a lot but I thought it was too soon to know
whether this was love. With a tone of unmistakable certainty and slight amusement in her voice, Becca again declared her love and said she had decided to follow her bliss."

Spring smiled as she remembered how Becca came to Washington every weekend after that to follow her bliss. She waited patiently for her love to be recipro-
cated while Spring cautiously guarded her heart, watching for any signs of
rejection that might threaten to break it. One day, Spring's love unexpectedly
bubbled out in words, surprising both of them. Red-faced with embarrassment
and wishing she could grab the words from the air and stuff them back into her

mouth, she announced that she didn't want to talk about it. Becca just quietly smiled. At that moment Spring knew she couldn't leave her. Not long after that she decided to stay in Washington and work toward her PhD degree.

In Becca's arms, Spring's body and soul came together in a full blossoming of her sensuality and sexual energy. Her skin tingled with each gentle caress. Her body cried out for release and when it came she soared so high she almost stopped breathing. Never before had she experienced such precious moments of wholeness when heart and mind, soul and body, spirituality and sexuality came together as one.

Spring smiled, then turned to Sky and Gritty as she continued, "We spent every weekend together for months and eventually we had to tell our families about our relationship. Becca's mother was the first. After Becca brought me to her house for Thanksgiving dinner, her mother called the next day to talk with both of us. She had figured us out by herself. She welcomed me into the family, saying that she wanted Becca to be happy and she could see that she was very happy with me. Then she said how relieved she was that I had worn a beautiful dress to her house, that she had worried that I would be wearing leather and chains. I laughed. I always wished that I had responded by saying I never wore my black leather outfit with chains on holidays.

"Becca told her daughter next. Cindy was eleven years old and adorably precocious. I was very fond of her. When Becca told her that she was in love with me, her pre-adolescent response was, 'tell me something I don't already know!' followed by her childlike response, 'She's *my* friend too, you know, not just yours!'

"I was afraid to tell my family for a long time. Finally I wrote a letter about finding the love of my life. I told them it had taken me a long time to understand and accept my sexual orientation and I expected they would need time to adjust to the idea as well. I promised I would be patient. Then I braced myself for rejection."

Spring knew that when she told her family the truth about who she was, she plunged them into a journey they didn't want and for which they weren't prepared, one that pitted Church teaching against their love for her. The struggle was long and hard and they alternately ignored, denied, disputed, and prayed over it as they searched their souls. For years they valiantly walked the painful journey that had been thrust upon them until they got to the other side of their fundamentalist religious beliefs and to the core of their love for Spring. Through it all they had steadfastly refused to reject her.

Then Spring thought about the newness of her love for Becca. Even though they no longer kept their relationship from their families, it was still complicated to navigate in a society where many feared and abhorred their love. She had to learn when it was safe to hold hands and show affection and when to be careful, when to be open about their relationship and when to keep it a secret. Sometimes she and Becca disagreed and fought about it.

Spring now knew that when she first looked into Becca's eyes, their souls had touched. At that moment she unconsciously knew they had been together many times before in different roles, in other Earth lives—that was the power she felt. Little by little the reasons for their reunion were revealed. They were to learn from each other, help each other grow.

It wasn't easy but they had waited until they were ready to face the many challenges that pushed each of them toward the light of who she was meant to be. Spring had trouble asking for and receiving help while Becca needed to be helpful. They both needed to fix things, including each other, but their motivations were different: Spring feared anger and conflict while Becca feared not being useful. Spring wanted to do everything herself and refused to be rescued while Becca was a rescuer. Both of them were fully competent and self-sufficient, but Spring could be a martyr about it while Becca felt her life would fall apart if she wasn't. Spring needed to toughen up while Becca needed to soften her rough edges. Spring needed to express her feelings while Becca needed to think before releasing hers. Neither of them had learned how to be spontaneous and exuberant as children. Together they would learn to come out and play.

Spring's memories brought her back to the quiet of a morning long ago when she saw two birds outside the window. At first she wondered why they were fighting and then realized it was spring and they were mating. That was how she often experienced her relationship with Becca. To get to each hard-won lesson, they rocked the boat a lot—something Spring had feared all her life—and to their amazement it rarely tipped over. On the few occasions when it did, they braved the wake and righted it together. The deepening of their love reminded Spring of some trees she saw once.

"One morning," she said to Sky and Gritty, "I went for a walk in the misty rain. I was thinking about how my love for Becca had deepened over the years and probably wasn't paying attention to my feet. On a steep slippery incline, I slipped and fell. I wiped the mud from my hands and then my jacket and jeans, checked my arthritic hip to be sure it wasn't broken, and pulled myself up with the help of my walking stick. As I stood I saw some trees that stopped me cold.

"I didn't know what kind of trees they were. I'd seen them before but now it was like seeing them for the first time. The one directly in front of me was covered with a dark brown, almost black, bark but part of its thick protective outer shell had peeled away to reveal another layer underneath in a rich deep red. In some places the red layer of protection had also peeled away, exposing a smooth surface in beautiful bright ochre. Another tree, free of both the dark brown and deep red layers of protection, was completely smooth and radiant like a rose.

"I thought about how my love for Becca had been like those trees. Our relationship kept peeling away my thick dark protective cover, exposing the blood red of my pain and reaching for the smooth bright ochre of my soul. After years of rocking the boat and exposing our hurts to each other, our relationship smoothed and deepened into a brilliant deep rose.

"Then a song called 'Rose of my Heart' came to mind and I hummed its tune, thinking about how Becca was the rose of my soul."

Sky and Gritty smiled and floated around the library, feeling joyfully light. They told Spring how happy they were that she finally became her own person, that she overcame her demons, that she found not only love, that she also found peace.

Spring didn't want to tell them they were mistaken. Some of what they said was true but she knew her latest Earth journey wasn't over. Her ultimate story was yet to be told and before launching into that difficult terrain, she needed a rest. So she just thanked them and suggested a break.

Then she left the library. As she floated through space drinking in the peaceful beauty of the vibrant multicolored lights, she longed to stay in this Spirit world forever. Yet she knew that she was not yet ready to do so. She had still been unable to subdue her fear. It lingered along with her negative premonition of what was to come. She knew she had to face it.

PART VIII

▼

THE BIG ONE

"COME TO THE EDGE."
"No, we will fall."
"COME TO THE EDGE."
"No, we will fall."
They came to the edge.
He pushed them, and they flew.

—Apollinaire

Spring was once again at a crossroads, the persistent feeling of foreboding intensifying as she floated aimlessly through space. The premonition that something bad was going to happen seeped through her energy, threatening to drive her spirit back to the physical, back to Earth where she could succumb to her fear. She wanted to rage at whatever she felt like raging at and just be a bitch and a shit if she wanted to. Why was everything so hard? How come she couldn't seem to shake her fear?

Sky and Gritty waited in the library. They had finished telling their lives but knew more insights awaited them from Spring's story. They admired her and appreciated the wisdom they inevitably gained from her persistence and resilience. Neither of them had the stamina nor the will to do what she had done time and time again. Her accelerated development would eventually result in her moving to a more evolved group. They watched her energy carefully for signs of deepening hues, anticipating their loss.

Sky had always trusted Spring's abilities without question but now she was troubled. She turned to Gritty and said, "I'm worried about Spring. She suffered a lot on Earth, particularly in recent lives, but I have never seen her struggle and suffer this much when we were together."

"I agree," Gritty responded, "and *what* has been going on with her in relation to Suma?"

All of a sudden Spring's fear descended into the room, its staggering power gripping Sky and Gritty like a vise. They looked at each other with alarm. Was it possible that Spring couldn't face whatever was to come? Had she decided to quit?

They knew they were being called into action, that Spring needed their support and encouragement. Quickly and without hesitation they left the library. They flew apprehensively toward the central receiving area and were relieved when they didn't find her there, but after circling back and forth among the multitude of lights they realized their search had been futile.

Sky and Gritty returned to the library with their energies intertwined in mutual comfort and resignation. Frightened, they went to their places at the table without speaking. Maybe it was time to ask Suma for help. Surely she would know where Spring was or how to find her.

"Maybe we should just wait awhile longer," Sky finally said, "and be patient."

Before Gritty could respond, an anxious voice from across the table asked, "Wait for whom? Is someone going to join us? Who? Is it bad?"

They had been so consumed with worry that they hadn't noticed Spring sitting at her usual place. Gleefully shooting across the table to embrace her, they screamed their welcome.

"We have been looking for *you*, Spring," Gritty exclaimed, "we know something very difficult is going to happen and we wanted to provide you with our support and encouragement."

"We knew," Sky added breathlessly, "that you were afraid. We wanted to tell you everything would be okay!"

"Take it easy," laughed Spring. "you are right. I should have talked with you about it. I still have a premonition that Suma has a big surprise for me."

"For *us*," said Sky, the words spontaneously gushing forth like a geyser.

"Perhaps, but whatever it is or whoever it is for," Spring said, "I don't think I am going to like it one bit…so I decided to fortify myself."

With that, she opened her storybook, hoping to gain strength from the Earth scenes they were about to see. Sky and Gritty relaxed. As images of Spring unfolded one after another they uttered sighs of happiness and even bliss with increasing frequency. They saw that: Spring was accepted into a doctoral program with a full scholarship—she experienced enormous pleasure in her sharp intellect and keen curiosity—her self-confidence flourished as she conducted research on difficult organizational issues and investigated how commitment to social change developed—her passion was ignited by issues that spoke to the core of her inability to accept that life was unfair—she was ecstatic at her easy grasp of statistics—she spent many rewarding hours in the computer lab excitedly awaiting the results of each statistical test that might answer some of the many questions that seemed to strike her regularly like bolts of lightening—she became a mentor to other doctoral students.

"Talk about fortifying yourself…and us!" exclaimed Gritty.

Spring bobbed up and down with satisfaction.

"For the first time in my life," she said, "I felt happy and serene. I studied and worked hard during the week and played with Becca and her daughter on the weekends. In record time I finished my course work and then my dissertation. At a grand ceremony Becca and her daughter listened with pride as I delivered the commencement address for my class.

"After graduation I eagerly explored new research questions and proffered new ways of thinking about old ones. I wrote several books and numerous articles and soon became nationally and internationally known for my cutting edge theories about how nongovernmental organizations can create positive change in the world.

"When I became Vice President of a big human rights organization, Becca's support was incredible. She sold her house and together with her daughter we created a new home and family in the city. I plunged into the new position with enthusiasm and confidence, trusting that my past experiences would provide the essential grounding to face the complex challenges. I became quite adept at handling thorny situations like an administrator having an affair with a female student, a rejected boyfriend stalking and threatening to kill a staff member, ideological differences, staff relationship and performance issues, workload conflicts, budgetary constraints, community controversies and grievances, politics and political rivalries.

"Six years later another opportunity appeared and I became President and CEO of a prestigious national drug and alcohol program with treatment centers in several major cities. It was perfect. National headquarters were in Washington, D.C. so we didn't have to move, I was ready for another challenge, and the organization's mission—to provide treatment to people for whom access had been historically denied—was my heart. I was at the pinnacle of my success and confidently began leading an organization that seemed to be at its pinnacle of success as well."

Spring then looked at Sky and Gritty and concluded, "Okay, if that doesn't bolster me enough, nothing will!"

*   *   *   *

As she opened her storybook to a new page, Spring knew that the time had arrived. This was going to be tough. She took a deep breath and pulled her energy up as if ready for a fight, then deflated it just as quickly.

She slammed her book shut and wailed, "I can't do this! I'm sorry but I'm just not ready. I need time. Please help me!"

Then her energy flattened onto the table, oozing despair.

Suma was there in an instant, tenderly pulling Spring's energy up while at the same time gathering Sky and Gritty into the circle.

She knew that Spring needed more than her stories of triumph. Her wounds were too deep and the success bandages she had plastered over them hid the pain but could not heal it. There was no easy way out. She would have to go through the dark cavernous abyss.

Knowing that Spring was ready, Suma gently declared, "It is time for you to go to the Place of Healing."

She left no room for argument.

Enveloped completely by Suma's energy and accompanied by Sky and Gritty, Spring surrendered and went willingly. They glided away from the library and moved smoothly through space—passing around and through the innumerable lights, soaring over the central receiving area where they paused momentarily to soak in its orderly excitement, and finally making their way purposely toward what looked like the opening to a cave. Suma explained that once inside Spring would be returned to physical form.

"We will wait for you here," she said, "but you must go in alone. You will be met by someone you know at the other end."

Noticing her hesitancy, Suma gently pushed her.

Spring practically flew through the opening, a bit piqued by the potency of Suma's authority. Once inside, the sight before her was temporarily blinding. When she blinked, she realized she was seeing through physical eyes. The cave was like the tunnels carved through mountains on Earth, this one so incredibly long that Spring couldn't see to the other end. Its walls and rounded ceiling reflected colors that gradually changed in sequence, their shades overlapping as they emerged. The colors first appeared at the entrance and continued to the far end of the tunnel—from red to bright pink to blue to purple to green to yellow to gray, then back to red to repeat the cycle. Soft, soothing sounds accompanied each change of color, reminding Spring of the music played in a massage therapist's office.

There were two moving walkways. The one on the right carried people away from the entrance, deep into the tunnel. Their physical bodies were bent over, weighed down by heavy packs on their backs and they walked very slowly or let the moving walkway carry them. The walkway on the left brought people back to the entrance. Spring noticed that people moving toward her walked briskly, a spring in their steps, and as they approached the entrance—now exit for them—they started evaporating, their energy colors beginning to replace their bodies.

First their arms disappeared, then their legs, their torsos, and finally their heads. By the time they reached the end of the walkway, they were a glow of pure unburdened energy.

Spring headed tentatively toward the right. As she stepped onto the walkway, she felt her legs try to move but a heavy weight on her back pulled her down and the familiar pain in her arthritic hip momentarily jolted her. She allowed herself to be carried by the moving walkway, the changing colors and soothing music putting her in a trance. When she neared the end of the tunnel and heard the words, "Please watch your step as you exit the moving walkway," she carefully stepped off and found herself in a waiting room.

The room was pleasantly decorated in muted and calming colors, a small lamp in the corner illuminating a sign on the wall that said, *Please sit down*. Spring sat on the couch and settled into its comforting softness to wait. Soon a door opened. Her therapist appeared and, just as on Earth, motioned for her to come in to her office with a simple nod and slight smile. Spring was thrilled to see her and stifled an urge to throw herself into her arms. She walked into the office, headed for the comfortable chair that was her favorite, and immediately relaxed.

When she saw the equipment resting on the table—earphones and two small gray pebbles attached to wires—she assumed they would use the Eye Movement Desensitization Response (EMDR) process for this Suma-ordered healing session. That was fine with her. She and her therapist had used it many times and she was comfortable with the technique. Safely wrapped in the familiar, she was ready to get started.

Smiling sadly at her therapist, Spring began, "You already know about my shame and the hidden message under it that in my eyes I am unacceptable. That message was my mantra before I had language and I clung to it for more than six decades. I really thought I had finally let it go. Apparently not. It seems to have been reactivated by a trauma that I have been unable to talk about."

She stopped and smiled apologetically. Of course her therapist already knew everything, including the story she had been unable to tell Sky and Gritty.

Pleased with Spring's readiness and ability to get to the core of things so quickly, her therapist encouraged her to go on.

Spring traced her shame all the way back to the crib, briefly recounting how her lifelong belief in her unacceptability had been born in terror and maintained in perfectionism. She remembered the horror that descended on her as she ecstatically played with her food as an infant and the same horror that crushed her sandcastles and fantasies a few years later—how she quickly learned to avoid punishment by sitting perfectly still, not getting dirty, just being good—how she was so afraid of making a mistake that she couldn't learn—how she bit her nails until her fingers were bloody.

With each tale, she choked on the shame that clogged her veins and arteries with the murky foul-smelling debris of her life script.

Her eyes closed, Spring then allowed herself to be guided through the EMDR protocol. With the earphones on her head and a small gray pebble in each hand, an alternating beeping sound moved from her left ear to her right ear, corresponding to alternating vibrations of the pebble from her left hand to her right. She felt her shame with each repetitive beep from one ear to the other and with each repetitive vibration from one hand to the other, the vibrations synchronized with the beeps. She heard the message "I am unacceptable," from left to right to left to right to left, over and over, marching through the deeply carved groove in her brain that formed an unending crevasse of shame.

Then, as if in a dream, she saw herself running through a gigantic ancient building with long winding staircases and tall marble columns. She gasped for breath as she ran without stopping, not looking back. Emerging from the building she saw a little house by the side of a pool and was relieved to see that she was home. She took off her clothes and dove smoothly into the water, hoping to cool down and rinse the perspiration from her body. Suddenly she felt something slimy crawling over her, winding insistently around her legs and arms and waist. She screamed and jumped out of the pool, frantically pulling the slime from her body. In wide-eyed horror she looked into the now murky water and saw countless monsters of varying sizes and shapes slithering over and under the water and along the sides of the pool.

Terrified, she recoiled in the face of their ugliness. Shivering in disgust she caught the creatures in a big net attached to the end of a long handle and dropped them into a large bucket of water. She drained the pool, scrubbed its sides and bottom until they were sparkling clean and refilled it with pure fresh water.

Then she reached for the bucket...and carefully dumped the monsters back into the pool.

Spring sobbed and gasped for breath as she gave final expression to the pain that she had contained and carried all alone for so long, the pain that she had run from, the pain that was represented by the monsters in the pool that she could not let go of, that she had carefully kept alive. She felt raw and unprotected and little, oh so little. She cried for the little girl playing with her food, playing in the mud, sitting on the bench being careful not to get her dress dirty as she longingly watched the other children at play.

Loving the little girl fiercely, she pulled her to her breast and held her as tightly as she could. Heaving sobs wracked her body as she whispered: "I will take care of you. You are beautiful just as you are. You can get your dress as dirty as you want. You can create and run and jump and play in your food and it will all be a delight, it will all be wonderful because you are wonderful and you don't have to be perfect. I love you so very, very much just as you are. I promise I will protect you. I won't let anyone yell at you again or tell you that you are bad or evil. You are pure, good, smart, creative—and you are enough. You are *more* than enough."

Then Spring thought of the young nail-biting woman studying for hours without learning, fearing exposure of her stupidity. Her sadness turned to anger and then to rage at the unfairness of what the young woman had endured. She defended her with the ferociousness of a protective mother bear who would kill for her cubs, vowing that she would destroy anyone who ever told her again that she was not smart enough, that she didn't do enough, that she was not enough because she *was*, she was enough, she did enough, she had enough and damn it, those shrieking gargoyles that screamed "who do you think you are?" were dead meat!

Spring entered the woman whose Earth name had been Sheila, moving with determination into her cavernous solar plexus, the deep place within that carried her self-loathing. At first it was quiet and seemed empty but then she saw them, the ugly little creatures starting to poke their heads out from the dark corners in which they skulked ready to jump and dance and shriek their taunts. She stood boldly in the middle of the cavern and stared them down, one by one. They immediately slunk away, cowards that they were. Ordering them in a firm commanding voice to never *ever* come around again, she drove them from the cave and carefully sealed it with a protective shield to keep them from coming back.

She went back to the pool by her house and drained it, leaving the monsters on the bottom to die, gasping for water. When they were all dried up like petrified wood from the hot sun, she scooped them into a big bucket and threw the entire thing into a garbage truck that was on its way to the dump. After scrubbing and sterilizing the pool until it sparkled, she once again filled it with pure clean water.

Then she picked up the pool and carefully placed it in Sheila's solar plexus. There, at the core of her, she created a sanctuary of healing, the calm pool reflecting the bright white-tiled dome cover that she had protectively sealed many times to deny access to the gargoyles and other monsters. She then invited Sheila to this sacred place and watched as she floated on her back with arms outstretched, the healing waters flowing over her naked body, gently caressing her, healing every wound. She could rest in this inner sanctum any time she wanted with the assurance that there was no shame here, only serenity and peace.

It was over. A healing balm radiated through Spring as she carefully placed the earphones and the pebbles on the table and sat back in her chair. She had gone home to her deepest self and the loving and divine power within her had cleared her core of its infection and healed her shame wound. She had kissed all the broken places in herself and love bloomed.

Their work completed, she felt a surge of gratitude as she bade her therapist goodbye, certain that she had known her before and would surely know her again. She left the office, walked through the waiting room and joined the many other people who stepped onto the moving walkway to go back through the tunnel. Her step was light and she walked briskly in her eagerness to get back to Suma, Sky, and Gritty. When she reached the end of the walkway there was no message of *please watch your step* for she was floating and no longer in physical form.

She had done it. She had descended into the depths of the tunnel where the core of her most profound anguish resided and had now ascended into the light of freedom.

When Spring emerged from the tunnel Suma, Sky and Gritty were waiting, as promised. Like balls of sunshine they bounced up and down with joy at the sight of her fresh new energy. When she saw them Spring laughed with such contagious heartiness they were soon rolling around in side-splitting laughter, their rejoicing spreading uncontrollably to others who emerged from the tunnel. Spring commented on the hilarious sight, which set off more peels of laughter.

Sky and Gritty noticed that Spring's light blue energy looked darker and they knew it was more than just a reflection from the lights.

With their energies intertwined and Spring at the lead, they darted away from the tunnel and headed back toward the library. They arrived in record time and when they resumed their places at the table, they noticed that Suma was not there.

"Damn," exclaimed Spring, "I wish she wouldn't keep disappearing like that! I wanted to give her a hug before she left!"

*   *   *   *

Spring didn't dawdle. She quickly reopened her storybook to the page she had dreaded, now ready to tell Sky and Gritty the tale they had been waiting to hear.

"My first weeks as President and CEO were filled with promise. There were welcoming receptions, an introductory staff meeting at headquarters, visits to the various treatment centers in a whirlwind of appearances where I was hailed as their highly qualified and exciting new leader, meetings with major donors upon whom the organization depended. I relished every opportunity to speak about my vision for the organization and my commitment to its anti-oppression mission.

"Like a bird that soars and then suddenly takes a dive, however, my optimism soon turned to deflating misgivings. I discovered a level of organizational dysfunction at corporate headquarters that was far greater than anything I had ever imagined or experienced and for which I could not have been prepared. Decades-old ideological conflicts festered and oozed with deep-seated resentment. Psychopathic narcissism and pathological lying characterized the individual pathologies of some administrators and staff. There was unresolved grief over past loss. Political alliances and power grabs were disguised as ideological truths. The organization was consumed by a shame that encouraged workaholism and promoted fear of inadequacy even as its prestige peaked.

"It all added up to major organizational distress and dysfunction, which unfortunately converged into one massive projection onto me as the new leader. The first attack occurred within weeks of my appointment and I weathered it with all the compassion, faith and good humor that I could muster. But the attacks continued unabated and I became disillusioned and increasingly apprehensive. I also sensed the blowing of fate in the wind.

"Like a mirror I reflected back the projections directed at me and my role as leader. Some people, in their frustration at my steadfast refusal to absorb their projections, began to smear my name with half-truths and non-truths, label me as crazy or incompetent or a liar, and twist my successes into failures. In response, support for my leadership also grew, adding to the divisions.

"A small group of staff and administrators who were committed to gaining and maintaining power mounted a life or death struggle against me. I knew that this always happened when someone dared to challenge or disagree with those who aspired to power. I also instinctively knew that grudges and revenge were a formula for the kind of horror I was witnessing, although I didn't fully comprehend either the source or depth of the decades old resentments. But understanding wouldn't have made it any easier."

Spring turned to the next page of her storybook and an ominous pall fell over the library. Sky and Gritty's anger and dismay grew as they watched the new Earth scene unfold.

Spring was leading a staff meeting with over a hundred of the headquarters' staff in attendance. She was poised, competent, and compassionate in the face of the troubled and frightened staff. She looked damn good for someone over sixty years old.

A middle-aged woman stood. Curls of streaked dishwater blonde hair framed her pinched face. She looked like a wasp poised to sting in her black jacket with bright yellow stripes tautly covering her rigid torso. Her rage, along with a markedly cruel disposition, was palpable.

"You are not accepting responsibility for the situation," the woman shrieked at Spring, "What have you done to deal with it? When did you first realize it was a problem? Why did it take you so long to do something? Who did you talk to? Why aren't you being straight with us?"

Spring listened as the woman's sharp tongue pierced the air with a rapid succession of questions, like a lawyer trying to provoke a witness to confess to a crime he didn't commit. But what she was accusing her of doing had occurred in a previous administration, long before Spring had even heard of the organization.

Jabbing a pointed finger at Spring, the woman's tirade ended with an angry shout, "We need some strong leadership around here and you're obviously not it!"

Tossing her head back with an audible snort, the woman sat down and glanced with a triumphant nod and smile at someone on the other side of the room.

Spring was devastated. Never before had she experienced such a humiliating public attack. She prayed for strength and was given the gift of detachment. As if she were watching a movie, she curiously wondered why the woman was so mean-spirited and what she might be projecting onto her. Then Spring observed the worried and irritated faces of staff as they silently cringed at the woman's spitefulness and at that moment saw how critical her leadership was for them.

She remembered a movie she had seen recently about a woman who wanted to be a boxer and imagined herself in a boxing match, defending her title. Her opponent was a vicious underhanded competitor who ignored all rules of decency and fair play in order to knock her out. Like the boxer in the movie, Spring knew she had to remain standing now and do so with skill and strength. She fended off each fast-coming and potentially fatal blow to the head by alternately dodging and confronting each assault, her movements a dance of grace. As she answered each question objectively and non-defensively, not a single blow landed. Just as importantly she did not respond by striking any blows in return.

When it was over Spring stood tall, composed and with the dignity of her position and personhood intact. A collective sigh of relief blew through the room. After the meeting she went to her office and shut the door. Then she cried.

Sky and Gritty shook their heads, then braced themselves as they watched the next scene unfold, knowing that things were about to get worse, shuddering at the reality of Earth's cruelties.

A couple of staff members huddled in the hallway, heads together and lips pursed with whispers of gossip and vile innuendo. They moved into a conference room where six others were already gathered for an unofficial meeting. The same woman who attacked Spring at the staff meeting snarled an invective of manufactured accusations against her. Excited chatter ensued with people throwing rumors around that began with "did you know" and "well, I heard" and ended with "we've got to do something about this!" With each assertion, they built their case against Spring: weak leadership, not astute enough, not right for the job, lacking the right background—she hadn't done this, she had done that, and on and on. A middle-aged man, heavyset and of moderate height with hair graying at his temples, sat quietly in the corner. The furtive glances that sought his approval or instructions revealed that he was covertly in charge even though he didn't speak.

"I knew that a small group was meeting behind my back," Spring said sadly as she looked away from the scene, "but I didn't know what to do about it. Things got pretty crazy. I had to constantly and diligently guard against being blind-sided by an unexpected attack when someone who had been part of the solution on one issue became part of the problem on another, when someone who did good with one hand did bad with the other."

"Who was the middle-aged man in the last scene?" Sky asked.

"His name was James," Spring responded, "he was a recovering alcoholic who had garnered a Native American scholarship after he quit drinking, earned a master's degree, and worked his way up in the organization over many years. He never spoke in meetings and was charming on the surface so at first I thought I had his support. Later I learned how different he was behind the scenes. From the beginning he told people he thought the Board had made a mistake in hiring me—that I was a borderline personality, wasn't smart enough for the job, didn't know what it was like to be an addict, couldn't relate to either the organization's mission or its clientele who were predominantly people of color since I was white.

"James was very intelligent. He cleverly sniffed out the self-interests of others then used that information to win them over for his own purpose, which was to get rid of me. I believed he wanted someone in the position who wouldn't upset the delicate balance of power he had built. Beneath his charm and ready smile there seemed to be a deep rage, a seething resentment. Staff was cautious and wary of him. They knew if they blocked him or even just disagreed ideologically, he would stop at nothing to destroy them and their careers. They had seen him do it many times."

"What was his story?" Sky probed, swatting at the pesky feeling that buzzed around her like an annoying horsefly.

Spring remembered a conversation she had with James once when he told her about his childhood. She thought he had cunningly revealed the information to provoke her empathy and disguise his true intentions.

"I thought a lot about James," she responded, "Finally I just gave up trying to understand him and decided that he was a sociopath…or maybe evil."

With that last statement, she looked over at Gritty who had come to understand human evil in her life. She wondered fleetingly if she had been too hard on James to think of him in such strong terms.

Sky felt driven to persist in her inquiry.

"But did you ever learn anything about his life?" she asked again.

"A little," Spring replied. "He grew up in a white foster home and was resentful about being robbed of his native culture during his formative years. Yet he spoke kindly about his foster parents, saying wistfully that they loved him and treated him well. Both of his natural parents were alcoholics and James started drinking at age ten or maybe even younger. He was very smart—brilliant according to some—and in spite of his drinking problem was the first person from his reservation to graduate from high school."

"Wait a minute," Sky said, confused. "I thought you said that he was raised in a white foster home and was robbed of his culture. Then you said he was the first person from his reservation to graduate. What does that mean?"

Sky thought she already knew the answer but hoped she was wrong.

"James was returned to his natural parents," Spring said, "and actually grew up the major portion of his childhood and youth on the reservation. Oh, my God…!"

Could James be Jamie, the Native American child that Sky had taken from his white foster parents and returned to his natural parents when he was six years old?

With bated breath, Sky asked what James' last name was.

Spring looked down, unable to face her.

"Buckley," she whispered.

As the truth seeped in, Sky was surprised at how serene she felt. She had wondered and often worried about what happened to Jamie. Now she knew. He had not recovered from the trauma of his childhood and in his rage he traumatized others and poisoned an organization. She did not blame herself now as she once would have and said a silent prayer of thanks for the insights she had received in recovery. Then, seeing Spring's anger, she calmly floated above the fray where she waited with unshakable faith that everything was okay.

Spring was furious. She raged through the library, bumping into the walls, hurling her energy from one end to the other, over and over, until she was in a frenzy.

"So this was your surprise," she flared, "well, fuck you, Suma, just fuck you! Why the hell did you put James in my life? What were you *thinking?* You knew how horrible he was—how sinister—how much grief he would cause—how toxic he would be to the organization. You had to know how traumatizing it would be for me! And didn't you realize what this lovely little surprise would do to Sky? How could you do this to both of us? Why, Suma, why?"

Gritty looked sympathetically at Spring, at the same time noting Sky's contrasting composure. She believed that everything happened for a reason and was curious about why Suma had done this.

Meanwhile Suma calmly floated over them unnoticed. She didn't seem at all surprised by Spring's reaction nor did she seem ruffled by it. She watched and waited with a full heart.

Once her emotions were spent and her energy completely depleted, Spring saw Suma. But instead of lashing out in fury, she was now ready for an explanation. Like a frozen mannequin she stared into space and waited for one.

"First I want to remind you," Suma began, "that James chose his life issues just as you chose yours. He just agreed to play a role in your lives in the process."

Spring remained quiet and attentive though she was not appeased. Sky and Gritty leaned forward with keen curiosity as Suma continued.

"I will tell you what happened to Jamie as a result of being taken from his natural parents at birth and from his foster parents six years later. His natural parents were consumed by shame at having failed their youngest child and Jamie took their shame into himself and made it his own, wearing it within like a loyalty oath. In his child's mind, he figured there must be something wrong with him or why else would his parents have left him in foster care when they brought their other children home. His belief was further confirmed when the foster parents who said they loved him let him go so easily.

"Jamie concluded—just as you did as a child, Spring—that he was fundamentally flawed, deficient, *unacceptable.* And then, of course, his belief was reinforced by the many ways society oppressed Native American people."

Spring's fury dissipated.

"So you're telling me," she asked, "that James had the same struggles that I had, that his purpose in life was to overcome shame just as mine was? Did he fail in his purpose? Surely he must have!"

"His story is not over yet," Suma replied, "but the important thing is the role he played in helping you to achieve *your* purpose, Spring. We already know how he helped Sky."

"I'm sorry,' Spring responded, her anger returning, "but I'm having trouble seeing how he helped me right now. All I got from him was a return of my shame."

"Exactly!" Suma looked at her lovingly and patiently explained, "You see, by reactivating your shame James provided the opportunity for you to overcome it forever. He helped to create a shame-based organization where people said out loud what you had always believed—that you were unacceptable. All the worst possible conditions were provided for you, everything that would cut deep and touch your inner core of shame.

"It was all given to you," Suma emphasized with a smile, "because you were ready."

"I guess I should take that as a compliment," Spring grumbled.

It was ironic, she thought, that she was beginning to feel compassion for her nemesis, James—and even a hint of gratitude.

Sky smiled and added, "I learned that we were never given more on Earth than we could handle, so the experience you were given really was a compliment of the highest sort, Spring."

Gritty was literally blown away by it all. She marveled—once again—at how things were not always as they seemed. For a while she had been pretty sure that James personified human evil; now she was reminded that when it came to labeling people as evil, the utmost caution was required. She thought that what happened to Spring had been a disaster and now, to consider the trauma as a *gift*—well, that was just too much!

Sky thought more about Jamie. Now she felt love and compassion not only for the hurt innocent child he had been but also for the sinister and difficult man he had become. She turned to Suma for assurance of a positive outcome for him.

Suma simply responded that the Place of Healing was there for everybody when they were ready and if they were willing.

Gritty wondered if Suma worked with Jamie's spiritual group like she worked with theirs, if she was his assigned guide, if that was how she got him to volunteer to help Spring and Sky on Earth. She timidly asked and when Suma said, "No," they all heaved a sigh of relief.

Then Suma waved goodbye with a big smile and a promise to return soon.

Spring waved back, half smiling as she shook her head and said, "Damn that Suma, anyway! I have never had so much trouble with her before! Don't you think she's been just *impossible* this time? I tell you, if she has any more surprises for me, I think I will have a heart attack. Oh—that's right—I already did that, didn't I?"

Sky and Gritty laughed along with her. Happy to have Suma's latest surprise behind them, they joked and speculated about what else Suma might have up her sleeve. Spring was pretty sure that James must have been the last big surprise. Sky and Gritty knew better though they didn't know why.

✻   ✻   ✻   ✻

Suddenly Sky and Gritty realized they still didn't know what had happened to Spring in the midst of all that organizational turmoil. They were sure if they had been in the situation that they would have quit on the spot, but Spring had never been one to cut and run when things got tough.

"So tell us," Sky urged, "what did you do? Did the stress from all that dissension cause your heart attack?"

Sky and Gritty huddled close as Spring continued her story, "The attacks continued. I insisted on not striking back but in my determination to take the high road, I failed to recognize the power of pathological lying. Without remorse or moral constraints—and with belief in its own falsehoods—deceitful strategies were planned that hit below the belt and put me at a disadvantage. One carefully calculated allegation that pierced my heart was that I had used the oppression of others to enhance my own career."

Spring remembered sadly how her despair had deepened, compounded by her refusal to accept life's unfairness. Many sleepless nights she wrestled with her old shame as it threatened to unite with the organization's shame and bring them both down. She searched for courage but as she tossed and turned in the dark hours of terror, the shrieking gargoyles told her she was a failure. With wicked delight, they squealed her fear. Her inadequacy had been exposed. Finally everyone would know. The monsters said her self-worth hinged on her ability to turn the situation around. If she were smart enough she could do it. She had believed them.

"For several years," Spring then continued, "I had held tightly to the egotistical illusion that I could be the one to heal an organization that was deeply entrenched in longstanding sickness. After spending a lifetime thinking that my home was in professional success, I now felt like a refugee wandering in the wilderness. One night I couldn't take it anymore. I got on my knees."

Spring saw Gritty smiling like a Cheshire cat and smiled back. She wondered if Sky had ever gotten on her knees. That would make it unanimous.

"When I finally surrendered, I accepted what I could and could not do for the organization. Healing it would not be one of my successes."

She then pointed to a scene as it emerged from her storybook. Sky and Gritty looked on with curious anticipation.

Spring had called a special staff meeting and the room was packed. She looked good in a perfectly matched ensemble—a brown jacket decorated with a delicate scarf in gold, green and brown hues, a beige silk blouse, and dangling gold earrings. As she stood behind the podium at the front of the room, her head held high and her voice filled with confidence and determination, she announced her plans to retire when she turned sixty-five. She then outlined the goals to be accomplished during her final year and a half as President and CEO. After the meeting, staff flooded into her office. Some brought flowers. Others wrote notes. They mourned their loss. They worried for their future.

As the scene faded Spring marveled at how good she had looked. Her shame had very effectively covered the crisis in her soul with its usual façade of competence. But if her body had matched her traumatized spirit that day, staff would have seen her doubled over in pain, covered in bruises of black and blue, dripping with blood from deep wounds, crying in despair. She teetered on the brink of collapse, in grave danger of finally succumbing to her lifelong script. Professional success had been her only weapon against shame and she was running out of ammunition.

Spring would need help to make it through to retirement and Becca could no longer be her sole counselor. Becca had run out of emotional energy and physical stamina after years of opening her loving arms to her battered partner when she arrived home from the office shattered and crying night after night. Spring knew she would have to find help elsewhere.

Looking up from her reflections Spring then said, "I braced myself for more hard times. Becca told me I needed to see a therapist and wisely suggested one who specialized in trauma recovery. As usual, she was right.

"Something about the therapist drew me to her right away. Her name was Ann. She was my age, tall and large-boned with shoulder length white hair and modest attire that hinted of a simple lifestyle. Her large green eyes reflected wisdom as deep as the ocean, a razor sharp intellect and an old soul's compassion. Of course I didn't recognize it at the time, but I saw Suma in those eyes and knew I had landed safely in strong capable hands.

"Our sessions were intense from the beginning. Ann and I explored how I had desperately clung to my shame, fearful that it was all I had, that without it I would not be the accomplished star it had made me. We talked about how I had let go of it bit by bit, a slow uneven process that happened on different levels—when I stopped biting my nails, told myself I was okay, explored my sexuality, trusted my intellect. But when the new job plunged me into a sinkhole of fetid turbulence, I naturally went back to my old familiar self. Shame was all I knew in a crisis and I took it back and embraced it even as it threatened to crush me.

"Then I went deeper. Ann held up a mirror to my shame and guided me to its depths. With the earphones on my head and a little pebble in the palm of each hand, shame oozed slowly like thick hot lava burning through every vein and artery, every muscle, every organ in my body and I screamed in pain. Then a light blue liquid slowly flowed through me, starting with my head, throat and lungs and streaming down through my torso and out to my extremities—cooling, refreshing and soothing each burning place of pain until my entire self glowed with Grace. All traces of the toxic lava were gone. With Ann's help, I had found the courage to go to the exquisite edge of my shame and was released. I wasn't completely healed—as you know, that happened when I went to the Place of Healing—but my soul no longer felt as bruised and battered.

"One day Ann asked, 'Have you noticed how the sun radiates through my office window whenever we meet, even when it's been cloudy all day?'

"Yes, I was being transformed from darkness into light. When trouble stirred I now had choices and most often chose to fill my spirit with the light blue liquid. I continued to look and sound fine but now my insides actually matched my outsides. At work I felt strong, powerful, in charge. I was the leader. I felt, talked and acted like it. Even when chaos, fear and anger raced through the halls, I was flooded with a comfortable, natural sense of humble confidence.

"My remaining time with the organization was just as challenging as I had expected, but I was fine. I began to trust that things were unfolding just as they were supposed to and that I was being carried.

"My confidence showed. Staff regularly expressed their appreciation for my strong leadership, told me how they were going to miss me and how sorry they were about the behavior of some of their colleagues. I noticed that their opinions were unimportant to me. For the first time and in a most profound way, I knew the extent of my personal strength and power. I needed no external confirmation."

Sky and Gritty clapped.

"Do you remember," Sky asked, "how we chose to live as women in the second half of the twentieth century in order to find strength and influence and learn leadership in a world still dominated by men?"

Gritty nudged Sky playfully and added, "and didn't Spring show what leadership was about in a most *elegant* way when she inhaled the negativity of an awful moment in the life of that organization and exhaled something positive?"

"She sure did!" Sky replied.

Then she looked directly at Spring and said, "You transformed a traumatic experience into incredible personal and spiritual growth."

Spring smiled in agreement. Then she thought more about what she had learned about leadership. She discovered that many successful people on Earth suffered from what was called the *imposter syndrome*. Regardless of many notable achievements they were convinced they were scamming everyone about what they knew and could do and feared being unmasked. How ironic it was that she had been able to exorcise the imposter lie only when she felt she really *had* been found out. It was when some staff contended that she wasn't smart, capable or qualified enough to be their leader that she became a real leader.

Suma then appeared and said, "The turbulence of the whole experience turned you inside out, but you weathered the storm until the cramp in your soul loosened and your real self separated from your false egotistic self. You were released from the success identity that you had gripped so tightly. It was then that you birthed your real self.

"It took you a lifetime to learn that lesson—well, perhaps more than one lifetime. You were given many experiences over time, though never more than you could handle, and they all converged to make you ready for this particularly powerful lesson."

"There's something else," Sky then said to Spring, thoughtfully, "and it has to do with Jamie—or James as you knew him. I hope you can now see James as he was without taking what he did personally. He lied not to hurt you but because he was afraid it would be discovered that *he* was not perfect. Whatever James or anyone else did or thought or said was not about you, it was about *them*."

"I get it," Spring affirmed, then added, "and even the opinions I had about myself were not true—so it was important not to take them personally either!"

She smiled and relaxed in the certainty that she had achieved her purpose on Earth, in spite of all the fears she'd had to the contrary. She looked to Suma and when she saw that she was gone realized that she didn't need her confirmation either.

Spring then remembered her retirement party. It had been magnificent, filled with accolades about what she had done for the organization and her lifetime contributions. But she knew that her achievements were tarnished by their unhealthy motivation to cover the empty darkness of her shame. Her success had been detrimental to her. It had kept her from discovering the divine within. Now that she was home in her true self she knew she was flawed like all human beings. Within the reality of her own imperfection she had found peace.

She then told Sky and Gritty that she wanted to finish her story with one final scene. She called it the grand finale and a counterpoint to all her struggles.

*   *   *   *   *

Spring opened her storybook to the last page. All three of them burst into laughter as they watched the unfolding Earth scene.

Spring stood in a circle of twelve women. They were keening over a covered body lying on the floor. In the dim light she saw two feet—so very white and still—sticking out at the end of a navy blue blanket. The women swayed back and forth in the circle, keening to the slow rhythm of a drum. The death ritual felt spooky to Spring. When a woman uttered a eulogy and another offered a prayer, her throat and stomach muscles tightened as she tried to stifle an almost irresistible urge to laugh. What the hell was she doing here? The ritual then turned from death to rebirth as the women threw the blanket aside and pulled the woman who had been under it up into the bright light of transformation. Then they all danced together. Spring doubled over with laughter.

As she watched herself laughing, Spring was reminded of the Place of Healing and how the tears she had shed for what she had lost had turned into laughter and celebration for what she had found. She marveled at how she had come, at age seventy-two, to that circle at a women's retreat in California—a place where vegetarianism, pot smoking, drumming, rituals, bodywork, and who knows what else, were the norm.

She focused again on the scene and watched as she luxuriated in the crystal clear water of the hot tub under a full moon, surrounded by lush fruit trees bearing fragrant apples, peaches, and pears. She looked around at the loving symbols of hearts and hands in that special sacred space and felt triumphant and whole. There was no shame.

"I was free," Spring interjected as she looked up to see Sky and Gritty fully rel-ishing the scene, "deliciously free from anyone's opinion of me, either positive or negative—including my own!"

The memory of that night made Spring smile. She had felt free to be curious and compassionate and to laugh at how she had come to such a crazy place of authenticity with the group of women with whom she engaged in ritual and cele-bration. She had let go of the past and what life had taken from her and was fully alive in the moment to enjoy the dream as it happened.

"That's it," Spring exclaimed, closing her book. "That's my story."

Just then Suma appeared and declared, "You are now ready to prepare to go before the Council."

*   *   *   *

An appearance before the Council involved a final life review before going to the Place of Life Selection where they would choose their next lives. But Spring wasn't ready to discuss future choices with the elders. Something undone nagged at her like a toddler pulling on her mother's leg for attention. She needed time to think and suggested a break. Sky and Gritty liked the idea of having some leisure time. Like Spring, they were in no rush to go before the Council.

Sky longed to experience some of her fond memories from Earth. She had loved the stillness of the lakes, the grandeur of the pine trees, and the simple home that she and Don had created. She would visit it one more time, sit by the water's edge and soak in the sun's rays, and remember the good and sacred of life there.

As Gritty floated away from the library she heard the sounds of harps and flutes and chimes and the rhythm of drums. Some spiritual dancing and singing might be just what she needed. She moved toward the music and joined a circle of souls in flowing harmony and melodic vibrations, feeling at one with all energy and thought, released from the past and the future as she swayed and laughed and danced.

Spring, ever the earnest and dedicated one, went to a quiet monastery for soli-tude and contemplation. She wondered why she didn't feel ready to appear before the Council and began to sort through the possibilities. There was no rea-son to be nervous about being judged by the elders; they always had great com-passion for her human imperfections and displayed infinite patience with her faults and bad decisions. The focus of the Council would be on how she handled the consequences of life events rather than the events themselves. She believed that she had done well in that regard. She tried not to retaliate when others hurt her. She focused on making the world a better place in spite of her shame. She followed a spiritual path. She learned compassion and forgiveness. She tried to do her best. All in all, she was certain that she had used life events in the service of her evolution.

Then she wondered if she was worried about her own advancement. She had always been an accelerated soul and in her desire to develop had never chosen easy lives. Maybe she was still too tired to consider another difficult life just yet. Or maybe the Council would decide it was time for her to move to the next level and she would need to make the transition away from Sky and Gritty. Naturally she had unsettled and complicated feelings about that. All of a sudden feelings of loss, excitement and renewed commitment poured through her like a swiftly moving stream until they reached a calm pool of acceptance.

Spring knew that what she did for others was more important than what she did for herself. She wondered if her quest to overcome her own shame had kept her from helping others on their paths. She had tried to be sensitive to the feelings of others, to understand them, to be an advocate for the human heart. She made a mental list of some specific actions that might qualify as helping and discovered that many had started with her own journey. She opened herself up to her sexual identity and had gone public in the face of discrimination and oppression—in the process perhaps she paved the way for others. Because she struggled with her own fallibility she became sensitive and accepting of others' shortcomings—surely that helped them. She developed into an articulate and effective leader and that impacted others. As a teacher she obviously helped her students. Her actions for social change—against war (the Vietnam War, the nuclear threat, Desert Storm, the War in Iraq), for human rights (civil rights, women's rights, gay rights, prisoners' rights), against the death penalty—hopefully paved the way for peace and social justice and maybe she had served as a model for others as well.

Spring's thoughts then turned to Suma and how uncomfortable and angry she had been with her. She knew she needed to make amends for acting out her own shame in their relationship but wondered if there was something else involved.

"I'm right here," Suma suddenly said, her energy floating around Spring and then settling down right next to her. "Don't forget to add the homeless man to the list of actions you took to help others."

"You were eavesdropping on my thoughts!" Spring playfully teased before asking, "What homeless man? There were so many of them in Washington D.C. I always worried about the men in the park across from my apartment, especially on nights when there were severe thunderstorms."

"Remember the one sitting in the doorway of a building on Connecticut Avenue in DuPont Circle?" Suma asked. "It was long before you moved to the District and you were there on business, staying at a very nice hotel."

"You mean the man with no legs?"

"Yes," Suma responded. "When you first walked by his outstretched hand you looked away. *That* man."

"Oh yes," Spring said with a smile. "I went back to the hotel and couldn't get him out of my mind so I went back and gave him some money."

"You gave him a twenty dollar bill," Suma said.

"But," argued Spring, "I gave it to him to ease my own conscience."

"Of course," Suma agreed. "the point is that you took many small actions that you didn't mention. No action is ever too small to count for the Council."

Spring smiled with gratitude and said, "I apologize for how crappy I have been with you this time, Suma. I appreciate how you made it possible for me to learn from it."

Suma just smiled, obviously pleased with Spring's awareness and humility.

"I think, though," Spring continued, "that the intensity of my feelings this time might be connected with something more but I can't seem to get at it. I am sure that you know what it is."

"I know what it is," Suma responded with a nod and an even bigger smile, "and so do you. Let's go back to the library and talk about it with Sky and Gritty."

∗   ∗   ∗   ∗

Spring happily reached out for Suma and they returned to the library as one. Sky and Gritty were already there, looking relaxed, sitting at their usual places at the table.

"You are almost ready," Suma announced with a take-charge manner and touch of pride in her voice, "but there is one more lesson before you will be ready to go before your Councils."

"You all know," Spring interjected, "about how my shame was the source of the trouble I've been having with Suma. But she and I agree there was more to it than that."

With that, Spring looked to Suma for an explanation that might confirm the little glimmer of knowing that twinkled inside her like a weakly flickering votive candle.

"When I tell you," Suma said, "you will know that I am simply articulating what you already know. Spring did play out her feelings of unacceptability and inferiority with me but the *intensity* of those feelings was related to the two of you as well."

Sky and Gritty remembered their premonition that Spring's story would involve them in the end. As they stared intently at Suma a light blue question mark appeared in the space above them.

"The three of you had the same life script," Suma explained, "but Spring carried it for you. This is how it developed. First, you learned as children that life was unfair. Later you realized that you couldn't make it fair. In your inability to accept either of those things, you believed that you couldn't make life fair because of your own inadequacies. Sky didn't have enough courage. Gritty didn't know how to act. And Spring wasn't smart enough.

"Finally, each of you concluded that you were deficient."

"So," Gritty and Sky chimed in with one voice, "all of us essentially believed that, because we were unable to make life fair, we were *unacceptable*."

"Right!"

Spring's energy was glowing with insight and inspiration as she joined in, "That's why I felt the shame with such rawness and poignancy! I was feeling it for all of us! We all needed to learn that we were enough and had always been enough—in our imperfect, flawed human way."

"In the end all of you recast your scripts," Suma added, "You spiraled through your soul journeys. You died, were reborn, died again as you went through each natural transition from birth, childhood and youth, adulthood, midlife, aging. Sometimes you fell overboard or lost your balance or had to slog through the muck of a crisis tributary, but each time you weathered the storm. And every time you allowed expression of the divine within, you took another step closer to the true self you were created to be. You never quit and each time crossed the sea to transformation. That made all the difference.

"You learned," Suma concluded, "how humans evolve in their imperfection."

"…that's for sure," Sky said, "each of us stumbled awkwardly from innocence and passion to reason and power."

"…and each of us learned how to work in an unjust world!" Gritty added.

"But we never accepted the unfairness of life, "Spring said, "That was our flaw and that was our salvation."

With excitement and increasing pleasure, they took turns articulating the lessons they had learned, spewing them out in rapid succession: They learned about the brutality of life. They developed sensitivity to others' feelings by becoming conscious of the impact of their own hurts. They discovered the extraordinary and surprisingly unexpected heroics that come from just trying to do a good job. They came to understand the pain involved in being advocates for the human heart. They learned what heroics really were—a combination of passion, self-knowledge, and an ability to articulate your cause. They became more powerful by developing a broader perspective about life. They learned that they could not really be powerful until they were aware of themselves. They understood and accepted the human condition as flawed and filled with contradictions. They addressed the big picture in increasingly effective ways. They realized that they were powerless to change everything and accepted what one human being could do. They didn't quit when they saw what they couldn't do. They learned to be leaders. They developed independence of thought and found their own authentic spiritual core. They persisted in their search for larger truths. In the end they found the home of their true selves.

"Bravo, bravo!" Suma applauded enthusiastically as their combined laughter filled the room.

"And now for the unification ceremony before you appear before your Councils!" she announced with pride as tall and big as a California redwood.

*   *   *   *

The ceremony was Suma's idea and she always enjoyed it more than anyone else. Sky, Spring and Gritty usually saw it for what it was, simply a time to assimilate the energy they had left behind in Suma's keeping when they went to Earth. They never brought all their energy with them on their Earth journeys. If they did they would remember too much about their life plans and that would defeat their learning purpose. They always liked to wait for reunification until it was time to appear before the Council so they could immerse themselves fully in the learning process. They didn't want fresh energy diluting their feelings and experiences from the last life while they studied.

Spring looked at Sky and Gritty curiously. They were laughing and crashing their energies into each other like bumper cars, squealing with anticipation. What were they so excited about? Assimilation of energies was routine. They had always just humored Suma about the ceremony.

As she opened the cabinet under the bookshelves, Suma seemed more excited than usual. One by one she pulled out three glass containers. They were perfectly square with beautiful etchings on each side and a glass lid on top that was secured with a gold clasp. With a flourish, she placed a container on the table in front of each of them—first Spring, then Gritty and Sky. Cheers rose up in the suddenly packed room where everyone who had played a role in their last Earth lives were now gathered to congratulate them for a job well done.

Suma picked up Spring's container and displayed it by holding it high in the air. The energy inside glowed weakly. She then emptied its contents into her hand where she held it briefly before dropping it over Spring like a thin veil of light blue gauze. Everyone watched as it melded quickly into Spring's blue energy and disappeared.

Spring was astounded. Her advanced energy was extremely potent so she only brought thirty percent of it with her to Earth. She could tell that Suma had returned no more than ten percent back to her. Where was the rest?

Suma seemed to be enjoying Spring's bewilderment. With a mischievous smile, she announced that she had a surprise. That set Sky and Gritty off into a twitter of giggles.

Like a deer staring into the bright headlights of a car, Spring sat frozen in place. Another surprise? What was going on? She looked at Sky and Gritty questioningly. That set them off into another round of uproarious laughter. Suddenly she felt very tired. She looked at the others gathered in the room and they seemed as baffled as she was about what was going on. At least that was a comfort.

Suma called for quiet and then proceeded.

"You will notice," she announced, "that I have returned only a small portion of Spring's energy to her. I will now return the rest!"

On cue Sky floated across the table and everyone gasped as they saw her energy enter Spring's empty container. Suma held the container that was now filled with Sky's energy in the air for all to see. Its light blue glow twinkled like a star. Then, with the flourish of a magician, Suma poured the contents from the container into her hands, enjoying the pleasurable gasps she elicited when she rubbed the energy into a bright glow of blue, deepening its hue with her warmth. In a grand gesture as if she were crowning a queen, she then dropped it over Spring.

Gritty immediately floated across the table and her energy entered Spring's container just as Sky's had. With a majestic movement Suma repeated the process that ended with dropping its contents over Spring.

As the energies from Sky and Gritty flowed into her, Spring felt the warmth of its glow. The merger left her feeling serene and peaceful, immortal. She relaxed into the resurgence of her energy as it returned to its full power.

Suma hurriedly lifted the container for Sky that she had pulled from the cabinet earlier. She displayed the bright energy inside for all to see and then poured it over Sky's place at the table. Everyone gasped as Sky reappeared at 100 percent of her light blue energy. Then Suma lifted the remaining container and repeated the process by pouring the energy within onto Gritty's place at the table.

With Spring, Sky and Gritty now returned to their full energies, Suma explained what had happened.

"Spring's ambition has been widely known for hundreds of years," she said. "With each Earth life she always aimed to accelerate her learning by taking on the most difficult issues and challenges. As a result she made outstanding progress in her evolution and was on the verge of transition. So when they planned their most recent lives, Spring, Sky and Gritty came up with a remarkable strategy to help her evolve to the next plane."

Spring nodded. With her vitality restored to full energy, she remembered everything. Suma's explanation was now for the benefit of the gathered crowd.

"Sky and Gritty decided," Suma continued, "to use only Spring's soul energy while theirs rested here. Spring decided to leave ten percent of her energy here and split the rest three ways. While Sky, Gritty and Spring lived parallel lives in three different bodies, they all used Spring's energy. So, voila, folks—they were all Spring! They were all her soul."

The crowd clapped and cheered, pleased to have witnessed such an unusual event, and then left.

Spring remembered how Suma had advised against their plan, warning her that the energy drain would be enormous. She had been right, as usual. Spring had been so exhausted through the whole learning process that she picked fights with Suma and almost quit a couple of times. She didn't know if she would ever divide her soul into parallel lives again.

"Now it is time for the three of you to go to your favorite place for a farewell feast," Suma announced.

Sky, Gritty and Spring glowed with rays of completion as they picked up their storybooks. Sky and Gritty gave their books to Spring who filed them under her own name in chronological life order with hundreds of her other books on the library shelf. As they headed toward the exit, Suma hugged them goodbye and assured them that she would join each of them at their individual sessions with the Council elders.

Suma moved away while the three of them floated purposefully through space toward the valley where they gathered each time when they first returned to the spirit world, toward the valley that was as familiar and as beautiful to them as they were to each other.

They didn't speak, each of them filled with love and hoping for the courage and humility to choose her journey into the next life.

Spring now looked forward to her meeting with the elders, ready for whatever was required of her.

Sky was grateful to Spring for carrying the burden of the shame lesson for all of them. Since she hadn't expended any of her own energy and was fully rested, she would be fine with being the first to return to Earth this time.

Gritty shook her head and thought about what an amazing discovery it always was when things turned out not to be as they seemed.

All of them knew that Spring would not be with them when they returned next time.

About the Author

While Dorothy Van Soest has published several books, this is her first work of fiction. Author, political activist, social worker, college professor and former university dean, she has taught and written extensively about diversity, social justice and peace issues. She began her career as a young teacher in Chicago and New York City, facing the challenges of gross inequity in education. Her lifetime commitment to justice has included working for civil rights and women's rights beginning in the 60's, anti-nuclear and anti-war activism, international human rights, and social change. A central focus of her life, which she maintains is essential for anyone engaged in social change efforts, has been her own personal and spiritual growth. In this debut novel, she synthesizes her personal recovery and change processes through fictionalizing her life experiences. She currently lives in Seattle.

Author's Suggestions for Using
Sheila's Trifecta

When I began writing this book, I used reflective journaling of real life events to recognize themes and then created fictional characters and stories. This process helped me to more deeply appreciate my own life through Spring, Sky and Gritty's reflections concerning issues that are deeply personal for me. I believe a similar process might be useful for any readers wanting to retrace the important events of their lives. For example, you might journal your thoughts and feelings and then write some of your stories based on real-life events and experiences. Or you might create fictional character(s) to provide distance and perspective from which to look at your own life. After self-reflection through writing, you might bring what you learned to your own support, therapy or educational group.

If you choose to use this book for your personal growth, I hope you will find the following questions and suggestions helpful.

DISCUSSION QUESTIONS AND SUGGESTIONS

1. Our first reaction when we have been wounded is to simply avoid similar situations or persons in the future. One of the lessons from this book is that the characters saw the injustices inflicted on them as containing some kind of wisdom about life that took them beyond avoidance and fear, enabling them to let go of their fear. For example, Sky came to understand the nature of forgiveness in her relationship with her alcoholic husband. All three characters found peace with their mothers, who had harmed them early in life.

Similarly, Spring found compassion and learned about gratitude from her nemesis, James, at work.

As you look into your own past you may see ways to find understanding and peace with your mother or another abusive or negligent person in your early life. Reflect on the positive things you have learned from your wounds. How did they strengthen you or give you knowledge you might otherwise never have had?

2. Think about a time when you hurt another person. How did that experience change how you feel or act toward others? What lessons are there to be learned from the pain you caused—whether it was inflicted intentionally or unintentionally? Look beyond self-justification, anger, self-blame and guilt and reach for deeper understanding of what you have gained from the experience. For example, when Sky played a role as a social worker in breaking the heart of a little boy named Jamie, she began to understand more about the complexities of life as well as her own codependent behavior.

3. What are ways you might transform woundedness—both your own and that which you inflicted on others—into useful insights and practices? In the book, for example, when Spring found the courage to look at her traumatized spirit, she became a powerful leader. When Sky dared to look at her own woundedness, she transformed the harm she did to Jamie as a social worker into constructive changes in the child welfare system.

4. It has often been said that our greatest personal power is hidden in the shadow side of our personalities—that is, the parts of ourselves that we want to deny. In the book, for example, the characters despaired about their human contradictions. Sky was a good girl and minister's wife but also a rabble rousing religious skeptic and later a co-dependent wife and social worker. She had a difficult time accepting these seemingly very different sides of herself. Similarly, Gritty was a committed teacher in the under-resourced inner city but also a lonely and increasingly desperate alcoholic. Spring was a notably successful achiever but also a nail-biting shame-filled woman. They all came eventually to understand what Suma meant when she said, "…your despair, though understandable, held the key to understanding for you."

How would you describe your shadow side—the parts of you that you might prefer to hide from yourself and the world? What wisdom have you gained from facing your own human contradictions? In what ways has your shadow side held the key to knowledge and understanding for you? What have you learned when you dared to look at your human weaknesses? What are some of the ways you might make use of the knowledge you have gained?

5. Try to imagine a timeline of your life from the year of your birth to the present. Along this line, note the major events that took place each year. What impact do you think those external events have had on your personal growth and development? For example, Spring, Sky and Gritty's journeys toward wholeness were shaped by external conditions and events of the second half of the 20th century, such as equal rights struggles and the nuclear threat.

6. The life scripts of the three characters in the novel—fear, guilt, and shame—are often seen as universal themes. How have your life issues been similar to those of Spring, Sky and Gritty?

SUGGESTIONS FOR FURTHER READING

Write from the Heart: Unleashing the Power of Your Creativity, by Hal Zina Bennett, New World Library, 2001.
A wonderful guide for writing as part of personal and spiritual growth, whether through journaling or writing for publication.

It Will Never Happen to Me! and *Changing Course,* by Claudia Black, Hazelden, 2002.
Two books about dealing with loss, abandonment and fear from growing up in an addictive family.

I thought It Was Just Me: Women Reclaiming Power and Courage in a Culture of Shame by Brene' Brown, Gotham, 2007.
An examination of our struggles with shame and valuable tools to become our best, most authentic selves.

The Spirituality of Imperfection: Storytelling and the Journey to Wholeness, by Ernest Kurtz and Katherine Ketcham, Bantam Books, 1994.
Stories from many spiritual and philosophical paths that speak to anyone who yearns to find meaning within suffering and to understand and accept the human condition.

The Booze Battle, by Ruth Maxwell, Ballantine Books, 1976.
The problems faced by those who are in relationship with an alcoholic, how the alcoholic views the world, and practical suggestions about how to bring the alcoholic to treatment and recovery.

978-0-595-41501-
0-595-41501-6

Printed in the United States
71193LV00004B/26